She watched the clock tick by for almost an hour—until she heard the announcement that her bus was boarding, and the line started shuffling sleepily forward.

Mira wasn't usually a person who broke rules, who did things she wasn't supposed to, who lived dangerously, who took risks.

But a week before her birthday, she boarded a bus to Beau Rivage—the city where she'd been born, the city where they'd buried her parents.

The one place her godmothers had forbidden.

OTHER EGMONT USA BOOKS YOU MAY ENJOY

*The Demon Catchers of Milan* by Kat Beyer

*The Mephisto Covenant* by Trinity Faegen

*The Rose Throne* by Mette Ivie Harrison

*Hourglass* by Myra McEntire

*The False Princess* by Eilis O'Neal

# KILL me SOFTLY

SARAH CROSS

**EGMONT**
USA
New York

*For everyone who loves fairy tales*

*"I don't want realism. I want magic!"*

—Blanche DuBois

Tennessee Williams, A Streetcar Named Desire

# EGMONT

*We bring stories to life*

First published by Egmont USA, 2012
This paperback edition first published by Egmont USA, 2013
443 Park Avenue South, Suite 806
New York, NY 10016

1 3 5 7 9 8 6 4 2

www.egmontusa.com
http://www.sarahcross.com/

THE LIBRARY OF CONGRESS HAS CATALOGED THE HARDCOVER EDITION AS FOLLOWS:

Cross, Sarah.
Kill me softly / by Sarah Cross.
p. cm.
Summary: When sixteen-year-old Mira runs away to discover her secret past, she finds a place where Grimm's fairy tales come to life, and she cannot avoid her accursed fate.
ISBN 978-1-60684-323-9 (hardcover) — ISBN 978-1-60684-324-6 (e-book)
[1. Fairy tales—Fiction. 2. Characters in literature—Fiction.
3. Blessing and cursing—Fiction. 4. Love—Fiction.] I. Title.
PZ7.C882742Ki 2012
[Fic]—dc23
2011045271

Paperback ISBN 978-1-60684-495-3

Book design by ARLENE SCHLEIFER GOLDBERG

Printed in the United States of America

*She'd never looked more beautiful, more*
*perfect, than she did when she was dead.*

BIRTHDAYS WERE WRETCHED, delicious things when you lived in Beau Rivage. The clock struck midnight, and presents gave way to magic.

Curses bloomed.

Girls bit into sharp apples instead of birthday cake, choked on the ruby-and-white slivers, and collapsed into enchanted sleep. Unconscious beneath cobweb canopies, frozen in coffins of glass, they waited for their princes to come. Or they tricked ogres, traded their voices for love, danced until their glass slippers cracked.

A prince would awaken, roused by the promise of true love, and find he had a witch to destroy. A heart to steal. To tear from the rib cage, where it was cushioned by bloody velvet, and deliver it to the queen who demanded the princess's death.

Girls became victims and heroines.

Boys became lovers and murderers.

And sometimes . . . they became both.

# CHAPTER ONE

"SWEET SIXTEEN COMING UP, MIRA," Elsa said with a grin, licking a stripe of sky blue frosting from her finger. "I'm taking your cake for a test run."

"Great," Mira said, forcing a smile. Her godmother had been wreaking havoc on the kitchen for the last hour or so, scattering measuring cups and batter-sticky bowls across every inch of counter space. Flour powdered Elsa's cheeks, and rainbow splotches of food dye stained her jeans. The kitchen was a disaster area—definitely not the place to sit at the table reading a nerve-wracking play like *Wait Until Dark*—but Mira had managed to block out the baking chaos going on around her. She had other things on her mind.

Mira's shoulders were hunched, as if to hide her guilt. Her hair kept spilling onto the book in front of her, obscuring the words. But it hardly mattered; she was too distracted by her plan—the culmination of eight months of deception—to concentrate on the story. The open book was her decoy. She could mumble one-word answers, and no one would worry that something was wrong—so long as she remembered to turn the pages once in a while.

Mira's other godmother, Bliss, darted in, her wide skirt swaying like a bell. Bliss was Mira's girly godmother: always dressed in frills, her hair in perfect blond ringlets touched with a few strands of silver. "Elsa, you're *ruining* the surprise!" Bliss scolded. "You can't make Mira's cake right in front of her! Besides—we agreed on pink frosting."

"No," Elsa said, "you *suggested* pink frosting. I chose to ignore your suggestion."

Bliss brought her fingers to her throat in a be-still-my-heart gesture. "That cake is going to make me ill before I taste it."

"We'll let Mirabelle decide," Elsa said. "Belle, what color frosting do you want?"

Mira shrugged. She wouldn't be around to celebrate. "Any color's fine."

Earlier, she'd crumpled the last of the love letters, the one that came out of the printer with the ink smeared, and stuffed it into her pocket. Her fingers went to it now for reassurance—like it was a charm from Bliss's shop.

*You can do this. You have to go or you'll always regret it.*

"Mira's distracted," Bliss announced, tapping a glass knitting needle against her palm. Bliss never knitted; she just carried the needle around, using it like a baton when she was making a point. Bliss was a little . . . eccentric.

Elsa, too. Her godmothers were unusual women: two friends who'd found themselves coparenting Mira when there was no one else to take care of her. Bliss ran a New Agey charm shop stocked with crystals, incense, and unicorn paraphernalia.

4

Elsa was a literature professor at the local university. Apart from a fine wrinkle and a new gray hair every year, they barely seemed to age.

Their lives revolved around Mira. Which made her impending betrayal even more despicable.

"Mira's always distracted," Elsa said, shooting Mira an affectionate look.

It was true—her godmothers were used to her daydreaming by now. But today she wasn't lost in fantasy. Today she just felt guilty, and was nervous about being found out, and struggling not to let it show on her face.

"If she wasn't distracted, she would no doubt choose *pink*," Bliss said, banging open the cupboards and peering inside. "Did you hide the red food coloring?"

"Maybe," Elsa said, before moving on to a more sensitive subject. Mira could sense the question before her godmother even asked. "You sure you don't want to have a party, Belle?"

They'd been over this before, and Mira's refusal to celebrate her sixteenth birthday was like a big sign stating I AM DEPRESSED. She'd always spent more time alone than with friends, but she did have them, and she'd always had parties in the past. Bliss and Elsa were big on birthdays. They said every year was a gift, not a guarantee, and ought to be celebrated accordingly.

Mira always felt that, under those words, they were talking about her parents' deaths. Two lives that had ended when Mira was three months old.

And maybe they were talking about her life, too.

Because Mira could have died that night. At her christening party, in the ballroom that had caught fire, the blaze

5

swallowing everything—including the life she'd been meant to have.

"Belle? Mirabelle? You listening?"

"Um, yes," she said, snapping back to reality. "Sorry. I was just thinking. . . ."

"You sure you don't want a party?" Elsa leaned against the counter, wiping her hands with a dish towel. "We could do something quiet at the house. Invite a few friends . . ."

Mira hated disappointing her godmothers. It would have been a lot easier to agree. Elsa and Bliss would have relaxed, stopped giving her those concerned looks. But she didn't have the heart to get their hopes up and let them plan a party she wouldn't be there to attend.

"You're breaking our hearts," Bliss teased, bending to kiss the top of Mira's head.

Mira took a deep breath—then exhaled slowly so it wouldn't sound like she was upset. One more day of lying. One more day until she ran away—to the one place her godmothers had forbidden her to go—and broke their hearts for real.

She'd have to get used to disappointing them.

The night she left, Mira scribbled her email password on a Post-it note and stuck it to her desk—the final touch. Then she counted her money, crammed the wad of bills in her pocket, and tiptoed into the hall, closing her bedroom door behind her.

It was after eleven and Bliss and Elsa were in their rooms, asleep. Other than the occasional tinkle of wind chimes outside, the house was silent.

Mira crept down the hall, barefoot and empty-handed,

doing her best to look innocent. If one of her godmothers woke up, she'd say she was going out to look at the stars—some dreamy excuse they'd believe.

But she hoped she wouldn't have to. If she lost her chance tonight . . . she might not be brave enough to try again.

Carefully, Mira unlocked the back door. She pushed open the screen door, which didn't creak because she'd oiled it two weeks ago when no one was home. Then she stepped out into the yard, like a thief in reverse: breaking and exiting. Stealing herself.

The air was damp, cool for June. It was drizzling, and the wet grass tickled her feet as she ran deeper into the yard, where the doghouse was. The doghouse had been there when they moved in, and stayed uninhabited since they didn't have a dog. Bliss had painted it Easter egg colors so it looked more like a dollhouse, and Mira had kept toys inside it when she was little.

Now Mira knelt in front of the doghouse and stuck her arm all the way in, feeling around until her fingers brushed the bulging nylon exterior of her duffel bag. Seizing the straps, she wrestled it through the opening, grunting a little as she jerked it free. It wasn't a large bag, but she'd packed it with as much as it could hold—even her shoes were inside. She'd hidden it that morning while Elsa was out running errands and Bliss was at her charm shop—then spent the day terrified one of them would find it.

Shivering as the rain pricked her arms, Mira got to her feet. She threw the bag's longest strap over her shoulder, took a deep breath—and dashed through the yard to the street. She ran until she got to the corner, bare feet slapping the pavement, then slowed to a quick walk. She kept her head down—and prayed that a police car wouldn't skim by on patrol.

She walked like that until she got to Rachel's house. Rachel was a girl she knew from drama class. They'd done scenes together, but Rachel was more of an acquaintance than a friend. She didn't like Mira enough to try to talk her out of this, didn't even care where she was going.

In other words: she was the perfect accomplice.

Rachel was waiting in her garage with her boyfriend, Matt, the two of them looking like twins in their dark jeans and T-shirts. Mira hurried up the driveway, a weight lifting off her now that she was one step closer.

"Hey," she said, out of breath and smiling. Her clothes were spotted all over with rain.

Rachel squinted; flicked her long bangs out of her eyes. "Mira, don't you need shoes?"

"They're in my bag," Mira said. "I was in a hurry."

"Prison break," Matt said, nodding like he understood.

It wasn't far from the truth. Not that her godmothers kept her locked up—they were just insanely strict. They protected her from everything—even things no normal person needed protection from.

Mira wasn't supposed to ride in a car unless an adult was driving, had to use a noxious-smelling depilatory because they wouldn't let her shave her legs, wasn't allowed to date, had to be home by ten on weekends, couldn't pierce her ears or wear makeup or have a cell phone. . . . The list went on and on.

She didn't like her godmothers' rules, but she followed them. Partly out of respect—she felt she owed it to Elsa and

Bliss to be obedient, after all they'd done for her. And they were so sweet, even when they were strict—she hated upsetting them.

But there was one restriction she couldn't accept: her godmothers refused to let her visit the city where she'd been born. After the fire, they'd taken her away and moved north to a college town in Indiana—and they had no intention of letting her go back. Mira pestered them about it a few times a year—and *always* on her birthday—and every time, they said no. Not "when you're older," not "maybe one day"—just a solid, unwavering *no*.

*Too many bad memories,* they argued. *It would be hard on you.*

But the only "memories" Mira had were their carefully chosen stories. How her parents had dressed her in lace and a dainty rosebud crown for her christening. How they'd danced together at their wedding, as if on air. Elsa and Bliss never told her anything new. It was as if they'd long ago decided on a handful of safe answers, and everything else was going to stay a mystery.

"Ready?" Rachel asked.

Mira nodded; handed over the money so Rachel wouldn't have to ask for it. "Cab fare," she said, per their agreement.

"And hush money," Rachel said with a grin. Not that she would tell Mira's godmothers. Rachel didn't care about rules—only her gas tank, and being compensated for her time.

"Man. I never would've guessed you were a bad girl," Matt said.

"I try to keep that a secret," Mira said, yanking her flip-flops out of her bag and stepping into them.

Rachel rolled her eyes. "You're both sooo bad. Get in the car."

They took their seats, Rachel started the engine—and they were off.

There were a lot of things Mira kept secret. Like how much she missed her parents.

It was embarrassing to admit she still missed them—so she didn't talk about it. It was easier to withdraw into daydreams when the loss hit her hardest, and imagine what her life would be like if her parents were alive. She'd re-create them from things her godmothers had told her, and she filled in the blank spots using characters from old movies, pieces of her own personality and the person she wished she could be—the person she might have been if she'd known them.

Rationally, she knew she should have gotten over their deaths a long time ago. She'd been lucky to survive, and she should focus on that, and be grateful. But the pain of losing her parents, of never knowing them, was always at the forefront of her heart.

She wanted to visit their graves. To tell their ghosts who she'd become. To see the city they'd called home, and get some closure. So she could—maybe—be normal.

She couldn't keep living like this.

Rachel drove with the radio tuned to a rock station, singing along whenever a song she liked came on. Matt turned around to loop his arms across the back of the passenger seat, his overgrown hair falling in his face.

"So where're you going?" he asked.

"San Francisco. To meet a guy," Mira lied, not caring about the rumors that would be circulating by the time she got back. They'd be better than whatever people already thought about her: a girl who was an orphan, who didn't date, who lived with two eccentric godmothers, and spent a ton of time in her own head. "It's been a long-distance thing," she said, filling out the lie.

"That's cool," Matt said, nodding.

"More like *weird*," Rachel weighed in. "That's a really long bus ride. This guy better be cute."

Mira shrugged. If Rachel thought long-distance romance was weird, she'd think the truth—a fake long-distance romance, complete with eight months' worth of love letters that Mira had written to cover her tracks—was a whole lot weirder.

Outside, dark houses in neat, quiet neighborhoods skipped by; and then they were on the highway, and Rachel was telling Matt to remind her when their exit was coming up, and Mira drifted and let them talk. She closed her eyes and saw the last line of the last letter she'd written:

*I'll see you soon. I love you. . . .*

Mira knew her godmothers pretty well—and she'd known that if she suddenly disappeared, Bliss and Elsa would assume she'd gone to the one place she was always pestering them about.

So she had to leave them chasing a false trail.

From November to June, Mira had written love letters to herself, and to a boy she invented, who supposedly lived in San Francisco. It had been a game at first—a plot that could be abandoned if she changed her mind. But the closer she came to leaving, the more determined she was to go through with it.

She'd sent the letters back and forth from two email accounts; and yesterday, she'd printed out a few prime examples—*I can't believe we're doing this! I can't wait to meet you!*—and planted them in her desk drawer.

She knew Elsa and Bliss would ransack her room once she disappeared, find the not-very-well-hidden letters detailing her plans to run off to San Francisco to visit "David," and decide that was where she'd gone. But even if they suspected the printed letters were a trick . . . once they broke into her email account (with the help of the password she'd written on the Post-it on her desk), and saw eight months' worth of progressively more impassioned messages . . . they'd be convinced.

Her godmothers hadn't raised her to be devious—and she usually wasn't. They'd never suspect she was deceitful enough, or crazy enough, to carry out such an elaborate plan. But turning sixteen was supposed to be special. She was willing to break the rules to ensure that it would be.

"Crap, I have to parallel park," Rachel muttered. Mira blinked her eyes open. Rachel had lowered the radio volume and was clutching the steering wheel tightly with both hands. The wet black road gleamed under the streetlights. Mira could see the bus station up ahead.

"Pull over; I'll do it," Matt said.

"I can do it, Matt, god!"

Mira leaned forward between the seats, eager to just *go* now that her destination was in sight. "You don't have to park. Just drop me off."

"You sure?" Rachel asked.

"Positive."

A moment later, the car jerked to a stop across from the station—and Mira got out, hauling her bag after her.

It was raining harder now. The drizzle had turned to a

steady patter, fat drops splashing her face, her shoulders. She waved good-bye to Rachel and Matt, then waited until the street was clear and ran across, tightening her toes so she didn't lose a flip-flop in the process.

"Good luck!" Matt yelled out the window.

"Be careful!" Rachel shouted.

"Thanks!" she yelled back.

Mira shoved through the bus station's grimy glass doors and went to the ticket counter, where she bought a one-way ticket with a handful of damp bills. She was shaking with excitement when she dumped her bag on the floor behind the last person in line, and sank down on top of it to wait.

She watched the clock tick by for almost an hour—until she heard the announcement that her bus was boarding, and the line started shuffling sleepily forward.

Mira wasn't usually a person who broke rules, who did things she wasn't supposed to, who lived dangerously, who took risks.

But a week before her birthday, she boarded a bus to Beau Rivage—the city where she'd been born, the city where they'd buried her parents.

The one place her godmothers had forbidden.

# CHAPTER TWO

SIX DAYS BEFORE HER SIXTEENTH BIRTHDAY, in a casino café called Wish, in the heart of Beau Rivage, Mira ordered her third lemonade of the night and spread a few cold French fries around her plate—artfully, so it looked like she was still eating, not just taking up space. It was one in the morning and she was alone in a strange city, with her duffel bag next to her, a play cracked open in front of her—and she had nowhere to go.

This was not the triumphant homecoming she'd imagined.

She was shivering from the air-conditioning. Her hair was even wavier than usual, made wild by the humidity and tangled from all the sweaty, plodding walking she'd done.

She needed a place to stay, but she was too young to rent a hotel room. Too skittish to camp outside. She'd trekked to three cemeteries that day, wanting, if she couldn't stay overnight in Beau Rivage, to at least see her parents' graves before she left—but all she found was sunburn and frustration.

By nightfall, her enthusiasm had vanished. The inviting

seaside city became a neon ruin. Dark figures stole through the shadows. Lights from the casinos rippled and flashed, drumming her eyes with violent starbursts. Humid air clung to her like an unwelcome admirer—and she'd hurried into the Dream Casino to shake it off.

That was how she'd ended up at Wish.

Casinos were open all night. She'd figured she could sit in the café, maybe doze off with her head on the table, and no one would care. But now that she'd been there three hours, Mira was starting to think her predicament was obvious. That some gambler would see a "helpless" girl in a frilly blouse and shorts and hit on her. Or some slot-playing grandma would spot a "runaway" and call the police. Or both.

She had the kind of innocent exterior people felt comfortable harassing: heavy-lidded, sleepy eyes, and a soft-featured face that made her seem gullible, though she wasn't. She kept her head down so as not to encourage any well-meaning Samaritans. Or perverts.

She was reading *A Streetcar Named Desire* for the nth time, mouthing words she'd nearly memorized, when she noticed a guy standing at the edge of her table. She moved her hand to the nape of her neck, worked her fingers through the knots in her hair, and prayed he would go away.

No such luck.

"I'm getting bored watching you," he said. "You've been reading that book for hours."

She raised her eyes and saw ripped jeans, black-ink sentences twisting across them like chains. A spiked leather cuff on one slender bronze wrist. A miniature chain-saw pendant dangled from his neck.

And then the kicker:

His hair and even his eyebrows were *blue*. Blue like sour candy, like poster paint. His hair stuck out from his head in spikes, stiff and sharp, and he had a smirk to match. A metal barbell pierced his left eyebrow.

Every part of him seemed calculated to drive people away. Like a plant studded with thorns, or an animal whose bright colors signaled *poison*.

Well, it was working.

Mira wasn't sure if he was flirting with her or harassing her for the fun of it—but she wanted him to leave her alone. And in her experience, the best way to get rid of an obnoxious guy was to be rude to him. She spent so much time being polite that she definitely knew how to be the opposite.

"I'm not here to entertain you," she said, putting on her coldest look.

The muscles in his tanned forearms flexed as he flattened his hands against the table and leaned over to read her page, undeterred. "What are you here for, then?"

"None of your business," she said.

"That's probably not true."

Mira ignored him, hoping he would get bored and leave.

"I'm Blue, by the way," he said.

She rolled her eyes. *Blue*. Right. "How nice for you."

Blue turned his attention to her duffel bag then: stuffed to bursting, the coded destination sticker from the bus company still stuck to the handle. "Are you lost? You're not an orphan, are you? My older brother loves seducing orphans."

The idea was absurd, but the word *orphan* struck a nerve. It always did.

Mira swallowed her initial reaction. "Is that so," she said flatly.

Blue nodded. "It's a sickness. So for your own safety, I'm going to have to ask you to leave."

"This is a public place," she argued. "I can—"

"Actually—" Blue started.

"Blue—you're being nice to her, I hope."

Mira turned to see a boy in a white oxford shirt, the sleeves rolled up to his elbows. He was cute, with honey-colored hair and an athlete's physique, but he seemed awkward, even a little embarrassed to be there. His eyes hovered around Mira, like a bee distracted by a flower.

She managed a strained smile, to be polite.

"This is Freddie," Blue announced. "He has a thing for damsels in distress." He said it almost derisively, and Freddie ducked his head and mumbled, "No."

"No, he's not being nice to me," Mira answered, since Blue was ignoring that part.

"I am being nice," Blue said. "I'm chasing you away."

She glared at him. "So I should be grateful you're a jerk?"

"Exactly." Blue leaned toward her again. "What are you doing here anyway? You're practically camped out."

"And you noticed because you have nothing better to do than stare at me."

"Yes," Blue said. "But it's also because I live here. The Dream is my dad's casino."

Mira took a shaky sip of her lemonade. *Great.* Maybe he was lying—but maybe he wasn't, and he was going to be a jerk and kick her out, because he could. Then she'd have to trek to one of the other casinos, when God only knew what kind of people were wandering around.

She grabbed her bag. "I have to use the bathroom," she said abruptly.

Freddie blushed and looked away.

"So you are human," Blue said.

"You thought I was something else?"

"No." Blue smiled. "Go ahead. We'll wait."


When she came back, Blue and Freddie had taken care of her check, and her glass of lemonade and the plate of fries she'd been "still working on" for three-plus hours had been cleared away. It shouldn't have been a big deal—but she'd been clinging to that table like it was her sanctuary. She felt like they'd stolen something from her.

"I wasn't done yet," she said. She imagined herself trudging through the city again, this time in the dark, her heavy duffel bag chafing her hip, the unnerving scuffle of footsteps behind her. . . .

"Don't bother thanking me," Blue said. "It's no trouble to comp your meal and your room. Really."

"I don't *have* a room here," she said, with growing irritation. "That's why I needed the table."

Blue's eyes lit up—and Mira got nervous: he seemed *way* too happy to find out she didn't have a room here. "Even better. I'll get you a room at the Palace down the street. It's a little sleazy—they have heart-shaped bathtubs and pink wallpaper and, uh . . . yeah." He gave her a fill-in-the-blanks look. "But no one will come by and grope you in your room. I can't promise you that if you fall asleep in the café."

She glared at him, as viciously as her face could muster.

Blue shrugged. "You never know. We cater to a filthy clientele."

"That's so tempting," Mira muttered. "But no thanks." She pushed past him and he grabbed her arm, bronze fingers tight against her skin. He didn't look like he was offering her a choice. He was trying to bully her into this, get her to leave the casino with him, and then . . . ?

"It's the middle of the night," Blue said easily, charm creeping into his voice. "Come on—Freddie and I'll walk you over."

Mira's blood was thudding in her ears. This had been a terrible idea. This whole thing . . . She jerked away from him. Her voice wavered as she said, "Did you not hear me? I'm not going *anywhere* with you!"

Blue's mouth snapped open like he was about to say something else. She didn't stick around to hear what it was.

The overhead lights in the casino blazed an ugly yellow. Mira followed the nauseatingly bold gold-black-violet carpet like it was the yellow brick road. Slot machines dinged and screamed en masse, like monsters at odds with each other. Cocktail waitresses wove in and out of the crowd.

It was 1:38 A.M.—there was no way she was going to wander the streets. So she found a secluded part of the elaborate fairy-tale garden in the Dream's lobby, climbed past the flimsy rope barricade, and settled at the base of a wisteria tree to wait until morning.

Mira checked her watch periodically, heart drumming nervously at first, wondering how long she could rest there before

19

someone kicked her out. But as 1:50 changed to 2:04 and then 2:15, she relaxed.

She was half asleep when she heard a female voice murmur, "Oh, look at her. I wonder what's wrong."

Mira snapped alert—and tried to pretend she hadn't heard. Maybe the woman wasn't talking about her. Or, more likely, she was—but maybe she would lose interest and go away.

She heard shoes sinking into the mulch that made up the floor of the garden, along with an annoyed masculine grunt as someone who would rather not be so nimble at 2:30 in the morning climbed over the rope and into the man-made fairy-tale forest.

Mira lifted her chin—just as the guy crouched in the dirt to be level with her.

She guessed he was twenty or twenty-one, which surprised her. She was used to college kids because she lived in a college town, and generally, they were such a mix of tolerant and self-absorbed that they didn't care what anyone did. She couldn't imagine one of Elsa's students checking on her.

But then, this guy didn't seem like a typical twenty-one-year-old.

He wore a dark suit without a tie, his shirt open at the neck. His hair glinted blue-black, and his eyes were just as dark—like sapphires, or a raven's wing. There was something not quite normal about him, something too beautiful, and strange, and she found herself watching him the way she'd watch a fire: captivated, and a little afraid to be so close.

He dipped his head and looked at her like he was waiting for her to tell him a secret.

"You don't look happy," he said.

"I'm okay," she said, aware of how false that sounded, considering where she was.

"Are you hiding from someone?"

"No . . . not exactly."

His dark eyes were taking her in, shifting from her bag to her wrinkled clothes to the unease that was probably all over her face. "You can tell me, you know. I might be able to help."

Past him, Mira could see the young woman who'd first spotted her, leaning sideways to peer through the lacy grove of trees. She had dark brown hair, a cute, heart-shaped face, and a cuter body—perfectly showcased by the tight green dress she wore. "Is she okay?" the woman called.

"She's fine, Cora." He lowered his voice and asked Mira, "So what's going on?"

Mira shrugged. "Some guy was harassing me in the café . . . so I came here."

"Some guy?" He raised his eyebrows. "You should introduce us. I'll make him apologize before I kick him out."

"I don't—oh?" A shiver crawled through her. Her eyes lingered on the blue-black of his hair, the bottomless blue eyes. "You—work here?"

"I run this place," he said. "Well, more or less. While my dad's away. And I love throwing people out. Just give me an excuse."

"Uh . . . I don't think you'll throw this person out. I think he's your brother. But thanks," she mumbled.

He laughed. The corners of his eyes turned up—and suddenly he was different. The cool expression left his face, and he was smiling. "Blue? Was my idiot brother bothering you?

You're right, I can't kick him out—but let me try to make it up to you. How about a spa session? Dinner at Rampion?"

He started tossing out options, like he'd be happy to give her whatever she wanted; and as he kept talking, she stopped hearing the words as the rush of blood in her head overtook them. The way his eyes locked casually on hers, combined with his body language, the timbre of his voice now that he was being nice made her realize—he was kind of sexy. And when his hand brushed hers by accident, a fizzy shock buzzed through her veins. This wasn't a kid with a skateboard, who smelled like body spray and laughed too hard at dirty jokes. He was something else, someone who lived in a different world, and she liked that.

"No, really, I'm okay," Mira said, embarrassed that she was reacting to this guy she barely knew, ten feet from where his girlfriend was standing. "I just want to sit here for a while."

He shook his head. "You can't stay in the garden. What's your room number?" He took his phone out. "I'll deal with your parents. Did you fight with them? Is that why you've got your bag with you?"

The girlfriend—Cora—was shifting her weight, rubbing her bare arms. She looked less worried now and more impatient. "Everything all right?" she called. He waved a hand in her direction: *wait.*

"I don't *have* a room here," Mira said. "I'm not with my parents. I'm here to *find* my parents." She exhaled a frustrated breath, already regretting blurting that out. She expected him to tell her how stupid that was. Instead, he seemed interested.

"Find them?"

"I'm looking for their graves. They died in Beau Rivage

a long time ago. But I don't know where they're buried. And I don't—have anywhere else to go right now." Mira fidgeted with the zipper on her bag, certain she would have to leave. Her muscles felt so worn-out from walking all day that she just wanted to sleep. Give up in every possible way.

"You don't have a place to stay, family here, anything?"

She shook her head, embarrassed. She'd been ruthlessly careful with every detail of her escape but had counted on her instinct, her affinity for her parents, to guide her once she got to Beau Rivage. Now she just felt stupid.

"You do now," he said. He lifted her bag before she could stop him, pressed down the rope barrier, and glanced back like he expected her to follow. "You coming?"

"Um—" She scrambled after him. "I can carry that. And I wasn't looking for a handout when I—"

"Relax," he said, turning so her bag was out of reach. "Let me help you."

Reluctantly, she climbed over the rope barrier, and he stepped down after. Mira wasn't sure where they were going—but she was sure Cora was less than thrilled. That much was clear from the dirty look the girl gave her.

"It's two A.M.," Blue's brother said. "And we have empty rooms that are going to stay empty. So the Dream is putting you up for the night. No arguments."

Mira nodded, abashed. "Okay. I mean—thank you."

"*Or* you could call the police," Cora said—her voice taking on a hardness that hadn't been there before. She crossed her arms over her chest. "Since there's probably someone looking for her. And she's not your problem."

A chill came over Mira. "I—no one's looking for—"

"Everyone in this hotel is my problem," the guy said coolly, eyes on his girlfriend. "And I'm sure that if she wanted to call the police, she'd do that herself. So how about you go play"— he dug a handful of betting chips out of his pocket—"and see how fast you can lose my money. Set a record tonight."

Cora made a face but accepted the chips, tucking them into her black clutch bag like she'd done this a hundred times. "Okay, but hurry up. I'm not feeling very lucky."

"I'll call you later," he said. He pressed the button for the elevator, and he and Mira stepped inside when the brassy doors slid open, leaving the other girl behind.

Mirrors on every side of the elevator caught their reflections— and showed Mira she was even more disheveled than she'd thought. Her wavy hair was tangled and sticking up in places, like she'd been rolling around in a forest, not just sleeping against a tree. She wanted to smooth it down but didn't want to seem like she was trying to look pretty for him. That would be more embarrassing than having messy hair.

He brought her to a room on the twentieth floor, opened it with his passkey, and set her bag down, then strode to the window and thrust the thick curtains apart. Moonlight swept into the room, edging the dark shapes with light.

He turned toward her but didn't move away from the window. "You just got in tonight?"

"Earlier today."

She drifted closer, lured by the view. Below, she could see the rolling dark waves of the sea, tinted silver by the moon. The Dream was so quiet, now that they were away from the clang of machines, the chaos of hundreds of voices.

"So you don't know the city very well?" he said.

"No," Mira admitted. "I have a map, but—it's hard to know where to start."

He looked at her carefully, like he was considering something. "If you're not in a hurry, I might be able to help you. If you're really serious about this."

"I'm serious about it," she said quickly. "I've wanted this for so long, I—it would mean a lot to me." She *was* in a hurry. But the thought of trekking through the city alone was so demoralizing she was willing to wait a few days if it meant she'd have help.

He nodded. "All right, good. Well—I can't promise you anything, but I'll see what I can do. And in the meantime, you'll be our guest."

"Thank you. So much." She felt like she was babbling, even when she barely said anything. He was being so nice—she should let him leave already. She started to move away from the window, and he said:

"So tell me your story." And she stopped. She could sense his attentiveness, like a hand on the back of her neck. Like his voice was touching her skin. "Who'd you leave behind at home?" he asked. "Foster parents?"

"My godmothers. They knew my parents. They were there when they . . . died. And they took care of me after that."

He leaned his shoulder against the window, tilted his head to look at her. The silver light turned his dark blue hair and eyes a midnight black. "Do you mind if I ask what happened?"

Normally, she didn't talk about her tragedy—but he was looking at her in a way that made her want to trust him. And he'd agreed to help her with this—this dream that meant everything to her. She wanted him to know.

Mira bowed her head. "I was three months old. We were at my christening party. . . . It was held in this beautiful ballroom, with a mural on the ceiling, like the Sistine Chapel, except with fairy-tale scenes. You could spin around and around and always see a different story. There was a red-cloaked girl running from a wolf, and a mermaid whose fins were splitting to become legs, and—a beauty taming her beast. . . . That's what my godmothers told me—I was too young to remember."

She took a deep breath, and paused. The tale of that night was whole in her head, in one piece like a bedtime story, because that was how her godmothers told it—but she couldn't tell it straight through. She had to split it into *before* and *after*.

"Then—the fire started. It spread through the ballroom, and crawled up the curtains and reached as high as the ceiling. Smoke filled the air, and beams were crashing down . . . and my parents were trying to save everyone. They handed me to my godmother Bliss, and she wrapped me in her shawl and ran through the smoke to safety. It was a party, and there were a lot of people . . . but my parents managed to get everyone out. Except, I don't think they realized they'd done it. Because they kept searching. So they were—" The words stuck in her throat, as hard as a stone. "They were the only ones who didn't make it out in time."

"How tragic," he said. "They were heroes . . . but they could have lived, if they'd known." He said it like he meant it. Like he understood how awful it was to have lost them that way.

Mira nodded. "That's the hardest part. I can't help

wishing they hadn't tried so hard to save everyone. Because—then maybe I'd still have them."

She waited for him to insist she didn't really mean that—like Elsa always did—or to say it was selfish to trade a host of lives to save two. But his mind was elsewhere.

"A christening party . . . So your parents were very traditional."

"They sort of look that way in pictures. I have maybe one picture where my dad's *not* in a tuxedo," she said with a smile. "But I don't know. I mostly think of them as perfect."

He tipped his head back, eyes closing, moonlight sliding over his throat. "I don't remember my mother very well. I never think of her as perfect. But that's probably because she left. When someone chooses to leave you . . . it's different."

"You lost your mother?" She hadn't expected to have that in common with him. She wondered if that was why he'd offered to help her.

"She left when I was eight. I think she was afraid of getting attached."

Mira nodded, not sure what to say. She couldn't imagine a mother cold enough to leave for that reason. "I'm sorry," she said.

He shrugged. "It was a long time ago."

They stood at the window a moment more, and then he went to the light and turned it on. The room expanded from a dark ocean overlook to a subtly glitzy suite; the shine and shimmer of the casino stirred with the colors of sea and sand.

Now that the room was brighter, it seemed less intimate, less a place for confessions. Mira unpacked her bag while he called the front desk, unrolling crumpled shirts and tank tops and skirts and trying not to stare at him.

"This is Felix," he said into the phone. "I need you to activate a key for room 2005 and bring it up here. Right. Just put that it's my guest. Leave the checkout date open."

He—Felix—hung up and faced her. Paused for a moment, watching her unpack. "Someone's bringing your key."

"Thanks," she said, pushing her hair out of her face, straightening up. Then it occurred to her that maybe she was being presumptuous. That it was rude to assume the room was free.

"I can pay," she said, reaching for her wallet.

Felix gave a short shake of his head. "Don't worry about it. I feel better knowing you're not on the street. Think of it like you're doing me a favor. Not like you owe me."

He smiled, and there was something unguarded about it, like they were friends. Mira smiled back—feeling safe, and less lost—and the tension she'd carried all day began to ebb.

A few minutes later, there was a knock at the door. A hotel employee had arrived with the key card. Felix took it and sent the clerk away, then set the key card on the desk next to a hotel notepad, where he wrote down the numbers she would need: the front desk, room service, his phone number—and that was when she finally saw his full name, the letters surging forward in a series of sharp slashes:

*FELIX VALENTINE*

"If you can't reach me . . . that probably means I'm dealing with someone high maintenance, or I'm in a meeting and can't answer my phone. It doesn't mean I'm ignoring you."

He stopped, lost in thought, and then laughed. "I never

asked your name. I was so caught up in . . ." He shook his head. "It's late, and I wasn't thinking. What should I call you?"

"Mira," she said. "Or Mirabelle."

"All right, Mira . . . I'll let you get some sleep. But call me if you need anything. And tomorrow or the day after, we'll start our search—whenever I can steal some time."

"If you're busy, I can look by myself. You've done a lot for me already; you don't—"

The words dried up in her mouth. Something about the way Felix was looking at her—his eyes dark, and very sure—made her feel like it was silly to keep offering him an out. He touched her shoulder and said:

"Mira, I spend every day doing things I don't want to do. But I *want* to help you. I can make time for that." He leaned in then, and his lips brushed her cheek; and for a moment he was all she could see. Her world was reduced to the warmth of his lips, the hint of smoke on his clothes, and the tang of his cologne.

And then he moved away. He was being friendly, probably. But she wasn't used to being kissed by anyone other than her godmothers. She wasn't used to kisses that were simultaneously startling and wonderful, casual and memorable. Her world was so much smaller than that.

"Okay?" he said with a smile.

"Okay," she managed, not sure she knew what she was answering anymore.

"Good." Felix stepped into the hall; paused long enough to tell her, "Hey—bolt the door after I leave. You can't be too careful around here."

"I will," she promised. But she didn't. Not immediately.

Her cheek burned like she'd been lying in the sun too long, and she stood perfectly still, not wanting to break the spell. The scent of Felix's cologne lingered on her skin.

When she closed her eyes, she could imagine he was there. She could relive that kiss one more time. All two seconds of it.

Exhaling slowly, Mira threw the bolt and kicked off her flip-flops. She let her fantasy float away—*it was the kiss equivalent of a handshake; nothing to get excited about*—and let the delicious freedom of being barefoot bring her back to reality. The carpet soothed her, because it wasn't a hot strip of road with no end in sight. She had a room; she didn't have to worry that someone would harass her or hurt her. She could rest.

But first: a shower. She was too sticky with sweat to sleep.

She padded to the bathroom—which was huge and had folded towels as thick as couch cushions, an entire wall of mirrors, and a deep Jacuzzi tub that was separate from the shower.

Mira shucked off her dirty clothes and stepped into the glass-walled shower. She scrubbed the day's travel grime from her skin, until she felt like a new person, with fresh hopes—and as she did, her fingers grazed the disfigurement at the small of her back.

The mark.

The mark rested at the base of her spine. It was wine red like a burn, shiny-smooth like a scar: a ring spoked by thin red lines, like a wheel. It was as big around as her fist.

Her clothes covered the mark if she was careful to wear long shirts, but her bikini never did. It looked like she'd been branded, and she hated it. One of the reasons she was growing her hair out so long was for extra camouflage. If she had hair down to her butt, she could walk around in her bathing suit without worrying what people would say.

Because she'd heard it all, since her first appearance at a pool party when she was twelve. Bikini clad for the first time, constantly hurrying out of the water for another trip down the waterslide, she'd heard:

*What's that thing on her back? Cancer?*

Giggles. Sounds of disgust and disbelief.

*Is that a tattoo? It's so ugly!*

She'd wrapped her towel around her waist as soon as she realized they were talking about her, then sat on the side, the fun of the waterslide forgotten, while she waited for Bliss and Elsa to ferry her home.

Ever since that day, she'd felt the mark like it was a living thing. Like an eye that followed her everywhere.

Her godmothers said it was silly to be self-conscious about "a little birthmark." *It's your body, there's nothing wrong with it.*

As if it was normal to have a hideous, wheel-shaped mark on your skin.

She felt a pang of guilt when she thought of Elsa and Bliss, and wondered where they were right now—whether they'd flown to San Francisco or were tearing the house apart in a panic. But she was too exhausted to beat herself up over it. She didn't like lying to them, but they hadn't left her much choice. She needed closure, needed that connection with her parents. She'd deal with the consequences when this was over.

Finished with her shower, Mira wrapped her soggy mass of blond hair in a towel, pulled on the pair of boxer shorts and the tank top she'd brought as pajamas, and climbed between the sheets, letting the covers swallow her up like quicksand.

She was so tired she could barely feel her limbs—but her brain wouldn't fall asleep. She stared at the blackness of the ceiling and wondered if she was crazy, coming all the way to Beau Rivage to kneel beside two graves. Breaking her godmothers' hearts to save her own.

*Of course you're crazy. It's a question of* how *crazy.*

The covers were heavy, like earth lying on top of her.

Normally, when she couldn't sleep, she took refuge in daydreams. She'd unroll a story for her parents like a velvet carpet, and guide them down it until she fell asleep. But tonight she felt too caught in the present to leave it.

She was in a new place, in a beautiful room that belonged to her. She thought of Felix, and how he'd kissed her cheek, and her heart raced like it wanted to remind her it was there. She'd spent eight months obsessed with her plan, writing love letters to a boy who didn't exist. It felt nice to have a real crush for once.

When she slept, she dreamed of the ocean, of wisteria petals fluttering onto her skin. Of Felix kneeling in the sand, sea foam dripping from his fingers, murmuring, *here they are.*

She awoke to a tremendous *bang.*

# CHAPTER THREE

PALE DAWN LIGHT BLED around the curtains—enough for Mira to see that the bolt on the door had been breached, and the door had been flung open and slammed hard against the wall. A slender, dark figure moved swiftly through the room—

And pounced on the bed.

Mira started to scream; she reached for the phone beside the bed as the intruder's body fell onto hers. A hot hand clamped over her mouth.

"What are you still doing here?" he hissed. "Are you crazy?"

Disoriented but filled with adrenaline, she bucked like a wave—she was stronger than she looked; she'd been dancing ballroom for years—and managed to roll him off her, his body thumping hard against the floor. Her instincts said, *fight, protect yourself.*

She leapt from the bed and landed on him, her knees striking his chest. Then she reached for the phone—and she would have smashed it into his head if he hadn't jolted his hips and knocked her sideways.

He grabbed her wrists and pinned her flat on her back. Leaned over her.

And in the dim hints of dawn, she recognized him. The spiky hair. The wiry frame that was working hard to keep her trapped. And her fear quickly turned to anger.

"You really are crazy," Blue muttered. "You need to get the hell out of here, *now*."

"Get off me!" she said, struggling to bring her leg up so she could knee him somewhere sensitive.

"I'm trying to keep you from getting killed."

"Yeah, right—"

The busted door had long since swung to a close, clicking almost shut. Now it opened again and Freddie's worried head peeked in. "Is everything—?"

When he spotted them on the floor, he hurried inside, looking mortified. "Blue, what are you doing?"

"You know what I'm doing."

"Get your stupid friend off me!" Mira said.

"You're the stupid one," Blue told her. "Because you're still here. Pretty sure I told you to leave."

*I hate you,* Mira thought, glaring up at him.

Blue's chain-saw pendant hung down as he hovered over her, the silver blade dangling in front of her face, taunting her. She wanted to knock it out of the way, but he had her hands. The floor that had felt so plush last night was hard under her shoulders; and in her skimpy, makeshift pajamas—fine for living in a house full of women, not for being assaulted by strange boys—she felt almost naked.

34

Freddie dropped down beside them, distressed. "Let go of her, Blue; that looks really bad."

"Feel free to stop him," Mira said, "instead of frowning at me like a sad puppy."

"Hey!" Freddie said, looking like a sadder puppy.

"I'm not going to molest you," Blue said.

"You're molesting my wrist," Mira said. "I don't want you touching me."

"I didn't want you to knee me in the lungs, so I guess we're even."

"We're far from even," she said through gritted teeth.

"Back to business," Blue said. "You need to get out of this hotel—and not come back. And if I have to carry you out, cart you to the Palace Casino or a Motel 6, I will. If I have to hurt you, I will—I'm *not* nice. So don't test me unless you want proof of that."

Mira answered him with words Bliss and Elsa never let her say. Blue smiled, like she'd told him he was a talented assailant.

Freddie looked stricken. "Ladies shouldn't talk like that."

"Oh, shut up!" she snapped.

"Be nice to Freddie," Blue said. "He has a crush on you."

"Maybe *I'm* not nice either," she said.

"Fine," Blue said. "Be mean to Freddie. But don't blame me if a lovesick sparrow pecks your eyes out. You've been warned."

Blue released her and got to his feet, watching her carefully, like he expected her to lash out. "Get your stuff. Then we're getting out of here."

"Those sparrows wouldn't hurt anyone," Freddie said. "A blue jay might. Or a hummingbird. But never a—"

Blue cut him off so he could yell at her. "Hurry up. You've

got two minutes before I pack your stuff for you."

"You're crazy," Mira said, pulling on her hoodie and zipping it up, since she wasn't wearing a bra and she'd had enough of these guys staring at her. "First, you offer to comp my room. Then you try to drag me off to some sleazy hotel. And when your brother is actually *nice* to me, you freak out and assault me. What part of that makes sense?"

Blue shook his head. "If I had put you up somewhere, you wouldn't have met my brother. I don't want him around you. End of story."

"I can't believe you're jealous of your own brother," she muttered.

"Jealous?" Blue narrowed his eyes, looking angry finally. It gave his face a different cast from the cocky obnoxiousness he usually wore. "You have *no idea* what you're getting yourself into. Now do what I say before I do something I'll regret."

Mira shoved her feet into her flip-flops, huffing like a bull, she was so furious. "I doubt you regret anything. You'd need a conscience for that."

"Yeah, yeah—let's go." Blue put his hand out and shoved her lightly between the shoulder blades. "You don't belong here. You have no freaking clue."

Blue and Freddie escorted Mira through the Dream's lobby and out the front door, where a valet stood waiting to usher guests in and out of cabs. He saw Blue and motioned for the hotel car—a black Lexus SUV—and saw them all in safely. Mira wondered if it would make a difference to the valet if she announced she was a hostage. She guessed no.

"Where to?" the driver asked.

"Take us to the Deneuve estate," Blue said.

"Viv isn't going to want to see us this early," Freddie said.

"I don't care what Viv wants."

"Do you ever care what anyone wants?" Mira asked sharply.

"No," Blue said.

Blue lowered the windows and slouched on the wide leather seat, his eyes closing, his body going limp like water—like he was determined to grab a few minutes of sleep. Mira had the urge to hit him while he was vulnerable, to get back at him for holding her down—but it seemed absurd to start fighting in front of the hotel's driver.

The whole morning was absurd. She'd never felt so angry, or aggressive, in her entire life. She didn't normally want to hit people, or even yell at them—because normally you could reason with people. And if you couldn't, you could avoid them. But Blue was impossible. He was so rude and belligerent and . . . relentless about it.

Mira settled back and did her best to calm down. Maybe Felix would punch Blue for her later.

They rode in near silence, Freddie periodically asking the driver whether he wanted to hear their band's CD, the driver always answering with a firm no. Tall buildings and silvery sheets of ocean gave way to roads thick with magnolia and oak trees as they left the city behind. A weedy green smell infused the car, so strong Mira could taste it.

By the time they reached the Deneuve estate—a white mansion located on the edge of a wooded golf course—Mira had gone from furious to annoyed, and was heading toward hopeful. *Viv* sounded like a girl's name. Viv probably wouldn't jump on her or order her around; she might even take her side and yell at Blue and Freddie—especially since they were bothering her so early in the morning.

As they climbed out of the car and headed toward the house, Mira saw that a well-built, dark-haired teenage guy was pushing a lawn mower across the sloping yard, easing it around the oak trees that punctuated the front lawn. Sweat slicked his chest, and bits of cut grass flecked his light brown skin. He wore a pair of maroon basketball shorts with a T-shirt tucked into the waistband.

He shut off the mower when he saw them—and scowled.

Mira hoped that wasn't Viv. But on the bright side: someone else was unhappy to see Blue and Freddie. The world was already making more sense.

Blue hiked up the hill as if the guy's pissed-off expression had energized him. Mira hurried to keep up.

"Would you like me to carry your bag?" Freddie asked. He looked a little guilty—but hopeful, too.

"No." She twisted the strap around her wrist so he couldn't take it from her. "Don't do me any favors."

"But I'd *like* to do you favors."

She glared at him. *"No."*

As they drew closer to the house, a woman rose into view on the veranda. She wore a sheer pink robe trimmed with marabou feathers, and held a martini glass full of what looked like orange juice. Her large, very perky—probably very *expensive*—breasts rose from the neckline of her negligee. They didn't so much as wiggle when she waved hello.

"Is that Viv?" Mira asked.

Blue burst out laughing. "You're lucky she didn't hear you say that."

"That's Regina, Viv's wicked stepmother," Freddie said. "Er, stepmother," he corrected. "*Normal stepmother* is what I meant."

"Um . . . okay," Mira said.

"And that's Henley," Blue said as they rounded the hill, gesturing to the lawn-mowing guy. "He works here as a gardener. Among other things."

When they reached Henley, he was wiping the sweat from his face with his T-shirt. He was their age, seventeen or so, but his forehead was already creased, like he'd spent years being on guard, waiting for something bad to happen.

"Why'd you have to bring Knight here?" Henley asked. His voice was deep and gritty, like the boys' at school who flunked everything but auto shop and were perpetually pissed off.

"Relax, Silva," Blue said. "Don't be paranoid."

"Henley thinks I want to date Viv," Freddie whispered to Mira—a bit too loudly to be subtle. "But I don't. I haven't made a single overture."

"Who's this?" Henley asked, eyeing Mira now.

"No one important," Blue said. "Just a random seduceable girl I'm protecting."

"I'm Mira," she said, sticking her hand out.

Henley's hot, sweaty hand engulfed hers. His eyes were narrowed and he still looked angry, but it didn't seem directed at her. "Nice to meet you, I guess. Too bad it's in the company of this asshole."

"Viv's alive, right?" Blue said. "You didn't cut her heart out?"

"What is wrong with you?" Mira snapped. "That's disgusting."

Henley's eyes were hard, his gaze heavy. "You're lucky I don't have an axe, Valentine."

"Aren't we all," Blue said. "So: Viv?"

"What do you want with her?"

Henley was the gardener, but he behaved like a gatekeeper. Mira wondered what that was about. Maybe he was Viv's boyfriend—or wished he was.

Blue shrugged. "I needed to get Mirabrat out of the hotel. Felix latched on to her and she thinks he's dreamy."

"Oh, shut up," Mira said. "You don't know anything about me."

"Anyway," Blue went on, "she doesn't have a place to stay, and I felt like bothering Viv. It seemed like a good idea when I first thought of it."

Blue glanced toward Viv's stepmother, who was leaning over the veranda, dipping her finger in her martini glass and peering at the group. "Is Regina watching to make sure the lawn gets done, or is she standing by in case you need her to lick the sweat off your chest?"

Henley bristled. "She just likes having breakfast outside."

"That's what I figured," Freddie said amicably. "She seems like a nice woman. Aside from the wickedness."

"Shut up, Knight," Henley growled.


Eventually, the four of them went around back, where Viv's balcony was.

The balcony overlooked a small garden made up of a stone well flanked by fruit trees. Birds dotted the branches like ornaments on a Christmas tree—until they saw Freddie, at which point they rushed to surround him, flapping above his head like a floating crown. Chipmunks emerged from the underbrush to squeak at his feet.

Freddie held out his hand, and a sparrow perched on his

finger. He laughed a pure laugh, and called, "Mira, look!" Then he beckoned her closer, saying, "Don't worry, this one won't peck your eyes out." But Mira kept her distance, too stunned to move.

The woodland creatures ignored Henley and Blue, but they couldn't get enough of Freddie. It wasn't a scary sight, but it was *wrong*. It went against nature. Mira squeezed her eyes shut, hoping that the adoring swarm of animals would disappear.

But when she opened her eyes, the animals were still there. Freddie was still laughing that sweet, ticklish laugh. And Henley was scowling at him like Freddie was a being of pure evil.

"Different mark, different destiny," Blue was saying to Henley, his voice low and calm. His eyes cut quickly toward Mira—then away.

"Oh yeah." Henley snorted. "Like she doesn't notice."

The French doors that led to Viv's bedroom were wide open, a breeze sucking the filmy white curtains in and out.

Henley cupped his hands around his mouth and barked, "Viv! Wake up!"

A minute later, a girl stepped onto the balcony. The sunlight revealed her slowly, like it was reluctant to touch her.

Her skin was chalk white, her lips were red-pink like pomegranate seeds, and her hair was as black as a stroke of Chinese calligraphy. She wore a nightgown that lay almost flat against her petite, boyish figure, and a red satin sleep mask that was pushed up on her forehead.

"Hey there, Vivian," Blue said.

Viv leaned her elbows on the balustrade, and three doves

fluttered down from the roof to join her. "God. First the lawn mower and now this. I need my beauty sleep, you know."

"You'll have plenty of that soon enough," Blue said. "Might as well stay conscious while you can." He grinned crookedly up at her, and Viv rubbed a hand across her face, looking miserable.

"If I could control these birds, they'd be shitting all over you," she said.

"Too bad you own their hearts, not their minds," Blue said. "Can we come up?"

"I guess," Viv said. "You're not going to leave until I say yes."

Henley led them through the back door and into the kitchen, grass clippings dropping to the floor as he tugged his dirty T-shirt on. He looked uncomfortable in the elegant house. Like he didn't belong there, and he knew it.

When they reached Viv's bedroom, Viv was dressed and sitting on the edge of an enormous red and black bed, her body standing out starkly against the bloodred sheets. Viv took a drink from a half-empty Coke bottle and grimaced. "It's flat," she complained. "And warm."

"Because you're too damn lazy to go downstairs and get a new one," Henley said.

"Because I don't want to see the bitch," Viv snapped back.

Blue flopped down on the bed and grabbed a pillow to get comfortable. "Hey, at least it's a breakfast she can't choke on."

"Shut *up*," Viv and Henley said at once.

Mira wondered what *that* was supposed to mean. Maybe Viv had choked on something once? And now they made fun of her about it?

42

Sighing, Mira sat down in Viv's desk chair, next to a Mac laptop. It was too hard to keep up with these people and their inside jokes; she didn't know what they were talking about half the time.

The laptop's Apple logo was covered by an X of black electrical tape. Mira narrowed her eyes at it. *Weird.*

"So what's up?" Viv asked, causing Mira to swivel around in her chair. Viv was staring at her, her dark eyes shining. "Is she ours?"

Blue shook his head. "Out-of-towner. Just doing guard duty."

Viv nodded, like that made sense to her. "Cute. But you need to get a new hobby."

A dove fluttered in from the balcony and landed on Viv's shoulder, cooing sweetly. A chain of blue butterflies followed, then drifted toward Freddie.

Freddie laughed again, and Henley grunted and hurled Viv's Coke bottle through the open French doors. The bottle failed to clear the railing, and brown liquid spilled all over the balcony.

"You're cleaning that up," Viv told him.

"Anything else you want me to do?" Henley snapped.

Viv rolled her eyes. "Take anger management classes? Stop being an idiot?"

"I vote for all of the above," Blue said, hugging Viv's pillow and rolling over so his back was to them. "You guys make it impossible to sleep."

"Says the guy who woke me up at seven in the morning!" Viv grabbed her pillow and wrenched it from Blue's grasp, then hit him with it until he finally sat up.

They were all quiet for a moment. A mouse with a daisy clenched between its teeth took advantage of the stillness to scurry across the floor. It dropped the daisy at Viv's feet, then darted beneath the dresser before anyone could step on it.

Mira wanted to ask, *Why is this place crawling with animals? Cute little animals that act like they're in love with Viv?* But the fact that no one else was asking it made her hesitate.

"You should come out with us," Viv said to Mira, bending down to dig a pair of sandals out from under her bed, and unearthing a tiny white rabbit in the process.

"I really just want to—" Mira started to explain why she was in Beau Rivage, but Viv interrupted before she could finish.

"Don't worry," Viv said with a smile. "We won't let anyone hurt you." She turned to the others. "You guys feel like going to Gingerbread?"

"Fine with me," Blue said. "Felix won't set foot in that place."

"That's because you guys own, like, five fancy restaurants. I wouldn't go either if I had my own sushi bar downstairs." Viv slipped on her sandals, winding their red ribbon laces around her ankles. "Just give me a minute."

Straightening, Viv went over and stood in front of a black-framed mirror. The mirror caught her reflection from head to waist, and Viv looked nervous as she stared into it. Twisting her hair into a messy spiral, she blinked at the glass as if waiting for its approval.

*"You look beautiful,"* the mirror said. *"Exquisite."*

The mirror . . . spoke? Mira squinted to see if there was a speaker box attached. Like . . . maybe you could buy a mirror that came with preset phrases: press a button and it would say, *"You're gorgeous!"*

But Viv seemed upset, not flattered. She swore and yanked the pins from her hair, black waves spilling to her shoulders, then flipped her head upside down and mussed her hair with her hands. "Worse?" she asked, with a pinched look on her face.

"*Still beautiful,*" the mirror replied. "*More beautiful than she is.*"

Mira made a choking sound, and Blue kicked his way off the bed, knocking another pillow down as his boots hit the floor.

"Could you stop playing with your mirror?" Blue asked. "You're freaking out our guest."

"I was just checking," Viv said defensively.

"Why bother? You already know what the answer will be."

"I know. But—" Viv shook her head. "Never mind."

Freddie got to his feet, sending the butterflies into a frenzy. "We'll go to Gingerbread House, Viv. Pancakes will make you feel better. And maybe you'll gain some weight and Regina will be happier for a while." He tried on a shining smile, but it didn't seem to improve Viv's mood.

"Regina's never happy." Viv sighed and left the room, her platform sandals clunking down the stairs.

Mira noticed that Henley watched Viv—watched the space where she'd been, once she was gone—with the same admiring gaze the mirror had fixed on her. The naked longing on his face made Mira shiver.

She felt like she'd stumbled into a world of strangers' secrets—into wonderland, instead of the city where she'd been born—and their secrets were like dynamite waiting to explode. She wasn't sure how much she wanted to know.

45

*"I held her life in my hands.*
*And then I took it away from her."*

# CHAPTER FOUR

GINGERBREAD HOUSE was a kitschy café, housed in a cottage that had been decorated with candy. The window frames were red and white striped, and lacquered strawberry squares, butterscotch medallions, rainbow-swirl lollipops, and peppermints stuck to the walls.

The early morning crowd was trickling in: a mix of solo diners, couples, and cops. A dozen girls in party dresses walked barefoot through the parking lot, carrying their worn-out shoes—like they'd spent the night clubbing and were reluctant to go home.

A party of middle-aged tourists, dressed in T-shirts that bore the name of a lighthouse they'd visited, was turned away at the door by a woman in a Bavarian barmaid costume, with the explanation that they needed a reservation.

Viv didn't meet the same resistance. She claimed an eight-person table in the middle of the cramped café, then took out her phone and started inviting people. A waitress hustled over to hand out menus, and poured them all cups of sludgy black coffee.

Mira found herself seated near the end of the table, next to Blue and across from Freddie. She'd had a moment in the car—crammed in the backseat with people she barely knew—when the situation had overwhelmed her. She'd felt a sudden burst of loneliness and helplessness—despair that she wouldn't find her parents' graves after all—and hot tears had slipped down her cheeks. She'd quickly turned toward the window and wiped them away. She didn't think anyone had noticed she was upset—and she didn't want them to.

"The pancakes are really good here," Freddie told her. "So are the waffles."

Mira scanned the menu. She tried to keep her voice light. "I'm looking for freedom with a side of restraining order, but everything just comes with bacon."

"The restraining order costs extra," Blue said, tearing open two sugar packets and dumping them into his coffee. "No substitutions."

"That sucks. I guess I'll go with bacon," Mira said.

While the others ordered, Blue brought his coffee cup to his lips and asked quietly, "Why were you crying before? Were you scared?"

Mira shook her head, not sure how much to say. "No. I was . . . thinking about something that makes me sad."

"Okay. I wanted to make sure we didn't scare you."

"You weren't thinking about that when you broke into my room."

Blue shrugged, looking guilty. "I did want to scare you then. But only to warn you. I never wanted to make you

47

cry—that takes things to a different place."

"What place?"

"A place where I'm hurting people, not helping them."

"So you still think you're helping me?"

"Whether you know it or not." And then he went quiet, shifted his attention to the waitress, laughed at some joke Viv made. He stood up to wave at a big, barrel-chested guy who was heading toward them. The guy looked like he hadn't gone to bed yet. He wore a wrinkled Hawaiian shirt and had lipstick-print kiss marks on his neck—in two different colors. His shaggy golden hair tangled around his face, and he managed to look smug despite his dishevelment.

"That's Rafe," Freddie said. "He's the one who broke your door down. He would have come in with us, but he had to . . . ah, escort some ladies home."

Mira nodded, eyeing Rafe warily. He had one strike against him, and she had a feeling there would be more.

Rafe flopped down next to Viv and slung his arm across the back of her chair—then proceeded to peer down her shirt. "Viv still doesn't have any boobs," he announced.

Henley smashed his fists against the table, rattling the plates and silverware. Then he muttered something about leaving before he killed someone, and left the café.

Viv sighed. "Stop talking about my boobs, jackass."

"Rafe, please show some manners," Freddie said. "At least pretend to have them."

Rafe ignored them both. "You lost the puberty lottery, Viv. Get your dad to buy you a pair. The same set your stepmom has."

Viv sipped her Coke, her eyes hooded and dismissive, like

she was used to this. "You know, if I had to break your curse, I would kill myself."

"I would, too. I need something to feel up if I'm fated to be stuck with one girl for the rest of my life."

"There are ladies present," Freddie said—his silver voice taking on a sharp edge.

Finally, Blue threw a piece of toast at Rafe. "Keep your curse talk to yourself, Wilder."

Rafe snatched the toast off his lap, folded it like a taco, and ate it in two bites.

"*You* don't get to complain," Rafe said with his mouth full, jabbing a meaty finger at Blue. "That's one problem you'll never have—being stuck with one girl. You can have as many as you want. Just keep going on to the next."

Blue glared at him, coldly, steadily—with genuine loathing.

Then another one of their friends arrived, diverting their attention and keeping Blue and Rafe from fighting.

"What's all this *curse talk*?" Mira murmured to Freddie.

"Just a joke," Freddie said, flashing an unconvincing smile.

Mira pouted at him. It was obvious there was something he wasn't telling her.

The new girl took a seat at the foot of the table, between Mira and Freddie, and when Mira looked at her—*really* looked at her—she forgot why she'd been pouting at Freddie in the first place.

The new girl was the most beautiful girl Mira had ever seen.

Glossy, straight, black hair hung to her waist. Her doe eyes were long lashed, so dark they were almost black; her skin gleamed like silk. Her face was so lovely that just looking at her made you happy, and she even smelled pretty—like honeysuckle. There were no butterflies floating around her head—but there should have been.

Freddie introduced them. "Mira, this is Miss Layla Phan. Layla, meet Mira."

"Hi," Layla said. Her voice was gentle, sweet—but there was something fierce in her expression when she looked at Rafe.

"You don't want to sit by me?" Rafe called to her with a grin.

"No, I don't," Layla said. "I wouldn't sit by you if every other seat in the room was on fire."

"Ouch." Rafe winced, then rebounded with a sleazy smile. "That would hurt me if I believed it. You know you're curious to go for a ride."

"About as curious as I am to get syphilis," Layla snapped.

"He meant a ride in his car," Freddie clarified for Mira, looking like he desperately hoped she was dumb enough to believe him.

"His car has syphilis?" Mira asked, feigning shock. When Freddie blushed, she said, "I know that's not what he meant."

Freddie nodded, abashed, and rubbed his hands over his face. "You're right, I'm sorry you had to hear that. He will—be reformed, eventually."

"He is such a tool," Layla muttered. Her hand was trembling against the table. "I would love to just shoot him with a hunting rifle when his transformation day finally comes."

"Transformation day . . . ?" Mira prompted.

Layla's big, dark eyes blinked at Mira and she seemed to remember where she was. "Oh. Nothing. Never mind. Hello. I forgot I don't know you. I . . . exaggerate. A lot. I don't even own a rifle."

"You can get one at Walmart," Viv said. "Charge it on my card. I'll use my coma as an alibi."

Mira focused on eating her pancakes, even though she was starting to feel sick. What was wrong with these people? Was *everyone* insane?

Next to her, Blue seemed edgy. He was breaking his bacon into pieces. His fingertips glistened with grease.

"I'm starting to think it was a mistake to introduce you to the whole gang," he said.

Rafe was still hitting on Layla; Layla was fighting with him, insisting that fairies didn't turn good people into monsters, they just exposed the monstrousness that was already there; and Freddie was doing his best to play peacemaker, or etiquette coach from 1850, or whatever he thought he was doing. Henley was watching the group from outside, leaning against the window, smoking a cigarette. Viv was sawing into an apple tart with a masochistic grin on her face.

"No wonder you're such a freak," Mira said finally.

"Oh yeah, I learned it from watching them," Blue said with a faint smile.

"I want you to know," Mira said, "that whatever your intentions are, even if you think they're good, I didn't travel all the way here to be shuttled around and babysat by crazy people. There are things I need to do here, and I intend to do them."

"Fine, just stay away from our casino."

"No," she said.

Blue turned fully toward her then; grabbed her wrist—hard, like he was trying to intimidate her—and she flung her syrup-sticky butter knife at him and twisted free from his grip. Causing a scene, of course. Sometimes you had to.

She sprang to her feet. "Don't tell me what to do. And don't manhandle me unless you want to be dismembered. This is your last warning."

"Will you keep your voice down?" Blue hissed.

"No, I *won't*," she said, getting louder on purpose. There was a syrup stain the size and shape of a gash on Blue's chest. People were staring at them, but oddly enough, no one seemed all that surprised by her outburst—and she didn't care if they were. Anger blended with the sugar in her body and made her feel nauseous. She just wanted to go. So she grabbed her bag and, for the second time in two days, stormed out.

"Always popular with the girls, Blue," Viv said. Mira heard a chair being pushed back like someone was about to chase after her, and then Blue's voice saying:

"Forget it, Freddie."

"But she's upset," Freddie said.

"She's a big girl; let her play with fire if she wants to."

"Nice ass," Rafe said.

And then the door swung shut behind her, mercifully silencing the peanut gallery; and Mira was plodding through the hot parking lot, her flip-flops squishing like they were about to melt on the steaming asphalt.

Henley looked up at her approach. "Need a ride?" he asked. He didn't look particularly enthused about giving her one.

"No," she said. "But thanks. Have fun with the crazies."

He snorted. "I wouldn't call it fun."

"I was being sarcastic."

Henley nodded, raising his cigarette to his lips, and she set off toward the Dream.

# CHAPTER FIVE

MIRA STOPPED IN ONE OF THE Dream's glitzy bathrooms, changed into wrinkled—but normal—clothes, and dug some defrizzing, detangling serum out of her bag and rubbed it through her hair. She still looked like a mess, but at least she wasn't wearing pajamas, and her hair was behaving a little. Then she went to the front desk and asked for Felix Valentine. Her heart was thudding like crazy. She wondered if the check-in woman could tell.

When Felix showed up, he looked even better than she remembered. His eyes were brighter, his smile came faster.

"Hey, Mira," he said.

She started babbling immediately. "I don't know if this is a good time. If it's not, that's okay. I would've waited for you to call, but your brother broke into my room this morning and made me leave, and I—I thought you should know."

"Wait—say that again? Blue broke into your room?"

"One of his friends busted my door and they forced me to leave with them."

"I can't believe no one told me about this," Felix muttered. "Give me a minute." He got out his phone and stepped away to make a call. She couldn't hear much—the lobby was bustling this time of day—but she could tell by his face that he was yelling at someone. When he came back, the irritation was gone from his face.

"It's taken care of," he said. "It won't happen again."

"Thank you," she said, scuffing one flip-flop against the floor. Suddenly, she felt shy. She wasn't used to people getting angry on her behalf—but she kind of liked it. It made her feel like she mattered to him.

Felix ran his fingers through his hair and cocked his head to look at her. "I need to get out of here for a while. You want to go searching today? I'm all yours if you want me."

She nodded, not trusting herself to speak.

They started their search in the largest cemetery in Beau Rivage, then moved to the most picturesque. Eventually, the sweltering heat chased them indoors, into a mostly empty Vietnamese restaurant, where they sat at a rickety black table for two hours, ordering iced coffees and summer rolls and dishes Mira couldn't pronounce, while caffeine and his undivided attention made her giddy.

Felix had changed before they left the Dream—out of his suit and into jeans and a plain white T-shirt that made him seem like a different person. He wasn't intimidating when he tramped through graveyards in the heat, getting just as sweaty and dirty as she was. He'd brought sunglasses, which she thought was unfair, since the bright white of the sun was making her squint; and at the restaurant, she swiped them and put them on, propped her chin on her hands, and dared him to steal them back with her best impassive diva face.

He raised an eyebrow at her. "I'm not fighting you for those. Those are my cheap sunglasses."

She scrunched her nose at him, channeling Myrna Loy in *The Thin Man*—and he laughed.

She drank so many iced coffees and looked at him so long her blood buzzed. Her heart wouldn't stop racing.

In the car—which was black, with tinted windows—Felix played jazz. Mira knew some of the songs because she'd danced to them, and Felix admitted that it was his mother's influence. One of the only things about her that had stayed with him.

"It was all she ever played when I was a kid," he said. "She'd give me a puzzle or something, turn on some jazz and get dressed up like she was going out, just to sway around her room for an hour. Music was her escape, I guess—from me, from my dad. Not that he spent a lot of time with us before she left."

Mira asked about his father—what was he like?—but Felix seemed reluctant to talk about him, so she let it go.

They sped past gorgeous old homes, deserted brittle buildings, stretches of brilliant white sand. She told Felix about her upcoming birthday, how she'd felt like it was time to stop wishing and finally do something. Then how nervous she'd been that she'd made a mistake . . . and how grateful she was to have his help.

They ended the day in an old, sad graveyard by the sea. Most of the headstones were cracked, the mausoleums had collapsed, but you could still read the inscriptions. Mira had actually been relieved not to find her parents' graves in this broken place.

They were sitting side by side on a stone bench, in the shadow of a tree that dripped with Spanish moss, when Mira took out the photograph she'd brought. The one she kept beside her bed at home, and whispered *good night* to before she went to sleep.

She held it by the edges, so as not to smudge it with sweaty fingers.

"This is a picture of my parents," she said. "If you want to see."

"Of course I want to see."

She handed the photograph to Felix. It was a portrait of her parents on their wedding day. Her mother wore an antique gown with a lace collar that crept all the way up her throat. Her father looked dashing in his black tuxedo, standing with his arm around Mira's mother, with the noble bearing of an army officer, or a knight. They were both so beautiful. So happy.

"Adora and Piers," Felix said, repeating the names she'd told him earlier. "They look good together."

"They were perfect together," she said. "I mean, I *imagine* they were. When I think about what they might have been like." Mira dipped her head, embarrassed. "I . . . make up stories about them. It's kind of weird."

"It's not that weird. I think about the past sometimes— how I wish it had been different. There are things I'd give almost anything to change."

"Like what?"

He laid the photo on her lap; lifted the stolen sunglasses

off her nose. "Driving you around isn't enough? You need to know my secrets, too?"

Mira laughed. "Of course."

Felix squinted at the sky, serious now. Leaves rustled above them, casting indistinct shadows that shivered across his face. "How should I put this? A lot of times . . . I'll think I know someone, that I can trust them. And then I find out I'm wrong. And I wish I could undo ever meeting them."

She watched him carefully as he tried to explain. She felt like she was seeing something he didn't want to show her, and she wanted to be worthy of that.

"I've been burned a lot," he said. "It makes you—after a while, it makes you feel stupid. I keep telling myself—" He tensed his jaw and went quiet, like he was debating even saying it.

"What?" she asked softly.

Felix sighed, wiped the sweat from his forehead, and glanced away, toward the sea. "I keep telling myself that love isn't something that destroys you. Because I don't want to believe that it is. That it has to be. But every relationship I've been in has ended in disaster. So it feels like . . . love destroys you. Like that's all it does."

Mira wondered how he'd been betrayed. What a girl, or girls, had done to break his heart.

And she told herself that *she* would never hurt him like that.

Not that she would have the chance.

Felix stood up, like the conversation was over. "Sorry, Mira . . . I didn't mean to unload on you like that."

He went and stood at the edge of the graveyard, amid

broken bits of stone angels, and stared out at the water. There was a crack in him, in the person he wanted to be. It was a crack she recognized, because it was in her, too.

Mira sprang up, the photo fluttering from her lap, forgotten. She tiptoed toward him, like it was a dance with very precise steps, and rested her fingers on his back. Lightly, just so he'd know she was there.

"It won't always be that way," she said, trying not to sound naïve. She knew she was a girl he could trust. If he wanted to . . .

The water glinted like glass, the sunlight breaking it into glittering shards. The endless heat, the moisture, and the heavy perfumes of summer made her aware of the physical, of every sense—and weakened the allure of daydreams.

She wanted to wrap her arms around him, press her cheek to his back, and hold on tight. But she couldn't make that leap. Not without some sign that he wanted that. It would be too humiliating if he pushed her away.

Felix was quiet so long she didn't think he was going to answer her. But then he turned, and her arms slipped around him before she could think about it—and suddenly he was holding her, too, very naturally, and he looked down at her, like he was trying to see who she really was. One side of his mouth turned up, so briefly it could barely be considered a smile—but at that moment, it was everything.

"We'll see," he said.

Felix dropped Mira off at the Dream, told her to charge dinner to his room, and gave her a key to his suite. He had to get back to work, but he promised he'd get her a new room later—one with an intact door, where Blue wouldn't bother her. Until then she was free to hang out at his place.

Now she lay on Felix's bed, leafing through an old fairy-tale anthology she'd found on his bookshelf, and daydreaming—remembering the way his arms had felt around her—while breaking apart the giant chocolate chip cookie she'd filched from the buffet.

The book of fairy tales was in bad shape. The cover wriggled loose from the binding whenever she moved it, the table of contents was missing, entire stories had fallen out and disappeared. But flipping through it, she found most of the famous tales, and many that were new to her.

"Cinderella." "The Red Shoes." "Beauty and the Beast." "The Juniper Tree."

Mira had seen most of the Disney fairy-tale movies, and had vague recollections of owning a Grimm picture book or two, but fairy tales hadn't been a big part of her childhood. Elsa and Bliss had plied her with classic novels from an early age, so she'd gravitated toward those—Frances Hodgson Burnett, Louisa May Alcott, Laura Ingalls Wilder—and had only scattered memories of kids munching on candy houses, "can't catch me, I'm the gingerbread man," geese that laid golden eggs, glass slippers, and sparkly transformation sequences.

Tonight, she'd chosen the book because it seemed an odd thing for Felix to have—a fairy-tale anthology surrounded by business tomes. But the more she read, the more the tales absorbed her.

In "The Juniper Tree," a boy who was decapitated by his stepmother came back from the dead to murder her. Cinderella's stepsister chopped off her big toe in an attempt

59

to fit into the too-small slipper and fool the prince. And "The Little Mermaid" was downright tragic. Every step the mermaid took on land was agony, as if her feet were being cut by knives; and in the end, the poor girl failed to make the prince love her, and was faced with the choice to either murder him on his wedding night or dissolve into sea foam, soulless and dead.

Love and death. Death and love and transformation. Mira read for hours, transfixed.

It was one minute after midnight when the door clicked open. Mira heard someone moving around the suite with an absolute lack of stealth, and then a muttered:

"Asshole. Where are you?"

So not housekeeping. And not Felix.

It was Blue.

Mira sighed and climbed off the bed to confront him. They nearly collided in the doorway.

"Stupid girl," Blue said, his lip curling.

"Miss me?" she said.

He made no attempt to move away from her. He stood so close she could feel the heat radiating off his body. He'd changed his clothes since this morning and was wearing a dusky purple shirt with an anatomically correct heart on the chest.

"At least you're not naked," he said.

"Because if I was, you'd pass out from the glory of it."

"No," he said. "That is not why. Where's Felix? He chewed me out on the phone over you. He must like you—for all the wrong reasons."

Mira rolled her eyes. "*Maybe* he doesn't approve of your

bad behavior. You know—breaking into my room, assaulting me, kidnapping me? I suppose that didn't occur to you."

"I know my brother better than you do. Bad behavior is his specialty."

Mira waited a moment, her spine rigid, staring at him while he stared back. Finally, she eased up on the teeth she'd been clenching and said, "Well, he's not here. Good-bye."

But Blue didn't move from his spot. He braced his hands on either side of the doorway, the muscles in his arms tensing. "So you fall for the same shit every girl falls for? You think you'll be the special one—the girl who lasts? That the rules don't apply to you?"

"What rules?"

"All *you* need to know is to stay away from him," he said, leaning forward aggressively. "That's your rule. Stay. Away."

Mira jerked back to avoid him—then was annoyed that she'd yielded. As soon as she moved, Blue pushed into the bedroom, eyes flicking to the bed.

"Reading fairy tales, how sweet. Is Felix your Prince Charming? Did he bring you flowers yet?"

"I don't see why you care. Can't you find someone else in this city to harass?"

"You're not my victim, Mira. If you were, you would know it." Blue sat down on the bed, one leg of his ragged jeans pulled onto the coverlet. " 'Cinderella,' " he murmured. "Do you like the part where the shoe fills up with the stepsister's blood? The prince thinks he's found his mysterious girl from the ball, and then a little bird tells him to check out the trail of blood; he's got an imposter on the back of his horse. It's pretty twisted."

"Just like you," she said.

"That's right," he said, his eyes meeting hers, something severe flickering in their depths. "Just like me. Just like my brother."

The way he said it made her shiver. She didn't want to be alone with him anymore. "I think you should go."

"Oh, do you now? Too bad. I need to talk to Felix. And unlike you, I actually live here." Blue resumed flipping through the book, ignoring her. Then he ate the rest of her cookie.

Irritated, Mira retreated to the living room and put on the TV. She got about two minutes of peace before Blue threw himself down next to her.

"So what kind of lines has he been feeding you? I'm curious."

"He's not hitting on me," Mira said through gritted teeth. "He's helping me find my parents. Taking time out of his busy life to help me with something that's important to me. What a crime."

"Find your parents?" Blue whistled. "So you are a lost little girl."

She twisted to face him, fists clenched, ready to punch him in his T-shirt's anatomically correct heart. "You're really pissing me off. I know that's your M.O., but I'm warning you: you need to stop, or I will snap and hurt you."

He smiled. "See, this is why I don't get you. You're so prickly and untouchable when you're with me . . . why can't you keep that up all the time?"

"Because. This might be fun for you—but *I* don't like being angry all the time." Her nails were digging into her palms so hard it hurt.

She relaxed her fists and climbed off the couch. She needed to get away from him before she broke something over his head—but he grabbed the back of her shirt and pulled her back down.

"Wait," he said.

*"What?"* she snapped, held in place by the fist clenching her shirt.

Blue smiled. He had one of those devastatingly charming smiles that made you hate him even more when you noticed it. It was like he was fighting dirty.

"Don't go. Tell me something."

"Tell you what?" she said stiffly.

"Tell me what you would do if I was nice to you."

"Not kill you," she said. She didn't even have to think about it.

He laughed. "How many people have you killed?"

"Five hundred." She rolled her eyes. "How many people have *you* killed?"

Blue let go of her shirt, rose, and wandered to the edge of the suite, where the minibar was. He twisted open one of the tiny clear bottles; swallowed before he answered—in a voice that was like choking.

"One."

~ঠ ৫~

*He kissed her like a man possessed.*

*It was the kind of kiss you vanished into. Everything disappeared except the sound of her breathing. The smell of her red hair: passion fruit and raspberries. He lifted his hands to push her hair away from her face so he could look at her.*

*It was a first kiss. It was a perfect kiss—she'd told him so, and he'd flushed with pleasure. Drunk on it.*

*He kissed her again. Deeper. Pulled her closer.*

*He heard his friends performing in the other room: Jewel singing, Freddie picking out the tune on his guitar.*

Happy birthday. Happy birthday.

Happy birthday—

*And then the strangest gasp. Eyes rolling back so the whites showed. Terror in his heart. Silence in hers.*

—to you.

Blue left Mira alone after that, mixed himself a drink, and didn't speak to her, not even to harass her. He sprawled on the couch and watched movies from Felix's vast collection; she took a bubble bath with the door locked. She thought she would feel better when he wasn't talking to her, but it was actually more unsettling—she wasn't used to his being quiet.

He was, however, inebriated. Which could be very bad . . . or it could make him let down his guard and answer some of her questions.

Mira sat in the chair across from him. Blue had slid halfway down the couch, a highball glass in his hand. She didn't even know what he had in there. Lighter fluid, judging by the smell.

"Hey, psycho," she said.

"Hey." His eyes were glued to the screen—an old war movie. It looked vaguely familiar.

"So tell me something: why are your friends so weird?"

"Freddie's not weird."

"Um, little animals flock to him like he's made of candy."

"That makes the animals weird."

She pressed her lips together, momentarily stymied.

"Is it because they're cursed?"

"The animals?" Blue took a slurp from his glass; grimaced like he really *was* drinking lighter fluid.

"Your friends."

"Probably. It creates a lot of drama. Sturm und Drang. Crap like that."

"I don't speak German," she said.

"Neither do I. Except for a few choice words. Like *märchen.*"

"What?"

"*Märchen,*" Blue drawled. "The flavor of the city, Fräulein."

Mira resisted the urge to dump his drink on him. Being obnoxious right back wasn't going to get her the answers she wanted.

"What kind of curse is it?" she pressed.

"An old one. Is there any other kind?"

"Well . . . there's the curse that has me constantly running into you. That's new."

"Ha." Blue smiled. His eyes were beginning to droop—either sullenly or sleepily, she couldn't tell. She was about to take another shot at him when she heard the *buzz* of an electronic lock opening. In another moment, the suite's front door clicked open.

"Hey, Mira." Felix slipped his jacket off as he came in, brows furrowing when he saw Blue. "I forgot to tell you to call security when he shows up."

"Just a warning: he's trashed," she said.

Felix went behind the couch, took the highball glass from Blue's hand, and leaned over his brother. "What are you doing here? I told you to stay away from her."

"I told you to kiss my ass," Blue said.

"You're not actually dumb enough to say that to me when you're sober. Get up." Felix gripped the back of the couch and rocked it forward to knock Blue off. Blue tumbled down, unfazed, and rearranged himself so he was facing the TV, on the floor this time.

"Later," Blue said. "I'm watching *Apocalypse Now*."

Felix stood there for a moment, his fingers digging into the back of the couch. Then he shook his head. "Whatever. I'm not in the mood to get into this with you right now. Mira— can I talk to you about something?"

"Sure," she murmured. She followed Felix into his bedroom.

It was weird seeing the two brothers interact—the obvious strain between them. She wondered if they'd ever liked each other. She could hear Marlon Brando's famous "the horror" speech coming from the TV behind her—"I've seen the horrors. . . . Horrors that you've seen"—and the creak of the leather as Blue climbed back onto the couch . . . before Felix shut the door.

Felix had brought the smell of the casino with him—the miasma of cigarette smoke from the pit had sunk into his clothes. His eyes were faintly red from it. He brushed a hand across them, looking irritated, looking like he was trying hard not to be.

"I hope he wasn't bothering you too much. He knows he's

supposed to stay away from you . . . but Blue doesn't like following orders. And I don't want to fight with him when he's drunk."

"I'm fine. Really," she assured him. "He's annoying but he didn't do anything."

She sat down on the bed, and after a moment he sat down, too. The book of fairy tales lay open between them.

"You wanted to talk to me," Mira ventured. "Did you find something?"

Felix shook his head. "Not yet. But I was thinking about you tonight, and I wondered: why didn't your godmothers tell you where your parents were buried? What didn't they want you to find?"

Mira was quiet, unsure how to respond. The possibility that Bliss and Elsa had hidden something from her—some secret about her parents—had never crossed her mind. "I don't know. Maybe they didn't think it mattered."

"You didn't ask before you left?"

"I didn't want them to know where I was going. They would have stopped me. They were pretty violently opposed to my ever coming here."

"Why? What's in Beau Rivage that's so dangerous?"

" 'Memories' I don't have," she said with a shrug. "They were afraid it would be traumatic for me."

"That sounds like an excuse. And not a very good one." He looked up, meeting her eyes. "I don't believe in coincidence, Mira. I think there's a reason you had to travel here alone. Something you were meant to find."

*Maybe it's you*, she thought, and then had the immediate urge to unthink it. She didn't want to be overeager, immature.

She didn't want to like him more than he liked her.

"We'll figure it out." He set his hand down on the book of fairy tales, seeming to notice it for the first time. "You were reading this?"

She nodded. "I was kind of surprised to find it on your bookshelf. I didn't really read fairy tales when I was a kid. I thought they were . . . I don't know, too juvenile? But they're different than I thought. Darker. So far, I think 'The Little Mermaid' is my favorite."

"You like sad endings?" he asked.

"Maybe." Mira swallowed. She hadn't thought of it like that, but maybe it was true. She didn't love the romance in the story; she loved the yearning, the despair, the mermaid's noble sacrifice. It stabbed her heart and made her *feel* in a way that happy endings didn't.

Because if you could love someone, and keep loving them, without being loved back . . . then that love had to be real. It hurt too much to be anything else.

"Sad endings are what I know," she said.

He frowned at her. "Nothing's over yet, Mira. We'll find them. We've barely started." He reached out and touched her face; turned her toward him. His fingertips sent a shivery burn though her, and she found herself staring at him a beat too long. "Not giving up on me, are you?"

She shook her head, not trusting her voice; and when her cheek burned hotter against his hand, she moved away—before she could do something embarrassing like close her eyes and *sigh*, or lean into his touch like a cat.

"What about you?" she asked, to change the subject. "What's your favorite fairy tale?"

Grimacing, Felix stretched out on the bed. "I don't really like fairy tales."

"But . . . you have this book." It didn't fit with the rest of his stuff. Why would he keep it if he didn't like it?

"It's been in the family a while," he said. "My dad would be annoyed if I threw it away. And I *used* to like them. But I guess the novelty wore off. I got sick of reading about torture and dismemberment and . . . happy endings that get handed out at random, to people who don't deserve them."

"Tell me how you really feel," Mira joked.

Felix cracked a smile. "They're not all bad. Sleeping Beauty's all right. She gets to sleep for a hundred years and not go to work tomorrow. I'd like to do that. And she gets woken up by a kiss. That's a nice change."

Felix lay on his back, eyes closed, his mouth relaxed—and Mira blushed, hyperaware of his position, of how easy it would be to lean over and kiss him. Had that been a hint? But . . . no, she couldn't. She'd die of embarrassment if she kissed him and he opened his eyes and said, *What are you doing?*

"Some curses are meant to be broken," Felix said. "And some just keep going until your life runs out."

"Curses?" Mira's breath faltered. There were no coincidences—that was what he'd said. Here was her answer, the truth she'd tried to drag out of Blue.

"Curses & Kisses. That's the name of Blue's band," Felix said.

"Oh." Her hopes deflated as quickly as they'd soared. "Was that . . . were you quoting a lyric?"

"Just talking. Tired, I guess. I should get up and find you a new room." Felix pushed himself off the bed, and she blurted:

"Or I could stay here."

Her heart seemed to hammer twenty times before he spoke, beating: *stupid stupid stupid stupid.* . . .

"You want to stay here?" Felix gave her an odd look, surprised. Pleasantly surprised? Did he want her to stay? Did she want him to want her to stay?

His eyes on hers made her dizzy.

"All right," he said finally, his expression unreadable. "Let me kick my brother out."

When Felix left, he shut the bedroom door, and Mira perched on the edge of the bed with her legs drawn up, wondering what he expected to happen, what *she* wanted to happen. Part of her knew she was asking for trouble if she stayed. The rest of her wanted to know what trouble was like.

A few minutes passed, during which she heard the brothers arguing in low, angry voices—but she couldn't make out the words. Something made of glass crashed, shattered. She heard a *thud* against the wall and flinched. Then Blue's voice came through the door, so close it was like a hand on her shoulder. "Mira, don't stay."

She didn't answer.

"Mira . . ."

And after another moment, she heard Blue cursing. She heard the hall door slam.

And then she and Felix were alone.

Felix emerged from the bathroom in a fog of steam, wearing black pajama pants, his hair still wet, a towel thrown over his shoulders. Tonight, for the first time, she saw his body, lines of lean muscle his clothes had only hinted at; and she stared at him like he was a picture, wondering what it would be like to touch him—and wishing she was wearing a sexy nightgown, instead of pajamas that looked like gym clothes.

He turned down the bed, yanking the coverlet off and letting it fall to the floor, while she stood awkwardly beside him in her T-shirt and girly boxers.

"I could sleep on the couch," she offered. "If you want."

He gave her a look like he didn't take her seriously. "You really want to sleep on the couch?"

"No," she admitted.

She hesitated—then climbed into bed.

She didn't want to sleep on the couch. She didn't know what she wanted—that was the problem—and she wasn't sure she'd know until it was too late. But maybe this was why she'd come alone to Beau Rivage. Maybe she was meant to discover something about herself. To grow up. Wake up.

When she was with Felix, she didn't lose herself in daydreams. She wanted things that were real.

The light clicked off. She could feel the mattress sinking under his weight, the sheets being tugged as he came closer. She lifted a hand to feel for where he was, and her hand found his bare chest and slipped over the muscles there, enjoying the feel of him before she turned self-conscious and stopped. He was leaning over her, the heat of his body warming the air between them.

"Hi," he said. There was a smile in his voice.

Her hand lay frozen against his chest. She'd never felt so tense.

"Don't be nervous."

"I'm not," she lied, wanting him to make a move so she could reject it or accept it . . . and stop waiting for something to

71

happen, wondering what it might be. His hand settled on her hip, familiar, and she stalled, nervous about what else might seem natural to him, but be monumental to her.

"Felix," she started, "why does your brother hate you so much?"

He sounded amused. "Did he say that?"

"Not exactly. He just . . . he says a lot of bad things about you. Like that I should stay away from you."

"Of course he does. I'd tell you the same things about him if I thought you were interested. You have to be used to guys fighting over you."

"Fighting?" She laughed. "Um, no. That doesn't happen."

His hand on her hip felt so heavy—she could barely pay attention to anything else. He was stroking her skin, kneading her hip, almost casually, and yet not casually at all.

"I didn't know you liked me like this," he said, his voice low, intimate in the dark. "I'm kind of happy about it."

"You are?" she said.

Felix laughed. "Why wouldn't I be?"

"I don't know," she said. "No one I know has ever . . . liked me like that."

"Either the guys you grew up with are blind," he said, "or your godmothers are jailers. All right: I'll tell you why I like you." He bowed his head close to hers. "You're brave, Mira. You're beautiful. And hopeful—and I'm not. But you make me feel like things can be different. . . ."

His voice turned tender, faded as he kissed the corner of her mouth, warm and soft; and his hand slipped up her ribs, his fingers catching her T-shirt and tugging it slowly up. She wasn't sure if she—

72

His hand grazed her breast, and her breath caught in her throat.

Felix stopped. He seemed like he was weighing whether that was a *yes* gasp or a *no* gasp. The moment passed, and he smoothed her shirt into place so it covered her again. She wanted to do something, to show him she could be natural at this, but—she couldn't. Her body had gone rigid with apprehension.

"You want to just sleep?" he said gently. She wondered if he was embarrassed for her, because she'd thought she could play in his world, and she couldn't.

Mira nodded, then remembered it was dark. "Okay."

"Come here," he said, kissing the edge of her ear. He pulled her backward against him, so that his chest was pressed to her back, his breath warm against her neck. He held her, not speaking, just letting her be.

"Good night," he said.

Mira lay still until she heard his breathing fall into the smooth, even rhythm of sleep. She touched Felix's hand; said his name. But he just pulled her closer, sleepily possessive, so she was fitted more tightly against him.

Gradually, the sound of his breathing calmed her down. Once there was nothing to wait for, nothing to decide, her breaths fell in sync with his. She felt safe then, with his arms around her. Like she was his—even if it was just another day-dream. Right then she felt like it was true.

"Good night," she whispered.

# CHAPTER SIX

MIRA WOKE RELUCTANTLY, her mind shaking off layers of sleep. She remembered, distantly, the warm pressure of a hand on her back, fingers rubbing up and down her spine. A whispered *good morning* that felt like a dream.

She lay on her stomach, her T-shirt pushed halfway up her back, the sheets kicked to the floor. When she felt the chill of the air-conditioning on her skin, she scrambled to pull down her shirt.

She wasn't naked—nothing anyone else would consider *private* was on display—but it was almost worse than being naked. Because she couldn't be sure how long she'd lain like that—and whether Felix had seen the ugly mark on her back.

As if she didn't already have enough strikes against her—now she'd be deformed in his eyes, too. An immature girl with a freakish mark.

She wandered out into the empty suite, trying hard not to cry. Her embarrassment from last night came flooding back.

Why had she been so eager to stay with him? Everything was ruined now. The curtains in the living room were wide open, and she could see the ocean far below. The sparkle of the sunlight hurt her eyes.

On a table near the couch sat a vase of flowers and a crisp white card, and a silver serving tray with a domed lid. Inside the tray, she found breakfast: French toast with strawberries. Opening the card, she found a message from Felix.

*Hey beautiful,*

*I tried to say good-bye this morning but you were impossible to wake up.*

*Playing catch-up today but I'll be free later. We can drive to some cemeteries if you want—then do dinner?*

*I didn't want you to feel trapped, so I left you my passkey. My home is your castle—you're welcome to explore, and charge anything you need to the room. All I ask is that you stay out of my other room (suite 3013). I keep some private things there that must not be disturbed.*

*See you tonight,*
*Felix*

The passkey lay on the table. Mira ran her fingers over it, feeling electric. He'd see her later. They were going to search again; he wasn't repulsed by her mark. And in the meantime, she was free to explore, go shopping, whatever she wanted. His home was her castle.

She liked the sound of that.

Mira spent the morning exploring the hotel. She roamed the

long halls of rooms, imagining the drama that went on behind closed doors. She even went up to the thirtieth floor, to check out the view—but she didn't go near suite 3013.

Afterward, she headed down to the casino. She threaded her way through rows of slot machines, hoping to run into Felix; then skirted the gaming tables very, very quickly, searching for a head of blue-black hair.

There was no sign of him. Maybe he was in one of the VIP rooms, or in his office.

Or maybe he was in suite 3013. But she wasn't about to barge into the one place he'd told her to stay out of. Maybe it was a test—and if it was, she was going to pass it.

The last place she explored was the shopping area. She browsed through designer jewelry and clothes, overpriced underwear, and even Dream memorabilia, like glittery T-shirts and magic wand earrings. Felix had told her to charge whatever she needed, but she didn't want to abuse the offer. In the end, she bought a red satin nightgown from a lingerie boutique called Cinderella's Secret—but she paid for that with cash, not Felix's card.

On her way out of Cinderella's Secret, Mira stopped to orient herself. The Dream's shopping area was themed, like the rest of the hotel: it was made up of a series of wide corridors decorated to look like a forest trail. Shop windows peeked out from between trees, and vines and flowers grew over everything. A trail of Hansel-and-Gretel-style "bread crumbs" was embedded in the floor. The whole area was called Forest Passage, and in addition to boutiques, there were several cafés, some of which had "outdoor" seating in the "forest."

Sitting at one of the outdoor cafés was Blue.

He sat with his back to her, at a small metal table, along with Freddie and a dark-skinned girl with a pink streak in her brown hair. Mira didn't recognize the girl. She was kind of fierce-looking, closer to the Blue end of the fashion spectrum than to Freddie. She wore a shredded T-shirt over a white tank top, black shorts, and boots made for stomping.

Blue was going on about something. It was noisy in the Passage, so Mira couldn't hear him, but she wouldn't have been surprised if he was complaining about her. She hung back and spied for a minute, and probably would have gone on spying if Freddie hadn't spotted her and waved her over.

Scrunching up her Cinderella's Secret bag so they wouldn't see the logo, she pasted on a smile and started toward them.

Blue regarded her with a bewildered expression that quickly cooled to indifference.

"You're alive," he said.

"I usually am," she said.

Freddie rose to his feet in an almost courtly way. "Mira, how wonderful! We'd love it if you'd spend the day with us. Um, of your own free will this time."

"Gee, thanks, could I?" she said.

"Yeah, spend the day with us," Blue said. "You're guaranteed one more day that way."

Freddie frowned. "Blue, don't be like that."

"Don't worry, I'm used to it," Mira said.

The girl with the pink streak in her hair put down her drink to join in—then pressed a handkerchief to her mouth before any words could escape. Her eyes watered and she started to cough, like she was choking.

"Are you okay? Is she okay?" Mira asked, searching their faces for answers. "Does anyone know the Heimlich—?"

The girl held up a hand to stop her, then breathed and wiped her mouth, clutching the handkerchief in her fist. A wet lavender petal clung to her lip. "I'm fine."

"Okay," Mira said, still feeling like she should do something. "If you're sure . . ."

"I don't think we've met," the girl said. "I'm Jewel." Her voice was husky, lovely, bluesy. Her dark hair was pulled into a high ponytail, the pink streak twisted through it like a ribbon. A diamond stud glittered in her nose, and her ears were pierced with a row of precious stones: emerald, amethyst, pink sapphire, onyx. "I sing in Curses."

"Oh, right. The band." Mira said.

"We have a show this weekend," Freddie said. "You should come."

"Maybe," Mira said. "I might have plans."

"You might not be here," Blue said. Then, turning to Freddie, as if Mira were already gone: "So there's no use inviting her to anything."

"I'll be here," Mira said.

"In theory," Blue said, not bothering to look at her.

"Uh . . . anyway," Freddie went on, his gaze passing awkwardly between them, "we'd love it if you'd come out with us today. Or come to the show. If you have time."

"We're not very good. Well, *we* are," Jewel said, "but Blue isn't. He kind of ruins us. We'd be a good band otherwise."

"If I was a competent musician, I'd be too sexy," Blue said.

Mira snorted. "I don't think you have to worry about *that*."

"Isn't that the whole point of being our drummer?" Freddie

said. "Nobody ever likes the drummer. Do you have to be bad, too?"

"Unfortunately, yes," Blue said.

Mira raised her eyebrows. "Are you telling me you have a drummer who can't keep the beat?"

Jewel nodded. "He's lucky we like him. And that girls come to our shows anyway to gawk at Freddie."

"They do not come to gawk at me," Freddie said. "They come to watch you."

"They do not," Jewel said. Then, to Mira: "Freddie plays hard to get."

"I don't play anything!" Freddie protested.

Jewel dismissed his claim with a wave of her hand. "Whatever, yes, you do. Freddie only dates princesses. He's a snob like that. And princesses are always in short supply, so . . ."

"You like your girls high maintenance, Freddie?" Mira asked. "Aren't those girls usually annoying?"

"I'm not . . . no, it's not like that." Freddie seemed flustered, unable to properly explain. "It's not like that."

"That's why he's still a virgin," Jewel said with a wicked grin—before being interrupted by another coughing fit. She pressed the handkerchief to her mouth, and when she pulled it away, Mira saw that the cloth was full of sodden flowers: shiny-wet violets, tiny daisies, delicate pink bleeding hearts. All fresh and flecked with blood.

Mira swallowed and felt like she had a rosebud stuck in her own throat. Her mind fought to make sense of this, to feel anything but numb horror.

She had to be misinterpreting what she was seeing.

Jewel couldn't be coughing up flowers.

Freddie was still stuck on Jewel's last announcement. He seemed to think Mira's horror was for him. "That's not why," he insisted, color rushing to his cheeks. "And . . . and it's not like that's a bad thing."

Blue shrugged, unfazed. "We're all virgins, except for you," he said to Jewel. "Oh, and except for Mira. She slept with Felix last night."

"*Slept* in the sense of *sleeping*," Mira said. "Not that it's any of your business."

"You just made it my business by telling me," Blue said. "So what happened? He decided he wanted to play with you a little first?"

"You know, you are the most . . . *despicable* person I've ever met." Mira's fingers tightened around the Cinderella's Secret bag. "You don't even know me, but you insist on being a jerk to me every chance you get."

"Only because I care," Blue said, grinning. She would've slapped him if she didn't think he would like it.

"Felix is *not* someone you want to hook up with," Jewel said. "You should stay away from him. Count your blessings and move on."

"I'm pretty sure I didn't ask for your opinion either," Mira snapped.

She knew it was rude, but she was struggling not to say something worse. Blue had no right to embarrass her in front of his friends. And she didn't need to be lectured.

Jewel shrugged. "Your funeral."

Mira told them she'd see them later, and left. She wasn't in the mood to argue about Felix. Blue would say something nasty if she stayed; she'd never be able to get him to back down—especially not while Jewel was agreeing with him.

It wasn't until she'd emerged from the hotel, and into the hot, bright light of day, that she remembered the blood-flecked flowers in Jewel's handkerchief—as unnatural and fantastical as the Dream itself. There had to be a reason, even for something as unreasonable as that.

Her throat tightened as Felix's words came back to her.

*I don't believe in coincidence.*

Maybe the curses Blue and his friends joked about, and talked circles around, were real.

Mira made her way from the Dream to the "beautiful shore" Beau Rivage was named for. She wanted to stroll barefoot through the white sand, and think—not daydream, but try to make sense of things.

What exactly was going on here?

And what—if anything—did it have to do with her?

Sun worshippers and day-trippers streamed past her, carrying beach towels and picnic baskets, dog-eared paperbacks, plastic pails, and shovels. They were a blur of humanity, redolent of banana and coconut suntan lotion—but occasionally, an individual would stand out.

The crowd would part around someone, and Mira's breath would catch. She saw a young man with a white-tipped cane, the skin around his eyes marred by crisscrossing scars. There was a girl whose hair frizzed around her head like dandelion fluff, looking harried as she darted through the crowd, a strange wooden doll clutched to her chest. Mira was tempted to stop her, ask her what was so urgent, but instinct told her not to. Besides, the girl was quick and out of sight before she could try.

Were these curses? Was that what she was seeing? Or was she just paranoid?

Mira was holding on to the railing of the boardwalk with one hand, peeling off her shoes with the other, when Henley and Viv stopped beside her, both in swimsuits. Henley was loaded down with a cooler and a cardboard tray stacked with French fries and hot powdered donuts. Viv was holding her car keys, hip cocked to one side as she fixed the knot on her red sarong.

Mira sighed. She hoped this didn't mean Blue was on his way. "There's no escaping you people, is there?"

"Excuse me?" Henley said, with his typical furrowed brow and humorless expression.

"Ha-ha, no, it's a small world," Viv said. "I'd like to get away from these losers once in a while, too."

"If I wasn't here, you'd have to carry your own shit," Henley said.

Viv rubbed his shoulder play-vigorously. "You're *right*. I'm so lucky!" She leaned in and kissed his arm, then kept her cheek pressed to his bicep, her dark eyes on Mira. "So, outsider, what do you say—join us? I can promise you no Blue, at least for a little while. And free food." Viv snaked a fry from its paper wrapper and bit off the end. "Deal?"

"Didn't you guys want to be alone?" Mira asked, watching Viv cozy up to Henley, totally confused by their behavior today versus yesterday.

"Um, no." Viv laughed, then started down the steps to the beach. "Come on," she called, waving at a red beach umbrella stuck in the sand. "That's my spot."

Viv ran ahead, her ghost-pale skin almost as white as her bikini, while Mira kept pace with Henley. She hooked her fingers inside the heels of her silver flats and carried them, letting her toes sift through the hot sand.

"So are you the gardener or her boyfriend?" she asked.

Henley glared at her. "You did not just ask me that."

"What? Am I supposed to just know?"

"It's complicated."

"Complicated how?"

Henley sighed roughly, the ice and drinks rumbling in the cooler as he shifted his weight. "You're an outsider. You wouldn't understand. So I'm not going to bother telling you."

"If *you* don't tell me," she said, "I'll ask Viv."

Viv was standing under her umbrella, the wind rippling through her red sarong as she peeled it off and flung it aside, like an unwary matador taunting a bull. Henley's face got tight as he watched her; there was an almost painful attraction there.

"I'm just her toy," he said finally. "She treats me like shit and then on off days when she's bored, I'm worth knowing. Is that what you wanted to hear?"

"Sorry," Mira said. "I just couldn't figure you guys out. . . ."

Henley continued across the sand, dropped the cooler next to Viv, and sat down like the seat he'd picked was temporary. Like he'd be ordered away soon enough.

He'd claimed Mira couldn't understand what was between him and Viv because she was an outsider. And she *didn't* understand—but did that mean there was some secret detail that made their relationship make sense? Something an insider would know?

They'd hinted at curses—and she wanted to know what they were. Was it a curse if bad things happened to you? If all your relationships were broken? If *you* were broken?

Mira had lost her parents to fire. She'd been born with a hideous mark on her back. She was saddled with a sorrow that never grew lighter, and now, with a realization:

Maybe she was cursed, too.

The sun blazed down, pale and furious. Viv was curled up on a blanket under her umbrella, every inch of her drawn into the shade. Henley crouched a few feet away, shooing away the seabirds that were desperate to get close to Viv.

Mira lay just beyond the umbrella's reach, rolling a wet plastic Coke bottle across her stomach to cool off. Pink light burned through her eyelids. She wasn't sure how long she wanted to stay, but Viv was quiet, peaceful now, and the crash of waves was a good soundtrack for thinking.

What kind of curse did they all have? And was there something wrong with Felix, too?

So far the most obvious curse was Jewel's: the wet flowers that rose from her throat, blooming in her waiting handkerchief like the blood of a consumption victim.

There was the odd allure Freddie and Viv held for animals. And Viv had said something about *breaking* Rafe's curse; Layla had threatened to shoot Rafe on his "transformation day". . . .

Blue was just obnoxious.

She wasn't sure that added up to anything.

But Viv seemed more open than the others; maybe Mira could get it out of her.

"Your house is beautiful," Mira said, to get her going.

"It's a beautiful prison," Viv said. "That's all. Like the rest of my life."

"Why a prison?"

Viv rolled over to squint at Mira. "Regina. My stepmother. She's obsessed with her looks—and obsessed with mine. She hates me."

"She probably doesn't *hate* you," Mira said.

Viv laughed. "Believe me—she does. She'll say stuff like *I used to have a body like that* or *I used to have skin like that*. It's like living in a cage, being scrutinized all the time. I used to feel guilty, like it was my fault she wasn't happy; now I just hate her. But I'm stuck with her every day, living way out there. My dad spends all his time on the green, avoiding us."

Viv glanced at her seabird-chasing boy toy. "And then there's Henley. But he's doomed."

"Doomed?"

Viv sighed, and propped her head on her hand. "We're all doomed here. You picked a crappy place to go on vacation, Mira. You don't like Blue, do you?"

"No," Mira said, caught off guard by the change of subject.

"I was worried he was doing his knight-in-tarnished-armor thing and it was winning you over."

"No, he's just irritating. I don't want to be around him any more than I have to be."

"Okay, good," Viv said, lying back down.

Mira draped a thick wave of her hair over her face, like it was a shield from the sun. It smelled like Felix's shampoo. *Felix.* She'd see him later and Blue would be a bad memory.

"How are you doomed?" she asked after a moment, hoping Viv wasn't tired of her questions. But Viv was on a roll.

"You know when you go to a carnival, and you get to drive an old-fashioned Model T car, but there's a metal track between the wheels, keeping you on course? So you get the impression that you're driving, but if you veer too far in either direction, the track jerks you back into place?"

"I think so. . . ."

"Our lives are like that. It feels like we can do what we want—but if we venture in a new direction, fate pulls us back. We can rebel, but we all know we'll fail. Which doesn't stop us from trying, I guess. Like Blue."

"How does Blue—?"

"Wait," Viv said, sitting up. She shaded her eyes with her hand and peered out at the water—and at a group of girls, all clamoring for someone's attention. Someone with Freddie's honey-colored head.

"I thought I sensed a flock of girls," Viv said. "Knight's here; I bet that means Blue's here, too. Looks like your sanctuary may be compromised."

"Great," Mira muttered. That meant now would be an ideal time to go—but she couldn't leave right when she was making headway with Viv.

Henley started back toward them, his warding job over now that the seabirds were fighting the girls for Freddie's attention. He ducked under the umbrella, hesitantly, as though waiting for permission and expecting it to be denied.

But Viv was in an affectionate mood. She extended her leg and touched her toes to his chest; slid her foot flirtatiously up and down. "Henley, would you be a sweetheart and get my camera out of the car?"

Henley nodded, transfixed.

"Thank you." Viv gave him a sweet smile and he slowly got to his feet, like someone waking from a dream.

"It's too hard to gossip with boys around," Viv said, once Henley had staggered away. "Now, where were we?"

"You were talking about being doomed. And how it's futile to try to escape fate. You said that hasn't stopped Blue. What did you mean by that?"

"Oh. Just that Blue still wants to believe his fate is in his own hands. But it's only a matter of time before he succumbs."

"Succumbs to what?" Mira asked.

"Instinct," Viv said, as if that was sufficient explanation. "I'm still waiting for things to happen to me, personally. It's embarrassing; I feel like such a late bloomer. I had two significant birthdays go by, and yet—*nothing*. Sometimes I get so fed up and depressed about it that I feel like choking myself just to set things in motion."

"Uh, you—what?"

Viv laughed uneasily. "Uh, I'm probably confusing you. . . ."

"Yes. But—feel free to explain."

"It's . . . hard to understand if you're not from here."

*That again.* Mira was about to argue when a rain of cold water droplets spattered her stomach, jolting her upright. It didn't take long to see where the "rain" had come from.

Blue was standing over her, shaking out his wet hair like an annoying blue dog. Beads of water clung to the muscle on his chest. He was wiry, not buff like Henley, but his body made up for size with definition. Nothing could make up for his personality.

"Stop dripping on me," Mira snapped.

87

Blue pushed his hand through his hair, flicking more water at her. "Move if you don't like it."

"If I move, it will be to assault you. I don't want to humiliate you in front of Viv."

"So considerate." He sat down, the sand sticking to his skin like powdered sugar, then reached across her to grab a Coke out of the cooler—dripping on her again. He grinned as she glared at him.

"I'm going to find Henley," Viv announced, tying her sarong around her waist and crawling out from under the umbrella. "He's either taking a smoke break or using my camera to photograph skanks on the boardwalk. Either way, he's in trouble. Remember what I said, Mira. About . . ." She jerked her head at Blue.

Mira nodded. Blue squinted after Viv as she left.

"What was that?"

"She said before that she's glad I don't like you. Maybe she was reminding me to make sure it stays that way—but that's one reminder I don't need."

"Good." He drank half the bottle of Coke, then capped it and lobbed it back into the watery slush in the cooler. The water splashed her leg, and she rubbed it away.

"You have gorgeous legs," Blue said.

She narrowed her eyes at him. "Are you being nice, or sleazy? Because I doubt that's a compliment, coming from you."

"Always assume the worst."

"I can't wait until I never have to see you again," she muttered.

She rolled over onto her stomach, tugged a cheap paperback out of her purse, and let her hair curtain her face so she could read. She'd almost succeeded in ignoring him when she felt his fingertip skim the back of her calf, from the hollow of her knee to her ankle. She flipped over and hurled her book at him, the open pages slapping his face.

"*Don't* touch me!" she yelled. She could still feel the line he'd traced on the back of her calf, cool against her skin, like the seam of a crooked stocking.

Blue shrugged, shameless. "I wanted to see if it felt as nice as it looked."

"It won't feel as nice when I kick the crap out of you."

Blue seemed to consider this. Then: "Are you a dancer?"

"Yes," she said through clenched teeth.

"I thought so. You couldn't be that sexy naturally. I figured you had to work for it."

She was working up a response—something that was more than an accumulation of curse words—when she noticed Freddie striding up the beach. He was carrying something in his cupped hands, water dribbling down between them, and he kept stopping and turning back to respond to his admirers—girls who trailed after him in a procession of sun-kissed cheeks and tiny bikinis.

When he reached them, he dropped to his knees in front of Mira.

"Mira, have you ever seen a starfish? I brought one so I could show you."

She glanced quickly at the purple starfish splayed across Freddie's hands, then back at Blue. He was like a thorn under her skin, constantly irritating her. She couldn't have a nice, normal conversation with Freddie when she felt like she was about to explode. "Why are you such an asshole?"

89

"It's a survival skill," Blue said.

"Really? How does being a jerk give you an edge?"

"It gives *you* an edge."

"Of course it does," she said, fed up.

"I think you're obsessed with me," Blue said. "But that's okay. I'm not going to judge you for it." Then he got up before she could hit him. Sand speckled his legs and his swim trunks. The sun had wicked the water from his skin; a few droplets dribbled down from his hair.

Blue turned, and Mira sucked down a bubble of air with her Coke and almost choked—because smack in the center of his lower back, crowning the waistband of his swim trunks, was a fist-size birthmark: wine red like a burn, shiny-smooth like a scar.

Like hers—only it was shaped like a heart. A perfect, dark heart.

"What?" Blue said, turning again. "You're sad that I'm leaving?"

"What—what is that?" she asked, pressing her fist to her chest, coughing like she'd nearly drowned.

"What is what?" he said.

"That mark. On your back."

Blue shrugged. "Nothing."

She didn't believe him. That mark *meant* something.

"Don't worry, it's not contagious," Blue said, before he ran down to the water. The sea ate him up in little bites, first his legs and then his waist and then his chest, until he disappeared beneath the waves. The sun glittered on the water and it was almost blinding; she couldn't watch anymore.

"Sorry about that," she said to Freddie. He was still

kneeling beside her, dejected but patient—or maybe just quiet. The starfish looked limp in his cupped hands.

"I'm going to put this back," he said. "Okay?"

Tentatively, Mira touched the starfish and then withdrew. She felt bad for ignoring him. "Thanks for showing me. I *do* think it's cool. I was just—mad before. I don't know why it seems like it's his goal to piss me off. I'd rather he just pick one: be nice, or leave me alone."

Freddie nodded. "Well . . . that would be better. But he doesn't have the self-control for that, I don't think. He just likes you."

She raised her eyebrows. "Um, have you been paying attention *at all*?"

"I didn't say he *wants* to like you. Just that he does. Maybe because you act like you don't like him, so he feels a little safer."

"Freddie, that doesn't make sense."

Freddie shrugged. "Blue has, um, weird issues with girls."

"Because his mom ran away?"

"I'm not sure how to explain it. Just that, I mean, obviously he likes you, but he doesn't want to, so he's going a little overboard to keep you at bay. But I think he's having a hard time just ignoring you because you genuinely don't like him. Which is strangely attractive to Blue."

"Like he hates clingy girls, but he gets turned on if he thinks you're playing hard to get?"

"Uh . . ." Freddie stopped to think about it, then settled on shrugging again. "I don't know, Mira. I don't know how to explain it."

"You could beat him up for me. That would solve a lot of problems." She flashed him a coy smile.

"He's my friend. I can't do that." But he smiled back, not at all offended, like he knew she was kidding.

She was *sort of* kidding.

"I'm going to bring this back now, okay?" Freddie gestured with the starfish, lifting his cupped hands, the muscles in his chest tightening with the motion. She nodded, and he trotted down the beach, relaxed and casual. It didn't take long for the girls to surround him again, and when they did, he sped up; his footsteps got clumsy on the sand, like a bear lumbering away from an upset beehive, paws full of honey. Except Freddie was the honey *and* the bear.

Mira didn't, as a rule, chase after boys. But when she followed Freddie with her eyes, paperback pressed to her brow like a visor, she saw herself reflected on his skin. Her wheel, her wine-red mark, was imprinted on the small of his back. They could have been twins.

*Twins.*

She shoved up off the ground and ran after him. Pushed through the swarm of admirers and grabbed his shoulders, spinning him around. His face was blank with shock. Sun-baked heat sank into her hands.

"What's going on?" she demanded. "You have to tell me what's going on here."

Her fingers dug into his shoulders, too hard. He stared mutely back at her, and she felt like she was touching fire.

*"If you wanted me, if you loved me,*
*I could take everything from you."*

# CHAPTER SEVEN

"YOU ATTACKED FREDDIE. You scared him," Blue said.

They sat at an outdoor table at Gingerbread House, the café where she'd thrown the knife at him. Just the two of them. Blue had appeared, dripping wet, while Mira was questioning Freddie, demanding to know what their marks were—and he'd pried her away with hands that were cool from the sea. He'd said that if she wanted to talk about this, they needed to do it elsewhere. He'd looked so serious that she'd agreed.

"I didn't attack him," Mira said. "I was getting his attention. I needed to talk to him."

The air outside the café smelled like brine and grill smoke. The sound of flags whipping and dinging against flagpoles mixed with the cries of gulls and the rush of cars. Mira rested her foot against the base of the table, then realized she was touching Blue's leg. She left it there, to see what he would do.

"He said it felt like your hand was on fire. What's that all about?"

"It was hot today," she said. "I don't know. I told you that."

Mira lifted her head to study his eyes, but he wouldn't look at her—not directly. He was knocking his wrist against the table, rhythmically, like he was trying to make it bruise.

"I saw that mark on his back," she said. "You both have one."

"And you're proving that you're rude enough to keep bringing it up. Maybe he's embarrassed by it. Just drop it."

"No," she said. "I'm not being rude."

The wheel spun slowly in her mind, like a windmill set off by a soft wind. The mark connected them somehow. She wasn't going to just let that go.

"Is Freddie an orphan?" she asked. "Did his parents die?"

"The Knight family is perfectly intact," Blue said. "He has two older brothers, Wills and Caspian. Loving mother and father. They all live together in a swank mansion. Always have."

"So he couldn't be my brother?" she forced out, swallowing hard afterward. Her heart thumped in the interim. Blue stared at her, mouth poised open, not understanding. Finally, he said:

"He'd certainly be disappointed if he was. Why would you think that? You don't look alike."

"I thought maybe we could have been separated. When my parents died. Like we could have been taken away by different guardians."

She lowered her eyes. Blue finally shifted his leg away from her. He cleared his throat.

"You were taken away? From where—from Beau Rivage?"

"I was born here. But I didn't stay long. Something bad happened—a fire—and I lost my mom and dad. My godmothers raised me. I'm here to find my parents' graves." Her throat grew tight. "You'd know that if you did more than fight with me."

"Sorry," he said. Then, more quietly, "That sounds . . . disturbingly familiar. Like a story."

"Isn't everything a story?"

"Maybe. But that's not what I meant. I mean it sounds familiar. Like a classic tale."

"I'm an orphan," she said, a bitter edge to her voice. "That's as classic as it gets—Oliver Twist, Sara Crewe. But being an orphan isn't a fairy tale. It's not romantic; it doesn't make me special. It just means I never had a chance to know my parents, and I never will."

"So you hoped you had Freddie?" he said, brows dipping as he tried to work it out.

"No, I'm just—I'm trying to make this make sense. *This.*"

Mira rose from her seat and jerked her blouse up from her waist. She turned so he could see the mark, his gaze like needles in her skin, in the vulnerable part of herself she kept hidden.

"I think maybe . . . I'm cursed, too," she said.

She shuddered when he touched her, his fingertip tracing the mark at the base of her spine.

Blue uttered a word she'd directed at him under very different circumstances. He whispered it, and his touch was like a whisper, too. She felt a fire more intense than the one she'd felt when she touched Freddie. That had been a surface fire, stinging and hot. This one was deeper, embedded in her core. It ignited something dark and secret within her, and she kept smoldering until he took his hand away.

"Oh," he said.

95

"Don't forget I loathe you," she said shakily.

"I know. Let's keep it that way."

She sat back down. His eyes ticked across her face like a pendulum.

"Well." He swallowed. "You're not his sister. For a start."

～◗ ◖～

*Happy birthday. Happy birthday, baby. You only turn sixteen once.*

*The room was full of balloons, the color of a castle at the bottom of the sea, blue and black and silver and green. They were dancing. Jewel was crooning a torch song on a miniature stage, her voice throaty and tender, black pearls dripping from her lips when she stopped to breathe. Everyone clapped, ecstatic. An explosion of gratitude, like firecrackers popping.*

*He was surrounded by everything he loved. Everything good.*

*Couples spun off into dark corners, private shadows. His father encouraged it, treated them like adults. Champagne foamed over bottle tops, and paper came off presents with a giddy ripping sound.*

*He tried to keep to his kind, he really did. To the girls who knew better. But he got caught up in the moment.*

*Tonight, her dress and her lips were as cherry red as her hair. And when she smiled at him—like it was time to stop pretending, stop avoiding each other—he felt too good to believe she could be anything but right.*

*But he should have known.*

*She led him by the hand to that dark back bedroom, tottering on red heels she could barely walk in, almost tripping over someone's purse, and she laughed and threw her arms around his neck to catch herself before she fell.*

*They froze for a moment. He felt her body against his, warm and wonderful, and his arms went around her to pull her closer. She kissed him, and he kissed her—*

*And he kept kissing her until he couldn't breathe. Until she couldn't.*

"How old are you?" Blue asked, taking her hand and turning it over, unfolding her pointer finger from where it was curled against her palm, and touching it softly, examining it.

"Almost sixteen," she said. "My birthday's in a few days."

"How many days?"

"Four."

"Oh," he said, his word cut short by breath. "Do you have any prohibitions on you? Restrictions?"

"What do you mean?" It was a struggle to keep her hand still, to keep from ripping it away or curling her fingers around his and holding them. Her nerves jerked each time he touched her. The softer he was, the nicer it felt, the worse it became.

"Things you've been forbidden to do. Things that have been kept from you."

"Sure. Lots of things. Everything. My godmothers are the most overprotective people on the planet. I'm not allowed to be here, for one."

"But anything specific?" he asked.

"I'm not allowed to ride in my friends' cars. I'm not allowed to get my license until I'm eighteen. I'm not allowed to date. Not allowed to watch R-rated movies. Not allowed to go for walks after dark. Not allowed to play with sharp objects. The list goes on and on."

Blue nodded grimly, like she'd confirmed something for him. "Okay. Well . . . I'm going to tell you something. You might not like it."

"About my . . . curse?" she said, still hoping that he would tell her no, she was mistaken.

But he nodded instead.

"Mira, you have what's called a märchen mark. *Märchen* is the German word for *tale*. As in *fairy tale*."

"What do you mean?"

"It identifies you. It places you in a role. It tells you what you're meant to do, or what will happen to you. It's like . . . your destiny. Your curse."

Blue laid his hands on the table, a slight tremor running though them. "There are certain places where our kind gathers. Beau Rivage is one of them."

"So your friends—they're all . . . cursed."

Blue nodded. "Yes."

"What does my mark mean? What's my role?"

"The wheel that you have, and that Freddie has, represents the spinning wheel from 'Sleeping Beauty.' "

Mira drew in a breath and held it. *Felix's favorite tale.*
*Fate.*

"You're a Somnolent," Blue continued. "That means you were cursed, probably when you were a baby; and that there is an object—not necessarily a spindle, since the tales evolve and that would be too archaic now—that is destined to send you into an enchanted sleep if it cuts you or pricks your finger or something. Possibly a very long sleep, depending on where your prince is when it happens. And whether he knows how to find you."

"My prince?" Mira blinked at him, stunned. "I have a prince?"

"Um, yeah. That would be Freddie."

*Freddie.* Freddie was nice. Freddie was sweet. And a chick magnet—not to mention a bluebird, butterfly, and chipmunk magnet.

But Mira couldn't see him as her boyfriend and curse breaker, the love of her life.

She let out a long sigh and stirred her melting milk shake. So far, fairy tales and happily-ever-after didn't seem to go hand in hand. And being a princess—if that was indeed what she was—wasn't the dream come true she'd imagined back when she was five, dancing around the house in a pink tutu and plastic tiara. If Bliss and Elsa knew the truth about her, she was surprised they hadn't burst out laughing at the sight: a real princess playing princess.

She swallowed a mouthful of runny ice cream, her throat clenching as she put two and two together. Elsa and Bliss.

"I am so dumb."

Blue arched his eyebrows. "Isn't that my line?"

"My godmothers. Are they *fairy* godmothers?"

"Probably," Blue said. "If they were entrusted with your welfare. But I guess they *could* be human. Stranger things have happened."

"Stranger things like us," she said.

She no longer thought it was cute that the café was called Gingerbread House, or that the walls were decorated with candy. She wouldn't have been surprised to find a boy in a cage in the kitchen, being fattened up by a witch like in "Hansel and Gretel."

One of the waitresses hovered nearby, wiping down tables that were already clean—she was obviously eavesdropping. *Stupid fairy-tale town.*

"Can we talk somewhere else?" Mira asked, nodding toward the nosy waitress.

"Sure," Blue said, getting up. "I wanted to bring you to Layla anyway. She'll explain this stuff better than I can."

By three o'clock, Mira and Blue were camped in leather armchairs by the wide front window of The Emperor's New Books used bookstore, waiting for Layla to go on break.

The shelves housed an eclectic assortment of books that Mira doubted anyone would ever buy: acrid-smelling romance novels from the 1970s, crossword puzzle books with half the answers penciled in, travel guides that hadn't been useful in decades. A plastic crate of record albums gathered dust on the floor, and just beyond it stood a wire rack stuffed with well-thumbed graphic novels—the only nod to the current century.

Mira got the impression the store was more of a hobby for the owner than a business. And from what she'd seen so far, the customers treated it like a library. The current sole patron—a young police officer who was flipping through baby name books like his life depended on it—was taking forever to leave.

Layla was sorting through a shipment, looking as effortlessly gorgeous as the last time Mira had seen her. Blue had poured himself iced coffee from the pitcher in the employee fridge and was absorbed in a comic book. And Mira, who normally would have been content in a bookstore, was too antsy to read anything.

"What's Layla's märchen mark?" Mira asked, leaning toward Blue, keeping her voice down.

Grudgingly, Blue abandoned the comic he was reading—a *Peter Pan* retelling, full of ethereal girls and fey lost boys. "Layla's Beauty, from 'Beauty and the Beast.' We all feel bad for her because she has to put up with Rafe."

"Oh my god, Rafe is the Beast," Mira said. She felt stupid; it was so obvious.

"Yep. Beastly on the inside, soon to be beastly on the outside, once a fairy sets the curse in motion. He's supposed to be redeemed by the end of it, but we have very little faith in him. It'll take a miracle to get Layla to fall in love with Rafe. We just hope he can still play bass with monster paws. Otherwise, we'll have to find a new band member."

"You say that like you think it's funny."

Blue shrugged. "Isn't it? It's what he deserves. Not that we don't like him, but sometimes you have to learn things the hard way."

Mira glanced at him. "And you? Did you have to learn something the hard way?"

"Nice try," he said. But the smile on his lips didn't quite reach his eyes.

What Mira *really* wanted to ask was what Blue's heart mark meant—and what Felix's mark was, if he had one—but Blue seemed to be going out of his way *not* to tell her. His reticence made her uneasy. She knew there were bad people in fairy tales: wolves that swallowed women whole, stepmothers who treated their daughters like slaves, tricksters who struck impossible deals—and so many more. Could Blue be one of the wicked?

She didn't want to fight with him. Not when they were finally getting along. So instead of pushing him, she asked, "What about Viv? Is she Snow White?"

"Bingo. She's a Somnolent, too—you guys have enchanted comas in common. Henley's the hapless Huntsman. One day, Viv's stepmom will order him to cut Viv's heart out and bring it back to her. That always adds an extra dimension of hilarity to their hookups."

"Oh my god." Mira recoiled. "He won't do it, though, right?"

"Who knows? She's such a bitch to him and he's so obsessed with her that he just might. He freaks out whenever he suspects some guy around here could be her prince; he's definitely not eager to hand her over to someone else. He'll be relieved when he finds out you have a claim on Freddie."

"I don't—" She shook her head, not ready to accept that. It was too weird.

"Freddie's not so bad."

"Nothing against Freddie, I just . . ."

"You don't like feeling trapped, like your future is already mapped out for you."

"Right."

"Trust me, no one does." Blue picked up his comic again, like he'd decided now would be a good time to avoid her. His head was bowed, and a maelstrom of blue spikes stared back at her, stiff from the salt water.

Mira batted the comic out of the way. "What about you? What's your trap?"

"I don't want to talk about it. Curiosity killed the brat."

She stuck her tongue out at him. It seemed appropriate.

"Sexy," he said, flicking his own tongue at her. She kicked him in the shin in response. Blue bent forward to grip his leg, cursing.

"Still sexy?" she asked. "What was that you said about learning things the hard way? Maybe that's your curse."

She let him read for a while, figuring she should give him a break, and she stared out the window, watching people go by and wondering how many were cursed. Had that old woman been a damsel in distress once? Would that boy grow up to slay a giant? And was that girl, the pretty one with the dirty face and the careworn clothes, heading home to clean house for a wicked stepmom and two greedy stepsisters?

It was strange to think of another world being hidden behind the regular world. An entire society where destiny ruled.

A triumphant "aha!" from the stacks caused Mira to glance over. The police officer with the baby name books was scribbling madly in a notebook, like he'd made some great discovery.

"Mix in some numbers and symbols," Layla advised as she whisked by. "They're savvier now at picking unguessable names. They learned it from Internet passwords."

The officer hissed through his teeth. "Damn it! This will take forever!"

Layla patted his shoulder. "Sorry, Leo."

Mira's forehead wrinkled with confusion. Sometimes this place was just too weird.

Finally, the young officer hustled out the door with his notebook of names, calling out a quick "Thanks!" as the jangling bell announced his departure. Layla flipped the CLOSED sign on the door and came over to join them. She had a thick leather-bound book balanced against her hip.

Layla had been yanking books down from dusty shelves all day, but there wasn't a speck of dirt or a drop of sweat on her. Her sleek, black hair was as frizz free as a Barbie doll's, and her dark eyes sparkled, even when she wasn't smiling. She was like a Renaissance painting—flawlessly beautiful—and there was a warmth to her beauty, too.

"I feel bad for Leo," Layla said with a sigh. "True names are much harder to crack these days. The troll is almost definitely getting that baby."

"Troll?" Mira said.

"Rumpelstiltskin curse," Blue explained. "Leo's the guy charged with finding the troll's true name, so the queen can save her baby from his clutches. Sucks to be him."

"Um, maybe someone should tell him it's *Rumpelstiltskin*?" Mira said.

Blue laughed. Layla gave her a small smile. "*Rumpelstiltskin* is the name in the tale," Blue said. "It's not the name of every troll. That would be too easy."

"Oh," Mira said, disappointed.

"Anyway," Layla said. "We're not here to talk about poor Leo's curse. We're here to talk basics. Are you ready, Mira?"

"As ready as I'll ever be."

Layla placed the leather-bound book on the table in front of them and opened it with a *whump*. The pages were gilt-edged, printed with dark brown ink. It seemed to be a sort of encyclopedia. The text was laid out in two columns, and each entry began with elaborate cursive—a work of art in itself. Some entries were accompanied by symbols—an apple, a braid, a crown—all inked in the same deep brown. Line drawings of fairy-tale scenes illustrated the text.

"I grabbed this from the back," Layla said, her expression colored by mischief for a second. "I'm *not* supposed to touch it—it's an antique. But my boss isn't here today, and I think Mira deserves something special for her introduction. If you spill coffee on it," she added, looking pointedly at Blue, "I will kill you."

"Understood," Blue said, shifting his iced coffee out of the way.

"What is it, exactly?" Mira leaned forward to peer at the pages. Layla had opened the book to a seemingly random place, and the first entry read:

*The Changed*
 *Those who are physically transformed by magic, for good or ill, often accompanied by discomfort, suffering, or pain. The curse can be undone, sometimes through true love, sometimes via other methods (killing the Enchanter, &c.).*
 *Some roles that belong to the Changed category are the Beast ("Beauty and the Beast"), the Mermaid ("The Little Mermaid"), the Kind and Unkind Girls ("The Fairies").*

"It's a taxonomy of curses," Layla said. "It explains our roles, our marks, lists the tales . . . and also the categories we fall into. For example, your *mark* is the wheel. . . ." Layla flipped ahead to the "Sleeping Beauty" listing, which was illustrated with the same wheel shape Mira had on her back. "Your *tale* is 'Sleeping Beauty,' your role is the princess, and your overarching *category* is Somnolent."

"That's a lot to keep track of," Mira said.

Layla shrugged. "It's mostly intuitive once you get the hang of it. Viv is also a Somnolent princess, but her tale is 'Snow White,' and her mark is an apple. So there's some overlap."

Layla leafed through the book, her fingers turning the pages almost lovingly. "Originally, this book was made as a reference tool for young fairies so they could learn the various curses and make the right choices about whom to bestow them upon. But now it's more of a collector's item. Fairies have easier ways of sharing information."

"But aren't we born with these marks?" Mira asked.

Layla shook her head. "Did someone tell you that? We're usually cursed when we're children, or older, once our personalities have made themselves known. There *are* some hereditary curses—curses that run in a particular family, that is," Layla said, glancing quickly at Blue. "And—"

Mira turned toward Blue, to ask him about it—but he just held his coffee up and away from the book, like that was the issue here.

"I'm not going to spill it," he said. "Don't look at me like that."

"Um, anyway," Layla continued a little awkwardly, "you were probably cursed as an infant, Mira—most Sleeping Beauty Somnolents are. Viv was cursed when she was a baby, too. But my curse was bestowed when I was ten, and Jewel was cursed only a few years ago. So it varies. Anyone with magic in their blood has curse potential, but it takes a fairy to awaken it."

"There's magic in my blood?" Mira swiveled her wrist to

look at the cluster of veins there, suddenly nervous about what they contained.

"It just means that somewhere in your family's history, there's an ancestor who wasn't fully human—a fairy, perhaps—whose magic was passed down to you," Layla said. "In a very diluted form, of course."

"Fairy-human relations are generally frowned upon," Blue said. "And by *relations*, I mean—"

Mira cut him off, heat spreading across her cheeks. "I get it."

"So our curses are punishments for those forbidden trysts," Layla said. "Fairies feel they have a right to test us—to make us undergo an ordeal. Although some fairies have a soft spot for us. Some are good. And these days, they don't curse everyone—lots of people get skipped. We call that having a dormant curse."

The talk of fairies brought Mira's thoughts back to Elsa and Bliss. Were they *both* fairies? Bliss she could sort of see as a fairy godmother, what with the frilly dresses and the bouncy steps and the charm shop. But Elsa seemed too practical to be magical. And she couldn't imagine either of them *punishing* someone.

Well . . . except maybe her. For disobeying them. And lying to them.

Thinking about her godmothers made her eyes well up. She could call them, tell them she was in Beau Rivage and knew the truth now—but what if they were furious with her? What if they overreacted and took her away again?

She wasn't ready to leave. Wasn't ready to surrender her independence either.

Layla was still explaining. "It's not just a matter of having magic in your blood—there's a social dividing line, too. Prince and princess curses are reserved for the people we call Royals. We call them that because their families were members of the nobility, once upon a time. They're usually rich—"

"Marrying the peasant who spins straw into gold—always a good move," Blue said.

"—and they're considered to be the fairy-tale elite, although their curses aren't necessarily more desirable—as I'm sure you and Viv would attest. But that's all subjective anyway," Layla said. "Traditionally, what's viewed as a bad curse is bestowed by an evil fairy. Rafe's Beast curse, for instance. Whereas my curse, which is *supposed* to be a good one—because I'm destined to break the Beast's enchantment," she said, rolling her eyes, "was bestowed by a good fairy."

"In other words, a fairy could view your curse as a reward, and you might still hate it," Blue said.

"Good and evil are *our* descriptors for fairies, by the way," Layla said. "It's best not to call a fairy evil to her face."

"I'll remember that," Mira said with a smile.

Someone banged on the glass then, startling them. It was an old woman whose hair hung down in matted orange, black, and white strips, like ragged cat fur. She was carrying a wicker basket and looked slightly crazed. Layla pointed to the CLOSED sign until the woman scowled and went away.

"We *do* have some power over our lives," Layla added, turning thoughtful. "We make our own decisions—it's just that fate has a way of twisting our efforts to meet its expectations. So there have been Cinderellas who've run away from the ball, fled their princes, and kept running until their glass slippers cracked. And there have been Wolves who chose not to devour Red Riding Hood or her grandmother and were accepted into the Hood family with gratitude, only to turn feral again weeks later and slaughter everyone—because murder is a Wolf's nature."

Blue's fingers curled around the armrest of his chair and dug in. Mira studied him, wondering—was he a Wolf? But a heart mark didn't make sense for a Wolf.

His head was bowed, so she couldn't read his expression. His knuckles were white.

"So . . . is it worth trying?" Mira asked. "To have anything the fairies don't want you to have?" She hoped Layla said yes. Layla *had* to say yes. Because Mira couldn't imagine giving up and accepting that Freddie was her future, prince or not. She wanted to believe she could fall in love and have it matter, not just fall into place like a puzzle piece.

Layla offered a commiserating smile—in a way, her fate was worse. She didn't have to worry about plunging into a hundred-year coma—but she was destined to be trapped in a house with beastly Rafe, putting up with his crap until "love" taught him not to be an asshole.

"It's difficult to escape your destiny," Layla admitted. "But in your case, your best chance is to figure out what your trigger is—the object that sets off your enchanted sleep—and avoid it. It probably isn't a spindle; you can't find those nowadays, and evil fairies don't take chances. Did your godmothers ever mention anything? An object you weren't allowed to touch?"

"There were so many things they wouldn't let me do . . . I really don't know," Mira said. "They had an entire ban on sharp objects. They wouldn't even let me use scissors unless they were those safety scissors you use in kindergarten."

"Maybe it's scissors?" Blue said.

Layla shook her head. "We can't assume that. Mira's godmothers were probably just being cautious. The only way to know for sure is to find a fairy who remembers the curse, and ask. We should ask Delilah."

"No. Absolutely not," Blue said, getting to his feet. "That's dangerous."

"It's the only way she'll have a chance to be safe," Layla insisted. "What if Mira goes off somewhere, and no one knows where she is, and while she's there, she pricks her finger on whatever triggers the sleep, and no one finds her for a hundred years? I'd rather ask the fairy."

"So would I," Mira said. "I'd rather know." She shivered, wishing the sunlight streaming through the window could chase off the chill that had settled over her. *Sleep for a hundred years.* And wake up to what? Everyone she'd ever met would be dead. The world she knew would be gone. She'd lost enough when she'd lost her parents; she couldn't bear to lose everything.

"I'd rather know," Mira said again. "So I can avoid it."

"In the Sleeping Beauty tale," Blue started, "the evil fairy who curses the princess states that she'll prick her finger and *die*. It was only through a good fairy's intervention that the curse got softened to enchanted sleep. *Delilah* is an evil fairy. If you confront her, who's to say she won't take the opportunity to curse you with something worse?"

Mira swallowed. She didn't want to think about what *worse* might mean. "That's a chance I'm willing to take," she said finally. "I've been in the dark too long—I don't want to stay there. I want to know the truth."

# CHAPTER EIGHT

"I'LL DO THE TALKING," Layla offered, crossing her arms and leaning against the gritty outer wall of the nightclub, looking a bit tougher than her delicate sundress should have allowed. "I'm Honor-bound; she can't curse me with anything worse than Rafe."

*Honor-bound* was one of the categories the Marked fell into, like Changed and Somnolent. *Honor-bound* meant that you broke enchantments. If a girl fell into an enchanted sleep, her Honor-bound prince could wake her with a kiss. If a boy became a Beast, an Honor-bound girl could teach him to love, and redeem him. The Honor-bound were protected from harmful curses because they possessed the power to undo them.

Mira knew this because Layla had spent the afternoon giving her a crash course in fairy-tale destinies.

Now it was evening, and Mira waited with Layla and Blue outside Stroke of Midnight, a nightclub where Blue's band played sometimes. They'd come here because Layla and Blue knew the fairy who owned the place. Apparently, fairies tended to be reclusive. Their homes were hidden, and they were hard to recognize because they went around in disguises most of the time. So Delilah, the fairy who owned the club—and who was well-known and approachable, if a bit evil—was their best hope. Unless they wanted to go on a quest, hire a go-between to track a fairy down, or ask Mira's godmothers—which Mira absolutely didn't want to do.

*I'm not ready to go home yet,* she'd told Blue when he'd brought up that option. *You don't understand how angry my godmothers will be. I really messed with their heads. This will all be over if I tell them. They'll take me away.*

And though Blue had tried to get her to leave from the moment he'd met her, for some reason, he accepted that without argument. And she felt weird, flattered, like maybe now he wanted her to stay.

Posters advertising upcoming shows were plastered all over the club's door and stapled to the telephone pole outside—including a Curses & Kisses poster with all four band members mugging for the camera. Jewel bit down on a gem the size of a jawbreaker, her lips curled back in a sexy snarl. Rafe was doing his best to look hot, Freddie was smiling warmly, and Blue was slouching, his hair spiking like a shark's fin, eyeing the camera like he wanted to mess with it.

Mira let her eyelids droop, tired from all the walking they'd done, the heat and humidity that never dissipated. The club wasn't scheduled to open for another few hours. It was dead quiet, and the stillness only served to highlight the general shadiness of the area.

Across the street, some guys were crouched, playing a

dice game, occasionally whistling at Layla; but Blue and Layla ignored them, and they never ventured closer. A woman with slumped shoulders trundled a shopping cart down the street, one broken wheel causing the cart to swerve. And a girl dwarfed by her fake-fur jacket clopped down the street in platform boots, her legs like matchsticks, her eyes sunken and haunted.

Mira hugged her arms to her chest, feeling uncomfortable. This place was a reminder that she'd been sheltered from more than curses.

"I still think it's better if we don't talk to her at all," Blue said. "We could ask a good fairy."

"We don't know where to find one on such short notice—certainly not before Mira's birthday," Layla countered. "And besides, Delilah knows everything. She'll have the answer we're looking for. Although, if you want," Layla said, glancing at her phone, "we could call Freddie for backup. One more Honorbound to keep you safe."

"Uh . . ." Blue hesitated. "I don't know if that's a good idea. I'm not sure how Freddie will react when he finds out about Mira. He's been waiting for her his whole life."

"That's true," Layla said.

Mira was quiet. She didn't know how *she* would react when Freddie found out. Because it wasn't that she didn't like him—she just didn't like him *that way*.

He'd been waiting for her his whole life . . . but she'd spent almost sixteen years not knowing who she really was.

"We could ask Felix to come," she said.

Blue glared at her. "No."

"Delilah does like Felix," Layla hedged. But she seemed uneasy at the suggestion.

While they were discussing it, a black town car pulled up to the curb. The men playing dice scattered like crows. Blue straightened, his posture as stiff as Mira had ever seen it, and Layla pressed her hands together in a supplicating gesture. Like they were both waiting for something terrible.

The car doors opened and an ogre in a black suit stepped out from the driver's side. A genuine ogre—there was no other word for the heavily muscled, gray-skinned man before them. His bald head was mottled with dark gray splotches, and his ears were malformed like a wrestler's. Broad shoulders strained at the seams of his suit.

The ogre clasped his meaty hands together and stood waiting while a willowy, raven-haired woman emerged from the passenger's side, one fishnet-clad leg at a time.

"Here she is," Layla whispered.

Delilah was dressed like she'd come from a funeral, or a fashion show. She wore a black blouse with an enormous, drooping bow at her throat, a knee-length black pencil skirt, fishnet stockings, and black boots with stiletto heels. A black velvet hat tilted across her hair, and a mesh veil draped one side of her face.

Crossing the street with choppy, hip-swaying steps, she gave them a curious smile. Her lips were the blue-violet color of a bruise.

"It's all right, Sam," the fairy said to the ogre—who was glowering at them suspiciously. "I know these children." She looked at Blue, who was avoiding her gaze. "Problem with the show Saturday? You'd better not be canceling on me, Valentine."

"No, nothing like that," Layla said quickly. "We hoped

we could ask you a few questions before the club opens. If you have time."

"Of course," the fairy murmured, standing back as the ogre unlocked the club's door.

The ogre sniffed in Mira's direction, his large nostrils flaring, and she shrank back a few steps. Maybe he ate people. Maybe he'd been displaced from his mansion in the sky by a sneaky teenage boy, and devouring teenagers was how he got his revenge.

The door opened and the ogre flicked on the lights, revealing the dinginess of the club. Stroke of Midnight might as well have been a warehouse; it didn't evoke the cool, decadent sexiness Mira imagined when she thought of nightclubs. Dents from drunken fists pitted the walls, stains ringed the floor, and the air held the faded scent of smoke and beer. Almost immediately, Mira's foot landed in something sticky. Her ballet flats made squelchy adhesive sounds against the floor.

They followed Delilah down a narrow corridor and into her office, which had no windows and was painted entirely black—walls, floor, ceiling, everything—so that it was like being trapped inside a coffin. Two acid green lightbulbs gave off a sickly radiance, but it wasn't enough to keep the room from feeling claustrophobic. Mira was starting to regret this. She wished Blue had argued against it a little harder.

"Now, what can I do for you?" Delilah asked, pivoting to face them. One of her legs was poised behind the other, so that her body seemed to narrow precariously from her hips to the floor. She looked like the blade of a knife.

Layla took Mira's arm, as if to reassure her—and also to lead her forward and present her to the fairy. "This is Mira. She's a Sleeping Beauty Somnolent. The princess."

"Ah! Welcome," Delilah said. "And you're looking for guidance?"

"Of a sort," Layla said. "She's a stranger to our ways. We were wondering if you knew which fairy had cursed her. Because we need to find out what her trigger is."

"No one ever told her?" Delilah asked, scandalized. "Where are her parents?"

"She was raised apart from them," Layla said. Mira squeezed the girl's arm. She was grateful Layla hadn't mentioned her parents' deaths to the fairy. It felt private, and a little like a weakness.

"I'll see what I can dig up," Delilah said. She motioned to Mira. "Turn around, dear. Show me your mark."

"I—but you already know—" Mira was still stammering out an excuse when Layla spun her around and yanked her shirt halfway up her spine.

"Just do as she says," Layla whispered.

Mira shuddered as Delilah's long fingernails scraped her exposed mark. The fairy's touch was rough and cold, like corroded metal against her skin.

"What's your full name, dear?" Delilah asked. Her fingernails stabbed lightly into the curve of Mira's waist, as if sizing her up for something.

"Mira. Mirabelle Lively," she stuttered after a pause. The fairy made her nervous. She knew she needed to cooperate if she wanted answers—but she found herself reluctant to feed the fairy information. Knowledge was power—and handing more power to Delilah seemed reckless.

"Who are your parents? When is your birthday? How old are you now?"

Mira answered every question, shivering at the sensation of the fairy's cold fingers on her skin. Delilah seemed intrigued when she discovered Mira's sixteenth birthday was approaching.

"Darling, what terrifying timing. I'll make it a priority to find out before then. Birthdays have a habit of being rather monstrous around here."

"Monstrous?" Mira asked.

"Oh yes," Delilah said, her voice a velvet purr. "Birthdays are days of change. Leaving one year and entering the next. It's a powerful time, and bad things tend to happen. We wouldn't want you to be unprepared."

Delilah circled around to face her, smiling—as if she hadn't just implied Mira's doom. "Are you coming to the show Saturday night, princess? With any luck, I'll know by then. We can chat about it."

Saturday was the day before her birthday. Three days from now.

In four days, she'd turn sixteen. But on the day when she was supposed to be celebrating—celebrating *life*, of all things— she could turn into a sleeping damsel, a princess in stasis. Just when the world was supposed to be opening up for her.

And right now she didn't know how to save herself.

"I—" Mira's voice felt fragile in her throat. She looked at Layla and Blue, but neither of them gave her a sign. It was her choice to make. "Yes," she decided. "I'll be here."

"Perfect," Delilah said. "Will that be all?"

"Yes," Layla said with an overly bright smile. She grasped Mira's arm—firmly—and ushered her out. "Thank you so much."

"Yes, thank you," Mira murmured as they hurried past the ogre.

Layla let out a sigh as the door swung shut behind them, and she practically dragged Mira down the dark hall.

"Sorry for rushing you," Layla said. "I was certain she'd ask for something in return. And when she *didn't*, I wanted to get away from there before she changed her mind."

"Does she usually ask for payment?" Mira asked.

"Yes! Of course!" Layla exclaimed, as if it should be obvious.

It grated at Mira that no one had bothered to warn her about that *beforehand*. But it was over, so she didn't complain. She'd gotten lucky. Inexplicably.

"There must have been something she liked about you," Layla said. "Maybe she felt bad for you. Even evil fairies must have hearts."

"Yes," Blue said—speaking up for the first time since they'd entered the club. "That's why they curse babies—because they really *feel* for the underdog."

Layla frowned. "You're such a cynic."

"And you're a sucker," Blue said. "Watch, you'll end up redeeming Rafe after all. The fairies picked you for a reason; they know what your heart's like. You're too good."

Layla muttered something about how no, she certainly was *not* too good, and hugged her arms to her chest. But the spark had gone from her eyes. She was obviously thinking it over— maybe even steeling herself against the inevitable.

What was it she and Viv had said? That you could fight your destiny—but fate had a way of twisting your efforts and steering you right back.

Mira didn't want to be steered. She didn't want to be manipulated, or feel like everything she did and felt was unimportant. She wanted a *choice*.

As they crossed the empty dance floor, shoes ringing hollowly on the cement, Blue reached out and took Mira's hand. His grip was strong, secure—he seemed less like the mouthy troublemaker of the past few days and more like someone she could trust.

"Delilah might ask you for something later," Blue confided, his voice low. "When she has the information you want. But if you tell me what it is . . . I'll do my best to help you."

"Thank you," she said, surprised. She could feel his supportiveness, his worry for her, in his touch.

He squeezed her hand in lieu of a reply.

Blue released her hand eventually—it would have been weird if he hadn't, though she noted its absence—but he grabbed it again as the streets grew more crowded, people spilling out of doorways and forming a snaking mob that allowed only foot traffic to pass through. Touristy shops had closed their doors, bars and restaurants had opened them, and a street fair had sprung up: kiosks and food carts filled the streets.

The air was thick with the scents of sugar and exhaust, fumes from roasted nuts and cotton candy machines, salt water and shrimp, sweat and perfume.

"Let's go this way," Blue said, tugging her down the packed street.

"Through the fair?" Layla called, grasping Mira's shirt to keep from being separated. "Why?"

"I want to show Mira."

"Show me what?" Mira asked.

"Things you didn't see before. Look between the cracks."

Mira studied the crowd before her, not sure what she was

looking for. A band played at one end of the street, and little kids danced to the music, waving balloon animals and toy swords. There were couples out on dates, hands creeping up the backs of T-shirts to fondle bare skin. Vendors hawked nylon fairy wings, funnel cakes, lemonade, art. Men and women lingered on the thresholds of bars, calling to friends, cozying up to strangers.

It seemed like any other place.

But then a pair of twenty-something girls caught her eye. Sisters, maybe? They walked with the same awkward gait— a kind of limping sashay—and had the same pert noses and cascading dark curls. They limped along in open-toed sandals, perfect pedicures marred by the white bandages they wore.

One girl's heel was wrapped—and oddly shaped, like part of it was missing. The other girl wore a thick bandage where her big toe should have been.

They were Cinderella's stepsisters, Mira realized—and this was the aftermath of their curse. In the tale, each stepsister cut off part of her foot in hopes of fitting into Cinderella's tiny slipper. Mira hadn't thought anyone would actually do that—but the sisters flaunted their injured feet like they were proud of them.

The sisters sensed her staring and glanced over, their eyes narrowing in unison. Blue waved hello, but instead of acknowledging him, they turned up their noses and hobbled away.

"They're still so snobby!" Layla exclaimed. "You'd think that amputation would have humbled them a bit."

"They think they're special because they avoided getting their eyes pecked out," Blue said. "But really, it was just their stepsister being nice to them. She let them wear goggles to the wedding. It's not that the birds didn't try."

"Of course not." Layla sniffed. "Birds are diligent."

"You know those girls?" Mira asked.

"Not exactly," Blue said. "We know *of* them."

Blue stopped on a corner where the crowd had opened up, outside a Mexican restaurant advertising a happy hour that had long passed. The door was propped open and the buzz of conversation floated out, along with the clink of silverware against dinner plates.

"There are a lot of cursed people we're not friends with," Blue continued, still peering ahead, his eyes seeking familiar faces in the crowd. "But we usually recognize an insider when we see one. There are things that make us stand out. Things normal people dismiss, because people believe what they want to believe. The difference with us is that we believe in everything.

"Occasionally we get surprises," Blue went on. "People who were raised outside and show up unexpectedly—like you. Like Viv's prince, probably, since there's no Snow White prince in our generation here."

"Speak of the devil," Layla murmured.

Mira stiffened, glancing around apprehensively. What now?

Blue caught her eye and nodded toward a family of four that was ambling through the fair. At first glance, they were beautiful—eyes bright like laughter, summer clothes in sherbet colors. The little boy and girl bounded ahead of their parents—then circled back so as not to lose them. Their handsome father was the picture of contentment. He kept one arm curved lovingly around his wife's waist. Supporting her, Mira realized. Because the woman was tilting. She could barely stay upright.

The woman shuffled forward like a sleepwalker. Her eyelids drooped; her ruby mouth hung slack. Her skin was the color of ginger, and beaded with sweat. She was still lovely— but it was a cold, sickly loveliness.

"Who is that?" Mira asked. "What's wrong with her?"

"That's Gwen," Blue said. "Another Snow White Somnolent."

Layla leaned closer to confide the details. "Prince Charming—that's him—fell in love with her when he saw her in her coffin. But after he woke her and they were married, things weren't the same. She wasn't the girl he'd fallen in love with."

"Yeah, because she was alive," Blue snorted.

At first, Mira thought he was being flippant. But when his expression stayed hard, she wasn't so sure. "Tell me you're joking."

"Mira, it was an accident that he woke her at all." Blue stared after Gwen, dark blue brows furrowing. "The prince thought she was beautiful, posed and frozen in her crystal coffin, and he decided to take her home—to keep her, just like she was. But then one of his attendants tripped while they were carrying the coffin, and the jolt dislodged the poison apple that was stuck in her throat—which broke the enchantment. That's how she woke up."

"Supposedly," Layla said, "once Gwen was herself again, the prince found her effervescence unbearable. And Gwen couldn't deal with losing him; she was already in love with him because he'd saved her. She had a pretty messed-up home life, like most Snow White Somnolents; she didn't have anyone else. So she let him drug her, to recapture his interest. Because he prefers her barely conscious."

"Oh god," Mira said, so stunned she felt sick. "That's not a life."

"That's the point," Blue said, looking uneasy, too.

Mira watched, helpless to tear herself away, as Gwen and her family disappeared into the crowd. For those few moments that Gwen was still in sight, Mira felt like she was watching a funeral procession: a woman carrying her body to its grave, with the short, shuffling steps of a bride.

"I need to sit down," Mira said.

Blue cleared a spot for her on the sidewalk and she lowered herself to the concrete, sucking in deep breaths of steamy air. Blue crouched in front of her, a penitent look on his face.

"Should I not have showed you that?" he asked.

"I don't know," she said. "Maybe I wasn't ready to know that things could be that bad. Like, before, I just thought I had to worry about my curse. Pricking my finger, falling asleep."

"Not how twisted your curse might be."

Mira nodded. Her lungs felt cottony, full of fear instead of air.

"It won't be like that for you," Blue insisted. "Don't worry. We're going to find your trigger. You won't even get that far."

"And you know Freddie," Layla said soothingly. "He's not a bad guy, not even close."

"But what if I fall asleep somewhere else? Some other prince could wake me. Decades later, even—right?"

Neither Blue nor Layla answered at first. Then they nodded reluctantly and spoke over each other.

"That's right," Layla said.

"Right," Blue said.

"And I'd be asleep. Love at first sight—with an almost

dead girl. Delilah mentioned my birthday. That's *so soon*. What if something horrible—"

Blue cupped her face in his hands. His skin was hot, snapping her out of her hysteria.

"Hey. *Hey*," he said, until she looked at him. Her gaze dragged up from the ground and met his eyes, which were staring into hers like he was trying to reach her—to snatch her back from whatever dark dream she'd fallen into. "That's not going to happen."

"You promise?" she whispered, not even sure why she'd said it. Just that she felt vulnerable, and needed someone to reassure her.

Blue laughed good-naturedly, caught off guard. "What good is my promise going to do?" Then he seemed to realize she was serious. "All right," he said. "I promise." He glanced at Layla. "Layla—what's the penalty for breaking a promise? Is there one?"

"Not for promises like this," Layla said with a smile, like she thought it was sweet.

Mira got to her feet then, embarrassed that she'd come apart. She felt so much younger than everyone here, so naïve. Seeing a sedated princess was nothing new to Blue and Layla. They dealt with this messed-up world every day.

Around them, the mundane world had surged forward to fill in the gaps. A mother struggled to tie a bouquet of helium balloons to her son's wrist. A girl licked a dot of mustard off her boyfriend's cheek, and laughed, like she'd surprised herself.

There were nods to the city's fairy-tale history—a candy apple stand selling apples that had been dipped in glistening red candy on one side, white chocolate on the other, like the half-red, half-white poison apple in the Snow White tale. There was an artist selling bejeweled nightingales in wire cages, and paper-doll ballerinas and tiny tin soldiers. But there were no more scarred beautiful people in view, spreading their pain for everyone to see.

Blue took her hand again—loosely, so she could pull away if she wanted—and she held on like he was her anchor in a world that was swiftly spinning out of her control. She clung to him, damp and heat sealing their palms together, so, so grateful not to be alone.

It was only once they had walked Layla home, and the last light of twilight had faded, that Mira realized how late it was. She and Felix had made plans to search that night—and she'd inadvertently stood him up. She wondered what time he'd given up on her, and whether he'd filled his night with someone else.

There was something about being near Felix that made her feel happier, more alive. So much had changed and become uncertain today; she wanted to talk to him. To feel that good again. She missed him—and while he had every right to be annoyed with her, she hoped he'd understand. This discovery today was bigger than her parents, bigger than romance. It had pushed everything else out of her mind.

She walked nearly shoulder to shoulder with Blue. He was quiet, too—as if he'd had the life-shattering revelation tonight. The lights of the Dream glittered in the distance, and they followed them like two explorers following the North Star.

Muggy, polluted air swirled around them each time a car sped by. On the other side of the four-lane highway, the Palace

Casino flashed an incessant neon assault, signs promising entertainment, money to be won, cheap food. Its gaudy pink façade was stacked with turrets and pocked with heart-shaped windows, making it look more like a Japanese love hotel than a casino. Mira recalled Blue's earlier threat to dump her there. He certainly wasn't threatening her now.

"You're not being a jerk," she said. "You haven't been for a while."

Blue's steps thudded heavily beside hers. His hands were in his pockets, his head bowed. "I guess I lost my enthusiasm for it."

"It stopped being fun?" She nudged him with her shoulder, not used to his acting so serious.

"Stopped being useful. I don't know." He sighed. "I guess I'm confused. I don't know what to do with you now. How to treat you. You're not what I thought."

Mira's silver flats crunched over a fast-food wrapper. *I'm not what I thought either.* "What was I before?"

"A normal girl. Someone who was leaving. And I wanted to make sure that you did. That you had a chance to. But now, who knows? You might stay. You want to know things. And I don't want you to know what I am."

"You can tell me," she said. "You can trust me. Or if it's too hard for you, I can ask Felix." She meant it as a way to make things easier for him—but he grimaced at the mention of his brother.

"Felix won't tell you."

"Yes, he will. Once he knows about me."

Blue just shook his head. "You don't know Felix."

She thought about reminding him that *he* didn't know

Felix, that the two barely got along—but it seemed point-less. As futile as everything else she tried to tell him about his brother.

When they finally reached the Dream, neither one of them headed toward the doors. Instead, they stood before the Dream's white marble fountain. Three cupid statues shot arrows of water into the pool below, which was illuminated by pink and red lights. The water splashed down like music, and a subtle melody crept from speakers hidden in the flower beds.

"I used to write songs out here," Blue said.

"You write songs?" Mira said. "But you can't even play anything."

"Of course I can play. I just suck at the drums."

"You're . . ." She shook her head. He just . . . baffled her.

"What?"

"I was going to say *an idiot*, but that seemed rude."

Blue smiled. "I guess. I mean, sometimes I am."

"Why play an instrument—*publicly*, in a *band*—if you're horrible at it? Don't you feel like you're shortchanging people?"

"Not really. I feel like I'm doing them a favor. Freddie has his way of dealing with the groupie situation—being polite and terrified, basically—and I have mine."

"You're that worried about groupies? You're worried too many girls will be obsessed with you? No offense—"

Blue feigned shock. "Did I just hear you say *no offense*?"

She swatted his arm. "Let me finish. *No offense*, but isn't that a little conceited?"

"I'm not worried about girls liking me. I'm worried I'll like one of them back."

Two lovers stopped before the fountain—easy to identify

because they stood so close to each other and stayed connected with small, affectionate touches while they spoke. Mira watched them, distracted now that she and Blue were no longer alone, and as she did, the lovers wrapped their arms around each other and shared a slow, mesmerizing kiss.

She stared, caught off guard by the display, and the couple, oblivious to anyone but each other, clasped hands and continued down the path to the street.

She realized Blue had gone silent, too. They'd both stopped to watch. And it occurred to her then what his mark might mean.

"Your mark is a heart," she said, growing surer as she spoke. "A heart means love. You're some kind of hero—Honor-bound or something. You fall in love."

"Mira . . ." Blue stopped and turned toward her, his face tight in an expression she couldn't place. "Do I seem like a hero?"

"Not really. But—"

"I fall in love," he said. "But don't assume anything else. Don't assume anything good."

And he walked away from her. Left her standing by the fountain, and pushed through the glass doors to the casino. In an instant, they were separate, apart again, and it was hard to remember what it felt like to be his friend—to feel close like that, to feel like they trusted each other.

Mira sat down on the rim of the fountain. The marble ledge was damp, and mist sprinkled her skin. Coins shimmered under the water like fish scales. She counted them, each one a wish, and wondered how love could be anything but good.

*Love destroys you.*

# CHAPTER NINE

WHEN SHE LET HERSELF INTO FELIX'S SUITE, the lights were on but the rooms were empty. It was ten o'clock. Probably too late to go tiptoeing around graveyards.

Mira's eyes stung at her carelessness. She'd missed him. Missed her chance. And she had only three days to find her parents' graves before her birthday—or she wouldn't be able to share it with them. Might not be able to share *anything*, with anyone, if she succumbed to her curse. She had to find them now—while her wants still mattered.

Maybe she could go alone.

She had a list Felix had made, with the names and addresses of all the cemeteries in the city. Mira stuffed the list into her purse, grabbed a flashlight, and hurried down to the valet station at the front of the hotel. She looked for Felix as she cut through the casino, but there was no sign of him.

Out front, the valet was ushering someone into a taxi. Mira

caught the shimmer of a silver evening gown before the door shut and the valet turned to see what she needed. He wore a dark blue jacket that resembled a soldier's dress uniform, and he stood at attention, his back straight, looking bored and hot and a little disenchanted.

"Somewhere you'd like to go?" the valet finally asked.

"I—hi. I'm Felix Valentine's guest. And I wondered— could I use the courtesy car?" She swallowed. If this didn't work, her only option was to get a cab to take her. And she wasn't sure she trusted cabs.

The valet looked her up and down slowly, then smiled as if he recognized her. "Of course. One moment."

He hailed one of the Dream's courtesy cars and asked for her destination.

Unfolding the list, Mira pointed to the cemetery she'd chosen. "Here," she said.

The valet raised his eyebrows, but didn't comment. She supposed it was his job to fulfill strange requests. He leaned in to inform the driver, then opened the door for Mira. "I hope you find what you're looking for," he said.

Mira thanked him and climbed inside. Then the door slammed and they were moving swiftly through the night, the glitter of the hotel lights receding behind them. Cinderella in a modern-day carriage, on her way to dance with the dead.

The cemetery Mira had chosen was called Enchanted Rest. She was getting used to the fairy-tale names of the places Blue and his friends frequented, so when she noticed the name on the list, it seemed obvious. If her parents—her fairy-tale parents—were buried somewhere, why not there?

But when the car pulled up, she was dismayed to see the cemetery wasn't the enchanted grove its name implied. The unkempt grounds were enclosed by an iron fence tipped with spikes and bordered by knee-high grass. No one had bothered to lock or even latch the gate, and as Mira pushed through, the hinges groaned like a tormented soul.

Anticipation made her shiver—the thrill of a bad idea mixed with the hope that she'd finally find her parents. Mira clicked on her flashlight and shined the beam on each headstone, mouthing the names, waiting for her lips to stumble across *Piers and Adora Lively*.

At first, she could hear the low hum of the driver's radio, but as she crept deeper into the cemetery, the sounds of civilization vanished, and all she heard were the wind rustling through trees, the shush of her footsteps, the chittering of insects. And her breath, coming too fast.

She forced herself to push on. She wouldn't let herself think about vengeful ghosts or deranged wanderers. Only about the happy ending waiting beyond one of these headstones.

Lost in thought, she collided with a spiderweb that stretched between two trees. She cried out as it stuck to her, panicked by the wispy feel of thread on her lips. Frantically, she brushed the webbing from her shoulders, her face. A flap of wings startled her and she spun around, but couldn't tell where it had come from. She heard the faint dirge of the gate creaking open and banging shut, and began to tremble, even in the heat.

*It's the wind. Keep going. You're almost there. . . .*

When Mira reached the last grave, she turned to look back at all the ground she'd covered—not wanting to believe that she'd searched the whole cemetery and not found them. She wanted to cry. She'd been so sure they'd be here.

Could she have missed them? Overlooked their graves?

Mira sagged against the iron fence and gazed out at the thick forest beyond it—as black and impenetrable as the night sky. Resting her hands on the top bar, she stared into the dark, imagining there were two more graves hidden out there: concealed by rosebushes or thick garlands of moss. But there, and waiting for her.

She thought of the Cinderella fairy tale she'd read the other night. The stepsisters' acts of mutilation had grabbed her attention, but there was another part of the tale that had resonated with her. After her mother's death, Cinderella planted a hazel twig near her mother's grave and watered it with her tears until it grew into a beautiful tree. Cinderella then went to the tree for comfort, because it was imbued with her mother's spirit. When she needed clothes for the ball, she went to the tree and asked for them, and a bird in the tree threw down a gorgeous gown and delicate shoes.

But it wasn't the gown and the shoes that appealed to Mira—it was the way the dead mother looked out for Cinderella. Watched over her, stayed with her . . . And if fairy tales were real—if there were things like curses and destiny—then maybe Mira could plant a hazel twig near her parents' graves, and they would be with her, in a way. Maybe she could ask the tree to make her stop missing them.

Half in and out of consciousness, fantasizing about her own little hazel tree, Mira curled her fingers around the fence—and sliced her hand on one of the spikes.

Pain swept through her like wildfire. She trembled when she saw the cut on her finger, the blood flowing freely. She didn't like blood—not the sight of it, not the slippery feel of it. Her knees went weak and she feared she was about to collapse—to pass into a life-stealing sleep. Lost in the back of a graveyard, prey to wolves and men and anything and everything for a hundred years.

If she screamed before she fell asleep, would the driver hear her? Would he know what to do? Would people think she was dead? *Would they bury her?*

"Mira!"

The call came from behind her—and she *did* scream. Her heart raced in her chest. And then two hands grasped her shoulders, and her mind caught up with her fear.

"Mira, it's me."

"Felix," she said. By the time she recognized his touch, his voice, she could barely hear herself over the pounding of her heart. "You scared me."

He pulled her into his arms. "You cut yourself."

Her knees stopped wobbling as she relaxed against him. She didn't collapse, didn't lose consciousness. The pain in her hand was still there, but the fence wasn't her trigger. It was a wound, like any other wound.

She clutched the arm that curled around her, unable to help herself; stained his sleeve with blood.

"Felix," she said again. "How did you . . . ?"

"The valet told me where you went." He shook his head and muttered, "I should fire him for sending you here. Cemeteries aren't safe at night. You should have called me."

"It was late when I got back. I didn't want to bother you." She didn't want to admit that she'd worried he'd be busy, or on a date with someone experienced, someone sexy, and she'd have to hear the girl's voice in the background while being turned down.

"You never bother me." He looked past her into the trees, eyes narrowed like he was searching for something. "What were you doing, staring into the dark just now? Was someone there?"

"No," she admitted. "I just—I do this thing where I space out and stop seeing what's in front of me. I disappear into my head. I always do that."

She was studying the night shadows that veiled his face and remembering the heart on Blue's back. "Felix, something happened today. I—" She stopped herself; took a deep breath, barely able to say it, to make it real. "Remember how you thought I came to Beau Rivage for a reason? That there was something I was meant to find here? I think I found it."

"What did you find?" His voice was low, appropriate for a graveyard at night, like he didn't want anyone to overhear, not even ghosts. He pulled her closer, his hands on the small of her back, and she let her arms go around him like they belonged there.

"I'm like you," she whispered. "I'm cursed."

❧

*She was the first girl he'd fallen for, and he was nice to her, he made her laugh and fixed her bike chain when it broke and he flirted with her and pretended to cheat off her history tests, when really it was an excuse to stare at her. At how her red hair fell over her shoulders and onto her desk, and how she'd fling it away, like it was a weapon she was losing patience with. He always got bad grades anyway. He was rich enough that it was okay to be an academic failure.*

*He didn't expect anything to happen between them because it couldn't* happen; *but he wasn't immune to wanting it. His heart surged every time she smiled at him. Surged with hope that this could be different. But he was careful. The one time she asked him to a school dance, he lied and said he wasn't allowed to go; his father was dragging him off to a business conference. She seemed to sense the lie and never asked again.*

*But then on his birthday . . .*

*He kissed her. He stupidly kissed her. And it was better than he ever could have imagined. Until it was over. Really and truly over.*

*He would dedicate a piece of his heart to her. He would never forget her—but that was all the recompense he could offer. He couldn't bring her back.*

*She'd never looked more beautiful, more perfect, than she did when she was dead.*

Mira told Felix everything.

Her curse. Her meeting with the fairy. Even how certain she'd been that she would find her parents at Enchanted Rest, and her disappointment when she hadn't. Felix listened as she poured out her heart, her confusion, and started to ask questions only when she'd worn herself out. By that time, they were tucked away in a rounded booth at Twelve, the Dream's jazz club, named for the underworld nightclub where twelve princesses were said to dance, night after night, until they wore through the soles of their shoes.

The Dream's version of Twelve was a secret cove of a room: rounded booths arranged in a half circle in front of the stage, shadows pierced by haloes of candlelight. Filmy curtains shielded each booth and could be drawn closed to give the booth the look of a sultan's tent. Silver plum branches served as centerpieces—copies of the silver branches from the Twelve Dancing Princesses fairy tale, branches the soldier-hero collected in the underworld as proof of where the princesses went to dance.

Mira slumped against Felix, as exhausted as if she'd danced all night herself, and his arm came across her shoulders to pull her close.

"How's your hand?" he asked, turning her wrist to look at it.

"Fine," she said. "The cut wasn't deep. I just don't like blood. And I was worried about . . . you know. I panicked."

"I bet," he said, stroking her fingers. It reminded her of the way Blue had held her hand when he'd first learned about her mark: examining her fingers, as if imagining the wound that would one day condemn her to sleep.

"You're not alone anymore," Felix said. "You have a place here. In Beau Rivage . . . and with me. So you don't have to be afraid of this. Of being cursed."

She burrowed into his side, taking comfort in his closeness. In belonging.

"There's still so much I don't know," she said. "Like . . ."

Felix's other arm circled around to grasp the one that held her, so that he was holding her against him, his arms locking her in casually but protectively. She wanted to stay there forever.

"Like . . . I don't know the truth about you," she said. "Or Blue. What your curses are. Everyone else seems to know, but no one will tell me."

She tipped her head to look at him. "Blue says you won't tell me either. Is that true?"

Felix stared steadily at the stage. She couldn't see his eyes,

136

but his throat didn't quiver with a swallow, his hold on her didn't tighten. He didn't show signs of being tense.

"I can't tell you. It's part of the curse: I can't reveal it."

"You can't tell me anything? But I know what your mark is—what Blue's mark is, at least. Can you tell me what the heart means?"

Felix sipped his drink. One song ended and the audience broke into applause as the musicians segued into another. Little by little, the amber liquid in Felix's glass disappeared.

"We're called Romantics," he said finally. "That much I can tell you. But that's all."

Mira tried to push the rest of her questions down—if he couldn't answer, he couldn't answer. But she wanted to know everything about him. If he had a dark secret, she wanted to know that, too.

*Romantics.* What was a Romantic?

So much of Felix's life was closed to her. She never saw him when he was working. The time they spent together centered on her, not him. And his suite was almost as anonymous as the rest of the rooms in the hotel. Other than his clothes and his movie collection, which was too varied to really tell her anything, his personal effects consisted of a fairy-tale anthology and some business books.

Maybe he kept his private things in his other room.

Suite 3013—the room that was forbidden to her.

But what did he *do* there? Why did he need another room when he barely made use of the first one?

"Tell me something," she said.

"Tell you what?" he murmured, head dipping closer. The scent of warmth and cologne wafted from his throat.

"What's in suite 3013?" she asked, careful to keep her voice casual. "Is it your office?"

"It's nothing that would interest you, Mira. Ask me something else."

He made it sound like it was no big deal. But at the same time, he was throwing up a wall. Maybe it *wasn't* a big deal. And there *were* other things she wanted to know. . . .

"Okay. You said that I belong here," she started. "That I have a place here."

"Yes . . ."

"What about you? Who are your friends? What are their curses?" The rest of the question lay under her tongue, unasked: *Who are you . . . when you're not with me?*

"My friends . . . there aren't a lot of them. Just a few people I hung out with in high school. I don't really connect with people that easily."

"Why not?"

He shrugged. "I don't have time, for one. My dad's been training me for this job since I was in high school. I turned twenty-one a few months ago. You know how I spent my birthday? In a conference room with my dad, going over work stuff so he could dump his responsibilities on me and take off for a while. Now he's out traveling the world, and I have a casino to run. It doesn't leave a lot of time for friends. Forget about college. I can't even imagine what that's like: spending four years figuring out what you want to be . . . when my life's been mapped out for me for so long."

His chest grew still for a moment. "So I can't relate to most people my age. They'd probably say I'm too serious. And maybe I am. But I've lost things, too, and most people . . . they have no idea what it's like to really lose something. They don't understand how that changes you."

"I know what it's like," she said.

"I know you know," he said into her hair. "You're too serious for your own good. You should stay away from me; I'm a bad influence."

"You don't make me more serious," she said. "You make me the opposite. I was morbid to begin with."

He laughed. "Were you? So I can only improve things."

"Exactly," she said, pleased. She fidgeted with his cuff link, twisting it between her fingers, contemplating a confession: *You already* have *improved things. I don't obsess over my parents' deaths when I'm with you. I don't think about what's missing. I think about what's* here.

*I think about* you.

But she wasn't brave enough. A confession like that would change things. Break things, maybe. It was more than just *I want you*. It was closer to *I need you* . . . and that was dangerous.

Instead, she asked, "What did you lose?"

Felix stiffened. This time she could feel the tension in his body: the intake of breath that didn't get released immediately.

"I don't talk about that," he said.

"You can trust me."

He shook his head. "It's bad enough thinking about it all the time. I don't want to have to talk about it, too. I'd rather focus on something nice. Like being here with you."

Mira closed her eyes. She'd sunk down a little, and her head rested against his chest. She could hear his heartbeat, and as she listened, Blue's mark—a heart as red as blood and as smooth as a scar—appeared in her mind. It was surrounded by darkness. A reminder. A warning.

Felix's curse had hurt him—that had to be what he meant. He'd lost someone because of it, and it still haunted him. But who?

She wished he would tell her.

She wanted to be the person he told *everything* to.

"Where did you go?" he murmured. "Thinking about your parents again?"

"I—" He'd already asked her not to press him. "A little," she lied.

"We'll find them," he said. "I promise. And you know what? When we do"—he unwound his arms from around her, slid out from the booth—"we're going to bring them something."

"Bring them something? You mean besides me?"

"Come on," he said, smiling. "I think you'll like this."

As Felix unlocked the door and led her into the flower shop, a sweet, wild perfume enveloped her, so intense she could taste an entire garden when she breathed. Mira found herself surrounded by bins of cut flowers in every shape and color. All waiting to be chosen.

"Sleeping Beauties are supposed to have an affinity for flowers," Felix said. "Is it true?"

"You mean . . . . because of the wall of roses that grows up around the castle when they—when we—sleep?" She lifted a white rose to her face. "I do like flowers. I like them better when they're out in nature. But this is nice, too."

"I thought we could put together a bouquet for your

parents," he explained. "Something to lay at their graves when we find them."

"I'd love that," she said, smiling. "Thank you."

She tried to picture her mother and father in this room. Which flowers would they like?

Mira wandered through the shop, choosing flowers as they called to her: lush red roses, purple iris, pink lilies that curled like starfish. When she'd gathered them into a thick bouquet, she handed the bunch to Felix, and he bound the stems and slipped them into a vase.

Mira watched him, still holding the white rose. Biting her lip, she asked, "Why are you so nice to me?"

Felix cocked his head. "Why wouldn't I be nice to you?"

"Not just nice. You go out of your way for me, and I . . . I don't think I've done anything to deserve that."

"You've lost a lot. I want to give you something to make up for that."

She blushed, regretting her earlier enthusiasm. "I take too much from you already. You barely have any free time, and I take all of it."

"Only because I choose to spend it with you."

"But what about—" She took a deep breath, not wanting to ask, but needing to. "What about that girl you were with the night we met? Cora. I don't leave you any time to see her."

"We're not—" Felix shook his head. "We're not together. And anyway—I'd rather spend the time with you." He took her hand and pressed it to his cheek, his eyes closed, like he was savoring the feel of her skin. His jaw was rough; the blue shadow of stubble lightly scraped her palm as he turned his mouth to her hand—and she savored every second, too.

Felix's lips brushed her palm, and then he kissed her there again, harder, marking her with the wet brand of his mouth. Mira shuddered, going light-headed. Her thoughts seemed to dissolve, like the world was falling away.

She forgot what she was asking. She just wanted his lips on her skin.

"Mira, are you all right?" he murmured.

She blinked and saw him standing in front of her, clasping her wrist and studying her, a dark vibrancy in his eyes.

"Yes," she said breathlessly. "I just—I felt lost. When you kissed my hand . . . I guess I like you too much."

It was probably obvious she liked him too much, but admitting it made her feel strangely vulnerable. Especially after last night.

Would he think she was too young? Or something pathetic, like *adorable*?

Felix stepped closer until his body was flush with hers, and Mira's breath caught in her throat. She found herself staring at his chest, her heart thudding painfully, unsure of what to do; and he tilted her head back gently, so she'd look at him. His eyes were the deepest midnight blue.

"You're not scared of this, are you?" he asked.

"No," she whispered. "Not this time."

A breath passed between them.

And he kissed her.

His lips pressed the world away, obliterated everything; and a slow ecstasy seeped through her, flooding her veins. As her nervousness thawed, she kissed him back. Tentatively at first, then with more confidence as his body responded to hers, and he parted her lips and pulled her closer. When he drew his mouth away, her legs trembled, like her strength had fled with his kiss. Like she'd forgotten how to stand.

Felix didn't seem alarmed by her sudden weakness. He lifted her like she weighed almost nothing, and sat her on the glass counter, next to the bouquet she'd made, and a spool of red ribbon, a pair of scissors, and scattered sprigs of baby's breath. He stood in front of her, so they were eye to eye.

"I feel like I'm melting," she said. "Like everything sturdy in me melted away."

Her emotions tingled on her skin like static electricity, like his touch had pulled them to the surface.

"At home," she began haltingly, "when my godmothers were gone, I used to pretend that my parents were there. I'd imagine them doing normal things, like cooking, or watching old movies with me, or asking what I did at school. I guess because . . . I felt less lonely that way. I could pretend there wasn't a hole in me. But when I'm with you, I don't need them. I want what's real."

She was shaking. It was hard to be honest, to open up, and reveal something that sounded crazy. Because once you told someone the truth, that person had a piece of you—and they could belittle it, destroy it. They could turn your confession into a wound that never healed.

But Felix didn't do that. He would never do that.

He understood.

"You're not the only one . . . who can't forget," he said.

He looked lost suddenly, and she didn't want him to be sad, to think about the past when she was here now, ready to do everything right.

She threw her arms around his neck, swayed toward him,

off balance, and kissed him violently, possessively. *Come back,* she thought. *Stay with me.*

"I bought—a sexy nightgown," she said. "Do you want to see it?"

His hands tightened around her waist, fingers clutching at her blouse. "Yes. But I don't think that's a good idea. I think—" His voice turned low, a jagged whisper in her ear. "I think—that if you're not sure about this—you should tell me. Right now."

"Who's scared now?" she whispered back. "Don't I feel shh—"

He kissed the words out of her mouth, swallowed her flimsy attempts at seduction, until she realized she didn't have to convince him. He was back with her, in the present . . . and he wanted her, too.

His lips tugged at hers and she clung to him, her hands slipping against his jacket like she was trying to take hold of water, like she couldn't pull him close enough. Every time they broke apart, their breaths cut the air with twin gasps; and then their lips met again, frantic, like kissing was more important than breathing.

Mira started to feel dizzy, high, like the world was spinning. She tipped her head back, giving in to it, and Felix trailed kisses down her throat, his arms wrapped tightly around her, his lips wet on her skin . . . until she became almost numb to his touch. The world around her grew tinged with gray, and the feeling in her body flickered out, like a dying light.

She shuddered when he let her go, suddenly cold, like her warmth had been stolen. Her strength was gone; her limbs turned heavy and the glass counter tilted to meet her. As she collapsed, she knocked the bouquet and everything else to the floor, then stared dazedly at the mess of spilled water and flowers. The crash had sounded muffled to her ears.

*I think I'm sick . . .* , she tried to tell Felix, but her mouth wouldn't form the words.

Across the room, Felix slid down against the wall. He'd torn himself away from her, put that distance between them as if it had to be done, and now he was speaking softly to himself. His eyes seemed to burn; he looked feverishly gorgeous—and haunted. Then he pulled himself together. He rose to his feet hesitantly, like he was wary of coming near her.

*Felix,* she tried to say. *Something's wrong with me. . . .* She lay with her cheek pressed to the glass, feeling like consciousness was a thin stream inside her that was slowly bleeding out.

At last, Felix lifted her off the counter and into his arms, cradling her head because her whole body was drooping, and carried her into the elevator. He didn't speak—was he scared? He didn't . . . but then she stopped wondering, because she was too exhausted. She gazed at their reflections in the mirrored walls instead. Felix was still lit up with that feverish glow, but Mira barely recognized herself. Her muscles were limp, her eyes dull.

The elevator doors dinged apart and Felix carried her down a silent hall. It looked exactly like all the other halls in the hotel: same carpet, same paintings, same row of white doors. Her eyes closed as he opened one of the doors and slipped inside. She felt him lay her down on an unmade bed, the sheets twisted like rough waves beneath her. And then he was gone.

*He's going to get help. . . .*

She slept.

145

# CHAPTER TEN

MIRA AWOKE TO HUSHED MALE VOICES coming from an adjacent room. She pushed herself upright and shoved her hair out of her face.

She was sitting in a messy king-size bed in a mostly dark bedroom, still wearing her street clothes but not her shoes. Daylight filtered in through the half-open door, and dimly, she could make out posters on the walls: skulls, band logos, a model posed in sexy lingerie. There was an electric guitar propped in one corner, an acoustic guitar on a stand nearby. Rumpled clothes covered the floor, and a pillow and blanket were stretched out on the floor next to the bed, like someone had spent the night there.

"She was *out* when I got here," the first voice said. "I thought she was dead until I found her pulse."

"I could kill him," the other voice offered politely.

"No." A sigh. "You couldn't. That's not what you do. That's not how we solve this."

Mira crept out of bed, her legs quivering like Jell-O, and grabbed the door frame for support. Peering out, she saw Freddie and Blue in the suite's living room. Freddie was pacing in front of the TV, the sleeves of his button-down rolled to the elbows. Blue perched on the arm of the couch, in a black Joy Division T-shirt and ratty jeans, looking agitated.

Was this Blue's room?

"Hello?" she called uncertainly.

Blue sprang up from his seat. "Hey, how are you feeling?" She could see his throat move as he swallowed. "You were out for a while."

Blue led her over to the couch, and she took his arm gratefully. She didn't feel like she could walk properly. Her knees kept buckling, and finally, Blue scooped her up and carried her. She was too embarrassed to even say thank you.

As Blue eased her down, she noticed Freddie watching her—his eyes shining, body leaning toward her as if under a spell—and she was sure Blue had told him about her mark.

"So," Blue started uneasily, "how much of that did you hear?"

"Just the part where Freddie offered to kill someone."

"That . . ." Freddie scratched the back of his neck, flustered. "That was . . . a misunderstanding."

"You guys, seriously, what's going on?"

Blue shrugged. "Nothing. Freddie was just talking. He does that."

"And if I were to threaten someone . . . I would only do it to protect you," Freddie added. "That's what I'm here for."

"I don't need to be protected," she told him.

"Actually, you do," Blue said. He wasn't being obnoxious—he was serious, which was worse. He was messing with something—turning a key card around and around in his hand.

"Is that my passkey?" she asked.

"*Was* your passkey," Blue said. "If you need to open any doors, you can ask me."

"Felix *gave* that to me," she said, bristling.

"I know he did." Blue folded his fingers around the card. "I'm taking it back."

"You can't just steal my property."

"I'd like to see you stop me. You can't even walk."

"I'm not some *outsider*," she snapped. "I belong here. I'm one of you. You can't keep hiding things from me."

"Hiding things," Blue said calmly, "is what I do. So good luck with that argument."

"Mira, he's just trying to help," Freddie said. "There are things about Felix you're better off not knowing."

"God. I am *so* sick of this! I get that you don't like him," she said to Blue. "And I get that you like me," she said to Freddie, "that I'm supposedly your princess, but you can't just—" She shot to her feet, her fists clenched; and then her legs gave out and she flopped back onto the couch.

*Pathetic.*

Freddie dashed to the minibar to get her an orange juice.

"You need to get your strength back," he said.

"I feel like crap," she complained.

"No shit," Blue said.

*No shit*, she mimicked in her head. *Jerk.*

At least he was acting like himself again.

She took a few sips of juice before she asked them where Felix was.

"In hell, I hope," Freddie muttered.

She glared at him. "A real answer, please?"

"Working," Blue said. "You'll have to deal with us. Do you think you can eat something?"

She shrugged, which he must have interpreted as a yes. He ordered room service, and while they waited for food to be delivered, Blue managed to find Disney's *Sleeping Beauty* on the Dream's movie channel, which she thought was particularly sadistic of him. Freddie hummed the songs and mouthed the dialogue as he watched, as rapt as a little kid.

Mira choked down breakfast, and little by little, her strength returned—but she was very, very tired. She wanted to curl up in bed, close her eyes, and sleep.

But *sleep* felt like a fateful punishment right now. If her curse went according to plan, she'd soon have more than enough of it. So she fought the heaviness of her eyelids and watched as Aurora, aka Briar Rose, aka Sleeping Beauty, returned to her ancestral home—her castle—after sixteen years of living peacefully in the forest, only to be lured to the top of a tower by a sinister green light, to find the last spinning wheel in the kingdom—the one that would spark her curse. And in the green glow that gave her the pallor of a corpse, the princess pricked her finger and collapsed into enchanted sleep.

"Can we go now?" Mira asked, swallowing the last uncomfortable bite of her toast.

"We haven't seen the prince save her yet," Freddie said.

Blue clicked the TV off. "You know how it ends, Knight. Let's do something else."

The three of them ended up at Rafe's house—a sprawling, dove-colored mansion where Rafe lived alone, unsupervised except for the police cruisers that came by almost daily to respond to noise complaints. Rafe was asleep somewhere, snoring like a bear, and wasn't expected up before late afternoon—but the band members all had keys to the house.

Curses & Kisses held their practices in the palatial foyer, under a gaudy chandelier dripping with crystal teardrops and women's underwear. Blue's drum kit took up permanent residence there, since he never practiced at home.

Mira settled on a torn-up antique couch to watch Jewel and Freddie run through an acoustic version of their set. The couch fit right in with the mansion's broken-down baroque decor: the velvet upholstery was held together with duct tape, and smelled like it had been marinated in beer.

Blue lounged at the opposite end of the couch, playing a racing game on his phone. Over the course of four songs—two about love, two about heartbreak—he didn't say a word. Mira got the feeling he was deliberately ignoring her.

"Am I that boring?" she finally asked.

"I'm trying not to like you," Blue said.

"You can't even talk to me?"

"I'm careful," he said, still focused on his game. "If I talk to you more, I might like you too much. If I like you, I might be nice to you. And if I'm nice to you, you'll start to like me back."

She laughed. "No, I won't."

"You're that sure."

"Positive," she said. "I don't like jerks. And as for former jerks . . . I don't forgive them that fast. So you can stop avoiding me," she said, poking his phone and sending his pixel race car off the track. "Why are you so opposed to people liking you anyway? You have friends." She gestured to Freddie and Jewel. "Are you just afraid to make new ones?"

"Freddie and Jewel grew up here. They know a lot more than you do."

Mira rolled her eyes. "So tell me what I need to know. I'm getting really sick of—"

Blue shook his head, teeth clenched. "I'm. Not. Allowed. It's part of the curse."

"But Freddie knows. Jewel knows. You guys are always making cryptic references to how 'dangerous' Felix is. How do they know?"

"They know because they know what signs to look for. And because they saw it in action."

"Can *they* tell me?" she asked.

"No. It's something you have to discover for yourself. And I hope you never do. That you never want to."

"You realize this is maddening, right? You guys keep telling me there's all this bad stuff I need to worry about . . . but *no one* will tell me what it is. No one wants me to *know* anything. What's the point of that?"

"I don't know. I guess I want to warn you. But I can't tell you the whole truth." He took a deep breath; blew it out, agitated. "Mira. If you were . . . innately horrible, if you'd done something unforgivable, something you could never make up for or take back . . . would you want people to know?"

"What did you do that's so horrible?"

Blue shut his eyes, like he couldn't bear to look at her. Then he got up abruptly and stalked out of the room.

She followed him.

*Until her head lolled back like a broken doll's, he'd thought that she was overcome. Swooning. Like he was doing, inside.*

*Her hair hung down in burning red ringlets, silky to the touch. Her pale eyelids were lowered, her skin cool. Her arms hung slack, bumping the floor as he lowered her, as he laid her on her back, his own heart racing in panic.*

*He pressed his ear to her chest, fumbled with her wrist, searching for a pulse.*

*Somewhere—in the light—the party was in full swing. His friends were laughing, having a good time. Jewel teased out the last notes of a song, and then Freddie's guitar tapered off, and the stereo came back on.*

*He pressed his lips to her neck, seeking the vital, vibrant feeling he'd had while kissing her. The sensation of being truly alive.*

*But she had no more life to take. And so he felt nothing.*

"I didn't mean to upset you," Mira said when she caught up to him.

Blue was crouched in the middle of a dim room; the sheet-covered furniture crowded around him like ghosts, the air thick with dust and the stuffy smell of windows that never opened. He was holding his head like it hurt.

"Be a good girl and go away," he said.

She lowered herself to the floor next to him. "Blue . . . don't be like that. Talk to me. Be honest with me for once. Just try it."

She bit her lip—not sure that this was the best tack to take. But . . . maybe, if she seemed calm, Blue would feel that way, too.

"You want me to be honest?" He lifted his head, unfolded his arms, and touched her cheek. His touch was so tender it shocked her—like cold water thrown in her face.

"When I first saw you, I thought you were beautiful. You looked like you needed someone—and I wanted to be that someone. I knew . . . that if I felt that way . . . Felix would, too. So I tried to get rid of you."

"Because you don't like fighting with him." Her breath felt like it was trapped in her chest.

Blue's fingers traveled up her cheek and into her hair. "Because I don't want him near you. I don't want either one of us near you. But . . . you asked me to be honest. So . . ."

"You were mean to me because you liked me," she said. "I don't get that. It makes sense if you're five years old. But—"

"Shhh." He pressed his forehead to her forehead. The heat from his skin sank into hers, became a part of her, and she closed her eyes. Suddenly, she wanted to be quiet more than she wanted anything. She was hanging on words he hadn't said yet.

"I didn't want to give you a chance. I didn't want you to give *me* a chance. It was bad enough I tried to give you a place to stay, come to your rescue, whatever stupid, clichéd urges I had. I should've been a lot worse. Because, see? You're still here. You're still talking to me. Still letting me say this.

"You shouldn't do any of that," he whispered.

His breath skimmed her face. His touch was soft and warm, and it was a little like lightning—sparking something in her. It didn't burn the way it had when he'd touched her mark. This was different. More intimate and more demanding.

"Blue, this is . . ." *Strange*, she wanted to say. But *strange* was a lie.

153

"I want to tell you how pretty you are. I want to dance with you," he said. "I want to know why you read plays and which ones are your favorites. I want to hold you on the beach at night; and I want to make you laugh. I want you to like me—that's my nature. That's what I have to resist. It's so much safer when you hate me, Mira. Because if you wanted me, if you loved me, I could take everything from you. Without even meaning to."

"What—what do you mean, *everything*?"

"I mean you'd have nothing left." His voice was raw, hollow. "But you don't like me. That's good. That's safe. Except Felix finally kissed you."

"What does that have to do with anything?" The spark she'd felt went cold, like someone had washed it away with the sudden, uncomfortable awareness that she was letting Blue touch her and confess things she shouldn't hear—when she'd spent the night kissing his brother.

"He kissed you and you . . . you must really like him. You must be in love with him or something." Blue shook his head, his jaw tight. "Because he's perfect, right? Too good to be true."

"I still don't see what that has to do with anything." Mira said it stiffly this time, already drawing away from him. Blue's words felt like an accusation—like being in love was a mistake she'd made. But he didn't *know* she felt that strongly about Felix; he had no reason to say that to her—unless he was messing with her head again.

She was so tired of that. Tired of trusting him, and then regretting it.

She backed away from Blue, and he retreated to the

window seat, coughing as more dust rose up around him. Mira started for the door, but he called after her.

"Wait," he said. "Whatever you do, don't go into the grotto. It's unsanitary."

*Idiot,* she thought. Back to being obnoxious again.

"I thought we were being serious," she snapped. "Thanks for letting me know this is all a big joke to you."

"Sorry," he said. "I just wondered if you'd listen. If someone told you not to do something . . ."

He sounded worn-out, defeated. Because he liked her and she liked his brother? She didn't know. She wasn't going to think about it anymore—not when it could be one big mind game. She never knew with Blue.

"I came *here,*" she said. "I came to Beau Rivage when my godmothers told me not to. So, no, I don't always do what I'm told. Don't tell me what to do and you won't be disappointed."

Blue grimaced. Raised his fist to his mouth and coughed again, so it sounded like his lungs were tearing. When he finished, his eyes were wet.

"Do one thing I tell you. Just one," he mumbled. "Felix and I are called Romantics. Find Layla. Ask her to tell you what that means. You need to know."

Mira moved into the light like a sleepwalker, leaving Blue behind in the dust, the unused room, the past.

She thought of the fabled hundred years that cursed girls like her had slept, and how, after that much time, everything would be covered by a thick blanket of dust, including the princess. The intrepid prince would have to trust that some-

155

thing beautiful was hidden underneath. He'd kiss her and the first color to be revealed would be the chapped pink of her lips.

Her eyes went to Freddie, playing his guitar and lit by the sun. She couldn't picture him kissing a girl coated by dust—he was too alive for that.

He was golden. And she . . . she was covered with death, with her grief over her parents. She'd tried to replace them with dreams, and she'd drifted through life in a haze, her eyes seeking ghosts instead of the world around her.

She was already asleep.

She had been for a long time.

Freddie and Jewel finished their song. They looked up and laughed at some mistake they'd made. Freddie set his guitar down, and Jewel paused to cough into her handkerchief, catching a spill of orange blossoms and pearls.

"Mira," Freddie said when he noticed her. There was so much warmth in his voice, so much affection—he said her name like he'd say *I love you*. She didn't know how to deal with that.

"How do you perform?" she asked Jewel instead, gesturing to the spilled pearls.

"Oh. That." Jewel wiped her mouth and tucked the hand-kerchief into her fist. "I hold it in until the end of a song. Then I take a moment to let it all out and catch my breath. It used to be really bad. I could barely get two words out."

"Does it hurt?" Mira asked.

Jewel nodded. "But it's a pain you get used to. It's supposed to be a gift. My sister, Aimee, has it worse. She pissed off the wrong fairy, and now she spews toads and snakes and dead leaves when she talks."

Mira felt sick. "Live snakes?"

Jewel arched an eyebrow. "Would it be better if they were dead?"

"Foul," Freddie said, wrinkling his perfect nose.

"My mom's house is crawling with lizards now," Jewel went on. "It smells like a stagnant pond. There are leaves decaying in the corners, soaking into the carpet. I moved out of there, obviously." Jewel spit a handful of diamonds into her palm—looking for a moment like a boxer spitting out broken teeth. She held her hand up to the light.

"I bought a condo with the fruits of my curse. I'm the Kind Girl in my tale, so you'd think I'd let my mom and sister move in with me—but I can't deal with that smell. Or Aimee's attitude. Once she bit off an anole's tail while it was crawling out of her mouth—just to be disgusting." Jewel shuddered, and Freddie shuddered, too. He didn't have much of a stomach for bad things.

"And there's no one who can break the curse?" Mira asked. "No one Honor-bound?"

"My sister can break her own curse if she stops being nasty all the time. But it's hard to be nice when you're vomiting reptiles every other word. And since my curse isn't a punishment . . . it's permanent."

Shrugging, Jewel tucked the handkerchief into her pocket. "It could be worse. I could be like Layla and be charged with humanizing Rafe after he gets Changed. He's been such a tool lately, it can't be long before he insults an evil fairy and gets turned into a Beast. Then Layla's going to be Honor-bound to redeem him. She says she won't bother, but I know her; her conscience won't let her abandon him. I can—"

Jewel stopped to pluck a string of bleeding hearts from her lips; managed a wry smile. "I can handle *this*."

"Speaking of Layla," Mira said, "do you think we could get her to come over?"

"She won't come to Rafe's house," Jewel said. "Not until she has to."

"Oh." Mira sighed. "Because I kind of need to talk to her. I guess—later." She was about to sit down on the trashed couch when Freddie got to his feet.

"As you know . . . I am always at your service," he said. "I could drive you."

"Oh no, I don't want to interrupt your band practice—"

Jewel waved her hand at the mostly empty foyer. "What practice? Rafe will sleep until three, then spend an hour grooming himself. Blue's playing will *not* be improved—we know that by now. So . . . go. Have some fun." Her eyes glittered suggestively.

Freddie flushed. His normally proud shoulders were stooped with embarrassment, and Mira realized what Jewel meant by *have some fun*. She was teasing, but . . .

Mira hadn't been alone with Freddie since that strange moment they'd shared on the beach, when she'd touched him and her hands had burned. Hadn't been alone with him since he'd known, for certain, that they shared a destiny. It gave new meaning to the word *awkward*.

But she did want to talk to Layla. . . .

"You really don't mind?" she asked.

"You heard the boy," Jewel said. "His carriage awaits."

# CHAPTER ELEVEN

FREDDIE'S CAR WAS SILVER AND SHINY on the outside, with leather and new-car smell on the inside—predictably perfect—but it was cluttered with an unexpected number of guitar magazines, empty candy boxes, and . . . what looked like sword catalogues.

Mira grabbed one of the catalogues and flipped through it. It was from a mail-order smithy that sold medieval weapons and armor: broadswords, chain mail, decorative letter openers. Freddie had drawn circles around the things he wanted, like a kid marking up a toy catalogue to make his Christmas list.

"You like this stuff a lot, huh?" she said.

"It's an interest of mine. I—" He turned to her, frowning apprehensively as he backed down Rafe's driveway. "You think it's strange."

"No, no, it's just different. I didn't know anyone still made stuff like this." She kept flipping, fascinated. "How many of these do you have?"

"Swords? Just one. It's in the trunk."

"The *trunk*?"

"You never know when you might drive past a house covered in briars. Where a princess is sleeping. It's good to have something to hack through them. So you can rescue her."

"Wouldn't a hatchet work better?"

"A sword is more heroic," Freddie mumbled.

They drove past mansions spaced out like castles among the trees—home to quite a few Royals, Freddie said—and on toward cuter, cozier neighborhoods, where curses mingled with good and bad luck. Trees leaned across the road, dappling it with shadows; and then the trees cleared to reveal sun-baked yards, where children in bathing suits dashed through sprinklers. Old women held court on porch swings, and ladies in floppy hats did battle in their gardens, yanking out weeds by the roots.

A lovesick mutt chased Freddie's car for a few blocks—tongue lolling, tail wagging—until Freddie stopped to play with him, afraid that if he ignored him, the poor dog would get hit by a car.

When they resumed their drive, Mira stayed quiet. She could sense that Freddie wanted to talk to her, but she kept her eyes on the sword catalogue, skimming the descriptions even as she started to feel carsick—anything to keep from discussing their shared fate. It began to feel a little like a bad first date. She couldn't wait to get out of the car—and it must have showed.

"I think . . . you don't like me," Freddie said.

Mira hesitated. "Of course I like you."

"You're mad because of what I said about Felix."

Of course it would come back to Felix. "If that's true, then I'm mad at everyone."

"But, Mira . . ." He sighed. "We wouldn't all say it if it wasn't true."

And that was when she snapped. She was sick of the secrets, sick of the intimation that she should do whatever they said, without an explanation, because *they* knew better—as if everyone was a better judge of her situation than she was.

"No one is saying *anything*, except stay away from him," Mira countered. "Do you have some real reasons for me?"

"Mira, you passed out. When Blue found you, you were unconscious. You stayed that way for eight hours."

"It's called sleeping."

"It's *not*. Felix hurt you. You couldn't—your body couldn't—"

"You know what?" Mira said. "Maybe you're right. Maybe I *don't* like you." She shifted so she was facing the window, and did her best to ignore him. But it was impossible to tune out his sighs of frustration or the smack of his hand against the steering wheel.

"I never imagined you'd be so difficult," he muttered.

"Maybe that's why you're supposed to meet me when I'm unconscious. So I don't burst your bubble right away."

"Don't be mean, Mira. I haven't been mean to you." She could hear the hurt in his voice, and she squirmed, feeling guilty. He was right. And he *was* trying to help her—even if he was wrong.

"I'm sorry. It's just—I don't like being pressured to feel a certain way. Or told that the guy I like is bad for me, when he obviously isn't. I wish you guys would just trust that I'm not stupid. If we were friends, that's what you would do. You'd want me to be happy."

"No one thinks you're stupid. And I do want you to be happy."

"Then let me be."

"But that's not happy! You can't live happily ever after when there's no after!"

"Freddie!" she snapped. "Happily-ever-after isn't real! Not everything is a fairy tale!" Her voice seemed louder suddenly, and she realized he'd shut off the car. They were parked in Layla's driveway, in front of a small white house trimmed with flower boxes and crawling with honeysuckle.

Mira opened the door and stumbled out before he could say anything else. Freddie existed in a fairy tale more than any of them. With his replica swords, his animal magnetism, his unrealistic hopes, and his Once-Upon-a-Dreaming . . .

It wasn't her fault that she didn't live up to his expectations. His dream wasn't her life.

The birds at the bird feeder had sensed Freddie and were already in flight. Like prince-seeking missiles, they shot straight toward him, then landed on the hood of his car and began to serenade him. Freddie stayed holed up inside, unresponsive to their devotion.

Mira pressed down on the doorbell, shaking.

She wanted to be one of them, she was *supposed* to belong . . . but she still felt like an outsider. Like they were all ganging up on her. She didn't know all the secrets they knew, and that made her seem stupid, naïve. And she was tired of that.

She missed Elsa and Bliss. She missed feeling safe—and

for a moment, she considered calling her godmothers, coming clean about what she'd done. They were fairies; they knew this world better than she did. Maybe they could help her. . . .

*No.* Mira shook her head. They wouldn't give her answers. They'd decide for her—like they always had—and decide she was better off not knowing. They would take her away. She couldn't let that happen.

Layla yanked the door open, and Mira snapped out of her daydream. "Aah. Mira. I thought someone was in trouble out here!"

Mira flinched as Layla grabbed her finger and lifted it off the doorbell. She'd lost track of what she was doing—and had barely noticed the nonstop ringing.

"Sorry," Mira said. "I was . . . distracted."

"It's okay. What's up? What can I do for . . ." Layla peered around her. "Is Freddie not coming in?"

"Um . . . we had a fight," Mira said. "Nothing to worry about. Listen, can I talk to you? It's important."

"Of course," Layla said, stepping aside. "Come in."

Layla's house was cozy and rustic, full of mismatched furniture, country quilts draped over couches, New Age goddess paintings side by side with classic fairy-tale prints and framed family photos. It reminded Mira of her own house, and the cluttered, a-little-of-everything style her godmothers preferred. The living room smelled like honeysuckle and coffee. Books were piled on a low table: academic texts about fairy tales, obscure classics, and the libretto booklet for Puccini's *Tosca*, flopped open upside down to mark the page.

Layla sat down in a comfy easy chair and drew her legs

up onto the seat. She grabbed her coffee mug, then stopped. "Oops, sorry. Did you want anything to drink?"

Mira shook her head. "I just want to talk."

"Okay. I'm a bad hostess—just so you know. No one ever comes over, so I'm out of practice. Most of them get twitchy if they're not in a mansion. Also, my dad's a little weird. That might be the real reason."

"Weird how?"

Layla sighed. "I might need a real drink if I'm going to explain *that*. Kidding," she added—although she looked like maybe she wasn't. "My dad's a gambler. You may have noticed the casinos all over Beau Rivage? Yeah, so that's a problem. He's not very good at it. And he doesn't know when to stop. So on the rare occasion that people visit, he'll usually try to sell them something from our house to help pay off his debts. He knows most of my friends are rich. Which I guess to him means they're fair game and I shouldn't mind."

"Can't your mom get him to stop?" Mira asked, glancing at the family photos—all of which showed a very young woman with baby Layla and her father, if they showed her at all.

"She's dead. Like most moms around here." Layla sighed again. "Anyway. I'm sure you didn't come over to hear about my dad. What's up?"

Mira hesitated. After this, she'd know something about the Valentine brothers that neither one had wanted to explain. She was a little afraid to find out, because she was pretty sure *Romantic* didn't mean *buys you flowers and brings you candy*. Although Felix had that part covered if it did.

"Blue told me I should ask you about Romantics," she said.

Layla set her cup down with an awkward clatter. "Really?

I . . . I wasn't expecting that. He's usually pretty private. All right."

Layla got up to search for a book, running her finger across the spines.

"You can tell me?" Mira said. "It's not part of the curse that you can't?"

"I can tell you what a Romantic is," Layla said, returning with a heavy leather-bound book similar to the one she'd shown them at the bookstore, but more modern. "I can't talk about Blue's specific curse. Any secret that's meant to stay secret, I can't utter. The magic in our blood acts like a leash— or a muzzle, in this case. It prevents us from breaking taboos."

Mira nodded, disappointed. "Okay. Well, then, I guess tell me whatever you can tell me."

Layla turned to *R*, and pushed the book closer. Mira drew in a breath—

### Romantics

*Natural charmers who feed on love, drawing it from the lover's body through kisses and caresses that drain the lover's life force, often until there is nothing left. The stronger the love, the easier the life will be to steal.*

*No*, she thought, her limbs trembling as she recalled the weakness she'd felt last night. The numbness. The way the world had turned gray around her.

"That's—that's what Blue is?" *And Felix. And Felix . . . oh my god . . .*

"Yes," Layla confirmed.

"He can't help it?"

"Sadly, no. It's part of his curse. Blue must be worried about you, if he wanted me to tell you. He doesn't—for obvious reasons—like for people to know."

"Yeah, I can see. . . ." *Until there is nothing left.* "I can see why."

This was what Freddie meant by *no after.* No happily-ever-after. Because the person she loved could kill her.

"What tale is that?" Mira asked, searching for some shred of the tale in her memory. "I don't remember any fairy tales where . . . where someone drains the love from someone else's body. And . . ."

"It's not that specific in the tale," Layla said carefully. "You have to keep in mind that the people transcribing the tales weren't the same people living them, in most cases. They came across them through hearsay, in bits and pieces. A lot of the elements are captured, but some things are hidden. Some curses are also secrets. Secrets you shouldn't try to reveal . . . ever."

Layla looked torn, like she wanted to say more, but couldn't. Her eyes glimmered like she was upset. "You're not going to listen, are you?"

Mira stared at the entry until the words blurred together, a tangle of rusty brown—the color of dried blood. "What does it feel like when someone drains the love from you?" she asked.

"I'm not sure," Layla said. "It's never happened to me. Or to anyone—we know." She seemed to stumble on the last part, and Mira looked at her, searching for an answer—but Layla just shook her head. "I'm sorry. That's all I can say."

"Okay," Mira said. "Well. Thank you. . . ."

She headed to the door, conscious of the feeling of the

166

floor beneath her feet. The sensation of her muscles shifting as she crossed the room. The smooth texture of the doorknob in her hand. All things she wouldn't have felt last night, when her body went numb after Felix had kissed her and kissed her and kissed her. And then abandoned her.

Because he was afraid. He was afraid of draining her away to nothing. Because she cared for him too much. Or he cared for her too much. Or both.

Mira stopped at the door, not ready to face Freddie. To face anyone, really.

"Layla," she said. "Is it possible to avoid your destiny? Like if you're fated to be with someone, but you can sense that it isn't right between the two of you?"

Through a pane of glass in the door, she could see Freddie still in his car, leaning his head against the steering wheel.

"I don't know," Layla said. Her voice was fragile—this was a sensitive subject for her, too. "But I hope it's possible. That what we want—what we're willing to fight for—matters as much as, or more than, our curse."

Mira nodded, swallowed to force down the lump in her throat, and stepped out into the heat. The screen door banged shut behind her—and before she'd made it halfway down the driveway, a rust-eaten Camaro pulled in behind Freddie, boxing him in. A slim older man with black hair like Layla's sidled up to Freddie's car and knocked on the window.

"Frederick! Freddie Knight!" the man called. "Hey, buddy—I have something for you; open up."

Freddie seemed disoriented; he scrambled out of the car, struggling to get a polite smile on his face. "Mr. Phan," he said. "I'm sorry, I didn't realize you were . . . am I in your way?"

"Not at all, not at all! Take a look at this." Mr. Phan produced a ragged-edged vintage movie poster and showed it to Freddie. "What do you think this would set you back—normally, if you got it from an antiques dealer and not from a friend? Give me an estimate."

"Um . . ." Freddie faltered.

Mira heard the house door bang open again, followed by Layla's shoes clattering quickly down the driveway. When she reached Mira, instead of continuing on toward her father, Layla linked arms with her, and leaned her head on Mira's shoulder like she wanted to hide there. "Oh dear god," she muttered. "You're about to see the salesman in action."

"What do you think—one hundred, two hundred dollars? Either of those would be a deal. A steal, even." Mr. Phan leaned in, an easy confidence in his movements. "But I'll give it to you for eighty dollars. That's practically free!"

"Um, you see, I don't—I don't exactly have that much cash on me," Freddie fumbled, eyes darting toward Layla with a save-me vibe. "So while it's a generous offer . . ."

"You know what?" Mr. Phan clapped Freddie on the shoulder. His face broke into a charming smile. "I trust you. You're good for it, if anyone is. You can pay me the rest later. How much do you have on you now? Fifty? Don't tell me Philip Knight lets his boys walk around penniless! That would be a disgrace!"

"No, I have money—I mean—" Freddie stammered. He was already getting his wallet out, though he still looked like he wanted someone to save him.

"Aren't you going to intervene?" Mira whispered.

"I would," Layla whispered back, "but we really *do* need the

168

money. So I'm just going to leave my dignity on the driveway, and then go hide under my bed and try to pretend this never happened."

Freddie was counting out bills from his wallet now—he ended up giving Layla's dad fifty dollars in exchange for the old poster.

"Here you go," Mr. Phan said. "Enjoy it. I can't believe I gave you such a bargain. I've got a soft spot for you, I guess. You remind me a little of myself."

"Oh, er, thank you," Freddie said, stuffing his empty wallet back in his pocket. He tossed the movie poster into the car without looking at it, like he didn't want to be reminded that he'd dropped fifty bucks on it—and still owed thirty more. "Good to see you, sir."

Mr. Phan's eyes found Layla. He grinned. "Hey, baby! Guess what I brought you? You don't think I'd come home without a present for my girl, do you?"

Layla cringed. "Dad, I told you to stop bringing me things every time you go somewhere. We don't have the money."

"What's this, eh?" Mr. Phan fanned out the bills in his hand. "Looks like money to me. You let your dad worry about the bills. He's got everything under control. Now close your eyes."

Sighing, Layla did as she was told—but Mira could see the tension on her face. "Dad . . . I'm serious. You have to stop."

Layla's dad sauntered over, as upbeat as Layla was down. Drawing a slim jewelry box from his pocket, he opened it to reveal a pearl pendant, then undid the clasp and secured it around Layla's neck. She shuddered when the pearl touched her collarbone.

"Not jewelry . . ." she protested.

"Don't worry so much," Mr. Phan scolded. "Tonight's going to be my lucky night at the tables. You'll see. Nice doing business with you, Frederick!" he called over his shoulder. "Bring that other thirty when you get a chance!"

Once her dad finally disappeared into the house, Layla let out a sigh and yanked off the necklace. "Here, Freddie," she said, forcing it into his hand. "Pawn it or something. You can probably get eighty dollars for it."

"No, really, Layla," he said, pushing the necklace back at her. "It's okay. I wanted that poster. It's—your father gave me a good deal."

"You're just being nice," she mumbled, sagging against his car.

"So let me be," he said, lightly touching her arm. "It's no big deal."

Layla pressed her palms to her face. "Don't pity me. Please. That makes it worse."

"If I pitied you, don't you think I'd slay Rafe and make him into a carpet for you?"

Layla laughed a sniffly laugh, and Mira realized the girl was crying. Layla hid it well—her eyes didn't get red and swollen. She was as pretty as ever—just with two perfect tears sneaking down her cheeks. Wiping them away, she said, "Okay . . . maybe you should pity me a little."

Freddie smiled. "That's better."

"Thanks for your help, Layla," Mira said, stepping around to give her a hug.

Layla hugged back. "Anytime. Don't be a stranger, okay? It gets lonely in this crazy house."

"I'll come back," Mira said.

"Is that a promise?" Freddie asked.

"Uh—I guess." Mira eyed him oddly. "Why?"

"Well, if it is . . . then you should stay away from Felix. Or you might break your promise. Inadvertently."

Mira glared at him until he averted his eyes. Freddie shrugged, as if she couldn't blame him for saying it. And the sad thing was, she couldn't; a chill had gone through her at his words. Because he was right. She *did* have to be careful now. And she was afraid.

By the time they got back to the Wilder mansion, Rafe was awake. Practice began in violent, cacophonous earnest, and after an hour of playing audience, Mira left to sit in the rose garden outside. Curses & Kisses was half good (Jewel and Freddie), one-quarter okay but too full of pelvic thrusts to be enjoyable (Rafe), and one-quarter intentionally offbeat and horrible (Blue).

In the garden, the atmosphere was different—serene and romantic. It was the perfect place to get lost or hold a secret rendezvous. Roses bloomed everywhere, in nearly every color: red for love, pink for romance, white for innocence, lavender for enchantment.

If the tales were true, one day, a single stolen rose would seal Layla's fate. Too noble for her own good, the girl would trade her freedom for her father's and agree to live with the wretched Beast. And if Mira's curse took hold, one day, a bower of roses would form her prison—a coffin of thorns instead of glass. And yet the associations didn't frighten her. She felt at peace sitting on the stone path that wound through the garden, inhaling the heady blend of perfumes.

By sunset, Mira was propped against the base of a Greek goddess statue, deep inside the garden. She was reading one of the skinny paperbacks she always had in her purse, barely aware of the fading light, when Blue dropped a ruby into her lap.

She closed her book, startled.

Seeing him—the blue hair, the violent jewelry, the sharp expression—was more of a shock than it usually was. Because now when she looked at him, she could see inside him, too. Deep into the secrets he didn't want anyone to know.

For the past few hours, Mira had done her best to put the word *Romantic* out of her mind. But she couldn't ignore it when he was right in front of her.

"Technically, that's yours. Jewel dropped it when she was talking about you. It's kind of our rule." Blue sat down across from her, flipping her book up so he could see the cover.

Mira tried to play along. "What was she saying about me?"

"None of your business, nosy. Nah, actually, she was counseling Freddie."

She sighed. "Oh . . . Freddie drove me to Layla's, and we . . . we didn't get along like he'd hoped we would."

"Yeah, I was there for that part of the counseling session."

They fell silent. It was useless to pretend they could make small talk while the weight of Blue's confession hung between them. A hush fell over the garden. Even the birds had ceased their evening song. Not a sound reached them from the street; no voices carried from the house. It was as if the whole world was waiting for him to speak.

Blue drew his knees up. He reached back to mess with

the spikes on his head. "So . . . you talked to Layla?"

Mira nodded, heart in her throat. "She told me about Romantics. The reason you think I'm in love with Felix—"

"Is because you wouldn't have been that weak if you weren't in love with him. Romantics can only . . ." Blue kept his eyes on the stone path, tracing one finger through the grooves. "We can only take love that's freely given. That's meant for us. That's why . . ."

"That's why you make sure no one gets close to you," she realized. *Why you can be so cold, rude, confusing* . . . "You're afraid of that."

"Sometimes, you don't know," he said. "You can underestimate the depth of someone's feelings. Or be caught up in how good it feels to be near them. When it first happens . . . you're not sure how much of that feeling is natural—you know, happiness. And how much is the euphoria you get from stealing love. All you know is you never want it to end . . . and when you're lost in it, you can take too much, too fast. And that's dangerous. So I try to avoid it. To never get to that feeling in the first place."

He was nudging a piece of grit along the grooves between the stones. Focusing on it instead of her. Like maybe it was easier to be honest when you could pretend the other person wasn't there.

"I killed a girl," he said. "At my sixteenth birthday party."

Mira's breathing stopped. She waited, her chest growing tighter—but she didn't move. Didn't dare.

"I was in love with her. Like, the kind of love you fall into when you fall for the first time. I watched her for years, but . . . I knew what I was—I *always* knew. So I never tried to win

173

her over. And then it just . . . happened. She liked me anyway. More than liked me. And I got stupid, I gave in to it, but I—I didn't expect it to happen so fast. For her to . . . for it to be over . . . so fast," he said quietly.

"I didn't try hard enough. I didn't act like I did when I first met you. I thought if I didn't ask her out, if I was busy when she wanted to do something . . . that would be enough. But I had a hard time not showing her how I felt. It's just, it's natural for us—for Romantics. We fall in love, and we want to make you happy so badly, to give you what you most want, need, desire . . . it's like this selflessness that's the ultimate selfishness. Because we do it all so we can have you. We need that . . . love. But once we have it, it means we have to lose it. And we don't like letting go."

Her heart ached for him. She didn't want it to be true. Didn't want to believe that he was doomed—along with anyone who loved him. Blue didn't deserve that. No one did.

And . . . if Romantics were doomed, what did that mean for her and Felix?

"Isn't there some way around it?" she asked.

"It's our *curse*," he said bitterly.

"But . . . there has to be a way. You can't live without love." It sounded trite, but she meant it. A loveless life would destroy a person. She'd been yearning for things she couldn't have long enough to know. "It's not healthy to lock up your emotions and push everyone away from you."

"That's true," he said. "I can't live without love—without stealing it. Without feeding off it. Do you know that it's compulsive? That it's like breathing? I've been holding my breath for a long time. Over a year since—"

She nodded so he didn't have to say it. She knew the words hurt him.

"But as far as it not being healthy . . . it's not healthy for me to kill someone I love either."

"But if you're careful," she insisted, "if you stop yourself in time, like Felix did with me, couldn't you . . . ?"

"Couldn't I what? Couldn't I be like Felix? I don't want to be like Felix. I don't ever want to be like Felix." Blue's eyes were dark, like a river at night. In the harsh light of sunset, the pupil and iris blended together, hardening his gaze.

"Relax," she murmured.

"I *can't*," he said.

"What will happen if you . . . if no one ever loves you again? If you don't *breathe* like that again?"

From somewhere beyond them, she heard a door slam. The hum of insects stirring. A peal of Jewel's laughter floated on the warm, rose-scented air.

"I'll die," he said. "I'll finally be punished. And it'll be long overdue."

~ ⚮ ~

*Once upon a time, he believed he could be the exception.*

*He wasn't a hero; he knew that. But years ago, he and Freddie had saved a life.*

*They'd been inching toward thirteen, too impatient to sit quietly in the car while Mr. Knight dealt with some business in the bank—so they were hitting each other with toy swords, using the seat backs as shields.*

*But then Freddie busted a knob off the dashboard. He was trying to fix it while Blue played lookout, when Blue spotted the girl.*

At that age, hardly any of their friends were marked. Renee had yet to become Jewel; Rafe's best claim to beastliness was an obsession with girls' bra straps. But they knew enough to recognize a curse when they saw one.

Beau Rivage was in the grip of a cold snap, and that evening, the wind blew bitterly—but the teenage girl he saw wore nothing but shorts and a thin T-shirt. She crouched in the shadows, in an alley between two buildings. Every so often, there was a flicker of light before her eyes: a tiny flare that trembled and then faded, making the evening gloom seem darker by comparison.

She was freezing, likely starving—and lighting match after match, entranced by the beauty of the flame.

"Freddie!" he hissed, his heart pounding with excitement. "Look. A Match Girl."

Freddie abandoned the knob to peer through the windshield, just as another match flared. "Ohhhh!" he exclaimed. "Let's help her!"

They scrambled out of the car and stopped at the mouth of the alley. This close, the girl wasn't an obvious Damsel: she didn't have the fine features of a Cinderella, whose regal bone structure would be evident even under a layer of soot. The Match Girl was dirty and desperate, her hair a greasy tangle, a sour odor emanating from her clothes.

She was marked to suffer, and then be extinguished without fanfare.

But Blue refused to let that be her destiny.

He crept closer until he was a handsbreadth away from her. He grabbed her box of matches and she gaped at him, bewildered at first—but he knew if he didn't take it, she'd keep lighting the matches until she died, too absorbed by the dancing flame to do anything else.

They helped her stand; supported her as they brought her to the car. Then Blue darted through traffic to a fast-food restaurant across the street, where he bought her dinner, and a hot chocolate, and they set forth on their quest to rehabilitate her.

The Match Girl became their pet project. They harassed Mr. Knight until he agreed to bring the girl home, where Freddie's mother ran her a bath and gave her fresh clothes, complaining only once in her overdramatic voice that if the girl had brought lice into the house, she (the sensitive Mrs. Knight) would be "done for, simply done for."

The Knights kept the Match Girl as a lodger for a few weeks (the family's heroic legacy made it hard for them to say no) and Blue and Freddie tended to her the only way they knew how: they made pests of themselves. They drew her out of her shell with board games, staged sword fights, bad impromptu rock concerts, until she was healthier, and smiling, and no longer drawn to self-destruction like a moth to a flame.

The day they said good-bye to her was a moment of triumph for all three of them. They'd fought for her, and they'd saved her—a girl who'd been doomed by her curse; and for years afterward, Blue had clung to that memory as proof that destiny could be overcome.

He'd thought he had a chance, too. That if he was vigilant and determined, he could fight his own fate. He'd believed it with the pure heart of an idealist, a child who'd never been tested.

Now he knew better.

He wasn't a hero; wasn't anything close. He was every bit as dangerous as his curse intended him to be.

He couldn't hope to be good. All he could hope for was the strength to resist temptation—until his life flickered out like one last match.

# CHAPTER TWELVE

EVENING BLURRED INTO NIGHT. The stars were bright above her as Mira traipsed through the foam at the edge of the beach, leaving footprints in the damp sand. Jewel, Viv, Rafe, and Blue sat farther up the beach, talking. But she couldn't hear them. All she could hear was the sea.

She'd spent the whole day with Blue and his friends, away from Felix, away from her search for her parents' graves. Secrets flowed toward her and away, like the tide. She felt like she had learned so much—and yet there was still so much she needed to know.

Where were her parents buried? What was her trigger? Who was Felix—really? And what would become of her, now that she loved him?

Maybe she would never find her parents' graves. Maybe all she could expect to find—here, or anywhere—was herself. But the one thing she hadn't expected to find was a kiss that could destroy her. A kiss that—if it hadn't ended in time—could have been her last.

She shivered all over at the memory. Both terrified and wanting it to happen again.

She hadn't expected to feel so connected to Blue either. He'd killed a girl who was in the same position she was in—young, and in love for the first time. The parallel didn't elude her. But she wasn't afraid of him—she felt bad for him. She knew what it was like to lose someone.

Stepping carefully over driftwood and broken shells, she made her way to where Freddie crouched with his two older brothers at the edge of the sea.

The Knight brothers looked remarkably similar, except for their coloring and their expressions. All three had their pants rolled up to their knees. One brother, whose face was even more guileless than Freddie's, waded into the water, humming a little under his breath as he went.

Mira sat down on the piece of driftwood they were using as a bench, and Freddie introduced her. His oldest brother, who had dark brown hair and a smug air about him, was Wills; the boy already waist-deep in the ocean, sort of floundering in the waves, was Caspian. His hair was as black as the water at night.

"What's he doing?" she asked, meaning Caspian.

"Oh." Freddie sighed. "Tempting fate. He can't swim very well."

Wills smiled. He was squatting in the sand, watching the waves. "He was in a boat accident a while back. Fell overboard during a moonlight cruise on prom night, hit his head, and went under. He woke up on the shore, with a beautiful girl singing to him, and . . ."

"Let me guess. Mermaid?" Mira said.

Wills nodded. "That's what he thinks. He wants to see her

179

again, but he isn't sure how to find her. So . . ." He motioned to Caspian, who was splashing around, the water up to his chest now.

"You can't trust mermaids," Freddie grumbled. "They'll drown you as soon as they'll save you. It all depends on their temperament. Most of them don't like humans."

"Since when are you anything less than the spokesperson for fated romance?" Wills asked with a cocked eyebrow. He glanced at Mira. "Something go sour between you two?"

Freddie bowed his head, concentrated on dragging a stick through the sand. "No. Just . . . you know. Mermaids."

"Uh-huh," Wills said. The corner of his mouth crept up. Mira felt awkward, and oddly exposed. It was weird how they all seemed to know what was going on. Everyone here was so well schooled in curses—not to mention the drama that went with them.

"So are you all Honor-bound?" Mira asked.

"We're mostly Honor-bound," Wills said. "Although the only curse I'm meant to break is the curse of poverty and ser-vitude. Cinderella," he explained. "Still waiting for 'the one' to show up at one of the family galas in a secondhand party dress. Once she's done cleaning chimneys for the day. She'll be pretty and sweet . . . I just pray she knows how to read."

"Don't be callous," Freddie said. "Maybe she's been work-ing too hard to learn how to read. You could always teach her."

Wills stretched out on the sand. "I'm too lazy for that. She'll have to draw pictures. At least to write the grocery list."

Freddie sighed, and Wills laughed—then settled his head on his crossed arms. "You're too uptight, Freddie. You have your girl here; you won't have to go on a road trip searching for an overgrown briar patch. It's time to relax."

"I'm *very* relaxed," Freddie protested. "Usually . . ."

"He doesn't have me," Mira said.

Wills lifted his head, a look of surprise on his face. "No?"

"My mark doesn't brand me as Freddie's. It just says that he serves a purpose in my life."

"You're a *feminist*," Wills said, like that explained everything.

"I'm a *person*," she said.

Wills shrugged. "Call it what you want."

Freddie got up, undid the buttons on his shirt, and threw it onto the sand before treading dutifully into the water. He grabbed Caspian in a bear hug from behind and hauled him up the beach. "That's enough for tonight," he told his shivering brother.

Caspian blinked his big, limpid eyes. Water dribbled from his soaked clothes and into the sand. "She didn't come. Do you think I imagined her?"

"You'll see her again eventually," Freddie said. "But I don't think drowning yourself is a good plan. Let's get you dried off." He put his arm around Caspian and led him toward Blue and the others. And since it was either follow them or be left behind with Wills, Mira followed.

"Does anyone have a towel?" Freddie asked.

Rafe, Blue, Viv, and Jewel were sitting around an open cooler, bottles of beer jammed into the sand in front of them. Jewel had gathered her long T-shirt into a pouch and was storing stray gems in it.

"I have a blanket in the back of my van," Rafe said. "And a mattress, if anyone needs it."

"Really?" Blue said. "Because I was looking for a van to have sex in."

"Uh . . . sorry, buddy." Rafe clapped Blue on the shoulder, wincing slightly. "It's available to everyone but you. It's not cool to leave dead bodies back there. You understand."

"I was being sarcastic, but thanks for that." Blue stood up with his fists at his sides, agitated. Then he stalked away toward the parking lot.

Jewel picked a gem from her lap and pinged it off Rafe's broad forehead. "God, Wilder, could you be any stupider?"

Rafe rubbed the sore spot. "How am I supposed to know when he's kidding?"

"Like he'd be *serious* about that?" Viv said.

Rafe shrugged, blowing it off, then tossed his keys to Caspian. "Dry off, man; a blanket is better than nothing."

"Is it . . . contaminated?" Freddie asked.

Rafe gave Freddie a dirty look, and Viv rolled her eyes and said, "Since when does Rafe make it back to the van in time?"

"This is my booze," Rafe reminded them. "Watch it or you bitches are getting cut off."

Mira grabbed a beer out of the cooler—a beer she didn't even want—just out of spite, and followed Freddie and Caspian to the parking lot. Blue was there when they climbed over the last sandy ridge.

Caspian opened the back of Rafe's van apprehensively, like he expected to find a girl handcuffed inside. When he saw it was empty, he relaxed, and tugged the blanket out to wrap it around his shivering frame.

Freddie went over to Blue. They spoke in low voices that

didn't carry over the wind. Mira sat down on the hood of Viv's candy-apple red sports car. She busied herself trying to twist the cap off the beer bottle while she watched them. The metal ridges dug into her palm. Blue kept shaking his head; Freddie was leaning in, insisting on something, his face earnest and intense; and finally, the bottle cap went flying and beer sudsed up and spilled onto her lap. Mira shrieked and flung the bottle away from her, shaking foam from her hands.

"Can't handle your alcohol, Mira?" Blue called over.

"I didn't expect it to go everywhere! Now I smell like beer."

"It could be worse," Blue said. "You could smell like Rafe's sex life, like Caspian does." Poor Caspian was huddled in the blanket, staring longingly out to sea, oblivious to their conversation.

"That was low," Freddie said, hiding a grin.

Blue shrugged. "So what did you want, Mira? Are you our third musketeer? Or just having second thoughts about Freddie?"

She watched him, wondering at her own reaction as she did. After what she'd learned about Blue—what he could do, what he'd already done—she felt like she should have been wary of him. But she wasn't. Instead, her defenses were lowering.

She could see the prickly outside, but now she recognized the wounded heart underneath. And she found herself trusting him, worrying about him. Looking at him like a friend. A friend who needed her, maybe . . .

"You were upset," she said. "I thought maybe I could help. I don't know. Isn't that what people do when they're not assholes?"

"You expect me to know?" Blue asked. But he was smiling now.

"Come over here so I can wipe my hands on your shirt," she said, holding up her beer-sticky hands. Eyebrows raised in amusement, Blue did as she asked. He stood between her legs at the front of the car, his knees against the bumper.

"Go for it," he said.

Her wet fingers grazed the muscle of his abdomen as she fumbled to dry her hands on his T-shirt. Blue sucked in a breath when her hands brushed his skin, and something electric ran through her. A flush burned her cheeks. She made herself focus on the artwork on his T-shirt.

"Now the ick is on you, where it belongs," she said.

"You are a very nasty princess," Blue said.

"Are you flirting with me?"

He shrugged. "Probably. Is it working?"

"Not at all," she assured him. "Being told I'm nasty doesn't do it for me."

"I knew there was a reason I liked you." He grabbed her sticky hands and tugged her off the hood. "Should we get out of here before Viv shows up and wants to know who spilled beer on her car?"

Mira nodded. "Sure. Where are we going?"

"Casa del Knight," Blue said.

"We have a pool," Freddie said, as if that would sweeten the deal.

"A pool that Rafe has never had sex in," Blue said.

"That's what makes it different from Rafe's pool," Freddie explained.

Mira grimaced. "One day, you guys will have to tell me

*why* you're even friends with Rafe. But not today. I'll give you time to do some soul-searching first."

"Thanks," Blue said. "We appreciate that."

"Caspian, come on!" Freddie called, waving him over. "And don't bring that blanket."


"It's easy—like this," Mira said, lying on her back in the Knights' pool, letting the water support her, and showing Caspian how to float. She was trying to teach him to swim. For someone determined to find a mermaid, she figured it could only help.

Caspian clung to the side of the pool. "I don't know, Mira. I don't think my body is designed to do that."

"Everyone can float," she said, pulling on his arm. "Do you want to find your mermaid or not?"

"All right," he said with a sigh. He made a gulping sound—and then he let go and immediately began to sink.

"Just relax," Mira tried. "Lie on your back and—"

It would have helped to grab him and support him, turn him onto his back manually, like swim coaches did for little kids. But touching a guy's wet, bare skin seemed too intimate, if you weren't flirting. If you didn't hope to be touched back.

"Um, or we could try treading water," she said. She demonstrated, pedaling her legs, moving her arms a little.

Caspian's wide gray eyes blinked nervously as his limbs wavered underwater. He was cute, like Freddie, but he veered even further toward adorable. It wasn't hard to picture him falling off a boat. In a prom tuxedo, no less.

"Your hair flows out like a mermaid's," Caspian said.

185

Mira glanced to the side, took stock of the dark gold waves floating on the water. "I guess it does."

"Only it's lighter," Caspian said. "Mermaids have dark hair. Well. The one mermaid I saw did. If she really was a mermaid. I guess she could just be a girl who hangs out in the ocean, waiting for shipwrecks."

"I think that's even less likely," Mira said.

Caspian smiled, his whole face brightening. His arms were moving more smoothly through the water now. "That's why I think it has to be true. That a mermaid saved me. Her voice was so beautiful. . . ."

The look on his face was clearly *love*. He'd transformed from sad to smitten in an instant.

It was strange, seeing all these romantics in their different incarnations. There were regular romantics, like Freddie and Caspian: boys who got lost in daydreams, like she did. Then there were cursed Romantics, who were easy to fall for, who loved love and stole love. Love was what they needed to survive.

The Knights' back door slid open and a parade of people came streaming out: Viv in her teeny white bikini, Blue and Freddie and Wills in swim trunks. The boys jumped in. Viv set a raft on the pool's surface and wriggled onto it, hissing a little when water slithered up the sides.

"It's not even cold," Wills said. He smacked the water next to Viv, so a tiny wave splashed over her ice white abdomen. "Unless you're afraid the chlorine might bleach you. Oh, too late."

Viv gritted her teeth. "And you guys wonder why I hate everyone."

"I'm swimming," Caspian announced. "Sort of. Do you

think that will interfere with my mermaid search? If I fall into the ocean and I'm not drowning, do you think she'll bother to save me?"

"I think your mermaid probably has a life," Wills said. He'd stopped tormenting Viv and was floating in the deep end, hanging on to a foam noodle. "You can't count on her to be waiting around for you every day. So drowning on purpose just makes you an idiot."

"Yes, please stay out of the ocean, Caspian," Freddie said. "Wait for her to make a deal with a sea witch and come to you."

"But what if she *doesn't*?" Caspian asked.

No one had a good answer for that.

After a while, Henley came around the side of the house. He was dressed up—for him—in nice shorts and a button-up shirt thrown over a tank top. He sat down on one of the poolside lounge chairs and watched Viv like she was a silent movie. His gaze was lovesick and sad, but vicious, too, like his eyes could somehow punish her for not giving a damn that he was there.

Viv lay stretched out on her raft, still as death, staring up at the stars. Freddie was demonstrating how many underwater somersaults he could do in a row. When he came up for air, Caspian exclaimed, "You're like a dolphin!"

Mira frog-kicked over to where Blue lazed at the end of the pool, half hidden beneath the low diving board. His fingers clung to the board. Beads of water slid slowly down his face, his neck.

"You're awfully quiet," she said.

"I don't have any dolphin tricks."

"I'm sorry," she said. "That must be hard for you."

He nodded, a wry smile creeping up. "It is."

She reached up and grasped the diving board so she wouldn't have to keep treading. The motion carried her forward, and her bare legs brushed his. The sensation was unexpectedly alluring, and when she didn't rush to move away, he hooked his leg around hers. Neither one of them said anything for a while.

She stared at him—at that cool, impassive face—and wondered why this was so easy for him. How he could like her and make her hate him; and then make her want to be near him. How he could touch her and make her not want to move away. The definition of *Romantic* flared up in her mind.

He and Felix were supposed to be natural charmers. She wondered if *charmer* meant liar.

"Does Felix lie to people?" she asked.

"Ah, we're talking about Felix again."

She shrugged, her arms making a kind of pull-up motion so that her chest rose out of the water.

"Felix lies to people all the time. Our whole business is about deception: drawing people into the casino with hope and an impossible dream, and sending them home with less money than they came in with. He doesn't wear a sign that says *The House Always Wins*. So, yeah, he lies."

"You know what I mean."

Blue raised his eyebrows. Of course he'd known. "You mean does he lie to girls? To get them to fall for him?"

She nodded. Waited.

"You're the one who hangs out in his bedroom. Shouldn't you be able to tell?"

His leg was rubbing against hers, ever so slightly, almost

188

like it was an accident, but it wasn't. It was too regular not to be deliberate.

"Why are you doing that?" she asked quietly. She was grateful for the dark, for the water that hid whatever it was they were doing, for the laughter and splashes—and, yes, even the dolphin tricks—that let the others ignore them.

"I don't know. Why are you letting me?"

"I don't know," she said.

Once upon a time, she would have slapped him for touching her. Thrown a knife at him, a book at him. So what was this?

"I've never lied to anyone. To get them to . . ." Blue hesitated, until she nodded, to let him know she understood. "But I've left things unsaid. I'm sure he does that, too. And he might lie. But he might not have to. Why? Are you afraid you're in love with a lie?"

"No . . ."

"Then it doesn't matter what I say, does it?"

"It's just . . ." Mira bit her lip, tasting chlorine. "He never told me the things you told me. That's the only thing I'm worried about. Why wouldn't he tell me that he's dangerous? That he could hurt me without meaning to?"

"Because he doesn't want you to know. Come on, Mira, don't let love make you stupid."

"Did you tell that girl that you . . . that you—No, right?"

Blue stared at her for a long time. "Do you think that would've happened if she'd known?"

"So I should ask him about it. Let him know that I know."

Blue shrugged. "If you want to. Just stay out of his room."

Her breath caught. "His bedroom? Or suite 3013?"

Blue's eyes flickered with something strange, but all he said was, "Both."

"I'll have you know," she said, breathing shallowly, "that girls get kissed in rooms other than bedrooms. He kissed me in the flower shop. After hours. The night that I . . ."

"The night he almost killed you."

"The night I passed out," she corrected.

"If that's what you want to call it," Blue said. "But I think part of you knows the truth. And that's why you're here with me, instead of back at the Dream with Felix."

"I'm here because I'm trying to be nice. I'm trying to be your friend."

Maybe that was too much for him—right now when their naked legs were touching, playing at being casual. Maybe *friend* was too close to *I like you*—and that was closer to trust, attraction, affection than Blue was comfortable with. Because there was a change in him; his expression turned cocky, silly.

He was about to break the spell. She braced herself to go back to the way things had been before. Joking. Bickering. The shift was almost like an insult. Because he knew she trusted him—and he wouldn't trust her back.

"Is that what this is?" he said. "What does *friend* qualify me for? Can we be friends with benefits?"

Mira had the urge to hold his head underwater until he broke free and spluttered to the surface, coughing and promising not to be a jerk anymore. She was sure her irritation showed on her face—and just as sure that he was pleased about it. "You know, it's hard to knee someone in the balls underwater," she warned him. "But it's not impossible."

Blue's eyes glittered. He was back in his element: playing

around, abrasive and safe. "Hey, as long as I repulse you, I can't hurt you—there's no love to steal. So a friends-with-benefits thing could work for us."

She knew he was joking. She knew, but it wasn't funny.

"*No,*" she said, threatening him with a pathetically slow kicking gesture.

"You're right. You'd probably be disappointed. I haven't had a lot of practice, for obvious reasons. How's Felix? Amazing?"

"Felix . . . has had a lot of practice," she said dully, not liking the direction this was going in. "That's what you're trying to say."

Blue shrugged. "It's not like I read his diary. Just something to think about."

"Maybe I don't want to think about it."

"Well, maybe you should."

She closed her eyes; let the subtle rocking of the water carry her. "Shut up, Blue." The water was almost as warm as her body. If it wasn't for Blue's leg touching hers, it would be like floating in a sensory deprivation chamber. Instead, it was almost hypersensory. Every time he touched her, something new unfurled inside her. "Shut up or I'm leaving."

"Fine," he said quietly. "But only because I don't want you to go."

# CHAPTER THIRTEEN

AFTER SWIMMING, they all crept into the Knights' house, their swimsuits dripping water on the floor, their feet tracking grass onto Persian carpets. Every room was decorated to within an inch of its life. Years of wealth and influence had gathered there like dust.

Freddie shushed their laughter. It was late, he said, and his mother was hypersensitive. She'd wake at the slightest sound.

The boys descended to the basement, unbothered by the cold swimsuits clinging to their legs. Mira's hair was soaked, and she was hugging her towel to her body, missing the heat of the pool. Viv brought her to Freddie's room to change.

Moonlight streamed through the windows, casting a bluish glow on old Little League trophies, Freddie's guitars and amp, and a messy twin bed stripped to the fitted sheet. The rest of the covers slumped sloppily to the ground, like they'd been kicked off during fitful sleep.

Mira changed back into the clothes she'd worn earlier. Viv flopped down on Freddie's bed, still wearing her wet bikini. She stared at the ceiling, arms limp at her sides. Like an actress auditioning for the role of a corpse.

"Do you think I'll look pretty when I'm dead?" Viv asked.

Mira's mouth opened without a response.

"That's what I'm afraid of," Viv went on, teeth scraping her ruby lip. "I mean, I am, and I'm not."

Mira could hear the *tick* of a tiny clock, the blood moving through her head. She barely knew what to say. "What's on your mind, Viv?"

"Not dead, exactly. In an enchanted coma. Don't you worry about that, too?" Viv sighed. "No, I suppose not. Who's afraid of Freddie?"

"I worry about it," Mira admitted. "I don't want to not be in control. I don't want to be at someone else's mercy." She went and sat at the end of Freddie's bed, next to Viv's feet, which were pointed delicately like a ballerina's.

"Same here," Viv said. "But my whole life going forward is going to be like that. I'd have to keep a perfect balance to avoid it. Pretty enough to make Henley the Huntsman want to save me . . . but not too pretty, because too pretty is what sets my stepmother off. And she wants me gone—she wanted me gone years ago."

Viv twisted restlessly. "I don't know what she's waiting for. Waiting to make him hate me, I guess. Make him loyal to her so he'll cut my heart out when she asks him to . . . And then if Henley *doesn't* kill me, there's the matter of being pretty enough to attract some necrophiliac playboy. Someday my prince will come—and be enamored of my lifeless body. There's some happily-ever-after for you."

The image of Gwen shuffling through the street fair arose in Mira's mind. She imagined the moment when the prince must have found her—dead to the world, numb. He was so in love with her perfect little doll face that he felt compelled to bring her coffin with him so he could look upon her always. Like she was a souvenir, not a person.

Until she woke up, and ruined his fantasy.

"Blue and Layla told me about Gwen," Mira said, unsure how to offer comfort when everything she'd heard about Viv's tale was twisted and dark. "The other Snow White Somnolent. But I don't—I don't think it always has to be like that. Your prince could . . . take pity on you, maybe. Feel bad that your life was cut short. And not want to leave your coffin in the woods, or wherever he found it. He wouldn't necessarily be a bad person."

"No," Viv said, shaking her head, wet tendrils of hair writhing against the mattress. "The only person who'll pity me is Henley . . . that's the only way he won't kill me. If he decides not to anyway."

"I don't think it would be pity, Viv," Mira said, but Viv wasn't listening.

"Regina had a glass coffin built when I was thirteen," Viv said. "She put it in the sunroom and she tends to it like it's her baby; she polishes it every day. It looks like a display case, and that's what it is. A display case for my corpse, so she can use my so-called beauty to her advantage, flash my undead pallor at potential suitors, like: *here, take her, please.* She wants to get rid of me . . . she wants me in someone else's house, as someone else's problem."

Viv sounded upset, not blasé like she probably wanted to.

Mira laid her hand on Viv's ankle, just to remind her she was there. That Viv wasn't alone right now. Wasn't dead, or in danger. Mira knew she sometimes needed reminding of that herself.

"Couldn't you tell your dad it bothers you? Having the coffin in your house?"

"I've tried—but he doesn't want to hear it. He's spoiled because his curse is dormant, so he never had to go through any of this when he was younger. His only role to play is the inept, worthless father—which he's perfect for. When I complain, he says we need to learn to get along; he has other problems, he's not going to fix ours. And then Regina tells me I'm lucky my dad's so uninterested in my life. I could have a Donkey Skin curse, and wouldn't *that* be awkward?"

"'Donkey Skin'?" Mira didn't know that tale. "Is that—a princess turns into a donkey?"

Viv laughed. "Oh, Mira. That's cute. No—turning into a donkey would be fun, compared to this nastiness." She sat up, directly into a slice of moonlight. Her skin glowed like a ghost's.

"In the Donkey Skin tale, the princess's mother dies young—like most of our moms—"

Mira's hand trembled against Viv's ankle, and she brought it back to her lap before Viv noticed. That was her mother's fate—her mother's and her father's both.

"—but not before telling the king he can't marry anyone whose beauty doesn't surpass her own. Years go by, and naturally, no one's beauty compares to the dead queen's . . . until one day, the old lech notices that his daughter is the hottest thing on two legs."

Viv raised her eyebrows, daring her to make the connection.

A sour taste crept into Mira's throat. She hadn't known her father, but in her mind, fathers were heroes, protectors. "You're not saying—?"

"So the king decides to marry his daughter. He pursues her, no matter what kind of roadblock she throws up, and she has to dress in the skin of a donkey and pose as a filthy urchin to escape. Then she toils as a servant in another kingdom before she finally gets her Cinderella ending, when the local prince notices that the urchin cleans up nice on special occasions. But who knows what went on in that house before she ran away?"

These tales got worse and worse. Mira's hands twitched into fists at her sides, nails digging into her palms. A fairy had to *choose* that curse. Had to bestow it on a girl no older than Mira, knowing what would happen to her.

Her thoughts went to Delilah—and how cruel a fairy had to be to inflict that on someone. She wondered how much evil Delilah was capable of. And what the fairy had in store for her.

"Like all curses," Viv said, "your mileage probably varies. But trust me when I say I'd rather have my heart cut out by my boyfriend than deal with my dad trying to sleep with me."

"Henley wouldn't really . . ." Mira couldn't contemplate the other half of Viv's statement.

Viv flopped back down on the bed, in the same pose she'd take in her glass coffin. She was shivering, her voice trembling with the vibration. "Who knows what he'll do. He's crazy. I don't even care."

There was a knock on the door then. Light, polite, so as not to disturb anyone.

"It's open," Mira called, grateful for the interruption. She was afraid that if they kept going, Viv would sink so deep into her own darkness that she wouldn't be able to dig her out.

The door opened and Freddie slipped in. He bowed his head, as if to apologize for intruding.

"Hey, lover boy," Viv drawled.

Freddie ducked his head again, embarrassed this time. "Viv. Don't say that. Henley's in the house, you know." He cleared his throat. "How are you, ladies? I've been sent as an emissary to make sure everything's all right."

"We're done here," Viv said, pushing herself off the bed. "I need a cocktail anyway. Is the bar open?"

"Wills is mixing drinks," Freddie said. "But, Viv, you probably shouldn't—"

Viv dismissed his words with a wave, as if his worry buzzed around her like an annoying mosquito. "Enjoy the dark, kiddies. I'll give you some alone time." And then her pale slip of a body was gone, padding soundlessly down the hall.

Freddie sat down on the floor, next to a hamper overflowing with boxers and T-shirts. Mira had intended to follow Viv, but the way Freddie planted himself in the room made her think that he wanted to talk to her—even though he didn't say a word.

Silence descended, making every outside sound seem louder. Faintly, Mira could make out a high-pitched trill of feminine agitation—a damsel in moderate distress.

*It isn't funny, Philip! I'm going to have a bruise on my spine!*

"Is that—?" she asked.

"My mother," Freddie said, plucking a stray guitar pick from the floor. "Probably thinks there's a pea under her mattress. She's hypersensitive, and it's made her into a hypochondriac. Although there might really be a pea there. My father plays tricks on her sometimes."

"So your parents are cursed, too?"

Freddie nodded, leaned back on his arms, then drew one knee up, restless. "Both sides of my family have a long history of active curses. They're proud of it. Being marked, as a hero, especially, is an honor. It's a sign of good faith on the fairy's part—that she thinks you're worthy of it."

Mira wondered if her parents had been cursed. If they'd had to fight to be together—only to lose everything at her christening.

Lost in her thoughts, she was surprised when Freddie asked, "Are you scared, Mira?"

"Scared?"

"Your sixteenth birthday is approaching. And things tend to change on days like that. I wondered if . . . I mean, you seem distracted. I thought maybe . . ."

"Oh."

The memory of Delilah's cold nails on her skin came back. Tracing her mark, sizing her up. She could almost hear the fairy's voice, sweet like caramel and sharp like steel.

*Darling, what terrifying timing.*

"You don't have to be afraid," Freddie said. "If something happened, I would wake you. If we didn't know where you were when it happened . . . I would search for you."

And he would. She knew he would. But . . .

"I don't want to owe you anything," she admitted.

He looked stung by her remark. "You wouldn't owe me anything. I'm not out to gain something from waking you."

She was sorry she'd hurt his feelings—again. But that didn't make her worries less valid. He *thought* she wouldn't owe him anything. He believed that *now*. But how would things change if he restored her to life? How would he feel once he'd saved her and she was as standoffish as before?

Mira didn't want that rescue hanging over her head, pressuring her to fall in line like a good princess and show her gratitude by . . . by doing whatever was expected after that.

Marriage. Dating. Sex. She wasn't sure how things worked here, how much the fairy-tale community's reliance on tradition had kept them from evolving with the rest of the world. But clearly, there would be pressure to conform—either social or magical—or Viv wouldn't be as scared as she was. Not just of her enchantment, but of what came after.

Mira didn't want to be resigned to her fate. Didn't want to be mired in hopelessness, like Viv was, like it was quicksand—a trap that only grew tighter when you tried to escape.

"Can I ask what I'm doing wrong?" Freddie said finally. His mother's complaints had quieted, giving way to the heaviness of sighs, the flick of Freddie's nail against a guitar pick, the rustle of Mira's legs shifting on the bed.

"Nothing," she said. "There's not a checklist of things I want that you're not doing. I just—my heart is somewhere else."

She felt cruel saying that. But it was true.

Blunt rejection seemed to embolden him. "I'll wait, you know," he said, with a resoluteness she hadn't heard from him before. "I know you don't like me now. But I think you might,

199

eventually. And I would be good to you. I would never hurt you—the way Felix will."

Mira closed her eyes. Not that again. Not that—always. Her chest tightened, squeezing the air from her lungs. Freddie didn't understand. He couldn't see the way Felix treated her. He saw only the curse, the black-and-white doom of it, the fact that Felix wasn't a hero, wasn't a prince. There was a delicate line between love and death for Romantics, but she was sure Felix would tread it with the utmost care. Hadn't he already?

"People who care about you won't hurt you, Mira. Not even if they can't help it. That may not matter to you now, but one day, it will."

"You don't know anything about the people who care about me," she said, feeling surly, defensive. He was insulting someone she loved, and it brought out the worst in her. "You only know how *you* care about me. And you don't even know me; you'd feel this way about any princess who shared your curse. So don't lecture me like your love is so much truer than anyone else's."

Struck dumb, Freddie just stared at her. His usual expression—earnest, hopeful, kind—crumbled, and he looked like he was trying not to cry.

Mira felt awful. She hadn't meant to lash out at him. She'd just wanted him—wanted everyone—to stop attacking her, stop slandering Felix, and making her feel stupid.

"Get off my bed," he said. Wordlessly, she did. He scraped toward it like a sleepwalker, collapsed onto the mattress, with his face mashed into the pillow so he didn't have to look at her.

"Freddie, I—"

"I don't feel well. Please go away." His voice was muffled,

but the meaning was clear. He wanted her to leave before anything else could change. Before he broke down, or said something nasty, if he was even capable of that. Before she could be meaner to him.

Mira tiptoed to the door, utterly disgusted with herself. Before she left, she stopped in the doorway to get a few words out. "I'm sorry," she said. "I didn't mean to snap at you. I really do appreciate the things you said. It's just . . . this is hard for me. Please believe me."

She waited a few heartbeats for his answer, some indication that he could forgive her. But none came.

Mira needed Freddie. She didn't want to need him, but she did; and she knew that was where a lot of her frustration originated. It chafed at her that their fates were intertwined.

When she trudged into the basement, Wills was at the bar, shaking a cocktail shaker. Viv was perched on a barstool, rimming a glass with sugar. She wore a floppy, feathered hat and knee-high cavalier boots, like a stripper musketeer. Her tiny apple mark—not bloodred but cherry-blossom pink—showed above the waistband of her bikini bottoms.

Blue, Caspian, and Henley were gathered around a low table, in the shadow of a taxidermied grizzly bear. Blue was dealing hands for a game of poker.

"Suit up and I'll deal you in," Blue said, nodding toward an old steamer trunk full of silk scarves, velvet jackets, strange hats—like the stuff Viv was wearing.

"Suit up?" she said.

"We're playing strip poker." Caspian went on to explain, and Mira realized it was the tamest version of strip poker imaginable. It involved piling on clothes from the costume trunk, so there was very little danger of getting naked unless you wanted to. Mira set to work creating a winning ensemble, hoping she could bury her guilt in ridiculous clothes and stop thinking about what a jerk she'd been to Freddie.

Blue was sticking a villainous fake mustache to his lip—skinny, twisty, and black—when Viv joined them, narrow hips swaying, pink cocktail in hand. "That does not count as a clothing item," she said.

"It does if you can take it off," Blue told her.

"Then my earrings count," Viv argued.

Wills came down from the bar and sat between them. "By the time you get to your earrings, you'll be so drunk you'll just throw your top off."

Viv punched Wills in the ribs, and he grabbed her fist and started wrestling with her. Viv was shrieking, laughing, swatting ineffectively at her tormentor. The tendons were standing out in Henley's neck. He was mangling his cards like he wanted to mangle Wills.

Blue pointed to the mark on Wills's lower back: a bloodred high-heeled shoe. "Not her prince, Silva. Relax."

"Cheaters," Viv accused, once she'd caught her breath. Her cheeks were flushed the same pomegranate color as her lips, and she was tucking her hair behind her ears repeatedly, like she was suddenly shy. Wills pulled Viv into his lap, and she settled there without complaint.

But not everyone was so content.

"This game is going to be boring," Henley said. "All guys and one girl."

"Two girls," Caspian corrected, pointing them out. "See?"

Henley peeled his cards off the table—an attempt at non-chalance. "Yeah, but I've already seen Viv naked. So like I said: boring."

Viv's cheeks flushed pinker—two fevered flares. Her hand flinched in front of her glass, like she wanted to break it, or throw it at him.

"You should learn to close your drapes, Viv," Wills said coolly. He eyed Henley as he bit the tip of Viv's ear. "You can't trust the garden boy not to spy on you."

"So . . . *poker time?*" Mira said—a little too loudly. She slapped her palms down on the table, gave the boys her best can-we-end-this-pissing-contest? glare, and Caspian flashed her a grateful smile—so maybe it worked.

In any case, they shut up and played.

An hour later, Viv and the Knight brothers stumbled upstairs to raid the kitchen, and Henley slipped out the back, lighting a cigarette and muttering shit about Wills—leaving Mira and Blue alone in the basement, surrounded by oil paintings of hunting parties, the glassy-eyed heads of long-dead animals, and furniture that reeked of cigars.

Blue was still wearing—and villainously twirling—the skinny fake mustache. He wore baggy pajama pants that were half soaked from the wet bathing suit underneath, topped off by a jester's cap, and reindeer slippers that fit only halfway on his feet. A black silk necktie hung from his neck. He'd ditched his shirt a long time ago.

"I can't believe they left you alone with this sexy miscreant," he said.

She touched her hand to her heart in mock distress. "Neither can I. Your curse is that girls fall for you . . . right before you tie them to train tracks, right?"

"Muahaha . . . exactly." Blue twirled his fake mustache—
until it fell off.

Above them, someone stomped or fell hard against the
floor. Drunken laughter broke out, and it was probably only
a matter of minutes before Mrs. Knight arrived to scold the
revelers.

Mira thought of Freddie upstairs in his room, probably
wincing at the noise, hyperaware that they were bothering his
mother . . . all the while languishing alone with his broken
heart. And she thought of Henley outside, doing God knows
what—hopefully getting out his aggression on a mailbox,
instead of on Wills or Viv.

She hated that it was so easy for all of them to hurt each
other—and that it was Henley's *role* as Huntsman to hurt
someone he cared about, someone who also seemed to hurt
him on a regular basis. How tempting would it be when
Regina gave the order? Could love really drive you to murder?

"Their relationship is so messed up," she murmured.

"Blue and Mira's? I think they just need to make out."

She threw her costume-trunk fedora at him. "I'm serious.
I'm talking about Viv and Henley. It freaks me out that they're
sort of involved, and yet, one day, Viv's stepmom is going to
order Henley to kill Viv."

"Tell me about it." Blue switched to an exaggerated shrew-
ish voice. "*By the way, garden boy, when you're done trimming
the hedges, could you cut out my daughter's heart and bring it to
me so I can eat it?* That's a lot to ask of someone you're paying
minimum wage."

"It's even worse that they know about it—that they're

cursed and they expect it." Mira hugged her knees to her chest. "I don't know how you guys can live like this."

"We just do," Blue said. "We have to."

Mira closed her eyes, arms locked around her knees, as if she could shut out the world, but dark images filled her mind. She used to imagine her parents and happy endings she would never have. Now she envisioned torments that were all too real.

She pictured one of Cinderella's stepsisters planting her foot on a cutting board—and biting down hard as the cleaver chopped through the bone of her big toe.

She imagined a princess used to safety, luxury, throwing the rank hide of a donkey over her shoulders, its boneless face drooping past her forehead like a hideous veil.

And she imagined her future self, flat on her back in bed, limbs as heavy as if they'd been chained down. Mice scurried across her body, leaving footprints on her dress. Spiders spun an entire trousseau's worth of silk and draped her in it, so it appeared she wore a gown of the finest lace, adorned with rose petals and ensnared butterflies. Beetles nestled between her fingers like jeweled rings—lovely from a distance, horrific up close.

No one would come for her; no one would wake her. She'd be repulsive, not enticing, and she'd pushed away the one person who might have saved her. . . .

When she opened her eyes, Blue was staring at her, his eyes traveling her face. Maybe troubled by what he saw and didn't fully understand.

"I feel sick," she said, her fingers absentmindedly twisting a lock of wet hair. "Let's talk about something else."

"Like what? Felix? That makes *me* feel sick."

She wasn't in the mood to be teased. "Very funny. Why do you care so much?"

"Why do I care? I'm pretty sure I told you." He crawled toward her, shedding the jester cap and reindeer slippers as he went, until he was so close she could see that his eyelashes were blue, too. "Because I like you. Because I don't want him to hurt you."

"He doesn't want to hurt me either."

"You think his intentions matter if he ends up killing you? I don't."

"I know you didn't mean to—" Flustered, she ducked her head. "What happened to that girl. I know you didn't mean to. It *does* make a difference."

Blue paused, like his breath was frozen in his chest. Every mention of the girl he'd loved seemed to reopen the wound. It was a moment before he spoke.

"Not to her," he said. "Not to anyone who cared about her. She's gone."

"It was an accident. You can't keep blaming yourself."

"Who should I blame, Mira? The evil fairy who cursed me? Jane, for lo—" Blue stumbled on the word. "For . . . loving . . . me?"

"Her name was Jane?" she asked softly.

Blue nodded. "She was great. Really funny, really smart . . . her only flaw was that she couldn't see through my bullshit. *I* couldn't see through my own bullshit then. I still thought that love conquered all. But all it conquered, all it crushed was the girl I cared about."

Mira bowed her head. She thought of all the time she'd spent grieving, blaming herself for her parents' deaths and wishing she'd never been born—so that *they* could have lived. She'd believed her willingness to suffer would somehow make things better. She couldn't let Blue give in to that fallacy, too.

"Punishing yourself won't bring her back," she said.

"No. But it's a debt I have to pay. For what I took from her." Blue's mouth was a sharp, unforgiving line. His gaze was turned inward, into the past, and his eyes were as glassy as the stags' on the wall. "I have to lose something, too."

"But . . ." Mira took his hand and held on tight. "Don't you see that you have? That you did lose something?"

"It doesn't compare, Mira. It's not even close to being the same. Look at my life: I *stole* hers, but I still have everything. Why do I deserve that?"

She wanted to comfort him, to find the perfect words to convince him that he deserved forgiveness. That he could still be a good person. Could be redeemed, because he had a good heart—why would he torture himself if he *didn't* have a good heart? But her mind kept drifting to Felix. Felix was older, more sophisticated, *experienced*. Which begged the question . . .

Had Felix ever killed a girl? Stolen everything from her?

He'd said that love destroyed him. But he'd never told her what that meant.

Was he carrying around a wound like this, too? A secret despair?

Or . . .

The alternative—that Felix was a predator, smoothly seducing and then robbing girls of their lives—was too terrible to consider.

It was one thing to love and leave someone. To kiss and tell. There were all sorts of risks when you gave your heart away. Everyone had secrets.

But the truth was that Felix had saved her. He'd kissed her, and kissed her, and when she'd grown too weak, he'd pulled back. He'd taken her somewhere safe.

Whatever he'd done in the past . . . he was making up for it now. She couldn't blame him for a curse he had no control over. She *wouldn't*. Just like she wouldn't blame Blue.

"Are you thinking about him?" Blue asked.

Mira nodded, embarrassed. He probably thought she was obsessed. And maybe she was. But this was what she did when she fell in love. She'd fixated on her parents, on their imaginary lives, for years. Nothing in her real life had been able to tear her away from that. Nothing until Felix. Until she'd fallen in love with something real.

"This is so hopeless," Blue muttered.

"Can't you just be happy for me?"

She felt stupid as soon as she'd said it.

Blue barked out a laugh. "*No*. No, you idiot. I couldn't be more *un*happy. You know, I don't usually know the girls he likes. Not like this. I look the other way most of the time. But I met you first. I knew you first.

"I wanted you first," he said.

"You have . . . a funny way of showing it," she said, awkwardness making it hard to speak.

"I know. I know, and I'm still . . ." He scrubbed his hand over his face. "I don't know why I'm telling you this. Because I don't want you to like me—I would hate it if you did. And yet I hate it that you don't."

She stayed silent. She wasn't so sure he was right about that anymore—about her not liking him. The more he opened up, his armor peeling off to reveal who he really was, the more she felt connected to him.

She never felt nervous around Blue. She could hold her own with him, laugh at him, and, if necessary, slap him. There was something reassuring about that.

And, she realized . . . he told her the truth. Even when it might make her look at him differently or fear him. He took that risk. And that made him brave.

She wished she knew how to say that to him. But she was afraid of what it would mean. Afraid that it would scare him like it scared her.

"Okay," Blue said quietly, resigned. He put his arms around her, and laid his head on her shoulder—like someone who needed a hug, not someone who was giving one. She rubbed his bare back lightly, her fingers drawn to the smooth heart mark at the base of his spine. It was more than the sign of his curse. He wore his broken heart on his skin.

She didn't know what to do.

# CHAPTER FOURTEEN

AROUND 3 A.M., Blue brought her back to the Dream. He walked with her to Felix's suite when she said that was where she wanted to go. But when they got there, he leaned against the door, as if he could block her from ever going in.

They'd shared a day full of secrets and bad music and laughter. Confessions in a rose garden, flirtation in a moonlit pool.

And now it was over.

"You don't have to go back there," he said. "You don't have to stay with him."

She'd been about to knock when Blue wedged himself between her and the door. Now he was so close she could touch him with the slightest flutter of her fingers. One more step and she could press herself against him, lean her head on his shoulder. Forget—for a little while longer—that she'd almost died last night.

"I know," she said. "I'm not here because I have to be. I . . ."

She lowered her eyelids against the glare of the lights, and against the worry in Blue's face.

She'd spent a whole day away from Felix. She'd had twenty-four hours to recover, both physically and emotionally. And she was torn. The thought of him—of his mouth, soft and insistent against hers—still made her heart race, made her as dizzy as no sleep and too much caffeine and stolen love.

The thought of the end—when he'd torn himself away from her, then left her in Blue's bed without a word of reassurance—crushed the air from her chest.

Blue was expecting an answer, and she didn't know how to explain. She was scared to see Felix again—but more scared *not* to see him. She didn't want to walk away from this.

"You could stay with me," Blue said.

*That's the last thing I can do.* She shook her head. She couldn't spend the night with Blue. She was involved with his brother, and things were already too complicated.

"You can stay anywhere you want. Just tell me where, and I'll take you. God . . . anywhere but here, Mira."

With her eyes closed, she could imagine this wasn't hurting him. Wasn't scaring him. She didn't have to see the pained expression on his face. She could hear the worry in his voice, but she could ignore it, pretend it was exhaustion that made him sound like that.

"I don't know where I'm going to stay yet," she said. "But I need to see him."

Blue made a fist and banged it against the wall. "This is so stupid," he muttered.

He took her passkey out of his wallet. When she reached

for it, he said, "I told you: this is mine now," and stuffed it into the slot. The green *open* light blinked on.

Mira pressed down on the door handle. "Good night," she said, hesitant to go. "Thanks for—"

But Blue turned his back on her before she could finish. He headed toward the elevators; vanished around a corner without saying good-bye.

It hurt to watch him walk away like that.

But she supposed she deserved it. They were never going to agree on this.

Mira took a moment to swallow the emotion rising in her throat. Then she slipped into the suite.

Felix was awake, sitting on the couch in the dark, his features lit by the glow of the TV. Shifting light played over his cheekbones, revealed the angry set of his jaw before masking him in shadow. He was arguing with someone on the phone. His legs were kicked up on the table—like he was trying to unwind, but it wasn't working. An old noir movie flickered on the screen.

Mira shut the door. Felix didn't look up.

"If you don't think I can handle it, then maybe you should be here doing this stuff yourself," he said into the phone. "I told you, it'll get done. I've been busy . . . No, not that kind of busy. None of your business. No—I don't care what Villers told you. Uh-huh. Right . . . What?" He snorted. "Hire a tour guide; I don't know. Take her to the Eiffel Tower. I really don't care, Dad. Impressing your girlfriend is your problem. Oh, and it's three in the morning here. So if you're done . . . Yeah. Okay. I know. I know. Talk to you later."

Felix tossed his phone on the table and finally glanced over. He let out an angry sigh.

"Your dad?" she said.

He nodded. "Checking up on me. He can't relax if he doesn't question my judgment once a day." He leaned forward to stop the movie he'd been watching. The screen filled with a glaringly bright commercial—primary colors, some local restaurant—and they both watched it for a moment, not looking at each other.

Mira didn't know what to say. It was like they'd been in one place when they'd gone into the flower shop, and now—now that she knew what he could do to her—they were in another, and there was no easy bridge between them.

"You were out late," he said finally.

"Sorry," Mira said, not wanting to explain. Her arms and the crook of her shoulder still held the memory of Blue's embrace. She felt guilty. She wasn't sure *how* guilty she should feel; but she couldn't not think about what had gone on between them.

"It's okay," Felix said. "I'm just glad you're here now. I thought . . . maybe you weren't coming back."

"Oh?" Mira set her purse on the table. So he knew something was wrong; they both knew something weird had happened last night. But he didn't know she knew his secret—and she wasn't sure how to behave. Should she pretend everything was fine? Confront him?

What other secrets was he keeping?

Before she could decide, Felix came and took her hands. There was a gentleness and familiarity in his touch that made her feel safe, despite what he'd done. These were hands that had held her close, slipped across her skin, and taken her breath away. Hands that had brushed tall grass back from untended graves, to check for her parents' names.

"Feel like going out?" he said.

"Now?" She tipped her head back to meet his eyes. Felix was luminous, bright with stolen love, and so startlingly beautiful she didn't want to look away.

It was her near-death she was seeing, *her love* that burned in his veins—and it should have frightened her . . . but she was mesmerized. The dark gleam in his eyes, the warm curve of his lips drew her toward him; and her mouth wavered open as if for a kiss.

He didn't kiss her. He tightened his grip on her hands.

"There's something I want to show you," he said. "You'll want to see it. Trust me."

*Do I?* she wondered. *Should I?*

She'd never doubted him before. But he'd kept the truth from her—failed to warn her. He could have *killed* her, and he should have let her decide if that was a risk she was willing to take.

"I . . ."

"Mira?" His brows came together in concern. "Are you okay?"

But . . . but he couldn't have known she'd loved him already—why would he suspect she'd surrender her heart so soon? And she could see how it could be nerve-wracking, heartbreaking to say, just when you were kissing someone you cared about: *I could kill you. This could kill you.* You could lose everything before it began. Maybe he'd been afraid of that.

She could understand being afraid. He'd wanted her, he liked her, and he'd gotten carried away. Blue had said a Romantic could drain too much love too fast if he got lost in the emotion. And maybe that had happened to Felix.

But he'd protected her in the end. He'd stopped himself.

Mira exhaled shakily, forced a smile to her lips. "Where are we going?"

His eyes were shining. "You'll see when we get there."

Mira hadn't been able to discern much through the tinted windows of the car; and when Felix opened the door for her, he insisted she close her eyes. He made his hands into a blindfold and guided her forward, his body just behind hers.

"Walk straight," he told her. "Careful; there's a step."

Her shoes clicked on pavement. It wasn't the squish of grass she'd expected, or the crumbly feel of gravel. It wasn't like any of the graveyards they'd been to before. "Why can't I look?"

"I told you. I want it to be a surprise."

At last he came to a stop, and released her, but he didn't say she could open her eyes—so Mira kept them closed, fidgeting and scuffing her shoes on the pavement. But when she heard the clink of a key and the labored creak of hinges, her eyelids sprang apart. Where had he brought her—to a mausoleum?

They stood before a heavy wooden door carved all over with figures. The dominant carving—the only one she could make out—was of a withered old hag proffering an apple in hands that had been chipped away by time. There was a terrible look in the hag's single intact eye.

Mira stalled. "Felix, I don't know if I want to—"

"Wait."

Felix heaved the door open and pushed her ahead of him, into the dark room beyond. It smelled like rainwater and mold, and when she plunged in farther, she could see a scrap of black

215

sky, littered with stars, through a jagged hole in the ceiling. The skitter of something darting through the debris startled her, nearly made her lose her footing. Her breaths came faster, and the ripe scent of decay filled her lungs. Her heartbeat thumped violently in her ears.

"You wanted to bring me . . . here?" Mira took a few steps away from Felix, careful not to trip over any of the wreckage. Falling was the surest way to disaster in a horror movie—was that what this was becoming? Had Felix brought her here so he could drain the life from her, then abandon her where no one would find her?

This wasn't a place she wanted to be. It wasn't romantic; it wasn't a place you took someone for a surprise. Maybe Blue had been right.

*Mira, don't let love make you stupid.*

There had to be another way out of here. Somewhere . . .

She searched, trying not to seem frantic. Just calm, and . . . inching away . . .

"Look up," Felix said. He pointed his flashlight at the ceiling, and she instinctively followed the beam, blinking as she waited for her eyes to adjust. Sweat dripped down her sides and she was suddenly freezing, afraid something was coming for her, about to drop on her, she'd made the exact wrong decision, just following blindly, but then—

Above her, she could make out a faded mural. Like the Sistine Chapel's, but woven of fairy-tale scenes. A red-cloaked girl strolled with a wolf down a tangled forest path. Twelve princesses, dripping with jewels, danced holes into their shoes. An old man stole a rose while a beast raged behind him. On and on it went, tale after tale, all coming together and blurring at the edges. A world of fairy tales. A city full of curses.

It was the ceiling from her godmothers' stories.

This was the ballroom where they'd held her christening party all those years ago.

Mira stared with her mouth open, turning in a slow circle to see it all.

"Oh my god," she said. "How did you find this?"

Felix shrugged, his lips fighting a proud smile. "You described it to me, and I wondered if it might still be here. So I made some calls, and . . ."

Mira was overcome. She'd dreamed about this place—the last place she and her parents had been together. So to see it, to be here . . . Her eyes welled up, both happy and sad.

". . . and I found out," he went on, "that there was never a fire here."

"Never a—?" She blinked at him, uncomprehending. "But it's—" She gestured to the rubble, the broken ceiling.

"That happened during the storm. A lot of buildings were damaged then."

"There was never a fire," she repeated. She felt numb. "I don't understand. What happened? Were they murdered? Is that why my godmothers didn't tell me?"

"Mira." Felix came to her and put his arms around her. "That's not what I'm trying to say." The flashlight beam tilted toward a weather-ravaged wall. Chipped plaster lion heads clung stubbornly to the molding, and she counted them, afraid to breathe, afraid to even think about what might have happened that day.

Felix rubbed her back. And said the last thing she expected. "Your parents are alive."

* * *

She felt number than numb. She couldn't even tremble with the shock of it.

*Alive* meant real. Meant she could see them.

It also meant they'd abandoned her. *By choice.*

"That's impossible," she said. She felt like her voice was coming from someone else. Her lips and tongue were too dead to move.

"It makes sense, if you think about it. They wanted to protect you from your curse, so they sent you away from Beau Rivage. They let you believe they were dead so you wouldn't be tempted to come back. Everyone wants to fight fate," he said softly.

"And I'd bet," he continued, "that they intended to find you once they felt it was safe. On your birthday, maybe."

She blinked hard and sent tears racing down her cheeks. Felix caught them on his thumb.

"I didn't mean to make you cry. Isn't this what you wanted?"

"I wanted to see them. But—I never knew they *chose* to leave me. This—changes things."

She breathed sharply, tears caught in her throat. It was humid in the crumbling ballroom. Fetid with rot and mold.

She'd always thought of her parents as perfect—everything she needed, but couldn't have—and no one had ever been able to replace them. Bliss and Elsa were wonderful, but they were real; they restricted her, tried to protect her from the world. Whereas her parents . . . her parents were her own heart, better versions of herself: stronger, more understanding, and noble— they'd died because they were *too good*. She'd never imagined them arguing with her, or being disappointed by her, or . . . abandoning her.

But now they were real. And they *had* abandoned her.

Maybe they'd been forced to leave her—by a curse. Maybe they'd suffered every day. Or maybe they were glad she was gone.

It was impossible to know.

So as much as she longed for them . . . she was afraid.

What if they didn't want to see her again? What if they'd meant for Bliss and Elsa to keep her forever? Fairy tales were rife with child abandonment stories. Hansel and Gretel's parents stranded their children in the woods. Rapunzel's parents forfeited her to a witch after stealing herbs from the witch's garden. Sometimes your parents didn't want you. Sometimes they could never get you back.

"Where are they?" Mira asked, gasping a breath. "In Beau Rivage?"

"I don't know," Felix admitted. "I just found out this place was still standing today. But I'm looking for them. I've been asking around. I'm trying."

Felix was busy soothing her, unaware that she knew his dark secret and that she was upset about that, too. He thought he could make everything better; that was what Romantics did, what they wanted—wasn't it?

She stared at the sculpted lion heads on the wall, at their open jaws and teeth.

"Don't worry," he said. "Everything will be fine. I promised I would help you find them. And I will."

*"I lost her. I destroyed her. But I never forgot her.
I never let her go."*

# CHAPTER FIFTEEN

TWO DAYS BEFORE HER BIRTHDAY, her self-imposed deadline, Mira's search for her parents' graves had come to an end. She'd come to Beau Rivage looking for closure, hoping to find some sort of peace—but now that she knew her parents were alive, she felt anything but calm.

She was terrified she'd disappoint them, or that they wouldn't want her—but worst of all, she was afraid her curse would strike before she had the chance to find out. Dread and anticipation twisted inside her like a tightly wound spring. There was a ticking, a kind of countdown in her heart, akin to waiting for a monster to leap out from the dark.

She woke around noon, after spending the night alone. Felix had told her it would be better if she had her own room again, and she hadn't argued. Given what his touch could do to her, his bed was probably not the safest place for her to be.

She got dressed and went downstairs to kill a few hours in Forest Passage, not wanting to leave the hotel in case Felix had news. She found herself studying the crowds of shoppers, wondering if her parents had ever passed through these halls, if they might be here *now*—and then looking for them, looking for anyone too beautiful or too damaged to be normal. And as she looked, she thought about Blue.

Last night, he'd reached out to her and she'd hugged him for a long time, like he was broken and she was holding the pieces together. She'd felt his heartbeat, the heat of his skin against hers. She'd felt like he needed her, like he was finally admitting it.

And then Viv and the Knight brothers had bounded down the stairs, and they'd quickly pulled apart. It was better if no one asked questions. Mira herself didn't know what was going on. Were they friends? You didn't confess your darkest secrets to someone you didn't trust. Did he care about her? And if he did, after all he'd told her about Romantics—what did that mean?

She kept seeing Blue the way he'd looked last night when he'd dropped her off at Felix's door, his eyes dark and sad. That resigned shake of his head, like: *Never mind. Do what you want . . . That's what you'll do anyway.*

Maybe she should stop by his room. Just to let him know she was okay.

Things had been so much easier when she'd wanted to avoid him. . . .

Mira rode the elevator to Blue's floor. She had no idea what to say to him. *Hey, I came looking for you because . . . I keep thinking about what happened last night—whatever that was—and I was wondering: where do we go from here? Now that I know you like me and you know I like your brother and I don't know if I like you but we both know it's better if I don't. . . .*

She knocked on his door and waited. Knocked harder—and kept it up for about thirty seconds, in case he had headphones on, or was feeling lazy and didn't want to answer. When she was on the verge of leaving, sure that he was out—Blue finally opened the door. He had a bent-up spiral notebook in one hand, open to a page that was covered with messy handwriting.

He looked surprised to see her, and made a big production of peering out into the hall. "Did you . . . come here of your own free will?"

"Are you going to let me in or not?"

He propped the door open and stepped out of her way. "Enter."

Blue's suite was still a mess. His clothes were strewn everywhere, like he never got undressed in the same place. A mountain of notebooks was piled on the table. And the oak doors of the TV cabinet, which were closed now, had been defaced with a Sharpie—as if a vandal had gotten tired of scrawling obscene messages in the boys' bathroom and decided to use Blue's room instead.

She was pretty sure Blue was the vandal.

Mira sat down on the couch, which seemed to be where he'd set up for the day, judging by the half-empty Chinese takeout containers scattered around it, and the guitar he'd left behind. The tang of sweet-and-sour something hovered in the air—along with a scent that was distinctly Blue. Metal and industrial-strength styling wax.

"So what are you up to today?" Her long skirt had twisted beneath her when she sat down; now she focused on straightening it, feeling awkward, already regretting coming here. She never purposely sought him out. Obviously, he would think this was weird. . . .

Blue waved the notebook. "Writing. Pouring out my pain."

"Are you writing songs?"

He flopped down next to her. "Trying to. It's all crap right now."

"Can I see?"

"No."

Mira paused, trying to think of the right thing to say. She was afraid that if she misstepped, he would bring up Felix, that his tone would turn sharp, and it would pop whatever was in the air between them. This fledgling friendship, trust. She didn't want to lose that.

"So what do you write about?" she asked.

"Whatever I need to get out of my head. Usually something dark. If I'm lucky, Jewel will like it and we'll be able to use it. Work it into something she can sing."

Blue flicked his pen against his notebook, leaned back to get comfortable. "So . . . you're here. You're okay. Can I assume you took my advice and ditched Felix, and I don't have to worry about you anymore?" His mouth turned up, like he was teasing, but his eyes glimmered with nervousness. He wanted her to say yes.

"Felix isn't what you think." She stared at her hands. Why did they have to talk about this? "Last night he brought me to . . . the place where I was orphaned. The ballroom where my christening party took place. I thought it had burned down, but Felix found out there was never a fire there. He thinks my parents are still alive. That they sent me away to protect me from my curse . . . and we can find them."

"Felix is a regular Nancy Drew," Blue said flatly.

Mira frowned. "Don't be like that. I thought my parents were dead and they're not. This isn't about Felix."

Blue leaned his head on his hand, his arm propped on the back of the couch. "I know, I'm sorry. Why didn't you tell me about this right away? I mean, that's a big deal. Did you think I wouldn't care?"

"I don't know. I guess—I'm afraid of them. Of meeting the *real* them. That sounds bad, I know."

"Of course you're afraid. You don't know them. You just have this vision in your mind of what they're supposed to be like." He brought his leg up onto the couch and started picking at the frayed parts of his jeans. "I have this image of my mom that probably isn't even true—and I *sort of* remember her. You're working from scratch, from other people's memories, right? So you created something safe, something perfect, and now that's going to be tested."

She nodded. That *was* how she felt.

"But even if you don't like the real them," Blue went on, "you'll be okay. If you meet them, and you hate them, or they're mean to you—or they're just not perfect, and you feel guilty about being disappointed—you can come talk to me. Cry on my shoulder. Or knee me in the lungs. Whatever makes you feel better."

"I'll knee you in the lungs," she said, a small smile crossing her face.

"Yeah, I kind of figured I'd regret offering that."

She smiled bigger, biting it back so he wouldn't see it, and let her eyes stray to the legs of his jeans. There were words scrawled all over them in black ink, the handwriting even messier than what she'd glimpsed in his notebook. Bitten-off phrases and lyrical experiments. Like he needed a place to put his thoughts when he didn't have a notebook handy. So nothing was lost.

"How old were you when your mom left?" she asked.

"Um. Four, four and a half. I remember she smelled like . . . I don't know the name of it, but there was this perfume she always wore, and I forgot about it until my dad bought a bottle for one of his girlfriends, and she wore it out to dinner with us, and this memory of my mom came rushing back. Just a flash of her hugging me, but for a split second, I was right there. It was weird." He shook his head, a pensive look on his face, like he was still trying to make sense of it.

"But I don't have a lot of real memories of her. Just flashes like that. And I remember her as always being nice to me, but she must have gotten pissed sometimes. I don't know. I know she didn't love my dad; they had more of, like, a business arrangement. And I hope she's happy, wherever she is. But I think I'd be nervous to see her again. So it's not just you. Scared doesn't mean you're not happy they're alive."

Mira nodded. "I guess I was worried I was being ungrateful or something."

"Nah, you can't force yourself to feel a certain way. You have to just feel what you feel."

"Do you?" Her heart beat faster and she held her breath, wondering if he realized what he'd said.

*Come on. Just believe it for once . . . that you can't force yourself to never fall in love.*

"Okay, correction." He cleared his throat. "*I* can force myself not to feel things I shouldn't feel—because I have to. It's different for me; you know that."

"You can't," she insisted. "You can't do that to yourself. You can adapt, maybe be a little more careful—"

"A little?" He laughed.

"Fine, a lot," she corrected. "But that's different from cutting yourself off entirely, denying that part of yourself forever."

"Okay," he said. "If you're so sure you're right about this, Mira: hypothetically, if I started to feel that way about you—what should I do? Advise me."

"Hypothetically?"

"Purely hypothetically."

She sighed. How had she gotten herself into this?

"Hypothetically, you should do nothing. Because . . . I'm involved with someone. So there you go."

"So I should do exactly what I'm doing now. And ignore your advice about feeling what I feel. Perfect, thank you." He sank back and propped the notebook on his knees. "What rhymes with 'gives bad advice and is a hypocrite'?"

She rapped his kneecap with a chopstick he'd left on the table. "Don't write a song about me! Especially not a stupid song."

"Now my songs are stupid? You are so mean. Do your parents know you're so mean? No wonder you're scared to meet them."

"I'm going to hurt you," she warned, untangling her long, twisty skirt from her legs, and kneeling up on the couch—so he'd know she had every intention of throttling him.

"Please do."

She went to whack his head with the chopstick; then reconsidered and stuck it into his hair instead. It stayed there, balanced between two spikes, and he glared at her with exaggerated loathing.

"You did not just stick a chopstick in my hair."

"I think . . . hmm." Mira rested her chin on her fist, pretending to think it over. "No, I'm pretty sure I did."

"Sticking chopsticks in my hair is forbidden. *Verboten*. It is *an act of war*."

"But you look pretty," she said, struggling to keep a straight face.

She shrieked as he grabbed her and threw her down on the couch, high-pitched, screamy giggles exploding from her throat. She couldn't stop laughing; she could barely breathe. Tears wet her eyes as he tickle-attacked her and made ridiculous threats, until finally, she couldn't take it anymore and agreed to surrender, and instead of a peace treaty he penned a new mark on her forearm: a musical note with some kind of amoeba surrounding it, which she was pretty sure would have been a circle if she hadn't been wriggling around so much.

"This is not a märchen mark," Blue informed her. "This is a stupid idiot mark. It signifies that you agree you're stupid and belong in my stupid songs."

"If it's a stupid mark, shouldn't you have one, too?" she asked innocently. "Or is that why you have that bolt through your eyebrow? Is that like a permanent stupid mark?"

Blue sighed. "You know, I really thought you were going to let me spare you—but apparently, you won't be satisfied until you are destroyed."

And the war resumed.

They fought and wrestled and shrieked and kicked over

half-empty cartons of Chinese food until they were both on the floor, exhausted, chests heaving, irrepressible smiles on their faces.

Blue had her pinned and was hovering over her, his hands on her wrists. "Admit that you lost," he panted. "Admit that you bear the stupid mark with pride."

"No," she said. "I accepted that mark under duress. I refute it."

"Then you will pay the price—" His last word hissed out into a smile, and his expression turned soft, hazy. His lips parted for something other than speaking; and she felt the attraction in the air between them, felt herself willing him closer, like there was something in the look she gave him that said *okay*, that said *kiss me*—before she realized she was doing it. It just *felt right*.

But—it was wrong. And they both knew it. Blue abruptly pushed away from her, sprang up, and mumbled, "Sorry, Mira. I don't know what came over me. . . ."

"Yeah, I don't know either," she said, blinking the kiss-me look out of her eyes.

"Good thing you still hate me," he said with a weak laugh. "You still do, right?"

There was a pause while he waited for her.

"Definitely. There's still—yes. That hatred. It's—going strong."

"Okay, awesome," he said. Then they just stared at each other. Mira broke away first.

"Well—I only meant to drop by for a second," Mira said. "So I should probably . . ."

"Yeah, I should get back to . . ." Blue held up his notebook.

228

"You're coming to the show tomorrow night?"

"Sure, if you guys want me there. And I'm supposed to talk to Delilah."

"That's right."

They smiled and nodded at each other like two dumb bobbleheads, to the point where it was embarrassing. But she supposed it was awkward for both of them, at least.

Blue let her out, and when she stepped into the elevator, she took a deep breath, trying to force the tightness out of her chest. She felt like she hadn't breathed since he'd almost kissed her.

She wondered if it would've been so bad, if he'd actually done it. . . .

A part of her felt like she was still waiting for it.

But then she got hold of herself.

*Yes, it would be wrong! You're in love with his brother.*

*Unless there's some truth to this stupid mark.*

She turned her forearm to examine the mark Blue had given her—the now smudged musical note with the wobbly circle bubble—and licked her thumb and started rubbing it away, the ink smearing until it was almost indiscernible.

Getting so much attention from both brothers made her feel like a kid in a candy store. It was like Hansel and Gretel: they came across the witch's candy house, and they lusted after it, and they were young and stupid so they devoured it without a second thought. Mira had never felt as wanted, as attractive as she did right now; and the heady pleasure of it had made her reckless.

So many fairy tales were about breaking taboos, and being punished for crossing lines you shouldn't have crossed.

Touching a spindle you'd been forbidden to touch. Inviting a witch into your cottage, and accepting the shiny apples she brought you, even though you knew better, because you *wanted* them.

And while most heroes and heroines managed to scratch or scheme their way out of peril, it was easier to avoid doing something stupid in the first place. Smarter, better, and infinitely less fraught with regret.

When the elevator opened onto the glitz of the ground floor, Mira went into the bathroom and washed the last traces of Blue's mark off her arm. There wasn't room in her heart for more than one person. There couldn't be.

By midnight, Mira was more restless than she'd been in her life.

Being alone left her with no distractions—nothing to do but fixate on her fears. Stress over the impending reunion piled onto her worries about her curse, and made her sick to her stomach. She couldn't concentrate, couldn't read or watch TV. She needed to be around people.

But Felix was busy. Blue, she'd decided, was off-limits. And the idea of calling anyone else, and begging them to relieve her of her anxiety, was too embarrassing.

The night was slogging toward 1 A.M.—too, too slowly— and Mira couldn't stand it. So she slipped into her new red satin nightgown, which could pass for a dress, and slicked on lip gloss that looked like lava, shining and melting at once. She went down to the casino, where the party was. Where the life was.

She felt sexy, dangerous, free. Tonight, she didn't look like she needed permission—for anything—and no one questioned her. She made nice with strangers: celebrated their wins, sympathized with their losses. She drank in the manic energy and let the noise push her out of her head, away from her mental list of the ways everything could go wrong. And when she'd had enough, she wandered away from the crowd, and stopped at the mouth of a narrow hall that ended in a set of double doors.

She'd never been down this way before. It wasn't a place for guests. It was spare and uninviting; it led to an employees-only area.

The hall was empty, but as she stood and stared down it, the double doors opened outward, and four men and a woman pushed through them.

One of the men was Felix.

Mira squeezed her body between a pillar and the wall, so that she was hidden from sight.

As she stood and watched, keeping silent, she saw that the larger two men were holding a lanky third between them, and that he was cowering, his head forward as if he were being dragged to a hangman's scaffold. His shirt had come untucked and hung loose and wrinkled over his pants. Sweat filmed his face.

The two large men flanked him, their heavy hands shackling his arms. One of them—a member of the Dream's security team, judging by his bearing—had a thin, vaguely lupine face and a weak chin that seemed at odds with his burly arms and chest. The other large man had round, pink cheeks, and a layer of fat covering his muscles—so that he looked like a cross between a little boy and a wrestler. His lips were candy red, and even now he was cracking a peppermint between his teeth. His bite made a loud, shattering *crunch*.

Felix stood a short distance from the men, and the lone woman—a curvy, well-dressed brunette—stood across from him, so that they formed a triangle in the hall. The woman's tailored black suit suggested that she had an official position at the Dream. Mira couldn't guess what it was, but she radiated authority, and her sly, dark eyes held an eagerness that made Mira uneasy.

Felix was focused on his BlackBerry, his head bowed as if the others were of no concern to him. He wore a charcoal gray suit, a shirt the deep violet color of a plum. Long seconds ticked by before he spoke—and when he did, his tone was as cool as a blade.

"Card counting. In my casino. That was ballsy. Doesn't seem like such a good idea anymore, does it?"

"I won't—be back!" the captive man gasped. "You'll never see me again. I swear!"

"You're right." Felix lifted his head. "No one steals from me twice."

Shifting his attention to the woman, Felix said, "Gretel. You can take this from here?"

Gretel nodded. Her lips curved into a hungry grin. "Bring him down to the Box, boys. I have some toys we can play with."

Grunting affirmatively, the thin-faced guard and the candy eater dragged their charge through an unmarked door. The card counter moaned and managed to sputter a few pleading words before the door slammed coldly behind him.

Left alone in the hall, Felix sighed and ran his hand through his hair, face tightening in frustration. Then it passed, and his face slipped into the cool, unruffled expression he wore so often. He strode calmly down the hall toward the heart of the casino, and didn't look back.

Mira had never seen Felix when he hadn't known she was watching. Never seen that side of him. And his ease at dealing with the card counter—who had surely not been escorted outside and released—sent a chill creeping through her, a sick, damp feeling. She was still suffering the queasiness of that memory when there was a knock on her door.

The clock read 3:57 A.M.

She considered feigning sleep. It was late; the bolt was drawn; she didn't have to open it.

But she did.

Felix slipped in and shut the door behind him. A single lamp burned in the room, but it was enough for her to see that he was pleased about something. A clear energy ran through him, when he should have been weighted down by what had happened earlier, when he'd sentenced the card counter to . . . whatever the man's fate was.

Maybe he was used to dealing with people like that. But it bothered her that there had never been a hint of that coldness, that ruthlessness in him before. He'd seemed—like a good person. But that wasn't all he was, or could be.

Mira was still wearing her red satin nightgown. She'd wrapped herself in the suite's king-size bedspread, so that it draped her body like a cloak. A shield to keep him at bay.

Felix didn't seem to notice that she was being distant. He laughed softly, and fingered the edge of the bedspread. "Did I wake you?"

Then he wrapped his arms around her and hugged her hard, like he'd longed to hold her all day. "You could have stayed in bed," he murmured. "But I'm glad you didn't."

It took all her willpower not to burrow deeper into his embrace. Having his body so close to hers was like a drug that sent reason spiraling away from her, and she had to stop and remind herself that all wasn't well.

"I was awake," she said, pulling free less than gracefully. Her voice came out colder than she'd intended. And when she wedged herself into a corner of the couch and tucked her legs inside her bedspread cocoon, Felix quirked his eyebrows.

"Did I do something wrong?"

"I—I don't know. Maybe." Mira took a deep breath to settle her nerves. "I saw you tonight. While you were working."

"You should've said something." He smiled, his face warm with affection, but when she didn't smile back, furrows of worry took its place.

He sat near her, but didn't touch her.

"Mira, what is it? Are you mad because I was gone all day?"

She pulled the bedspread more tightly around herself. "No . . ."

When she didn't elaborate, Felix rubbed his eyes, looking tired and irritated. "What is it, then?"

Mira's mouth hovered open. *Who are you?* she thought. But that wasn't something she could say.

He was Felix. Of course she knew him—she was in love with him. He was caring and capable, generous with his time and everything else. He was dangerous—she was proof of that—but he did his best to curb that danger.

Or at least, that was what she'd thought. Until tonight,

when he'd sentenced the card counter with a few harsh words.

She watched him, trying to figure him out. To see something new.

Normally, there was something exotic about his dark blue hair, his matching dark eyes: they lent him mystery and made him beautiful in a strange way—like a black rose or a yellow diamond. But tonight, he resembled a storm, a pulse of lightning in a roiling black sky.

He sat with his arm flung across the back of the couch, not cool and careful, but restless, frustrated, staring at her like his gaze could wrench an answer out of her. She supposed he didn't have patience for drama, or whatever he thought this was. If she wasn't going to be nice to him, he probably wanted to go to bed.

After a few minutes of silence, Felix took a square of paper from his jacket—a thin ivory sheet folded in half—and tossed it onto the table in front of her. "Here. This is why I came up here."

Loosening the bedspread enough to free her arm, Mira leaned forward. She unfolded the paper and found a phone number written inside. "What is this?" she asked.

"It's your parents' number. I tracked them down. I thought you'd want to know."

Mira froze. She stared at the numbers like they were going to disappear. The news seemed too amazing to be true. *Oh god . . .*

"Still mad at me?" he asked.

A laugh bubbled out of her. Or maybe she cried; she didn't know, didn't care. Ten numbers and she could speak to them.

Hear their voices. She would finally hear them say her name, say *I love you*.

She threw her arms around Felix and buried her face in his neck, needing to touch him to be sure this was real. He'd seemed so cold to her a moment ago, but his body felt strong and safe to her now. Her heart drummed wildly and she found herself kissing his face, her tears smearing his cheeks as she laughed. *It was real.* They were *alive*.

They were alive and suddenly it didn't matter if they liked her, if she was the biggest disappointment or everything they'd hoped for. They were *alive* and they had never burned or suffocated in a room full of fire, and that was a dream come true no matter what happened next.

"You really found them?" she asked. "I didn't imagine that?"

Felix laughed. "Call the number. You can talk to them right now."

Mira nodded, possibility held in her fist in the form of a scrap of paper. She wanted to hold on to it a little longer, and prepare herself. This was a big deal, and she wanted their first conversation to be just right.

"I will," she said. "I'm not ready yet."

"If you want me to be there when you call, just let me know." He squeezed her hand.

There was such a crazy, fluttery feeling in her blood—like her heart was about to burst. "Do you think they'll want to see me? Do you think they'll like me?"

Felix ran his hand over her hair, cupped the back of her neck. "They'll love you. Don't worry. It'll be fine." His face had lost its impatience, relaxed to something softer. "I'll

236

let you sleep. Maybe tomorrow you'll tell me what's wrong."

"Wait!" She grabbed his arm to stop him. "I'll tell you now."

Questioning who he was seemed silly, now that he'd given her the one thing she'd longed for her entire life. What percentage of his day was spent punishing people who tried to cheat his family's business—two percent?

He'd spent so much more time than that worrying about her, trying to make her happy. Could she really blame him for doing his job?

Felix sat back down, so close to her their bodies were touching. The bedspread had fallen away when she'd thrown her arms around him, and become a rumpled coil around her waist. Her red satin nightgown shined like fire in the lamplight, and she felt his gaze on her body, on the sheen of the satin and the curves beneath it, and the look on his face made her short of breath.

"I saw you earlier," she began, "with two of your . . . I think, security guards, and a woman, and there was a man you'd caught counting cards. You were threatening him."

"Oh, that," Felix said quietly. "Did that scare you?"

"A little. You seemed—like a different person. Almost cruel."

"Some people deserve it," he said. His hand went to her shoulder, caressed her bare skin. Like it soothed him to touch her, and like it did the opposite, too.

"You're sweet, Mira; I hope you'll always be that way—and I would never want to hurt you. But some people . . ." His hand stilled, and he met her eyes. "No one steals from me—from the casino. I don't allow that."

"So . . . what happened to him?" *Don't stop,* she thought, leaning into him so he would touch her again.

"We sent him home with a slap on the wrist. Will that help you sleep at night? Don't think about it anymore. I mean it—he's not worth your time."

Mira nodded. He'd glossed over her question—but in a way, that was what she wanted. She didn't want to hear the gory details any more than he wanted to tell her. And at this point, she had other things on her mind. Felix had insinuated his thumb under her nightgown's satin strap, and now he slid it over the rounded curve of her shoulder, the satin whispering against her arm as it fell, the bodice straining against her breasts.

The nightgown was tight; she'd had to wriggle to get into it, and it would take the same effort to get it off, but his hands didn't exactly seem discouraged. He bowed his head to kiss her neck, his lips trailing luxuriously over her skin, every nerve in her body startling awake.

Her breath sounded wild in her ears.

Last night, he'd shown her the crumbling ballroom under the stars—and then deposited her in a new hotel room, untouched. As if mindful of the strength he'd stolen.

The strength she had in abundance now.

Two days had passed since he'd kissed her in the flower shop—and he kissed her as if that had been two more than he could stand. She grasped at his hair as his mouth worked its way from her throat to her collarbone and lower, his tongue sending shivers all through her body. Her blood was burning; her dress was disappearing. . . . Her head felt like a feather, airy and light. She wanted to surrender to that feeling . . . but she was afraid to. Her life was precious to her; she didn't want to lose it.

"Who—who were those people you were with?" she asked.

Felix lifted his head and she squirmed away from him, shifting into a less kissable position. His mouth gleamed in the light. His dark blue brows were two puzzled arcs. "What?"

Mira adjusted her nightgown. "The security guards, and that woman, Gretel. Is she Gretel from the fairy tale?"

Felix nodded. "That was Gretel, and her brother, Hansel, and Louis—the Wolf from 'Red Riding Hood.'"

"Friends of yours?"

He studied her, like he wondered what she was up to. But then he must have realized, read it in the flush of her cheeks and the darting of her eyes. "Sure, you could call them that. They were blackballed by the Marked community. So I found a place for them at the Dream."

She'd only meant to interrupt—to delay him until she could think straight—but now she was curious. She'd known there were heroes and villains in the fairy-tale community. She hadn't considered that there might be outcasts.

"Why were they blackballed? I thought Hansel and Gretel were captured by a witch. How is that their fault?"

"It's not their capture that's a problem. Gretel was eleven when she killed the witch . . . in a particularly brutal way. It was self-defense, but she pushed the witch into an oven and she watched her burn. She doesn't feel remorse. She's strong— she had to be, to save herself. And people don't like that; it makes them nervous."

"She likes to hurt people," Mira said, as understanding dawned on her. "That's her job here, isn't it?"

"Let's just say she's fond of retribution."

"And the Wolf? People don't like him because he tried to kill an old woman, too, right? Red Riding Hood's grandmother?"

Felix grimaced, his gaze shifting past her, like he was revisiting a memory that was far too vivid. "He did eat her grandmother—although he never did swallow the girl. A hunter arrived and shot him. Then he cut Louis open to save the old woman, and filled his stomach with rocks and sewed him up again."

"That's torture," Mira said, disgust filling her. "What was the point of torturing him?"

Felix shrugged. "Fairy tales aren't pretty things, Mira. You know that. I'm sure Red Riding Hood thought the hunter was a hero. Anyway," he went on, "Louis would have died—but Gretel and I found him and brought him to Delilah, and she cleaned the rocks out and saved him. That was a few years ago."

"Delilah," Mira murmured. "Weren't you—aren't you—afraid of her?"

"Why would I be afraid of her?"

"Blue's afraid of her," she said.

"No . . ." Felix shook his head. His eyes went distant again. "Delilah has her price—for everything . . . that's true. But Blue isn't afraid of her. Blue's afraid of himself."

～♡ ᧐～

*There was no rest for the wicked.*

*After the party, when all he wanted was to sleep, or to take a page out of Viv's diary and drown himself in the Deneuves' well—his father insisted on a dinner.*

He was shell-shocked, barely able to speak, and he missed her—already, he missed the soft warmth of her in his arms, the brightness of her laugh. He wanted to see her. Wanted to be near her. Wanted to die.

Instead, he sat stiffly, almost catatonically at a table for four in one of the private banquet rooms at Rampion, the Dream's finest restaurant, waiting for their fairy dinner guest to arrive.

His father catered to VIPs every day—but fairies were in a class of their own.

Fairies were revered by the Marked community. Some people courted them, begging for a curse—like Viv's late mother, who'd pricked her finger when she was pregnant and asked for a girl as white as paper, as black as ink, as red as blood, because she wanted her daughter's life to be "dramatic." Then there were families like the Knights, who invited fairies to christenings to bestow virtues on their future heroes and heroines.

But ultimately, fairies had the power—to enchant you, destroy you. It had been that way from the moment fairy and human blood had mixed.

Once upon a time, fairies had been fairies and humans had been humans, and they were as separate as fire and water. Occasionally, a fairy would enchant a worthy human, but for the most part, fairies viewed humans as tedious creatures, as silly as butterflies or bees.

That was before love arrived, and changed everything.

Fairies were female, and solitary. And while they lived a long time, they did not live forever. Every so often, a fairy would seek out an enchanted male—the North Wind, perhaps, or Dawn, Day, or Night, who dragged the hours along on red, white, and black horses—and they would mate to perpetuate their race. They did not fall in love. They were too haughty and proud with each other to be *that vulnerable. And yet love called to them—from a very different place.*

*The fairies and their male counterparts discovered love by observation—by watching humans. They descended from their peaks of isolation, their palaces and clouds, not to interfere or enchant, but to fall in love; and they lay with human men and women for the pleasure of it. Such unions were forbidden, but they were kept secret.*

*Until the half-blood children were born.*

*Their existence was a scandal.*

*The hard-hearted fairies believed the impure offspring had to be punished. The kindhearted fairies fell fast in love with the children—and chose to protect them, to offer them gifts and assistance. They quickly split into factions, for and against.*

*And so the curses began. The tests. Rites of passage. Punishments. Rewards.*

*Happily-ever-afters, and utter ruin.*

*Over the years, as the population of part-human, part-magic children grew, the fairies relaxed their vigilance, choosing to curse some of their mixed-blood descendants, and not others. They groomed them to be heroes or villains—after their own hearts. And because their hearts were involved, even the wickedest fairies could become attached. They saw, in the villains they marked, miniature versions of themselves.*

*Delilah had that sort of affection for Blue's father, because he had made something of himself; he was smart, charismatic, unafraid. She hadn't marked any of the Valentines herself, but she knew Blue's curse had awoken, and she'd invited herself to dinner to celebrate.*

*Blue's father considered it a great honor.*

Delilah arrived twenty minutes late, while Blue's father was sipping champagne and quizzing Felix on something work related. She carried a thin parcel wrapped in silver-black paper and handed it to Felix.

"It's a book of William Faulkner stories," she announced before he could open it. Her eyes slanted like a cat's when she smiled, like Blue's mother's had. "I think you'll like them."

"Thank you," Felix murmured, too polite to show he was puzzled, if he was.

"It was Blue's birthday," Blue's father reminded her—scolding her playfully. "Did you bring him something, too?"

"I hardly think Blue wants another present from my kind," Delilah countered silkily. "He looks like he needs time to recover from the last one."

She smirked, and her expression cut him to the core; because she knew what he had done, and it amused her. Jane, though miraculous to him, was merely human. Barely worthy of the fairy's notice.

Delilah turned to his father, and the two discussed business, and gossiped about other Cursed, other fairies. Felix interjected when appropriate—just enough to show he was following the conversation. Mostly, he stayed silent, only breaking from his polite, attentive pose to unwrap the book under the table, and then to leaf through it out of boredom.

When Delilah ran her black-taloned hand across the back of Felix's neck and up through his hair, like he was her lover instead of a boy centuries her junior, Felix barely even flinched.

"How's Louis?" she asked pointedly.

"Recovering," Felix said, his gaze locked carefully on the book. "Thank you."

Their father laughed, a little drunk from champagne. Like

Felix was an innocent schoolboy Delilah was trying to seduce. Or already had.

Blue watched them through a haze of despair. Emotionally, he felt destroyed—and he clung to that destruction, to remind himself of what he'd done. Because physically . . . he'd never felt better. A delicious energy coursed through him, along with a hunger he'd never known. Because he'd never known what it would be like to give in to what he really was.

He would see a girl now—a laughing girl surrounded by friends, or a tear-streaked mystery girl—and his heart would beat faster, desperate to know her. His lips would burn with the need to kiss her, to feel her pulse throb beneath his lips. Pulse and pulse and drum with the thrill of it—then fade.

He needed love so badly he felt like he would die without it.

And he hoped he would.

# CHAPTER SIXTEEN

WHEN DAWN BROKE, Mira was lying on the couch with Felix, her spine pressed to the couch back, her legs tangled with his. Her skin burned hot when he kissed her, then cold as lost love chilled her veins. Late night rolled into early morning, and Mira's head swam with exhaustion, turned as muzzy as the light outside. Creaking carts and footsteps in the hall announced the new day.

"I should go," Felix whispered, his lips moving against her ear.

"I know." She put a hand out to steady herself, not sure which way was up and which was down; and he lifted her and carried her to the bed. She sank into the mattress, eyes fluttering as he helped her between the sheets.

"Staying?" she murmured. She was heavy . . . everything was . . .

She let her eyes close. *There.*

"Going," he corrected. "But not because I want to." His

fingers brushed her cheek. She mumbled something, a sleepy *mmm*.

That was the last thing she remembered.

She didn't open her eyes again until afternoon. She had a vague memory of trying to get up, and not being strong enough. And before that, she remembered Felix laying her down, pulling the sheets over her . . . but her brain was hazy, and confused.

She blinked at the room around her, and thought: *this is how it will feel one day when I wake up, but I'll have slept for years.*

Last night, she'd forgotten about her curse. She'd been too busy enjoying the present to worry about the future.

But her curse was real. As real as Felix's curse, which had left her woozy and delirious, her love swept up and inhaled like breath.

One day, she might wake and see a stranger hovering over her, a boy on whose kiss her life depended. It wouldn't necessarily be Freddie. She might not know or like her rescuer—but she'd have to be grateful all the same. Everyone she'd known might be dead, and she'd have to rely on a stranger, to whom she was no more than a destiny, a pretty face. . . .

It was a morbid thought to be dwelling on, and she quickly shook it away. No. She'd find out what her trigger was—from Delilah, tonight—and she'd escape her fate.

She was going to have a happy birthday. A sweet sixteen— the sweetest. And that meant keeping her fears in check so they didn't carry over to tomorrow and spoil everything.

She stepped out into the living room of her suite, and the door bumped into something, setting off the soft bobbing rustling of a roomful of helium balloons—and she decided she was off to a good start.

Balloons in every color floated overhead, long ribbons hanging down to tickle her arms as she walked through. A forest of pink, green, purple, yellow—all soft pastels, blown sheer like bubbles.

In the center of the room sat a pile of presents wrapped in rose-print paper. Perched on top of the stack was a card.

"My birthday isn't till tomorrow," Mira murmured as she opened the envelope, happy nonetheless.

She liked birthdays, liked celebrating an existence her god-mothers had taught her never to take for granted. And to wake up to this, to know someone had spent the time thinking of her, planning this, thrilled her more than the actual presents ever could.

The card was made of shimmering paper that said *Happy Birthday* in gold script.

Inside, Felix had written:

*Mira,*
   *I wanted to be the first person to wish you a happy birthday.*
   *Consider this a prelude—and come find me after the show tonight. I'll have another surprise for you then.*
   *Yours,*
   *Felix*

*What kind of surprise?* she wondered. The idea made her feel shivery, anxious, and excited. She set the card aside and moved on to the packages.

Opening the largest box, she pushed aside tufts of tissue paper to reveal an airy chiffon dress, white and patterned with red roses. It was sleeveless, tight at the waist, with a fitted top and a flowing knee-length skirt, sweet and sexy at the same time. She held it to her chest like a dance partner, and spun around in front of the mirror; then rushed back to open the rest.

The medium-size box contained a pair of red high-heeled shoes with roses on the toes.

And inside the smallest box was a teardrop-shaped bottle of perfume. She removed the stopper and the scent of roses wafted out.

By the time she'd finished trying on the shoes and the dress and dancing around the suite, it was time to get ready. Tonight was the night she would seize who she really was. Armored in roses, she'd discover her trigger—her secret weakness—and she'd see Blue and she would *behave*. And tomorrow . . . tomorrow she'd be a new person.

Mira dressed for the Curses & Kisses show like she was dressing for a ball.

She zipped into her new dress, dabbed rose perfume on her wrists, stepped into the red heels. She left her hair loose, hanging in long waves down her back.

The club was packed by the time she arrived. The opening act was onstage, the clash of their instruments making her ears ache. As she made her way through the crowd, she felt ridiculously conspicuous: most of the audience members were wearing jeans, miniskirts, tank tops, T-shirts. She was dressed for a garden party, not a night of thrashing in a grimy club.

Some wolfish guys leered and brushed against her, like it was clear she was an outsider.

Feeling dirty from the stares and the occasional anonymous hand, Mira pushed through to the greenroom, where Blue and his bandmates were hanging out, waiting to go on. The greenroom had all the charm of a garage: it was floored with concrete, too hot, and smelled like stale popcorn and wine. It was made even less charming by the sight of Rafe tossing jelly beans into a blonde girl's cleavage, while two other girls giggled appreciatively at his efforts.

Blue was lounging on a green couch, his arms stretched along the back. He had a drumstick in each hand, and was absently banging them on the couch back.

Mira was too nervous to talk to him right away. She wanted to treat him like she treated Freddie—not like someone she'd almost kissed, someone she hoped liked her dress and thought she looked pretty. And she felt too out of sorts to do that.

So she went over to Henley, who liked her about as much as most people liked being set on fire, and could be counted on to knock her off whatever syrupy cloud she was floating on.

Henley was sitting backward on a beat-up wooden chair, tipped back on two legs. He was watching Viv, who was sharing a pair of headphones with Jewel and bobbing to the beat in black boots, a denim miniskirt, and a white tank top with a red splotch over the heart, like a bloodstain.

"What role are you playing tonight?" Mira asked. "Chauffeur, chaperone, ex-boyfriend?"

"Chaperone," he said. "Her stepmom asked me to look out for her. Viv tends to party too hard. And she holds her liquor about as well as a nine-year-old."

"She weighs about as much as a nine-year-old."

"Exactly." Henley squinted at her. "What about you?"

Mira looked around, flustered, hair swinging heavily as she moved. "What about me what?"

Henley sighed and let the chair thunk to the floor. "What role are *you* playing? Felix's underage girlfriend, Blue's obsession, or Freddie's princess?"

"That's . . . rude," she said.

"It was rude when you asked me, too." He coughed and dug around for the pack of cigarettes in his pocket. "That piece of wisdom is yours free. Happy birthday."

"Uh, thanks," she said, taking that as her signal that the conversation was over. Well . . . she supposed her sappy birthday bubble had officially been popped. Maybe it was okay to talk to Blue now. At least to wish him luck. Or tell him to break both his legs.

He was already watching her anyway. He'd definitely noticed the dress.

"You dressed like a goddess just to hurt me," Blue said when she was close enough to hear, driving a drumstick toward his heart like a stake.

"I did not," she said, flushing with embarrassment. "Um, so, I have news."

Blue raised an eyebrow. "Yeah? Good news?"

"My p—" The momentousness of the announcement made her gulp down a breath and try again. "My parents—Felix found them. I have their phone number and everything."

"Ah, Felix." Blue flipped a drumstick and caught it. "Good old Felix. He's swell."

"Don't be mean."

He reached out and took her hand, like an apology. "It's cool that you found your parents. Did you talk to them yet?"

"Not yet. I'm trying to figure out what to say. And I guess I don't want to rush it. In case it's not what I hoped for, you know? I want to keep this feeling a little while longer."

"Do you need me to psych you up for it? Tell you how awesome you are so you believe it when you call?"

His fingers tightened around hers and she smiled. "I'll be okay. I'm just giving it time to sink in. It's still kind of surreal."

"Well, if things get awkward and you want to play the sympathy card, just tell them what kind of friends you've made in their absence. They'll be horrified, and spend the rest of their lives making it up to you. Trust me."

"Thanks," she said. "I'll keep that in mind."

They'd moved on to talking about whether Blue got stage fright, when a half-naked Freddie showed up. He was bare-chested and wearing jeans, and was in the process of turning a black T-shirt right side out. His normally perfect honey brown hair was now meticulously mussed, like someone had told him how to be a rock star and he'd done his best to meet them halfway.

"Hi, Mira," he said warmly. "I'm glad you could make it."

There was nothing strained in his smile, nothing fake about the kindness in his eyes.

She was shocked.

It was as if they'd never argued. Mira had been nervous that Freddie would hate her . . . but maybe, once he'd had some time to think about it, he'd realized that she hadn't meant to hurt him. That their relationship was just as frustrating and confusing to her as it was to him. For whatever reason, he was giving her another chance. And she was grateful. She met his smile with one of her own.

"Knight, stop flaunting your body," Blue said. "Mira's going to start thinking of you as a piece of meat."

"Mira can think whatever she wants about me," Freddie said, tugging the shirt over his head. "I consider it an honor that she thinks of me at all."

Blue laughed. "You're such a kiss ass."

"I am not!" Freddie insisted, sounding hurt.

"Freddie's just being inhumanly nice," Jewel said, coming up behind them and laying her hand on Freddie's shoulder. "As is his way. Hey, Mira. Sorry to interrupt, but I need Blue to get changed. We go on in ten minutes."

"Fine," Blue said, sighing like this was the most unreasonable interruption in the world. Jewel patted him lightly on his spikes.

"Thanks, Blue-noxious."

"Mira, I'm about to be naked," Blue said as he whipped off his belt and tossed it on the floor. "So watch out. Well, in my underwear."

"I've seen you in your bathing suit," Mira said. "It's the same thing."

"It is not the same thing," Blue said. "When it's accompanied by seventies porn music, it's an X-rated strip show." Blue yanked off his shirt. "Freddie, you're kind of slow on the uptake. *Eine kleine* porn music, please."

Freddie scrunched his forehead in distaste. "I don't want to plug my guitar in just so I can play some bow-chicka-wow-wow accompaniment to your strip show."

Mira laughed. "Bow-chicka-what was that, Freddie?"

"Bow-chicka . . ." Freddie flushed as he realized she was teasing him.

Blue kicked off his scrubby jeans, then proceeded to pull on the newer, neater, rock-starrier clothes that Jewel had brought over: jeans that had been distressed by the manufacturer instead of by real wear, and a black T-shirt printed with a silver heart bound in barbed wire.

Mira tried to convince herself that seeing Blue in boxers *was* just like seeing him in his bathing suit. But . . . it was different, more intimate. She'd wrestled with him; she knew what his body felt like, knew the hard feel of his muscles when he fought her playfully, when he laughed . . . when he almost kissed her. It was impossible to look at him and not see all of that. Impossible to look at him and not feel like he was hers.

*But he isn't. And he can't be.*

She swallowed, ashamed of herself, and turned away. She let her gaze drift across the room, like Rafe's jelly-bean harem was really fascinating.

Freddie came to her rescue. "Are you staying after the show, Mira? Will we see you later?"

"I think so," she said. "Unless the agony of listening to you guys drives me away." When Freddie did his sad puppy face, she grinned and swatted his arm. "Just kidding. Of course I'm staying. I need someone to walk me home."

"That would be me," Blue said. "Just meet us back here after the show. Or wait by the door if you get kicked out early for brawling."

"That's probably what will happen," Mira said.

"I figured," Blue said. "Just don't run off, okay?" He was

buckling his belt, but he looked up at her very seriously. "Make sure I see you."

"I will," she said. "Go ahead and get ready. I'll see you guys later! Don't screw up!"

She hurried out of the greenroom to join the audience, feeling lighter than she had in days.

The club was as dark as a pit, an abyss with a single spotlight. Stage lights illuminated the band, but only faintly. Most of the glow was on Jewel, who glistened with sweat, glittering like the gems that fell from her lips: sharp and raw and gorgeous.

The music was violent, explosive—like it wanted to make people bleed, or inspire them to break things. The crowd writhed to Rafe's snarly bass line, smashed into each other, screamed along. And when the song ended, and Jewel dropped to her knees and let a stream of pearls spill from her mouth to the stage, the audience shrieked with pleasure, hands scrabbling to claim a handful of the pearls that had touched her lips.

Magic was what they came for.

Mira felt light-headed, dizzy from the noise, overwhelmed by the crowd. She didn't want to be nicked by a sharp piece of jewelry or a safety pin—on the odd chance it would trigger sleep. She needed to find Delilah, and find out about her curse. This not knowing was no good.

Elbows out for protection, Mira pushed through the crowd: past girls in red capes, girls who smelled of the sea; past boys with vine tattoos and ash-smeared fireplace princesses. She shoved past one body only to be confronted with another. She practically had to swim through them to escape.

Once she'd broken free, she rubbed her hands over her bare arms. Still perfectly intact.

At the edge of the room, Wills and Caspian Knight leaned against the wall with the air of college guys back in town for a high school dance. Viv was with them, rhinestone stars sparkling in her black hair. They beckoned her over, but Mira declined. She had a mission she wouldn't be swayed from. A darker destination.

She had secrets to uncover.

The corridor leading to the rear of the club was crammed with overaccessorized girls and guys flicking lighters in the dark. She turned at a fork in the path and picked her way down an unlit hall—one none of the club kids dared venture into—until she reached Delilah's office. A strip of acid green light showed under the door.

Mira knocked. Her ears were ringing from the music; her breaths came with effort and she was shaking. In a moment, she'd know what to be afraid of. She'd know what could hurt her most.

Delilah's ogre henchman opened the door, his gray face wrinkling at the sudden onslaught of noise, then gripped her shoulder and hauled her inside. The scent of garlic and boiled meat rose from his pores. Mira held her breath and tugged free, but she could still feel the pressure of his palm as she moved away, as if his hand were clamped on her skin.

With the door shut, the office was surprisingly quiet. The bass thumped despite the soundproofing, but it was low enough that she could hear the ogre's breathing, could hear Delilah's long black nails scraping papers off her desk.

Delilah glanced up, her eyes gleaming a pale gold like ginger ale.

"Mirabelle Lively," she said. "You came seeking your trigger. And I have it, as promised." With a smile, the fairy drew a slender gauze bundle from a drawer, about the size of a small cocoon, hanging from a silver chain. "Come closer."

"Don't be frightened," the fairy said. "There will be no accidents here."

Tentatively, her ears still ringing, Mira approached her. Delilah held the bundled pendant by its chain, her long fingers unwinding the gauze wrapping until a razor blade shined in the greenish light. A hole had been punched through the blade, and the chain threaded through it, to turn the razor blade into a necklace.

Mira let out a gasp. This tiny thing. This everyday object. All she had to do was press the tip of her finger to the sharp edge.

One drop of blood. One bite of pain.

And that would be it.

"Your predecessors are many," Delilah mused, letting the razor blade sway at the end of the chain. "Talia, who fell victim to a splinter of flax and slept, even as a king claimed her, and only awoke when her children were born. *La belle au bois dormant*, who pricked her finger on a spindle and slept for one hundred years, until her prince arrived to rouse her. Brünnhilde the Valkyrie, sent into slumber by a prick from a sleep-thorn, and trapped within a ring of fire until she was freed by a fearless mortal. Briar Rose, plunged into enchanted sleep by the spindle, but awakened by true love's kiss.

"And now you join them, Mirabelle. Just one prick of a razor blade," the fairy continued, "and you'll succumb to an enchanted slumber for however long it takes your prince to find you. Assuming he still wants to find you," she added with a thin smile. "Men are fickle. Never fear, the curses will keep making princes. I'm sure that in the next hundred years, one of them will release you. But better to be safe. Don't you think?"

Mira nodded. So she would avoid razors—she'd been doing that anyway; they fell on her godmothers' do-not-touch list, along with nearly everything normal people used: scissors, earrings, matches.

Her godmothers hadn't left anything to chance. They'd forbidden so many things it had never occurred to her to single out one of their prohibitions and question it. No one forbidden activity had seemed so tempting that she'd be driven mad if she didn't try it just once.

Her godmothers had underestimated only one of her desires: to see her parents. It had been the one rule she'd been desperate—or maybe destined—to break.

Delilah rewrapped the razor blade, dulling the sharp edge with layers of gauze, until it was as harmless as the cotton that covered it. Delilah ran it across the flesh of her own wrist to demonstrate. "There. Perfectly safe. It's yours to do with as you wish."

"I don't want it," Mira said, taken aback.

Delilah held her gaze. Her pale gold eyes flickered like candle flames. "But it belongs to you. How can you refuse it?"

Without asking permission, the fairy draped the chain around Mira's neck.

The gauze-wrapped razor blade settled against her chest.

Its presence made her heart beat faster, as if the blade would somehow escape its bindings—and seal her fate.

"Now that you know your trigger, you can keep yourself safe," Delilah said. "It's the secrets that hurt us most."

The metal felt cold against Mira's chest—though she knew she was imagining it. There was nothing to feel. Just the innocuous softness of the gauze. It was her imagination, her old talent for daydreams, working against her now.

"You never know what people are hiding—that's the problem. Once you know, you can find a way to deal with anything. But so long as you're kept ignorant, the situation is hopeless. Poor thing." Delilah clucked her tongue. "That's been your lot since you arrived, hasn't it? Everyone hinting at secrets, talking over your head—that must be miserable. You're so strong to have endured it. But you have practice, I suppose— having the truth hidden from you. It probably doesn't even bother you anymore." She pursed her lips, lemon-sour. "Poor thing."

Heat was rising at the back of Mira's neck, creeping up her cheeks like a stain. She didn't like the way Delilah was look- ing at her, full of pity, as if she were a child content to go on knowing nothing.

"It does bother me," she said. "For your information."

"Nonsense," Delilah said. "If it did, you'd have done something about it. All the answers are within your reach. You just have to look for them. Don't you know the first thing about fairy tales, Mirabelle? *No one*"—the fairy leaned in, her breath smelling of green apples—"is going to spoon-feed you the answers. A curse is as much about courage as it is about growth. They're one and the same."

"I have looked. I've asked Blue about our marks. I've asked Layla about our roles; she showed me the book that explains them. But there are certain things no one is allowed to tell me, because it's part of the curse, which *you* should know—"

Delilah held up a hand to silence her. "You already have the key to answer all your questions about the Valentines. And I'm not being mysterious when I say that. You have the actual, physical key, Mirabelle. If you desire answers, you simply have to open the door."

Mira knew Felix had secrets. A past that was too painful for him to talk about, flaws he didn't want to reveal. And she'd accepted that. She hadn't liked it—she wanted to know him inside and out—but she'd backed down, because that was what he wanted. Because she was happy—and she wanted him to be happy, too.

But how long could they last if she didn't really know him?

Maybe he was afraid she'd change her mind if she knew his secrets, if he let her down. And it was true that she wanted him to be perfect. She didn't want to believe he was dangerous. Whatever Blue and his friends said about Felix, it wasn't true when he was with *her*.

And yet . . .

He'd never told her the truth. Never warned her what a Romantic could do, though it was within his power to tell her. And she had to admit . . . that her willingness to overlook the danger didn't mean it wasn't there.

Mira had spent her whole life daydreaming things into being, existing in a fantasy world to escape a reality she found painful. But there was a real world she wanted to be a part of now. And if she were ever going to belong, she needed to see every side of it. The good and the bad.

The safe parts . . . and the dangerous parts.

In the main arena of the club, Curses & Kisses was playing harder than ever. The stage was littered with gems. Jewel's husky-sweet voice had gone almost hoarse. Blue pounded away at his drums like he wanted to break them.

Too impatient to be controlled by the flow of the crowd, Mira shoved through with fresh determination, until she reached the vacant greenroom. Blue's street clothes lay in a jumble on the floor. She rifled through his pockets until she found his wallet, and the passkey he'd stolen from her—and she reclaimed it. Curled her fingers around the plastic card like it was her lifeline.

Felix had written in a note to her:

*All I ask is that you stay out of my other room (suite 3013). I keep some private things there that must not be disturbed.*

And she'd obeyed. She was a good girl, used to being told *don't do this, don't touch that.*

But following the rules, sweeping questions under the rug, and pretending everything was fine didn't get you anywhere. You had to be bold. *Bold, but not too bold,* she thought. There was a balance.

There was one thing Felix had denied her. One prohibition he'd set down—which made it something to fixate on and wonder about.

What was so secret about suite 3013?

He'd said it was private. That he wanted it left alone.

And if he'd told her about it . . . he'd told her for a reason.

Maybe, like the razor blade, the prohibition was for her own good.

Or maybe, like her godmothers' forbidding her to visit Beau Rivage, it was keeping her from learning something she desperately needed to know.

You couldn't hide from bad things and pretend they didn't exist—that left you with a dream world, and dream worlds eventually crumbled. You had to face the truth. And then decide what you wanted.

Perfume and fancy clothes were wonderful. But she needed more than that.

This last broken rule, she decided . . . would be her birthday gift to herself.

# CHAPTER SEVENTEEN

MIRA LEFT THE CLUB AFTER MIDNIGHT, while Curses &
Kisses was still playing. Boys in wolf fur–lined jackets loitered
outside, the tips of their cigarettes glowing like fireflies. Trails
of smoke made her cough; the humidity made her skin feel
liquid. She ran in her red-rose high heels, clacking through the
streets, too fast and frantic to care what lurked in the shadows
around her. Nothing could be worse than the uncertainty, the
shadows that lurked in her heart.

By the time she reached the Dream, sweat ran down her sides,
her thighs, her throat. Her feet were throbbing because she'd
been running in boutique heels, not dance heels. These shoes
weren't meant for action; they were meant for someone who
stood still and looked pretty. Someone who fell asleep and
dreamed.

But Mira refused to be trapped in a daydream. It was
time to face the raw things. Not her fantasy of Felix—the

best parts of him, the parts he wanted her to see—but all of him.

He didn't have to be perfect. Life didn't have to be perfect to be wonderful.

It just had to be real.

The Dream was buzzing with life—the dinging of slot machines, the cheering at the craps tables, dealers slapping down cards with practiced speed, cocktail waitresses parting the crowd. It was a party, an all-night, glittering party.

Felix would be in the pit, supervising, checking in with and charming VIPs. Nights weren't time for quiet work, or whatever went on in suite 3013. She could be in and out in ten minutes, see what there was to see, and if she didn't like it—if Felix was as bad, as dangerous as everyone seemed to think—she could disappear and never come back. If all was well, she'd slip out, and Felix would never know.

Her heart pounded painfully as she stepped up to the suite elevators and pushed the call button, watching her reflection in the polished metal doors until they split apart and took her image with them.

Mira had the elevator to herself. The air-conditioning had dried the sweat on her skin but not her dress, and the damp chiffon felt slick and dirty. Soft music played as she rose to the thirtieth floor, where she stepped out into a corridor that was an exact copy of every other corridor in the hotel. Except this floor was empty. Dead silent, no people—it might as well have been a ghost town.

Following the signs, Mira hurried all the way to the end of the hall, where she found suite 3013. The door was plain, marked only with a gold placard engraved with the room number. It was tucked away near the fire exit, in about the most unpleasant place in the entire hall.

Taking one last look around her, Mira slid the passkey into the lock, waited for the green light to flicker and signal *open*, then turned the lever and stepped into the forbidden room.

In the dark, suite 3013 smelled like Felix's cologne. It smelled icy, like frigid air.

And it smelled like roses.

It was the roses that gave Mira the courage to turn on the light. Because that was his theme for her birthday: roses for Sleeping Beauty. Maybe he'd kept her away from this room because he'd been planning a surprise here—for just the two of them.

As the light came on and the room blinked into view, Mira saw that the suite was different from the other rooms in the hotel. The sea blue color scheme had given way to white. White couch. White carpet. Shimmering white wallpaper, etched with ivory swirls. There were potted red rosebushes on the end tables, and a vase of red roses on the desk, along with a list of the birthday presents Felix planned to give her—all delivered, all crossed out except for *Dinner at Rampion* and the word *Dancing*.

Mira smiled. So this was his secret. This was where he plotted romance.

The walls were hung with art, like in a gallery. It wasn't the collection of mass-produced seascapes found in the rest of the rooms; these were originals, some too rough and strange to be anything else. The largest piece was a misty spring landscape, with a castle in the distance, all purples and greens. There were smaller, less accomplished paintings, too, along with framed pencil drawings that looked like they'd been torn out of sketchbooks—even a sketch of a boy looking down, flipping a poker chip between his fingers . . . a boy who looked like Felix.

Mira checked for a signature on the drawings, but couldn't find one.

Moving to his desk, Mira opened all the drawers, sifted through blank pages of monogrammed stationery, souvenir postcards from around the world (all signed by his father), scattered trinkets, and an old, tarnished key. At the bottom of one of the drawers, she found a photograph lying facedown. Someone had written *Felix 6, Blue 2* on the back in blue ink.

Mira pried the photo out carefully, expecting to see a snapshot of the two brothers. But the boys weren't alone. There was a young woman in the picture.

All three were posed on a bench, in front of a cluster of bushes and a dusty elephant exhibit—the zoo? Felix had a big, guileless smile on his face. He was hanging on the woman like a monkey, his arms around her neck, hugging her. Blue sat on her lap, looking pouty and chubby and confused, clutching a bag of cotton candy. The woman had an arm around each of them, and there was enough of a resemblance that Mira was sure this was their mother.

She was pretty, reed slender, a little gangly, and a little chic. Her straight black hair was half gathered on her head in a messy bun, while the rest hung loose. Her smile—amused and exasperated—reached all the way to her eyes.

She looked like she loved them. She also looked pale, and tired. Like someone who'd been sick. Only, Mira didn't think that was it. . . .

She remembered the way she used to throw herself at Elsa

and Bliss when she was little, how clingy and affectionate she'd been. And she imagined, if you were a Romantic, the toll that affection would take on someone who loved you more than anything in the world.

Felix and Blue wouldn't have had any control back then. They probably hadn't even known what they were. They'd just loved her. And they were dangerous.

That was why their mother had left. Not because she was afraid of getting attached, like Felix had said. Not exactly.

Mira swallowed. She put the picture back in the drawer. She felt like she'd disturbed something precious, blown dust off a secret she wasn't meant to see. A loss Felix wanted to hide even from himself.

There were no warning signs here, no boxes full of mementoes from old girlfriends, no red flags. Felix was just private. He spent so much time being available to the public, attending to the Dream's guests, that he wanted a room for himself, and only himself. A room he didn't have to see every day.

Mira felt a little guilty disturbing that privacy—but glimpsing these pieces of his private life, and the small things he valued enough to save, only made her love him more. So she felt like it was worth it. Even if he ended up getting mad at her.

Her last stop was the bedroom. The door was ajar, darkness showing through the opening—and the fresh rose scent seemed stronger here. She pressed the door open with one finger, her heart pounding nervously as she wondered whether the bedroom would be specially decorated—maybe even with rose petals scattered across the bed. Because he *had* said he had another surprise for her. And she wasn't sure if she was ready for that. . . .

A triangle of light crept in as the door eased open. Just enough for her to make out a figure in the dark.

Her heartbeat flooded her ears, pounded around her head like a fist. "Felix?" she called. "Are you there? Did you know I would—?"

But there was no answer. No movement. Whoever it was remained as still as a statue.

"Felix?"

She pushed the door open farther—until it thumped against an obstruction. Light flowed over the rest of the room. And she saw.

It was a girl.

A perfectly still, glassy-eyed girl.

And there wasn't just one.

Cora, the girl Mira had seen with Felix that first night, was slumped in a chair, her wide eyes on the door, staring at who-ever had the gall to enter. Her brown hair was a mess, and she wore the same green dress she'd worn when Mira met her. One arm hung limply over the side of the chair. Her head was propped against the headrest. Red lipstick clung to the edges of her lips.

Barely a week ago, Cora had sauntered through the lobby and spotted Mira in the garden. She'd had a sure look about her, sharp but lovely. And now she was blank. She stared and stared but there was nothing in her expression. No life. Her eyes were as empty as marbles.

"Cora?" Mira's throat constricted; she blinked away tears, her hand trembling on the knob. "It's me—Mira. Please say something. . . ."

But even as she spoke, she knew the girl wouldn't answer. Because Cora wasn't just one girl coldly holding court over the bedroom. She was part of a whole menagerie of lifeless girls.

A blonde in a slinky nightgown was curled up on the floor beside the bed. A dark-haired girl, dressed in pants and a thin T-shirt, lay with her head tipped back like she was waiting to be resuscitated, or kissed. She had bruises on her wrists.

Girls lay on couches. On the floor. Some were elegantly arranged, limbs posed to capture their beauty. Others were crammed wherever they would fit, like the room was a too-small suitcase someone had grown tired of packing. They wore evening gowns, tank tops and jeans, pajamas, blouses that had been torn open.

And at the center of the room stood the bed, neatly made with a thick white coverlet. Potted rosebushes stood sentinel on each bedside table, giving off a rich, morbid fragrance. Scattered across the bed were loose pages from an old book. They were yellowed, curling at the corners. And left there deliberately, like bread crumbs: pieces of a secret that could finally be revealed.

Shaking, Mira gathered the pages. This was his tale. The curse they hid from her.

The first page bore an illustration: a well-dressed man in a richly appointed mansion, presenting a ring of keys to an eager young girl. Mira's breath left her at the sight of the man's blue hair, his sharply pointed blue beard. He looked like a devil and a king both.

The next page featured the title.

*Bluebeard*

She didn't know this fairy tale.

Her eyes hurried down the page, missing entire lines, like the frantic beating of her heart had swallowed them—and she had to go back. Breath hard in her chest, she read.

In the tale, a man with a blue beard sought a wife. Women found his strange coloring repulsive, but he was wealthy, and eventually, the girl he was wooing was won over by his gifts and his attention, and agreed to marry him.

About a month into their marriage, Bluebeard was called away on business. Before he left, he gave his young bride a ring of keys that gave her access to everything in his mansion. Every door, every chest of jewels. They were the keys to his wealth, and more.

But there was one door his bride was forbidden to open: a little closet at the end of the great gallery.

*"Open them all; go into all and every one of them, except that little closet, which I forbid you, and forbid it in such a manner that, if you happen to open it, there's nothing but what you may expect from my just anger and resentment."*

His wife promised she would never enter the forbidden room, and Bluebeard embraced her and bid her farewell.

But as soon as Bluebeard had gone, his young wife rushed to the forbidden room, so rapidly that she nearly stumbled and broke her neck.

She unlocked the door and stepped inside—and there, in the forbidden chamber, were all the bodies of Bluebeard's former wives, the floor covered with their clotted blood. The young wife fled in horror, but not before dropping the little key on the ground, whereupon it was stained with blood, as if by magic, and no amount of scrubbing or scouring would remove the stain.

The rest of the tale unfolded as fairy tales did: Bluebeard returned home early and discovered his wife's trespass. He vowed to punish her, and took out his sword to cut off her head. There would be no mercy.

*"You were resolved to go into the closet, were you not? Mighty well, madam; you shall go in, and take your place among the ladies you saw there."*

In the end, the young wife was saved. Her brothers arrived just in time to interrupt the murder, and to slay Bluebeard.

But there was a room full of women who didn't have anyone to save them. Who had heard the words *you shall take your place among them* from Bluebeard's lips, and been cruelly murdered for their discovery.

Mira didn't want to believe it.

There was no blood on the floor, no blood anywhere. She crept toward Cora and touched the girl's shoulder, wincing as she did. Maybe it was an enchantment. *Please let it be an enchantment. . . .*

The girl's skin was cold.

Mira pushed harder, as if to force her awake, and Cora toppled off the chair. Mira cried out; she stumbled back to keep the girl from falling on her.

Coming closer, Mira knelt and touched Cora's neck, searching for a pulse.

Nothing. Nothing. Nothing.

None of the girls was asleep, drugged, playing, waiting.

They were dead.

They had been loved here. Killed here.

And some—some had tried to escape. Their torn clothes and bruises were testament to that.

"But it was too late," Mira whispered. The forbidden room was a trap.

Mira wondered how he'd done it. Not with a sword—that was where the tale diverged from the reality. Felix was a Romantic; he had another weapon at his disposal.

Had he kissed their mouths, slow and soft? Had his lips brushed their throats like vampire bites, each touch siphoning away more life? Had he—had he—?

She couldn't let her mind go further. It hurt her to see the evidence, the years of seductions. She was crying and choking, wiping her eyes whenever the tears blinded her, refusing to let anything hide the truth from her now. She wanted to be horrified. It seemed sick to be jealous, too, but she *was*. It hurt to know he'd loved so many other girls; that she was not special, not unique.

He hadn't pressured her when they'd spent the night together. She'd thought it was because he was a gentleman. But of course he hadn't pushed her; he didn't have to. He knew this moment would come. When she'd need to know him—all of him.

A night when he would claim all of her.

No. Not tonight. Not her.

Mira turned from the room, her heart in her throat, love and sadness making it hard to breathe. She loved him. She really loved him—even in the face of this, she wanted to somehow deny it, make excuses for him. She was full of emotion and her heart ached like it would kill her.

She would go. She would run away and never come back. Leave her books behind, her clothes behind, her friends, her memories.

But not her life.

At the door, her hand on the knob—she heard the lock buzz open from the outside. She fumbled for the deadbolt—panicking even more when she saw how many locks there were: bolts and chains and—but the door swung toward her and knocked her out of the way.

Mira stumbled backward, red roses blooming on the toes of her worthless, pretty shoes, and faced him, on the dawn of her sixteenth birthday. Felix seemed sad, fierce, perversely loving, and angry.

But not at all surprised.

"I didn't mean—Felix—You don't understand—" she stammered, fighting to explain, to save herself, with a mind that had gone completely blank.

"Oh, Mira." He shook his head, eyes burning with emotion; raked a trembling hand through his hair. "You had to come here." His mouth was caught between a grimace and a tight line of pain.

"I just got here," she swore, so vehemently she nearly believed herself. "I didn't see anything. I didn't touch anything. I just—let's go to dinner. Please. Or I can leave. If you want me to leave forever, I can leave—"

"I know exactly when you arrived, and exactly what you did," he snapped. "I don't need a bloody key to tell me that. This is a casino; we don't trust anyone. We have surveillance like you can't imagine."

Mira's eyes spilled over with tears. Admissions of guilt. *Damn it.* She wanted to stay cool and calm and lie, but she couldn't. She *couldn't.* The bedroom was full of girls he'd murdered and he was going to kill her next.

Something seemed to break in him when he saw her cry—but not the right thing. He was sorry—sorry for himself most of all—but nowhere in his face did she see mercy.

She moved toward him, hoping she could reason with him; grabbed the front of his jacket. "Felix—you have to let me go."

He sounded weary. "I can't, Mira. I can't let you leave this room. Don't you understand?"

She didn't understand; she *refused* to understand.

The door was behind him. If she could get past him, fling it open, run—

She lunged for the door and he caught her easily; shoved her hard and sent her sprawling to the floor. Her skin flared red where it scraped the carpet; her elbow throbbed from banging into the desk. He'd never been forceful with her before, and the violence was a shock, even now.

Mira staggered to her feet—her hope dying as he turned his back to her and started securing the locks on the door. It was like a switch had been flipped in him; he seemed to grow calmer as he went through the motions. His hands shook less with every lock.

"I never wanted you to see this part of me," Felix said. "I *tried* to be better for you. But this is what I am. When it comes down to it—this is all I am."

"No," she insisted. "It isn't. It can't be. *I love you*."

A strange look came over his face—mournful, affectionate, resigned.

"I know," he said. "They all did."

And then he pulled her into his arms, seizing her with such determination that her struggle collapsed almost before it began. A few days ago, she'd been so weak from his kisses

273

in the flower shop she'd barely been able to walk; now the strength she'd regained wilted beneath his. And like a conquering hero, or a bridegroom—or a lover-murderer—he carried her unwilling body to the bed.

He threw her down on the white coverlet and wasted no time climbing over her, pinning her down to keep her from escaping. The dead girls surrounded them, frozen in their positions, a limp, uninterested audience.

Mira's gaze swept the room, taking in every macabre detail. It was like staring at a wreck; she couldn't tear herself away—until Felix laid his hand over her eyes. "Don't look," he whispered, his breath hot against her ear. "You don't need to see them."

He'd released one of her wrists to cover her eyes, and now she reached for him, her hand trembling over his features. He cared about her—she knew he did. If she could just get through to him . . .

"You don't want to do this," she said. "I know you don't."

Felix grasped her hand, pried it away from him, and flattened her arm against the bed. His eyes bore down on her, sorry but hard.

"If what I wanted mattered," he said, "this room wouldn't exist. This *curse* wouldn't exist. I want to be happy—to have a real chance at that, like everyone else. And I could, if someone would just *listen*.

"Mira," he whispered. "Why does no one ever listen?"

"I don't know!" she cried. And then she remembered that it wasn't her fault; she could explain. She hadn't even wanted to come here. "The fairy! Delilah. She said I should—"

"It doesn't matter." His voice was gentle, tinged with pain, with the regret that had seeped out sometimes when he was with her. "There's one innocent person in this room. And it isn't me, and it isn't you."

*The first girl,* she thought. The girl whose death had been an accident, before there'd been a forbidden room to invade, a secret to uncover.

Before his curse had broken him.

*Love destroys you,* he'd said once, and this was what he'd meant. She hadn't thought it would destroy her, too.

*You shall go in, and take your place among the ladies you saw there. . . .*

"You can't keep me here," she said, holding very still, as if he were an animal that would attack if she moved.

"You're wrong. I have to keep you here." His hands clamped around her wrists, and his grip was so strong it felt like he could crush her if he wanted to. He was so much stronger than she was. He had his own strength and he had all the strength he'd stolen. "Don't fight me. Don't make this harder."

"You expect me to just—lie here and *die?*" She strained against him, struggled to break his hold, to throw him off her. The skin of her wrists twisted, chafed in the shackles of his hands. Her shoulders surged upward, her legs fought against his weight. But he kept her pinned, as if it took no effort at all. The body she'd once loved to be close to was now a prison she couldn't escape. At last, she lay still, sweat slicking her skin, panting, her wrists aching.

Felix didn't seem angry that she'd tried to free herself. He knew she wasn't going anywhere.

And now she knew it, too.

Mira turned her face away so she wouldn't see the decision in his eyes. There had to be a part of him that loved her enough to listen. "If you care about me," she said, "just let me go and I'll never tell anyone, I swear to god, I'll never—"

He stretched her arms above her head, laid his cheek against hers, so that his body covered her like a shroud. All she could see, all she could feel was him. "I would have done anything for you," he said. "Anything you'd asked. But this— Mira, stopping this, sparing you . . . that's the one thing I can't do. I'm sorry. . . ."

He was really going to—

She screamed—for help, mercy, anything—and he kissed her, his lips pressing hard on hers until the sound died in her throat.

The world turned gray for an instant, flickered with stars, like static. Felix kept kissing her—hard at first, and then softer as she stopped resisting, his lips as gentle as water, lovely and romantic, like this was a special night. More precious than a first time—because it was the last.

He ran his hands over her body, and there was something dizzying about his touch, something that made it easy to give in to, and hard to breathe. The softest death imaginable. She arched her back, and he bent his head to kiss her throat; and it was wonderful, like it always was—she never wanted it to end. It was horrible—it *would* end, and her world would end with it. She didn't want to lose him; didn't want to lose everything.

She hated that he could provoke these emotions in her, even when he was hurting her. *Murdering* her. She hated that her heart would fail her before it would fail him.

When Felix lifted up on his elbows to look at her, his

face swam above her like a mirage. She wanted him to stop. Wanted him to touch her again, so softly, but to say it was all a lie. That he could forgive her for intruding, for uncovering his secret. That he was sorry for every horrible thing he'd done—and he'd never do them again. He could change for her.

He brushed the tears from her cheeks, and the tenderness of his touch was like a language she didn't understand. "It was so hard," he confessed. "So hard to let you go once I knew you loved me. The feeling was so beautiful, so addictive . . . but I held back. I wanted to have something real with you. But you wouldn't let me. You had to be like everyone else. And ruin this . . ."

She'd always trusted Felix not to go too far, not to hurt her—even once she knew he already had. She'd forgiven his trespasses without an apology, any acknowledgment on his part that he'd done something wrong.

But he refused to forgive hers.

This time, he wouldn't hold back. He was going to take everything.

Felix kissed a farewell path along her body. Every touch stole her warmth, weakened the thread that bound her to life, that made her aware of the bed beneath her, and his weight above her, the scent of his cologne, the rasp of his breath as he coaxed yet another wisp of life from her body. His hair hung in his face, disheveled, wild, so different from before.

"At least you'll have your happy ending," he murmured. "I can give you that. This won't hurt. It will be . . . just like the other times. And I'll always love you. I'll never forget you. . . ."

"No . . ." she said feebly. "This isn't happy, Felix—please don't do this. . . ."

"You'll be happier than I'll be when this is done. At least you can know love without having to destroy it. I have to go on. I have to keep playing this game until someone listens. And we both know . . . no one ever will. No one ever does. This has to be your happy ending, Mira. Because this is the only ending you have."

Life and love swept away from her like a wave pulled into the sea. It was all Mira could do to hold on to consciousness.

She'd struggled at first—but she'd long since stopped fighting. One kiss and her resistance began to drain away; two and the weakness, the strange euphoria set in. Three kisses and panic warred with resignation in her mind, the only part of her that still seemed to function.

She felt like she had in the Knights' too-warm swimming pool: her body floating, gravity disappearing, only the brush of a hand against her skin reminding her that she had a body at all.

There was one thing she couldn't forget. One thing no amount of numbness could steal.

The pendant lay bundled against her chest like a chrysalis, a razor-blade butterfly waiting to be freed. She could feel it even as her senses abandoned her. The danger it represented weighed heavily on her heart.

And as her mind struggled to find a way out, an ending other than death . . . the blade began to seem like a second chance.

Love was something you had to do. To feel. It was active, not passive.

Could you love when you were asleep?

And if she didn't actively love Felix—if she were as cut off from her emotions as she'd be from the rest of the world—could he still tear that love from her, steal her life from her, kiss by kiss?

She brought her hand to her chest, slowly, and began to unwind the gauze.

Her fingers were as numb as they were in winter. She couldn't even be sure she was unwinding the gauze properly, but the primal fear that shook her each time she touched it made her think she was succeeding. The razor was her trigger. Her body didn't want to be near it. It told her in no uncertain terms, instinctively: *NO.*

Felix ignored her fumbling; he was too preoccupied with her murder. She'd stopped fighting, and was numbly letting him feed. Even as he robbed her, as he rid her of everything that mattered, he didn't tear her dress, or do anything they hadn't done before. It was ironic; he treated her body with a sort of polite consideration, but he had no qualms about killing her. She supposed she should have been grateful he didn't take her violently; she didn't need that trauma on top of everything else.

The ribbon of gauze fluttered into her palm.

She couldn't see Felix anymore; could barely feel him. Her thumb struck the metal of the razor blade, and it met her with a jolt of recognition: *You know me. I'll hurt you. Welcome home.*

Death or sleep. One or the other was coming for her now.

She didn't have time to regret this. The razor blade bit into her finger, drawing blood.

And the world disappeared.

# CHAPTER EIGHTEEN

AFTER THE SHOW, half the club spilled out of Stroke of Midnight and followed Rafe to a promised blowout on the beach. Blue tried not to think of Mira: why she'd left the club early, what Felix had said to make her go to him. It was after midnight, close to 2 A.M., so it was officially her birthday. . . . He wanted to wish her a happy birthday, but he didn't want to be angry or depressed right now—which was how he'd feel if he saw her with his brother, and she said, *I'm happy. Can't you let me be happy?*

He was grateful for distraction. He threw himself into the party wholeheartedly: drinking, mocking people who were drunker than he was.

Girls trailed after Freddie like seagulls stalking a fishing boat . . . and seemed to find it cute when he fled in terror. Jewel slipped away with a blonde named Luxe, one of the jaded, ever-bratty Kinders, who'd laid her claim to fairy-tale infamy back when she was a preteen, after pissing off and robbing a house full of bears. The two girls kissed for a few minutes, then came up for air so Jewel could wipe the gems from her lips and push them into Luxe's pockets. Rafe pounded empty beer cans against his forehead until he wore a crown of bruises.

And Blue missed Mira. He wished she were there to ask him *why* he was friends with Rafe. Or so he could tell her the Luxe-robbing-the-three-bears story, and make her laugh. Or stand in the surf with his arms around her, while she pretended not to like it.

Wills swung Viv around like a rag doll, his hands on her bare abdomen; he set her down to be confronted by Henley and suffered a punch to the face. Then all three Knight brothers ganged up on Henley, drunk and stupid with the hero gene, granting black eyes like wishes.

It turned into a brawl on the beach, with the lower-born Cursed coming to the Huntsman's aid. Slick bad Wolves and cocky Jack-the-Giant-Killer types. Blue didn't like fighting, but black eyes and bruises fit his anti-Romantic agenda, so he jumped into the fray for a few souvenirs. They fought until the cops came to break it up, and he and Freddie ran and hid until the chaos died down, feeling reckless and alive.

Dawn broke over the beach, chasing them home.

Blue and Freddie stood in front of the Dream, gaping at the sight before them.

The entire building was covered with thorns: spiked branches that scaled the hotel walls like razor-sharp ivy. A tangle of briars crisscrossed the glass entry doors and the windows, locking everyone in, locking them out. It wasn't until Blue tried to touch one and a branch zipped out and scratched him, drawing blood, that he realized it wasn't an illusion.

Mira's curse.

Blue swore. He turned to Freddie, whose eyes were shining with excitement—one person's tragedy being another person's treasure, he guessed. "I'll get my sword!" Freddie said.

"That sword isn't going to do anything." Blue groped for his phone. "I'll get Henley to bring an axe."

"Henley?" Freddie blanched. "But I—I hit him in the face with a piece of driftwood a few hours ago. Do you really think that's a good idea?"

"Fine—get your sword. But hurry up!"

Freddie was already on his way. "Don't worry!" he shouted—and took off running down the street. Freddie was Honor-bound; he finally had a princess to save, and nothing about that could be a bad thing, as far as Freddie was concerned.

Blue, on the other hand, didn't like that fate had chosen today to strike. Mira's sixteenth birthday; talk about ominous. It felt like everything was falling apart. . . .

There were more than fifteen hundred rooms in the Dream. Over a thousand places where Mira could have fallen asleep. But no matter how many rooms there were, there were only two or three places Mira was likely to be.

With Felix. With Felix. With Felix . . .

Viv's phone went straight to voice mail, so Blue rang the Deneuves' house phone—Regina would pick up. And she was enough of a bitch that she would happily disturb Viv's beauty rest to make her talk to him.

Viv would *love* being woken up by her stepmother. But he could deal with her wrath. He was ready to promise her anything, kiss her ass for the next hundred years, personally taste-test every apple she was offered for the rest of her life, so long as she got Henley to come down to the Dream with an axe and get him past those briars.

He needed to get in there. Needed to find Mira and make sure she was okay.

Because there was sleep—and then there was Felix. And he had no idea which one had gotten to her first.

"I don't think this'll work," Henley said. He'd arrived with an axe, a chain saw, and Viv in tow. Freddie wasn't back yet—which was why Blue wanted Henley to try to chop through the briars *now*. When he'd told Freddie to hurry, he'd forgotten Freddie would interpret that as *go ahead and shower and change and brush your teeth so you're minty fresh for your destiny. Then hurry.*

"Just try," Blue said. "Try before I throw myself through the briars. The last thing I need is Knight freeing my entrapped dead body with his sword."

"I'm just saying," Henley went on, "these briars are enchanted. They're only supposed to part for a prince. Hnnh!" Henley swung his axe, and the thorny branches cleaved in half at the touch of the blade, then shrank apart, turning silver and brittle. The glass door cracked from the force of the axe.

Viv examined a dead-looking branch. She touched one of the thorns, and it crumbled into dust. "Is Mira sick?" she said. "I don't think the briars are supposed to be this weak. Unless there's something wrong with her . . ."

"Axe in hand. Get. Out. Of. My. Way. Vivian," Henley ordered, readying the axe for a second swing.

Sick. Weak. Wrong.

Blue found his hands curling into fists. He wanted to kill Felix. Kill him.

"Get the door open!" he snapped.

Heaving deep breaths, Blue stood back as Henley hacked through the rest of the briars—each branch curling back pitifully once it was severed.

Every crack of the glass made Blue's heart jump. He needed to find Mira. Needed to believe she could be okay. That it wasn't already too late.

The last of the briars gave way, and Henley kicked in the busted panes of glass.

They stepped through the hole into a silent nightmare.

Well, not quite silent.

The Dream was always alive. Always buzzing with excitement and despair, voices filling the air like the rush of a waterfall. No matter what hour of day or night.

Until now.

The slot machines still made the same electronic racket. Rows and rows of dinging machines, the sounds overlapping each other so there was never a scrap of silence, never a moment of calm.

But the players slumped in their seats, cheeks smushed against video poker screens, slots waiting for another spin. Fat plastic cups lay on the ground or overturned on sleeping laps, coins spilling to the floor.

The roulette wheels had stopped turning. Dice lay frozen on craps tables. Full houses went ignored. None of the blackjack players hit or stayed; instead, they slumped on the tables or on the floor, limbs at awkward angles, cards scattered.

The cocktail waitresses had dropped their trays and lay unconscious in pools of liquor and melted ice. Pit bosses watched nothing but their dreams.

Every last person in the casino was asleep.

It was like walking into an apocalypse. An end-of-the-world movie in which the machines kept going—even when the people were gone.

"Where do you think she is?" Viv asked, her eyes taking in the sleeping guests.

"I don't know," Blue said. "But—I have a few guesses." He took out his wallet to get his passkey, identical to the key Felix had given Mira, and which he'd taken from her   and saw that one of the cards was missing.

She'd stolen it.

She must have taken it during the show. Because he'd had it before that; he remembered checking for it, paranoid that it would be gone.

So she had to be—

"You guys need to stay down here," he said, his hand shaking as he returned his wallet to his pocket. "You can't go where I'm going."

"Oh, Blue, you don't think . . ." Viv trailed off.

No one would finish the sentence.

They knew his tale; they knew the one place that was forbidden. And what went on there.

Henley took Viv's hand, and for once, she seemed glad; she curled into the space beneath his arm, fear in her dark eyes.

Blue just nodded. He was afraid he'd lose it if he spoke.

"You want the axe?" Henley said.

Blue shook his head. If he took the axe, he was afraid he'd use it on Felix. And no matter what Felix had done, no matter how much he *wanted* to hurt him, he knew he couldn't kill his own brother. He didn't need more regrets.

He turned and started running toward the elevators.

Suite 3013 was as tranquil as a tomb.

Spots of blood flecked the snow white carpet in a trail that led to the bedroom. A single sheet of paper lay on the floor. Everything else was in order.

But the bedroom door was shut.

Blue's eyes went to the trail of blood and stayed there. As if it wasn't enough to drain her. He'd hurt her, too.

Blue gritted his teeth and pressed his palms to his eyes. He breathed in and out a few times, trying to calm down. He couldn't give in to despair. Not yet.

The scent of roses met him as he pushed into the bedroom, pressing against the door both steadily and gently, afraid there would be a limp body blocking the way. He didn't want to disrespect it, harm it—even if all the life had been stolen.

He'd been in this room once before, when he was thirteen. And Felix had never forgiven him. They'd never had a great relationship, but Blue's intrusion into Felix's most secret place had destroyed what little friendship they'd had. It had ripped the veil off Felix's carefully hidden crimes—and destroyed the illusion that Felix was less of a monster than their father.

To enter a Romantic's chamber was the ultimate invasion of privacy, and it came with a heavy price. For most, that price was death. With the exception of blood relatives who shared the curse—and the shame—no one who entered could be allowed to leave, to reveal the loathsome secret. Intruders had to be silenced, and added to the collection. And if the intruders didn't love you, if you couldn't silence them and strengthen yourself through the theft of their love and their life, then you silenced them in bloodier, more traditional ways.

Hence the so-called *bloody chamber*. The clotted blood on the floor, the women hanging from hooks in fairy tales, the slit throats. But Felix never had to take those measures. He was the quintessential charmer, suave and generous, handsome enough to overcome the centuries of mistrust blue hair had fostered. And Felix didn't like getting his hands dirty. He would never cut someone unless he absolutely had to.

So if there was blood, Mira must have fought him. Or maybe she was stronger than most girls, because her blood thrummed with the magic of fairy tales, and he'd lost patience, panicked, feared there was no way to silence her except with violence.

It was too much to hope that she didn't really love him. Blue had seen the effect his brother had on Mira; had witnessed her weakness with his own eyes. He'd sat beside her while she'd slept in his bed, unconscious and impossible to wake—his eyes on the slight flutter of her eyelashes, the faint up and down of her chest as she breathed.

He'd thought that had been agony.

This was infinitely worse.

When Blue had entered his brother's chamber the first time, Felix had been seventeen. There had been two girls in the room then, both lovely and young—younger than Blue was now. They'd been lonely, friendless girls; pretty enough, but both so deeply wounded emotionally that they'd never found common ground with anyone else. And they'd gravitated to Felix, who accepted them, who knew exactly what they needed. Felix liked lost souls, orphans, runaways—just like their father did.

Because no one ever came looking for them.

Felix's first two girlfriends were still there—their clothes and hairstyles about four years out of date—but they'd been joined by almost two dozen others. The girls who appeared to have acquiesced—no bruises, no signs of struggle—sat or lay neatly on the furniture, or curled against pillows. The girls who'd fought had received more careless treatment, and been flung wherever they would fit. Two girls had even been stuffed into a wardrobe that hung open, their limbs tangled together, legs battered as if Felix had slammed them with the door while trying to force it shut.

Blue remembered some of these girls. The ones who'd been nice to him. The ones he'd tried, with no success, to warn off. These girls had flitted into Felix's life, and were soon radiant with love—but they never flitted out again.

They disappeared. And they stayed.

And then there was Mira.

Blue could barely see her through the canopy of roses that guarded her bed, a dense tangle of briars and bloodred blooms, covering her like a casket. Protecting her.

She lay perfectly still, her thick blond hair spread around her on the pillow, one hand resting on her chest, as passive and coldly beautiful as every other girl in the room. And when he reached to touch her—to claw through the briars to get to her— the branches slashed at him, pricked his skin in twenty different places, beads of his blood dripping onto her rose-print dress.

The thorns seized his arm like a trap; they wouldn't allow

him to touch her or get near her, or even to move away. No amount of struggle allowed him to free himself. And though he fought to get closer, to let his fingers hover above her lips, hoping to feel her breath, the thorns seized him and forced his arm in another direction, so that he became more deeply entangled, but no closer than before.

"Please be alive," he whispered. "Please just be asleep."

But there was no sign that she was either.

Felix had left her here. And Felix didn't leave things unfinished.

He wouldn't have left her alive.

These were the thoughts Blue kept coming back to during the hour he spent trapped in the briars. Thorny branches had tangled around his left wrist, his waist; his right arm was entirely imprisoned; thorns bit into his cheek. Blood dripped down his face, but he'd stopped feeling it. All he felt was despair, and the hopelessness of the situation.

He was staring at Mira's lips, her chest—desperate to see some indication that she was breathing—when he heard the first solid crack against the outer door. He turned his head toward it, trying to see through the bedroom doorway, thorns raking fresh lines across his face; and he saw the outer door splinter inward, a chunk of wood stabbing into the room. Gradually, as more of the door fell away, he saw that Freddie was in the hallway, chopping through the door with Henley's axe.

Blue gritted his teeth. Felix wouldn't forgive the intrusion—even if it was Freddie. What to do then? Make Freddie go away, or tell him to hurry up and get in here, so they had a chance of saving Mira—who might already be gone?

Freddie was his best friend; Blue didn't want to see him

hurt. But Freddie was also Honor-bound, and if his princess was trapped beneath a prison of thorns, possibly lost, definitely hurt, he wasn't going to leave just because Blue told him to. That decided it.

"Hurry!" Blue yelled.

"I'm almost through!" Freddie shouted back.

It seemed to take an eternity for Freddie to bust through the door, but at last, he made a hole large enough and rushed into the suite, axe in hand, a sword buckled to his belt. He was flushed and sweating, but had a determined look on his face as he strode toward the bedroom.

A look that faltered as soon as he crossed the threshold—and saw the dead girls inside.

"Oh god," Freddie whispered. He blinked a few times, and his eyes grew glossy and then spilled over. It was horrifying even if you expected it—even if you'd been brought up to be the same kind of monster, like Blue had. Freddie was too softhearted a hero to stand it.

"Try not to look at them," Blue said. "I know it's hard. I know it's horrible. But we need to help Mira. I don't—I don't know if we're too late. But we have to try. Concentrate on Mira."

*And hope she's alive,* he thought. Because if she wasn't—if Freddie had come here to be a hero only to discover she was dead—it would destroy him.

Freddie nodded, swallowing hard. "You're right. I will." It took some effort, but Freddie managed to tear his gaze away from the other girls. He approached the tangle of roses carefully, hand outstretched as if to ward off a dangerous beast—

And the thorns parted for him.

The branches curled back, tightening around Blue, and

created a passage for Freddie at the side of the bed, so that he could reach Mira.

Blue held his breath and watched as his friend leaned in, strong and sure and every bit the hero. He'd never envied anyone more than he envied Freddie in that moment.

They looked perfect together: Mira, beautiful and still, lips slightly parted; Freddie, fiercely protective and golden, his features strengthened by love. If she was alive, if she was okay . . . Freddie could kiss her, and he would never hurt her. He had a kiss that healed, that broke enchantments and led to happily-ever-after. He was marked to be good, and he never had to be afraid that he was otherwise, that he was wicked, a murderer, evil.

Blue's kiss could only take. Could only destroy.

He was almost grateful for the thorns trapping him, keeping him in place so he couldn't stop it from happening.

Because he wanted to be the one to kiss her.

Instead, he forced himself to speak.

"Is she breathing?" Blue asked.

"I'm not sure," Freddie said. His voice had turned quiet, both reverent and afraid. "She's not moving. Or if she is, it's so slight I can't tell. But—she's holding on to something. . . ."

Freddie took Mira's hand—the one that lay atop her chest—and pried open the curled fingers, revealing something silver. And a patch of scarlet on her skin.

Blue squinted to see past the thorns that crowded his vision. "What is it?"

"It's a razor blade," Freddie said, sounding troubled. "On a chain. And her hand is bloody. She was—clutching a razor blade . . . ?" He glanced up, his eyes meeting Blue's through the thorns. "Do you think she—would you say that's her trigger? Why would she wear this, if she knew what it could do to her?"

"I don't know," Blue said. "She was supposed to—"

She was supposed to see Delilah.

It clicked for him then. Mira had gone to see Delilah that night, at the club, to find out what her trigger was. Blue had been so disappointed that she'd left before he had a chance to see her again, he'd completely forgotten that something besides her feelings for Felix—or her feelings for him—could have sent her fleeing the club like Cinderella after midnight.

What had Delilah told her? She couldn't have spoken of the Valentines' curse, but she must have said something. Something that had made Mira steal his key and enter a room she'd resisted entering until now.

Evil fairies were evil through and through; they didn't have soft spots or emotional Achilles' heels. Delilah hadn't asked Mira for payment—because what she wanted from her was something only Felix could provide. And the fairy had to have known Felix had begun seeing Mira; Delilah made it a point to know these things, especially about Felix, who followed his curse perfectly, and whom Delilah adored for just that reason.

Sleeping Beauty's original curse was to prick her finger and *die*—but the curse was always softened by a good fairy, who altered the princess's enchantment so she was destined to fall into a deep sleep instead. But, of course, any evil fairy worth her wickedness wanted to see the Sleeping Beauty princess die. What better way to lead Mira toward her own destruction than by somehow tempting her to enter Felix's forbidden chamber?

Felix, who would take care of that transgression the only way he was allowed.

Blue was so furious with himself he could barely breathe.

"Damn it," he muttered. "I should have made her wait. I should have gone with her!"

"Blue?" Freddie frowned at him. Blue could see the worry in his friend's eyes, the uncertainty that hadn't been there before.

Blue took a deep breath to steady himself. "Freddie, you have to kiss her."

"If she's dead," Freddie began, lips trembling as he turned back toward Mira, "I . . . I don't know if I should. I'm not supposed to kiss the dead. I—I can't even find a pulse. But . . . I have to try. I couldn't forgive myself if I didn't try. . . ."

Freddie leaned in, his eyes closing, lips parting, a kiss in slow motion.

Blue tensed, every cut on his body burning anew. Every second of this was torture. Every second that he didn't know.

The thorns gripped him fiercely, and . . .

Freddie kissed her.

The world trickled back slowly, in lovely increments.

Chiffon.

The scent of roses.

A kiss.

There were soft lips pressed to hers, kissing her, and Mira's mouth fell in with the motion, as if kissing were the most natural thing in the world, akin to being alive.

*Alive.*

Her eyelids felt heavy. Her arms and legs felt distant, like her mind and her body were in two different places.

A hand touched her cheek, and it was so warm—almost burning her, but in a good way, infusing her with life—she didn't ever want it to leave her. She was cold, freezing—as if someone had stolen her body heat while she was asleep.

Stolen.

*Felix.*

Her attempt to save herself had failed.

Her eyes jolted open, her lips fought to pry apart in a scream. She heard her blood rushing like an explosion in her head. A moan of protest came from her throat. Black clouds floated in front of her eyes, dark splotches replacing her vision. She was dying. She was dying. She'd thought something had stopped it, interrupted it—she had a vague recollection of nothingness, a murky pause—but she was wrong, she was dying again . . . *must* be . . .

"Mira, you're all right, it's all right," a male voice hastened to say—a voice very close to her. He sounded worried and relieved all at once.

The second voice sounded weaker and farther away. "He's gone, Mira. He can't hurt you anymore."

"Who?" she said. It was more a breath than a word.

"Felix. Felix is gone. Freddie and I are here. We won't let anyone hurt you."

Blue. Freddie and Blue were here. Her heart nearly broke from relief, and she started to cry.

"I can't see," she whispered. She let her emotions flood her, as if the tears would wash her blindness away, like Rapunzel's tears had cured her prince after he'd fallen from the tower, and thorns had gouged out his eyes.

She felt someone pull her up off the bed, shift her body so that she sat cradled in warm arms, against a warm body; and from his build she guessed that this was Freddie, not Blue.

"Sorry. I hope you don't mind," Freddie said. "I couldn't bear to look at you like that. Lying there, as if you were . . ." He held her close, and she let her body sink against him. She felt him shudder. "And you're very cold."

Mira sat curled up in his arms, not sure for how long. Time seemed to stand still. They were all very quiet; they'd been through something traumatic, and no one knew what to say yet. From time to time, Freddie kissed her forehead or her cheek, and a little flare of heat woke her limbs, sparked some feeling in them. Her eyes began to clear, the black clouds fading to gray, the gray dissipating and leaving behind a blur, so that she could see shapes and colors, but nothing distinct; until finally, she found herself staring at Blue, who was caught in a dense tangle of briars, watching her.

She had the impression he'd been watching for a while. And when her eyes cleared, and he realized she could see him, he exhaled. His body sank down as he relaxed, and the thorn branches scraped and crackled against each other, cutting his skin. A tear slipped from his eye, and he grinned almost painfully as it ran down his cheek.

"You're crying," Mira said, stunned. She'd never seen him like this. Even when he'd told her the story of his sixteenth birthday.

"These thorns hurt," Blue said, still smiling—sheepishly this time. And she laughed. He was so full of it. Freddie laughed, too—that bell-like peal. They were all laughing and crying a little, and Freddie hugged her so tightly she lost her breath for a moment—but it wasn't a scary feeling. She felt safe with them. She knew they would never hurt her.

# CHAPTER NINETEEN

AFTER FREDDIE CUT BLUE FREE of the thorns, the three of them headed downstairs, where the slumberers were waking up. Groggy gamblers patted their cards. Cocktail waitresses pushed themselves off gin-soaked carpets and gathered their trays. Slot players scraped coins into plastic cups, and argued over what belonged to whom. There was no sign of Felix, and Mira wanted to get out of the casino before she saw him.

Blue had warned her, before they'd left the forbidden room, that Felix didn't leave things unfinished—his curse wouldn't let him. He'd only left her alive because her thorns had attacked him, walled her in and protected her, and prevented him from sealing her fate.

Felix would come back for her, and for Freddie, too. And while Blue and Freddie had vowed to protect her, she knew there was only one way it could end . . . and she didn't want it to end like that today.

They gathered Viv and Henley, who were waiting in the lobby—and left the Dream behind.

The five of them grabbed breakfast at a greasy diner no one they knew ever went to, and drank enough coffee to stay awake for days. When the air started to smell like burgers instead of bacon, they peeled themselves off the seats and went out to face the world. Viv and Henley went one way—and Mira, Blue, and Freddie went to Freddie's house.

Mira knew she couldn't go on with her vanishing act. She had to call her godmothers and confess, and she was determined to get it over with—today.

She wasn't expecting to see her godmothers in Freddie's backyard.

They'd gone around back in an attempt to avoid Freddie's parents, only to run across a small gathering when they got there. Tables and chairs and croquet hoops had been arranged beneath an outdoor canopy behind the house. Glass pitchers filled with iced tea and orange slices sat sweating on the tables.

Elsa and Freddie's mother were drinking tea and talking. Bliss was clutching a croquet mallet, her bell-shaped skirt flouncing up every time she bent to take a shot. Caspian was cheering her on, saying, "That's it, great job!" And Freddie's father sat by himself, smoking a pipe and reading the newspaper.

Mira froze.

"Word travels fast when one of the casinos ends up covered in briars," Elsa was saying. "Today of all days—we figured it had to be Mira."

Freddie's hypersensitive mother was fanning herself with

a Japanese fan, her lips pursed in a victimized expression. "I should have known he was breaking an enchantment. I heard him stumbling around the house this morning—putting on cologne at seven o'clock. I can't believe he didn't tell me!"

Freddie had stopped short at the sight of the gathering. Now he was motioning back the way they came, whispering, "Perhaps it's better if we go in the front. . . ."

But Elsa had already seen them. She caught Mira's eye and smiled. Freddie's mother followed her gaze and sprang up from her seat.

"Frederick!" she shouted. "How could you?"

"Ah—I'm sorry?" Freddie tried.

"Didn't you think I might like to take a picture? You didn't even warn me! Now all I have to look forward to is . . . a fish girl! And a dirty housekeeper who talks to mice!" Mrs. Knight's voice was wobbling up and down; with every breath, she sounded closer to tears.

Caspian looked wounded. "A fish girl? Is that what you think of her?"

Mr. Knight took his pipe from his mouth long enough to say, "Boys—don't upset your mother."

Freddie sighed and went to make amends, and Mira headed over to Elsa and Bliss. It was time to face them. She figured they'd be angry—she'd lied to them, upset them. But they had some explaining to do, too.

It was strange to look at her godmothers and see them not just as her guardians, but as fairies—their true selves. Back home, they'd made themselves look a little older every year. But now the careful wrinkles and the silver streaks in their hair were gone. Elsa looked like the college students she taught—

brown hair still damp from a shower, wearing faded jeans and a loose white shirt. Bliss looked even younger—like a porcelain doll brought to life. And yet they blazed with a quiet power, a majesty they'd always hidden.

They looked like they were waiting for her to speak, so she did.

"I know the truth now," Mira began. "About my parents. And my curse. Why did you lie to me? Why did you tell me they were dead?"

She caught herself, took a deep breath so she wouldn't cry. She didn't want to act like a child. She needed them to see that she could handle the truth—no matter what it was.

Bliss laid her croquet mallet on the grass. "Your parents didn't want you to know they were alive, Mira. They thought you'd be safer that way. We were carrying out their wishes."

"Come here, Belle. We know this has been hard on you." Elsa drew up beside her, and Bliss did, too. They each put an arm around her. "Do you want to know how it happened?" Elsa asked.

Mira nodded. There was a lump in her throat.

"You did have a christening party," Bliss said. "It was held in a beautiful ballroom in Beau Rivage—the same ballroom where your parents held their wedding reception. Your parents had been under the impression that they couldn't have children, and so when they were blessed with you, they wanted to do something extra special to celebrate."

"It's a tradition in the fairy-tale community to invite fairies to a christening," Elsa explained. "The fairies bestow gifts on the infant, in the form of talents or virtues. Usually, there are one or two fairies. Your parents invited seven."

"I bet they had to pay the party planner a zillion dollars to find that many," Bliss said.

Elsa nodded in agreement. "When it came time for the fairies to bestow their gifts, we went down the line in order of seniority. It was deemed that you would be pretty, and kind, have a lovely voice, be a good dancer, do well in school—that was my gift—and be graceful."

"I was the youngest fairy," Bliss said, "so I had to wait until the end. I was going to give you animal magnetism—I think Frederick has that—"

"Irresistible to squirrels?" Mira raised her eyebrows.

"It's *very* fairy-tale," Bliss sniffed. "Anyway. I was going to do that—but then an evil fairy showed up."

"No one knew who she was," Elsa said. "Even I had never heard of her. It would have been impossible to invite her. But she was furious—they always are. She was wearing a black feather cowl and a long black dress infested with beetles. The beetles were scurrying out from beneath her skirts and taking flight and landing on the cupcakes. Vanilla frosting topped with edible gold and black beetles . . ." Elsa shivered. "I'll never forget that. I had such a sick feeling. . . . I knew she was going to curse you. And we only had one fairy left who could temper it. So I shoved Bliss under the refreshments table and we waited."

"Those beetles kept landing on me," Bliss said. "That nasty fairy walked right up to you and touched you with her wand. It was a gold wand—not glass like ours."

Bliss slipped a slender glass wand from her pocket, and Elsa did the same. Mira had seen her godmothers carry these things around, toy with them absentmindedly . . . and all her life she'd thought they were knitting needles.

But they were wands. Of course.

Now Bliss touched the wand to her palm, like it helped her to remember. "The fairy stated that when you were fifteen or sixteen, you would cut your finger on a razor blade and die. And then she left, and it was my turn. I couldn't undo the curse, but I could soften it—in place of the gift I hadn't had a chance to give you. I made it so you wouldn't die when you cut yourself. You'd simply fall into a deep sleep: one that would last for a hundred years, or until an Honor-bound prince arrived to wake you with his kiss."

"After that, the party emptied out. You can imagine—no one felt like celebrating. And it was like you had a ticking time bomb right here"—Elsa tapped Mira's lower back, where her mark was—"and no one knew how best to protect you. Least of all your parents. Some of the fairies stayed behind to advise them, and ultimately, your mother and father decided to hand you over to two fairy guardians. Who would do their best to protect you—and love you," Elsa said, squeezing her. "And who would take you away, to a place where fairy tales were just stories, where you'd have the best chance to cheat fate. And in seventeen years, when the danger was over, they would bring you home."

"And I guess . . . the danger is over," Bliss said, and went quiet. Her fingers fumbled over her wand.

Mira closed her eyes. She felt, for a moment, like she was very small again. Very young. She'd spent her whole life with Elsa and Bliss. And as much as she was looking forward to meeting her parents, she didn't intend to just step out of her old life and into a new one, as if her time with Elsa and Bliss was a dress she'd outgrown. Her parents were her parents—

301

they were more special to her than they could imagine.

But Elsa and Bliss were her guardians, and always would be.

"What if," Mira said, "once the danger was over, I decided I already had a home?"

Elsa's eyes glimmered with emotion. She looked almost surprised—and then she smiled. "Well, I suppose we'd suggest they start with a visit, and go from there. Would you like that?"

"I would love that," Mira said.

Elsa tucked a strand of hair behind Mira's ear. "I'll make the arrangements. Today, you just enjoy what's left of your birthday, all right? Tomorrow, we can start all the changes. I have to get my old house straightened up. Now that we're back home, where we belong . . ."

*Home.* It felt good to think of Beau Rivage as home. As the place where they belonged, and could be themselves. All three of them.

Mira glanced around, aware of the world again. Freddie had managed to pacify his mother and was standing nearby, watching Mira as if waiting to be of service to her, oblivious to the small bird perched on the rim of his iced-tea glass.

"He's *cute,*" Bliss murmured in Mira's ear, tickling her to get a reaction. "Is he a good kisser?"

Mira's face flushed hotter than the air. *"Bliss."*

"Now let's get rid of this ugly thing." Elsa's fingers closed around the chain of Mira's razor-blade necklace. She started to lift it, and Mira clapped her hand over the chain to stop her.

"No," she said quickly. "I want to keep it."

Her godmothers didn't know what the razor blade meant to her. They didn't know it had saved her life—and she wasn't going to tell them. She wasn't going to tell them anything about Felix.

Felix would have to be dealt with eventually—Mira had no illusions about that—but she wouldn't give her godmothers a reason to torture him, like Louis the Wolf had been tortured. No one deserved that kind of cruelty. Her godmothers were good people, but if they knew he'd tried to kill her, there was no telling what they might do.

Elsa's eyebrows dipped lower, like she didn't understand. "Mira, that thing is disgusting—it's covered in blood. It's not meant to be a souvenir."

"You could cut yourself," Bliss said. "And it just looks bad. Like you're suicidal."

"I won't cut myself again," Mira insisted. "I don't care how it looks."

"Mira," Elsa warned.

"It's her choice," Blue said.

Blue had kept to the fringes of the gathering. He came closer now, his posture rigid, not quite making eye contact. She remembered that he'd been that way around Delilah, too. He didn't trust fairies. And why would he? An evil fairy was responsible for his curse. Good fairies viewed him as something to be destroyed.

Because he wasn't a hero. Heroes *killed* people like Blue. He was a villain.

Which was something Mira would never accept. Because Blue was a hero to her. He'd helped save her; he'd done his best to warn her while bound by the rules of his curse—and to push her away even when he wanted her near him. That meant more to her than destiny.

Elsa and Bliss noticed him, and bristled in a feral way.

"You *would* be in favor of her doing dangerous things, wouldn't you?" Bliss said.

"I don't want you anywhere near Mira," Elsa told him. "Do you understand?" She drew her wand like it contained all the power of a samurai sword. And maybe it did. Fairies cursed people with wands, drew magic from their blood and changed them—for better or worse.

"With all due respect," Freddie said, stepping in front of Blue. "I won't let you threaten my best friend."

"Don't be insolent, Frederick," Mrs. Knight scolded.

Bliss was shaking, with a fury that seemed completely alien to her. She aimed her wand in Blue's direction, though Freddie—noble, Honor-bound Freddie—made sure to shield him. "That boy is a villain, Mirabelle. A wicked, nasty little—"

"I know," Mira said. "He's a Romantic. I don't want anything to do with him."

She glanced quickly at Blue. He looked like she'd stabbed him.

She was sorry for saying it, but arguing in his defense wasn't going to get her anywhere. Knowing that she liked him, trusted him, would put Elsa and Bliss right back on alert. And she didn't want to be protected. She'd rather leave them in the dark for a while.

"Good," Elsa said after a pause. She didn't seem entirely convinced, but it wasn't as bad as it could have been.

"Lucky for you she's sensible," Bliss said. "Because I'm a good fairy, but you don't want to see what I do when someone hurts my Mira."

"Now take that necklace off," Elsa said.

"*No,*" Mira snapped.

Her godmothers looked aghast. She'd never snapped at them before. No matter how frustrated she'd been.

But . . . she'd gotten used to making her own decisions.

"Now, now, no need for frowns on these gorgeous faces," Mrs. Knight said. "How about a group picture? Freddie, you stand next to Mira."

Mira gave in to Freddie's mother's photo session. They did about fifty fake prom poses and some group shots, half of which were invaded by birds. Her eyes were focused everywhere but on the camera—seeking Blue.

She didn't know where he was—if he'd gone inside or left—but she hoped he'd stayed. She hoped he knew her well enough to know she would want him to.

# CHAPTER TWENTY

SUNSET FADED FROM THE SKY and brought the deep violet of night.

Paper lanterns hung around the pool in the Knights' backyard, glowing softly. Platters of food were set up on a table near the cabana. And Beau Rivage's fairy-tale finest were hanging out poolside. Viv had organized a surprise birthday party for Mira.

Layla was there, and Viv and Henley, and Jewel, and both of Freddie's brothers, and Rafe (who was behaving himself), and Freddie and Blue. They'd brought Mira last-minute birthday gifts, like a mix CD, a Curses & Kisses T-shirt, a chipmunk Viv claimed was tame (but wasn't), and Wills's car keys, which she was pretty sure she'd have to give back once Wills realized they were missing—but she thanked Henley for the Porsche anyway.

Mira had discarded her rose-print dress in favor of a borrowed swimsuit, shorts, and her new Curses & Kisses T-shirt.

There were a few hours left in her sweet sixteen, and she was determined to make the most of them. To squeeze some sweetness out of what had been one of the worst, and most important, days of her life.

Just before they unveiled the cake, Viv told Mira they had another surprise for her: wishes. Like at her christening party. Only this time, they wouldn't come true unless she made them come true. It was more for fun.

Caspian and Freddie built a fire, and Layla handed out strips of colored paper, which the guests used to write a wish for Mira. They took turns stepping up to the fire and reading their wishes, then casting the colored paper into the flames. The smoke feathered upward, carrying their wishes to the stars.

From Layla: *true love*. From Viv: *to only sleep when you want to*.

Henley wished her *patience*; Caspian, *that you'll always have mermaid hair*; Wills, *a bank account that never empties*.

Jewel said *magic*, and tossed in the sapphire that slipped out with the word. Rafe set his beer down long enough to wish her *eternal hotness*.

From Freddie: *trust*. From Blue: *hope*.

And when it was Mira's turn to make a wish, she stepped up to her birthday cake, airy vanilla frosting studded with pink and blue stars—and she blew out all sixteen candles in one blow, and wished *that things had been different*.

They didn't sing "Happy Birthday." Freddie got his guitar, and he and Jewel did "Summertime" instead, and "Wild Horses" as an encore. They ate cake, pink and blue frosting staining their lips. Wills got the hose and filled a bunch of water balloons, and they chose teams and had a water balloon fight, running barefoot through the grass, using the trees and the cabana as cover and then launching an attack. They battled until they were soaked, then stripped down to their swimsuits and jumped into the pool.

Mira stayed on land, though they shouted for her to join them. "Later!" she promised.

She watched her friends splashing in the pool, and she was filled with a very different emotion from the loneliness she'd felt in the past. There was a sense of belonging now, and happiness, though it was incomplete. Deep inside, she was aching; she'd been in love, and it had gone terribly wrong—but she wouldn't let herself be devastated by a broken heart this time. She could go on from that.

She knew she could.

The razor blade hanging from her neck made her feel brave. Honest. A naked blade hid nothing, feared nothing. She wanted to be like that. Because that was how you found yourself, created yourself. You didn't hide. You didn't wait for the perfect moment to settle on you like a butterfly, like magic.

You went out and *made* magic. Made your own wishes come true.

Mira filled another water balloon and tied it off, then carried the wobbling weapon through the leafy darkness of the backyard. Brushing aside willow fronds and swatting at mosquitoes, she crept deeper, until the moon revealed Blue sitting at the base of a weeping willow tree.

Her damp Curses & Kisses T-shirt sagged on her hips, heavy with water from the water balloon fight. When he looked at her, it made her conscious of her body. Of everything.

"Hey," she said tentatively.

"Hey, birthday girl." He lifted a hand in greeting. "So did you mean that before?"

"Mean?" She'd said so many things.

"When you told your godmothers you didn't want anything to do with me. At first, I thought you meant it, but I dunno; that sounds like something a smart person would say."

She'd been about to reassure him; now she bit her lip to keep a straight face, and prepared the water balloon for launch.

"Did you not notice that I'm armed?"

"Sorry to ruin your plans, Mira, but this isn't *The Wizard of Oz*. I'm not going to melt."

She tossed the balloon anyway, halfheartedly, and it burst near his feet.

"That was a waste of an attack," he muttered. He was so moody right now. . . .

Mira crouched next to him. "Of course I didn't mean it," she said—because maybe he needed to hear it. "I said it because I didn't want to argue. I didn't want to hear them say anything bad about you. I already know they're wrong."

Blue shook his head. "They're not wrong. That's the problem. I have the capacity—the destiny—to be a villain. Just like you needed to know the truth about Felix. And needed to sleep. We can fight it, but . . ."

"But fate has a way of twisting our efforts, to get what it wants." *Fate, or other people,* she thought bitterly, recalling the role Delilah had played in all this.

"Right. And I don't ever want to—I don't—" He gave up, frustrated. "You know what I'm trying to say?"

"You don't ever want to hurt me."

Blue nodded. "And you already saw how easy it is—how inevitable. So your godmothers are right. I mean, I didn't like hearing that, but they're right."

"It's not inevitable," she said. *Because you're you. Because you're not selfish.*

She knew that she would hurt herself before she would ever hurt someone she cared about, and she felt like Blue was that way, too. He'd shown her, in the things he said, the way he cut himself off from the love he desperately needed. Love that would be so easy to steal.

His regret over what had happened to Jane on his sixteenth birthday was for what *she* had lost—not what *he* would never have.

Blue touched his fingertip to the razor blade that hung around her throat. "I still think you should keep this if you want to. And . . . god, I can't believe I'm saying this, I shouldn't defend him, he's an asshole—but thank you for not telling them about Felix. Because those fairies would have—" He closed his eyes, like he was picturing something horrible. And he looked guilty when he opened them. Like there shouldn't be any mercy for someone like Felix.

Or for someone like him.

"I know," she said. "He's your brother. I understand. And I wouldn't . . ." She shook her head. "I'm not vengeful. I don't believe in torture."

"You're something special," he murmured, a sad smile forming on his lips as he lifted the razor blade from where it lay

310

against her chest. He raised the flat of the blade to his mouth and kissed it.

"Don't flirt with me, Romantic," she said. But she was kidding—she knew he heard it in her voice.

"I'm not," he said, still with that same sad smile. "I'm not this time, I promise. You're just—you're something else, someone really special, and I feel completely justified in being in love with you."

Her heart froze in her chest. Stopped like time had stopped.

"Blue . . ."

He laid his hot forehead against hers and whispered, "Don't say anything, Mira. I don't need you to say anything. I just need you to know."

They stayed like that for a moment, and Mira closed her eyes, conscious of the sweat slipping down their skin, their fingers slowly finding each other and twining together, tighter and tighter because this was good-bye.

"I'm going to go now," he said. "But thank you. Thank you for everything."

Their fingers unfurled, separated, so only the heat was left behind. He lifted his head from hers, and the night breeze swept in as he moved away.

When Mira opened her eyes, his back was to her. He was standing a few feet away, playing with the end of a willow branch.

"Wait," she called. "What if I don't like you? Like, really don't like you?"

Blue turned, studying her. "You really don't?"

She nodded quickly, her throat too tight to speak, eyes

filling with tears. *Don't leave me, don't leave, don't leave.*

He came closer, chest rising and falling with his breath, so nervous she could see it like an aura around him. "You really don't?"

"I really don't," she whispered.

Tentatively, he reached for her. His hand cradled her cheek, and his gaze held hers for the length of one slow breath—long enough to give her the chance to pull away.

And then he kissed her and the tears she'd been holding overflowed when she closed her eyes. He pulled her to him, crushed her against his chest, his heart pounding against hers; and she held on tight, so tight, because she might never hold him again and she wanted to feel all of him, to remember this, always.

She was lying. Could he taste the lie?

Because she could feel it: her strength draining away, her love leaving her. The sweet shock of his mouth was like touching her tongue to a live wire. It seared her senses; it made her feel alive, even as it sucked that life away—and she kept coming back to it, again and again. Waves of sensation pulled her under—drowning her. But Blue made drowning feel like the loveliest thing. Like she was losing her breath, but she didn't need it, didn't want it, only wanted him . . .

"Mira, god, Mira," he whispered. The hand not clutching her against him was in her hair, shaking now against the back of her neck, and she knew he knew. How she felt. What he meant to her. What she'd realized.

His skin was more vibrant, his eyes shining a beautiful night-sea silver in the moonlight, and she felt weak in the knees. Reckless, and happy. She'd felt her strength dissolve with every press of his lips. Every soft surrender had taken more from her, life energy slipping from her mouth to his—and it was worth it, it was all worth it. Because he'd taken a piece of her—but now she had a piece of him, too.

"You crazy liar," he said breathlessly.

"You knew I was lying."

"Not to—that degree."

"Okay, so maybe I like you a little," she said, before she dropped and his arm snapped around her to hold her up. He lowered her gently to the grass, and leaned her against him, his body strong like the trunk of the willow tree. It felt wonderful to be that close to him . . . and to not worry, for once, that it was wrong to want to be there.

"I'll be okay," she assured him. "I just need to get my strength back. Just don't kiss me again until I get it back. It always comes back."

"We can't do that again," he said.

"We can be more careful. We'll take it slow, we'll figure it out, and—"

"No," he said, sighing deeply. "No, we can't, we can't. . . . Don't ever do that again. And . . . shit," he muttered. He was searching for something, fumbling; and then he laid a flat plastic card in her hand, and folded her fingers around it. "Don't ever let me do that again," he said. "And . . . don't ever go into suite 3024 at the Dream. It's private."

Mira stared at him, openmouthed. His passkey was in her hand.

"You're kidding, right? You don't have a—a room—for . . ."

"You have to promise me. You can't ever go in there.

313

I'm serious. I'm not playing. Promise me," he said.

"Of course," she said softly. "I would never."

Blue was silent a moment. Her heart beat rapidly in her chest, as if trying to make up for lost time. When she reached for his hand, he pulled away. Gently, but with a finality that made her sad.

"I want to stay," he admitted. "I haven't felt this way in a long time. I feel like . . . like I came up from being underwater, and I can finally breathe. I don't want to stop feeling that way. That's how I know I have to leave."

"You wouldn't hurt me," she said. "I know you wouldn't. *I know you.*"

Blue shook his head. "You don't know all of me; *I* don't even know all of me. But I know that the more I'm with you, the more I want to be with you. It's been over a year since I last—" His voice broke, and he stopped.

Mira laid her hand over his. This time, he didn't pull away.

"I'm afraid I'll break down," he said. "I need what you have. How you feel. I need love like I need water or air. And I won't take that from you. I won't let myself."

"So you're leaving," she murmured. Again. She felt like she'd already lost him once tonight—and he'd come back to her. But he wasn't going to stay.

"I have to. It's the only way I can make sure I'll never hurt you."

She'd wanted to believe that Felix was worthy of her heart. She'd made excuses for him even when he'd hurt her, lied to her. She never had to make excuses for Blue. Blue was every noble thing she'd loved, and wanted Felix to be. It killed her that she'd been so blind to that. And that, just as she realized it, she had to lose him.

It was hard for her to speak. Every word hurt.

"What if it's worth it to me to take that chance?" she asked, knowing he wouldn't listen, but needing to try.

"Then you don't know what you're risking," he said. "I do. I know what you would lose. And nothing is worth destroying that."

"But you'll destroy yourself."

He nodded. "I know this sounds weird, Mira, but I'm not really scared of dying. I've been preparing for it my whole life. It's written in my tale that someone Honor-bound is supposed to kill me . . . and I'd rather be the person responsible for *my* death than become more of a villain than I already am. That can be my one heroic act," he said with a faint smile. "The one I'm allowed."

"Blue . . ."

He kissed the tips of her hair—lifted a golden lock to his lips, as if it were her hand, to bid her farewell. "Good-bye, Mira."

He was gone.

Blue left, and she didn't follow.

She knew that he was probably still at the party, letting his friends know he was leaving. Maybe Freddie would try to talk him out of it. Or maybe they'd all expected this: either his resistance would break, or he'd disappear. One way or another, it had to come to an end.

He was right to go. Rationally, she knew that.

Mira sat with her back against the willow tree. She felt

shaky, like she needed to eat, though that wasn't the problem. And while she knew her strength would return, there was no guarantee that she would survive every kiss, that they wouldn't get carried away and go too far, or touch for too long. She could end up as just another girl in a forbidden room, a sleeping beauty who would never wake.

He didn't want that for her. And she didn't want that either. It was the wrong kind of forever. A soulless, frozen love.

Wind rustled through the trees, a hushing whisper all around her. The willow fronds quivered, shaking like her shoulders shook as she struggled not to cry.

*You were never meant to be together. That's not why you came here . . . that wasn't your destiny.*

She didn't want to die in his arms. And the only way to ensure that was to stay apart.

But she also knew that if she let Blue go, he would die. Maybe not right away, but much too soon. And she couldn't bear that.

Mira went back and forth, trying to decide what she should let him sacrifice, what *she* should sacrifice. . . . She took a deep breath, and stared up at the black, sparkling sky.

She wished one of those stars was more than just a star, capable of granting a wish. Because she would give up her supposed "lovely voice" and her "perfect dancing" and her grace and beauty and whatever else those seven fairies had promised at her christening. She would give them all up to save him.

But you couldn't make trades. You couldn't undo what had been done. Even in the case of Mira's own curse, Bliss had only been able to soften . . .

*Soften.*

Maybe . . .

Maybe she wasn't done fighting.

Mira's chest swelled with a hope so immense it hurt. She was afraid to want something more and lose that, too. But she had to try.

Using the tree for balance, she pushed herself to her feet and waited for the dizziness to subside. Then she started back toward the party. Her legs felt leaden and like jelly at the same time. But she kept going. She wouldn't give up on him.

She spotted Freddie leaning against the pool fence, arguing with Blue. She wanted to go to them, and tell Blue there might be a chance—but she couldn't get his hopes up. Not until she was sure she could save him.

There had to be a way to save him. . . .

# CHAPTER TWENTY-ONE

THE KNIGHTS' HOUSE WAS DARK. The clocks read 11:29 and 11:31. Just a half hour of her birthday remained.

Mira followed the sounds of conversation to the far end of the house, where windows on both sides of the room stood open to let in a breeze. Mr. and Mrs. Knight and Elsa and Bliss were arranged in a circle of sofas and chairs. They stopped talking when Mira appeared, and looked up at her with their full attention. She felt horribly exposed.

She had to remind herself that they couldn't see into her head. Or her heart.

"Could I speak to you guys for a minute?" Mira asked her godmothers. "Privately?"

"Sure . . ." Elsa said. She started to get up, and Mrs. Knight shooed her into her seat as she and her husband excused themselves. When the three of them were alone, Elsa asked, "What is it?"

Mira tried to look upset. "You didn't get me anything

for my birthday. It's almost like . . . you forgot."

"Of course we didn't forget!" Bliss insisted, her doll face turning fretful.

"Well, my birthday's today and . . ."

"Come here, Belle." Elsa motioned for Mira to come closer, and she did, hoping that no one noticed the weakness in her steps. Elsa took her hand, frowning at the swollen red slashes on Mira's fingers. "You've been through a lot today, haven't you?"

Mira nodded, glad they couldn't hear the frantic beat of her heart.

"And you came through it all right. We *should* celebrate. Tell us what you want," Elsa said. The fairy's fingers were cool against Mira's, despite the heat.

"Could I have a wish?" Mira asked. "Like the gifts you gave me at my christening party?"

"You're already perfect to us," Bliss teased. "We gave you everything we could think of then. What more could you possibly want?"

"There's a lot I want," Mira said.

Elsa's mouth curved into a fond smile. "All right. I'll give you a wish. Just don't wish for something anyone could give you, like a car."

"I won't," Mira promised.

She took a deep breath, pacing herself. She was afraid to say the words aloud. To make the wish real, and find out it was impossible.

"I want you to soften Blue's curse," she said.

They both stared at her so blankly that, for a moment, she wasn't sure she'd actually spoken.

"You—what?" Bliss asked.

319

Mira pressed forward. "I know you can't undo it. But I want you to soften it. Like you did with mine."

"Where is this coming from?" Elsa asked. Her expression made it clear she felt she'd been tricked.

But honestly, Mira didn't care. They'd promised her a wish. It wasn't her fault if their expectations were different; they'd tricked her all her life. To protect her, maybe, but this was for a good cause, too.

And now . . . she had to tread carefully. Blue's curse was a secret. The only reason she knew it fully was because she'd entered Felix's forbidden chamber. If she said too much, they'd demand to know how she knew.

"I know his curse is something bad. It's painful to him. It's dangerous. And I want you to make it less of those things. Whatever you can do to help, I want you to do it."

"Mira, this is really . . . unorthodox," Elsa protested.

"It's what I want," she said.

Until she had proof that Elsa and Bliss *couldn't* do it, she'd stand her ground. She was prepared to beg, cry, make them feel guiltier than they'd felt in their lives—but she wouldn't accept the *no, absolutely not* answer they'd given her so many times before.

She'd fight for him.

"I gathered that," Elsa said. "What I want to know is why you want me to do this. Did Blue put you up to it?"

Mira shook her head. "It's not his wish. It's mine."

Bliss crossed her arms and sulked for a moment. "I thought you didn't even like Blue Valentine."

"I don't have to like him," Mira said. "I'm compassionate. A fairy gifted me with kindness, remember?"

Elsa sighed. "You're absolutely sure? Because I can't give

320

you a second wish if you change your mind."

Mira nodded, her heart ready to burst. She tried to stay composed. She was afraid that if they could see how much this meant to her, they'd take it back. "I'm sure."

"All right," Elsa said. "Then we'd better find him before midnight."

"Before midnight?"

Mira swallowed. The clock above the mantle read 11:47; that meant she had less than fifteen minutes to find Blue. And she didn't even know if he was still here. "I didn't know there was a time limit."

"Of course there is. It's a birthday wish. I can't just hand them out every day." Elsa rose from her chair; peered through the window that faced the backyard. "Where is he? By the pool?"

"I don't know. Maybe," Mira said.

"Let's be quick, then."

The party guests were all crowded in or around the pool. They called to Mira when she came out, but all she cared about was finding Blue. Her eyes did a quick search of the pool area and came up empty. He'd been there when she'd gone into the house. But now he was gone.

Mira felt like a fist had been jammed into her stomach.

"I don't think he's here, Mira," Elsa said. "I know you wanted to do something good for someone . . . but how about a wish for you?"

Mira shook her head, refusing to accept it.

"I'll find him," she insisted.

Freddie stood on the concrete patio beside the pool. His sword belt was buckled over his swim trunks, and he was talking to Layla, who was perched on the edge of a picnic table, her beach towel wrapped tightly around her torso like a minidress.

Mira hurried toward them. "Freddie!" she cried.

Freddie's head jerked up. He knew her voice well enough to recognize when something was wrong. "Mira?"

"Do you know where Blue is? Can you get him for me? Please?"

"Frederick," Bliss said. "Do you always bring a sword to a pool party? You are familiar with the concept of rust, I hope."

"I—yes, of course," Freddie said, looking as if he wasn't sure whom to answer first, but deferring to the fairy out of respect for his magical elders. "I have it in case there's trouble, and I need to decapitate Fel—er, someone. Anyone, rather. Anyone in need of decapitation."

"Frederick, that is very disturbing," Bliss said. "I do hope you're joking."

"*Where's Blue?*" Mira shouted.

Freddie blinked at her, shaken. "He . . . left. I thought he told you."

"Apparently not," Elsa said. "We're looking for him."

"We have to find him before midnight," Mira filled in.

"I can call him. . . ." Freddie turned and started toward the house, looking slightly disoriented—of course he had his sword at the party, but not his phone—and mouthed *what's going on?* to Mira. She didn't have time to answer; she just waved her hands in what she hoped was a *hurry* gesture, and did some extra pleading with her eyes, until he took off running. She glanced around quickly to see if anyone else had a cell phone, but they'd all left their belongings in the house.

"Even a car would be better," Bliss said. "You could wish for a really *exclusive* car."

"You're making a wish?" Layla asked, perking up.

"Trying to," Mira said. "For Blue."

"I didn't know that was permissible," Layla said.

"It usually isn't," Elsa said. "But Mira's our girl, and sixteen is an important birthday. So I can make it work. But midnight's the cutoff."

"Oh," Layla said, growing quiet. There was barely any time left.

"Eleven fifty-four," Elsa said. "Sweetie, I don't think he's going to make it. Why don't you make another wish, just in case?"

"Animal magnetism," Bliss suggested. "Or serenity."

"I don't want anything else," Mira said.

Time kept passing. The world kept turning.

The clock inched closer to midnight.

Mira glanced at the house, twisting her hands, wondering what was taking Freddie so long. Any other time, she would have gone after Blue herself. But she didn't have the strength, she didn't know where he was, she wouldn't get to him fast enough. "What time is it?"

Elsa laid her hand on Mira's shoulder. "Eleven fifty-eight. He's not coming, Belle. Make your peace with it."

Things could have been better. Blue could have had a chance. She'd come so close, only to end up with nothing.

She shrugged away from Elsa; turned her back to her godmothers in case she started crying. She didn't want them to see her fall apart. She clung to the razor-blade necklace, and she brought the flat of the blade to her lips, shivering as she did. It smelled metallic, like steel and blood. She kissed it where Blue had kissed it.

She locked him away in her memory. That was where he would have to stay.

If he couldn't get here by midnight, it was better that he didn't come at all. She'd have nothing for him then—nothing that could change things, nothing that would save him. And she couldn't bear to watch him leave a third time.

She started toward the house to tell Freddie not to bother.

Tears streamed down her cheeks and she rubbed them away with fingers that stung with salt, sweaty from when Blue had gripped them in his. She was barely paying attention to where she was going, too busy wiping eyes that kept clouding with tears—when someone seized her arms. Hard. She choked out a cry.

It was Blue—staring at her intently, his gaze demanding something. His palms were slick against her skin. The front of his shirt was damp. He'd run through the heat to get here.

"What is it?" he asked. "Freddie called me. He said something was wrong. That you needed—me." His voice grew lower, softer. "What do you need, Mira? Tell me."

"I need you to be okay," she whispered.

And as she said it, she heard the first somber *bong* of a church bell tolling the hour—the first of twelve.

Tonight was shifting into tomorrow. Midnight was descending, and Mira's birthday was at an end.

She thought the second bell would steal her breath, the third would stop her heart—and the twelfth would kill her. The bells were long, each tone stretching out over seconds, their solemn music lingering like they were signaling a death, not a new day.

But at the third bell, someone separated her from Blue. It was Bliss.

"Let go of her," Blue snapped. He was completely misinterpreting things; he made to grab for her arm and Bliss held on tight and pulled her out of his reach.

Elsa stepped between them.

The fourth bell tolled. The night was slipping away. . . .

"Please be respectful—and quiet," Elsa said. "I don't want to lose my concentration." She was wielding her wand, holding it aloft like a conductor's baton—and the gesture seemed so familiar that Mira knew she was seeing magic.

Maybe, if there was time—

The fifth bell tolled, its round, full sound rolling through the night.

"Get away from me," Blue said.

He was afraid. Afraid because of the way they'd threatened him earlier. Afraid Mira had told them. Afraid they were doing the only thing they could do to protect her—

"Blue, it's all right," she insisted, her voice high and strained, hope warring with impending hopelessness. There wasn't time, there couldn't be, how much time did Elsa need?

The sixth bell tolled, and already, it felt like midnight in her soul.

Elsa's thin glass wand lit from base to tip, a surge of iridescent light shooting toward Blue. Fear flickered in his eyes. He looked, for an instant, like a cornered animal; and then he relaxed. His muscles went slack, and he spread his arms out. He was surrendering.

He thought they were destroying him. He didn't care anymore.

The seventh bell tolled.

"Do it," he said.

Elsa touched the tip of her wand to Blue's chest, and his skin lit with the same rainbow-colored glow, like the magic was racing through his veins. Blue trembled. He gasped.

The eighth bell tolled.

Bliss hugged Mira harder.

"I lack the ability to undo this curse," Elsa stated. "But I have the power to soften it."

Blue's terrified eyes met Mira's. "What is she doing?"

"It's for you," Mira said. "To help you."

The ninth bell tolled, silencing them, like thunder.

The light that lit Blue faltered as Elsa paused, distracted. It flared to life again as she began to speak.

"Instead of draining his beloved's life force with every kiss and caress, the Romantic will love as a normal man."

Blue was watching her, openmouthed. Neither of them really knew what was happening, what this would mean for them. They could only imagine how it might change things.

The tenth bell echoed through the night.

"He will take no strength from his beloved, but neither will he require it to survive."

The eleventh ring was already sounding when Elsa moved on to the second part of the wish, her voice and her wand trembling as time began to run out.

"The punishment for invading the Romantic's chamber—"

The iridescent light faded from the wand. It faded from Blue's skin like Mira's strength had faded when he kissed her. Until all four of them were left standing in the dark, lit only by the moon and the stars. The twelfth bell stole their voices, their breaths, and marked the end of the night, the end of Mira's birthday, the end of the magic.

"But what?" Blue asked. "What about the room?"

Elsa shook her head. "I didn't manage to change it. There wasn't time. You'll still have to give out the key. And bring an end to any trespassers . . ."

"It just won't be a clean end is what you're saying," Blue said bitterly. "Because I've lost the ability to siphon life. I'll have to do it the old-fashioned way—make the room into a bloody chamber."

Elsa nodded. "It's unfortunate, and I'm sorry. I meant to soften that."

"So I'll still be—I'll still be a murderer. If anyone enters the room . . ."

Mira's eyes flooded with tears. Blue's kiss couldn't kill anymore—but it didn't matter. If he might have to murder the girl he loved, he'd be too afraid to really live. She couldn't stand it.

"It's not fair!" she burst out. "How can you leave him like that?"

"Mira, I'm sorry," Elsa said. "But the day has ended. There's nothing I can—"

Bliss raised her wand, and magic screeched through it like nails on a chalkboard. Her jaw was set, her eyes narrowed, and she was staring right at Blue. Mira's mouth opened in horror. Did Bliss know about them? Was she going to punish him? "Wait!" she cried. But it was too late.

Bliss raked her wand in a hard circle through the air, wrist jerking counterclockwise.

And the church bell bonged again. Rich, funereal—and familiar.

Elsa's wand flared with new light. Her mouth pulled into a thin, disbelieving line. "Bliss . . . what did you do?"

"Hush," Bliss said fiercely. "Allow me to worry about the trouble I'll be in; you won't have broken any rules. Now go on and finish. You only have eleven more bells."

The second bell tolled for the second time that night. A second midnight.

Elsa took a deep breath. She touched the wand to Blue's heart, and he shivered as the iridescent light poured through him again.

Elsa repeated the softening of the curse, reciting it quickly now. And when she reached the second part of the wish, just as the church bells were tolling the sixth ring of the midnight hour, she said, "The punishment for invading the Romantic's chamber will always be death. However, the Romantic will no longer be forced to tempt his beloved into betraying him. From this moment on, he will not be required to give his beloved a key to the forbidden room, nor to disclose the room's location. The secret remains with him."

The light broke over Blue like water, and fizzled away well before the twelfth bell tolled. It was done. The wish was complete.

"There," Elsa said, letting out an exhausted sigh. "I couldn't do anything about the room—that will always be taboo. But the curse is effectively harmless." She smiled, and Mira smiled back, determined to keep a pleased expression on her face.

She couldn't possibly tell them that Blue's curse was harmless to everyone but her. Or that she had the last key Blue would ever give out.

She could sense the passkey in her pocket—the same

phantom cold she'd felt when the razor blade had first touched her chest. She shivered at its dark promise.

"Thank you," she said, pulling her godmothers into a hug. "It's perfect."

"I don't like him," Bliss whispered in Mira's ear. "Just so we're clear. But I love *you*. And I know this is what you wanted."

"Will you get in trouble?" she asked Bliss.

"Maybe," Bliss said. "But I've heard fairy godmother prison is very nice."

"Hush," Elsa hissed, and Bliss giggled.

"Happy birthday," they said.

Bliss and Elsa left her alone with Blue. He closed the distance between them and took her hands, careful not to crush her wounded fingers.

"That wasn't just an elaborate light show, was it?" he asked. His breathing sounded shaky. He was looking down at himself—like he expected to have changed on the outside, too. "I'm a little afraid to believe it. It feels like it can't be real."

"It's real," Mira said. "It was my birthday wish—that they soften your curse, like they softened mine."

"You had a birthday wish? And you wasted it on me?" He grinned at her. It was the first time she'd seen him smile like that in a while, and she lit up, grinning back.

"What was I thinking?"

"Can we work out some kind of trade, so I can make it up to you?"

"There is still something I want for my birthday."

"Anything," he said.

*You,* she thought.

She draped her arms around his neck, feeling excited, and nervous, and afraid.

It was exciting to think they had a chance now . . . and scary to know their fates were in her hands. She was the one girl who could betray him. And if she did, she'd make him into a monster. He'd be forced to kill her, and it wouldn't be soft; it would be violent. The risk of death had always been between them . . . but now he could walk away from her, and never have to risk that again. She was nervous that he would want to.

"Mira," he said. "You know I trust you, don't you?"

"I know," she said. "It's just . . . you'd be safe with anyone else. You wouldn't have to worry—at all—and—"

"Mira." He took her face in his hands. "I'm not worried. You know what's there. You're not going to go in that room."

"I know, but—"

"And this is real, right? What your godmothers said. My curse is . . ."

He kissed her lightly on the nose, and she laughed. Blue eyed her with faux seriousness. "How was that? Any weakness?"

"No. But I don't think there would have been anyway."

"Well, then, how about this?" His lips brushed hers, his mouth teasing her lower lip, and her eyes closed and she shivered as his fingers caught in her hair. And then suddenly, there wasn't any space between them. The sensation of drowning was there, but it wasn't like her strength was leaving her. It was like she wanted to be part of him. Like she didn't know or care where she ended and he began.

When they drew apart, she whispered, "No weakness."

"Really?" he said. " 'Cause I'm feeling a little weak." She felt him smile against her mouth. And they both laughed, shook with it. Their faces were too close, noses and cheeks pressed awkwardly together, but neither one of them moved. She tightened her arms around him, and he held her just as tightly. His breath murmured against her cheek.

"You're safe with me, Mira. And I'm safe with you."

He kissed her again to prove it. And when the clock struck one—that lone, ominous tone hovering in the dark—they were still kissing. Her razor blade had snagged his shirt and nicked his chest, and they'd ended up lying in the grass, hidden inside a shadow, ignoring their names whenever someone called them. He traced her mouth again and again, like he still couldn't believe it was real.

There would always be a part of him she couldn't know. A secret place where his heartbreak was stored, where lost innocence and regret filled the air like smoke. She had no desire to open that door . . . but she didn't know if that would change one day. If the key would tempt her, if a fairy would manipulate her or she would just be curious. But she had to believe she could be strong enough to resist. That what she wanted—what they both wanted—mattered more than the path that had been laid out for them.

She let her hand slip under his shirt to touch the heart mark on his back, and he brought her other hand to his lips, and kissed every finger he'd entrusted with the key. He was so much more than his curse, and she was so much more than the girl who could betray him. Together . . . they could be anything.

331